PRAISE FOR
ELIZABETH BEAR'S
HAMMERED

"*Hammered* is a very exciting, very polished, very impressive debut novel." —Mike Resnick

"Gritty, insightful, and daring—Elizabeth Bear is a talent to watch." —David Brin, author of the *Uplift* novels and *Kil'n People*

"A gritty and painstakingly well-informed peek inside a future we'd all better hope we don't get, liberally seasoned with VR delights and enigmatically weird alien artifacts. Genevieve Casey is a pleasingly original female lead, fully equipped with the emotional life so often lacking in military SF yet tough and full of noir attitude; old enough by a couple of decades to know better but conflicted enough to engage with the sleazy dynamics of her situation regardless. Out of this basic contrast, Elizabeth Bear builds her future nightmare tale with style and conviction and a constant return to the twists of the human heart."
—Richard Morgan, author of *Altered Carbon*

"*Hammered* has it all. Drug wars, hired guns, corporate skullduggery, and bleeding-edge AI, all rolled into one of the best first novels I've seen in I don't know how long. This is the real dope!" —Chris Moriarty, author of *Spin State*

"A glorious hybrid: hard science, dystopian geopolitics, and wide-eyed sense-of-wonder seamlessly blended into a single book. I hate this woman. She makes the rest of us look like amateurs." —Peter Watts, author of *Starfish* and *Maelstrom*

"The language is taut, the characters deep and the scenes positively crackle with energy. Not to mention that this is real science fiction, with rescues from crippled starships and exploration of mysterious alien artifacts and international diplomatic brinksmanship between spacefaring powers China and Canada. Yes, Canada!" —James Patrick Kelly, author of *Strange but not a Stranger* and *Think Like a Dinosaur*

"Packed with a colorful panoply of characters, a memorable and likeable anti-heroine, and plenty of action and intrigue, *Hammered* is a superbly written novel that combines high tech, military industrial politics, and complex morality. There is much to look forward to in new writer Elizabeth Bear." —Karin Lowachee, Campbell-award nominated author of *Warchild*

"Even in scenes where there is no violent action, or even much physical action at all, the thoughts and emotions of Ms. Bear's characters, as well as the dynamic tensions of their relationships, create an impression of feverish activity going on below the surface and liable to erupt into plain view at any moment. . . The language is terse and vivid, punctuated by ironic asides whose casual brutality—sometimes amusing, sometimes shocking—speaks volumes about these people and their world. . . This is a superior piece of work by a writer of enviable talents. I look forward to reading more!" —Paul Witcover, author of *Waking Beauty*

ALSO BY ELIZABETH BEAR

HAMMERED

ELIZABETH BEAR

BANTAM BOOKS

SCARDOWN

A Bantam Spectra Book / July 2005

Published by
Bantam Dell
A Division of Random House, Inc.
New York, New York

ISBN 0-553-58751-X

Printed in the United States of America
Published simultaneously in Canada

www.bantamdell.com

OPM 10 9 8 7 6 5 4 3 2 1

This book is dedicated to

my parents, Karen Westerholm

and Steve Wishnevsky, and

to my grandfather Henry Westerholm,

for the run of their

science fiction collections

Acknowledgments

It takes a lot of people to write a novel. This one would not have existed without the assistance of my very good friends and first readers (on and off the Online Writing Workshop for Science Fiction, Fantasy, & Horror)—especially but not exclusively Kathryn Allen, Rhonda Garcia, Jaime Voss, Chris Coen, Tara Devine, Chelsea Polk, and Larry West. I am even more deeply indebted to Stella Evans, M.D., to whom I owe whatever bits of the medical science and neurology are accurate; to M.Cpl. S. K. S. Perry (Canadian Forces), Lt. Penelope K. Hardy (U.S. Navy), and Capt. Beth Coughlin (U.S. Army), without whom my portrayal of military life would have been even more wildly fantastical; to Leah Bobet, my native guide to Toronto; to Meredith L. Patterson, linguist and computer geek, for assistance with interspecies linguistic theory; to Dena Landon, Sarah Monette, and Kelly Morisseau, francophones extraordinaire, upon whom may be blamed any correctness in the Québecois—especially the naughty bits; to Sue Yurcic, former Boeing test pilot, for obvious reasons; to Dr. Jacqueline A. Hope, geophysicist, and Dr. Ian Tregillis, physicist, for making Richard sound like I knew what he was talking about; to Dr. Peter Watts, biologist, for helping make the aliens *alien*; to John Borneman for help with my math; to my agent, Jennifer Jackson, my copy editor, Faren Bachelis, and to my editor, Anne Groell, for too many reasons to enumerate; and to Chris, who is patient with the foibles of novelism.

The failures, of course, are my own.

Editor's Note

In the interests of presenting a detailed personal perspective on a crucial moment in history, we have taken the liberty of rendering Master Warrant Officer Casey's interviews—as preserved in the Yale University New Haven archives—in narrative format. Changes have been made in the interests of clarity, but the words, however edited, are her own.

The motives of the other individuals involved are not as well documented, although we have had the benefit of our unique access to extensive personal records left by Col. Frederick Valens. The events as presented herein are accurate; the drives behind them must always remain a matter of speculation, except in the case of Dr. Dunsany—who left us comprehensive journals—and "Dr." Feynman, who kept frequent and impeccable backups.

Thus, what follows is a historical novel of sorts. It is our hope that this more intimate annal than is usually seen will serve to provide future students with a singular perspective on the roots of the civilization we are about to become.

—*Patricia Valens, Ph.D.*
  Jeremy Kirkpatrick, Ph.D.

BOOK ONE

"Soldier,
I wish you
well."
—A. E. Housman

The *Montreal* has wings.

They unfurl around her, gossamer solar sails bearing a kilometers-long dragonfly out of high Earth orbit and into the darkness where she will test herself, and me. She's already moving like a cutter through night-black water when Colonel Valens straps me to the butter-soft leather of the pilot's chair and seats the collars. I'm wearing the damned uniform he demanded; it's made for this, with a cutout under my jacket for the interface.

Cold metal presses above my hips, against the nape of my neck. There's a subtle little prickle when the pins slide in, and my unauthorized AI passenger chuckles inside my ear.

Gonna be okay out there, Dick?

"With a whole starship to play in? Sure. Besides, I have my other self to wait for. Whenever Valens lets him into the system, pinions clipped." He grins in the corner of my prosthetic eye. Virtual Richard. I'll miss him. "I'll go when you enter the ship. They'll miss me in the fluctuation."

Godspeed, Richard.

"Be careful, Jenny."

Spit-shined Colonel Valens raises three fingers into my line of sight. I draw one breath, deep and sweet, skin prickling with chill and cool sweat.

Valens's fingers come down. *One. Two. Three.*

And dark.

My body vanishes along with Valens, the observers, the bridge. Cold on my skin and the simulations were never like this. Richard winks and vanishes, and my head feels— empty, all of a sudden, and ringing hollow. It's strange in there without him. And then I forget myself in the *Montreal,* as the sun pushes my sails and the stars spread out before me like buttercream frosting on a birthday cake. Heat and pressure like a kiss gliding down my skin, and the *Montreal's* sails are eagle's wings cradling a thermal.

Eagle wings. Eagle feathers. A warrior dream.

I pull the ship around me like a feathered skin and *fly.*

Valens's voice in my ear as Richard leaves me. "All good, Master Warrant?"

"Yes, sir." I hate the distractions. Hate him talking when I'm trying to fly. The simulations were mostly hyperlight; I didn't get to play much in space I could see. Only feel, like the rough curve of gravity dragging you down a water slide, and then the darkness pulling you under.

This is easy.

This is *fun. Richard?* I don't expect an answer. He's gone into the ship, part of the *Montreal* now with her cavernous computer systems and the nanotech traced through her hull, her skin, wired into my brain stem so her heartbeat is my heartbeat, the angle of her sails is the angle of my wings.

"Got you, Jenny," he says, and if my heart were my heart it would skip a beat. I can't feel myself grin.

Dick!

"Guess what?" His glee tastes like my own. "Jenny, the nanites can talk to each other."

What do you mean?

"I mean I can sense the alien ships on Mars—the ship tree and the metal one—and I can sense you and the other pilots. And the Chinese vessel following us."

The Huang Di?

"On our tail. No lag, Jenny."

I don't understand. *No lag?*

"No lightspeed lag. Instantaneous communication. I think I was right about the superstrings. It's not so much *faster-than-light* technology as . . . *sneakier-than-light.*"

Implications tangle in my brain. *Richard.*

"Yes?"

Can you feel our benefactors? Somebody alien left the ships on Mars for us to find. Somebody *alien* meant for us to come find them, too.

"And they can feel me," he answers. "Jenny, I can't talk to them. Can't understand them. But I know one thing.

"They're coming."

I almost stall the habitation wheel as the *Montreal* and I continue our ascent.

Three hours previous
0900 Hours
Thursday 2 November, 2062
HMCSS Montreal
Earth orbit

Don't all kids want to grow up to be astronauts? It's not a strange thing to ask when you are hauling yourself along a series of grab rails on your way to the bridge of a starship, floating ends of hair brushing your ears like fingertips.

Let me say that again in case you missed it.

A *star*ship.

Her name is the *Montreal,* and she's as cold inside as a tin can on an ice floe. Her outline is gawky, fragile-seeming, counterintuitive to an eye that expects things that fly to look like things that fly. Instead, she's a winged wheel stuck partway down a weather-vane arrow, a design that keeps the hazardous things in the engines as far as possible from the habitation module without compromising the angle of thrust. The wheel turns around the shaft of the arrow, generating there-is-no-such-thing-as-centrifugal-force, which will hold us to the nominal floor once we're on it. There's no gravity in this, the central shaft. You could float along it if you wanted, and never fear falling.

I prefer the grab rails, thank you.

The "wings"—furled against the rigging like the legs of some eerie spider—are solar sails. The main engines are not to be used until we're cruising well clear of a planet. Any planet. From the simulations I've been flying back in Toronto, the consequences might be just as detrimental to the planet as to the *Montreal.*

Don't ask me how the engines work. I'm not sure the guys who built them know. But I do know that the reactor and drive assemblies are designed so they can be jettisoned in the case of an emergency, if worst comes to worst. And that they're shielded to hell and gone.

Don't all little kids want to grow up to be astronauts?

Not me. Little Jenny Casey—she wanted to be a pirate or a ballerina. Not a firefighter or a cop. *Definitely* not a soldier. She never even thought about going to the stars.

I catch myself, over and over, breaking the enormity of what I'm seeing down into component pieces. Gray rubber matting, gray metal walls. The whining strain of heaters and refrigerators against the chewing cold and searing heat of space. The click of my prosthetic left hand against the railing, the butt of a chubby xenobiologist bobbing along the ladder ahead of me.

Did I mention that this is a *starship*?

And I'm expected to fly her. If I can figure out how.

Big, blond Gabe Castaign is a few rungs behind me. I hear him mumbling under his breath in French, a litany of disbelief louder than my own but no less elaborate, and far more profane. "Jenny," he calls past my boots, "do you know if they plan to put elevators in this thing before they call it flightworthy?"

I've studied her specs. *Elevators* isn't the right word, implying as it does a change of height, which is a dimension the *Montreal* will never know. "Yeah." Grab, pull, grab. "But do me a favor and call them tubecars, all right?" He grunts. I grin.

I know Gabe well enough to know a *yes* when I hear one. Know him even better in the past few hours than I did for the twenty-five years before that, come to think of it. "Captain Wainwright," I call past Charlie Forster, that xenobiologist. "How much farther to the bridge?"

"Six levels," she calls back.

"At least her rear view is better than Charlie's," Richard Feynman says inside my head. If I closed my eyes—which I don't—I'd see my AI passenger hanging like a holo in front of the left one, grinning a contour-map grin and scrubbing his hands together.

Richard, look all you want. I marvel at the rubberized steel under my mismatched hands and grin harder, still surprised not to feel the expression tugging scar tissue along the side of my face. It's almost enough to belay the worry I'm feeling over a few friends left home on Earth in a sticky situation. Almost.

A starship. That's one hell of a ride you got there, Jenny Casey.

Yeah. Which of course is when my stomach, unfed for twenty hours, chooses to rumble.

"Master Warrant Casey, are you feeling any better?" says Colonel Frederick Valens, last in line.

"Just fine, sir." *Not bad for your first time in zero G, Jenny.* It could have been a lot worse, anyway. Gabe had me a little too distracted to puke when the acceleration cut in the beanstalk on the way up. "I suppose I don't want to know what sort of chow we get on a spaceship."

"Starship," Wainwright corrects. "It's better than you might expect. No dead animals, but we get good produce."

"Whatever happened to Tang?"

Charlie laughs, still moving hand over hand along the ladder. "The elevator makes it cheap to bring things up, and life support both here and on the Clarke Orbital Platform relies on greenery for carbon exchange. No point in making it inedible greenery, so as long as you like pasta primavera and tempeh, you're golden. I'll show you the galley after we look at the bridge. Which should be—"

"Right through this hatch," Wainright finishes. She undogs the hatch cover and pushes it open, hooking one calf through the ladder for purchase, her toe curled around a bar for a moment before she pulls herself forward and slithers through the opening like a nightcrawler into leafy loam. Charlie follows and I'm right after him, feeling a strange chill in the metal when my right hand closes on it. The left one picks it up, too, but it's a different, alien sensation. After twenty-five years with an armored steel field-ready prosthesis, I'm still not used to having a hand that can feel on that arm. I rap on the hatch as I go through it, examining a ceramic and metal pressure door that boasts a heavy wheel in place of a handle. I pick up the scent of machine oil lubricating hydraulics; when I brush the hatch it moves smoothly, light on its hinges.

Except light is the wrong word here, isn't it? My left eye—prosthetic, too—catches the red glimmer of a sensor as I pass through. "Seems a little primitive," I call after Wainwright.

She propels herself down the corridor—a much larger one—keeping one hand on the grab rail for the inevitable moment when she starts to drift to the floor. She gets her feet under her neatly, but even Charlie follows with better grace than me. All my enhanced reflexes are good for is smacking me into the wall a little faster. I stumble and catch myself on the rail. Gabe muffs it, too, God bless him, although Valens manages his touchdown agile as a silver tabby tomcat.

"The ship?" She turns, surprised.

I amuse myself with the hopping-off-a-slide-walk sensation of each step heavier than the last as I close the distance between us. This corridor must spiral through the ring, to take you from inside to outside "feet-down." I speculate there's a ladder way, too. One I wouldn't want to lose my grip in. "The hatchways."

"Less to break." She shrugs her shoulders, settling her uniform jacket over her blouse. I make a mental note to requisition some jumpsuits, if they're not already provided. Valens always seems to think about these things.

Wainwright continues. "And if it does, we can fix it with a wrench and a can of WD-40. That might be important a few thousand light-years out. Saves power, too. They're just like submarine doors, but less massive."

Gabe lays a hand on my elbow as he comes up beside me, still soft on his feet for all he's got three years on me and I celebrated my fiftieth last month. "Let me guess," Richard says in my implant. "Ask about the decompression doors, Jenny?"

"Captain." I brush against Gabe as I move past him.

Valens's gaze prickles my spine as he dogs the hatch behind us. I swallow a grin. "What do you do if there's a hull breach?"

"Try not to be in a doorway. The habitation wheel is designed like a honeycomb, for strength. There are automatic doors for emergencies, and if the air pressure drops suddenly—they come down."

"They don't wait for pedestrians to clear the corridor?"

"No." She turns her back on me and walks away, leading us farther out of the floating heart of her ship, now my ship, too. "For Christmas, I guess we'll hang the mistletoe in the wardroom." She glances back over her shoulder with a grin that stills my shiver.

"Hostile environment," Gabe mutters in my ear.

"Enemy territory," Valens adds from my other side. "What's outside this tin can is trying to kill you, Casey. Never forget that for a second."

I square my shoulders and don't look up. He needs me enough that I can get away with it. "I'll bear that in mind, Fred."

He chuckles as I walk away.

The bridge lies near the center of the habitation ring. It's long enough I can see the curve of the floor, but not particularly wide. Remote screens line the walls with floor-to-ceiling images of blue and holy Madonna Earth on one side, Clarke Orbital Platform spinning like a fat rubber doughnut at an angle. "I've never felt claustro- and agoraphobic at the same time before," Gabe says. He brushes past me and rests one bearlike paw on a console, bending down to examine the interface. "Sweet."

I'm the only one to hear Richard chuckle.

I find myself staring at the padded black leather pilot's chair. *Leather on a starship? Well, why not; at least it breathes.* But it's not the look of soft tanned hide that pulls me forward, has me bending to trail my fingers down the armrest.

Most pilot's chairs aren't equipped with straps and clamps intended to keep the operator's head and arms immobilized. They don't have a glossy interface plate with a pin-port mounted on a cable-linked collar at neck level, either, and another one right where the small of your back would rest.

It looks like an electric chair. I sink my teeth into my lower lip and turn. "There aren't any physical controls?"

"That panel over there," Richard tells me, even as Captain Wainwright moves toward it and lays her dainty right hand possessively on padded high-impact plastic. It's a good three meters from my chair. The chair that's going to be mine.

"Somebody else flies her sublight," Wainwright says. "We save you and Lieutenant Koske for the dirty work. When she's moving too fast for anybody else to handle."

I nod, barely hearing her. Remembering the simulations, the caress of sunlight on solar sails. A little sad that I won't be feeling that for real.

"Jenny." Richard again. "Don't get greedy. You'll be driving faster than anybody else ever has."

Except for the pilots of the three ships that didn't make it. China's already broken two, the *Li Bu* and the *Lao Zi. Montreal* is Canada's second attempt. The first one—*Le Québec*—had an unexpected appointment with Charon. Pluto's moon, that is. These babies are very hard to steer.

I look from Wainwright to Valens and grin. "When do I get to try her, then? And who is Lieutenant Koske?"

"Your relief," Valens says. He moves to stand beside and behind me, just enough taller to loom.

I touch the interface collar, metal fingers clicking softly on plastic. "Do I get to meet him?"

"He's probably eating," Wainwright says, on my other side. "As for trying her out—how does this afternoon sound?"

Tall, dark, good-looking, without the faint mottling of repaired burn scars that mars my face—Trevor Koske *is* an asshole. I can tell from the set of his shoulders under his spotless uniform jacket as I follow Valens to his table. Koske sets his fork down, light glittering off slight scratches in his cervical interface, and turns to face us. Somehow, he and I managed to miss each other, despite getting the trillion-dollar-soldier treatment from Valens within the same few years. Admittedly, we guinea pigs weren't encouraged to fraternize. Some shrink probably thought being around normal people would encourage us to believe we still were. Normal, that is. How normal you can be when you can catch a bullet in your left hand, I'm not telling.

"Lieutenant Trevor Koske," Valens says. "This is Master Warrant Officer Genevieve Casey." Wainwright purses her lips at him as he usurps her role—*making friends already, Fred?*

I set my tray down and put out my hand. "Jenny," I say, determined to act like the civilian they won't allow me to remain. "Pleased to meet you."

Gabe, at my shoulder, grins and sticks his hand out, too. Koske regards our hands like a pair of dead eels, his fingers resting inches from the handle of his fork. "Charming fellow," Richard says. "I hate him already. Did I tell you about the time—"

Richard. I withdraw my hand, still smiling. *I took his job.*

"You merited his job."

Because I'm a freak. Nobody says another word as I

hook a chair back with my foot—a chair set on a swivel arm in the floor—and sit down directly across from Koske. I pull my tray closer and pick up the fork. Soba and a green salad with ginger dressing; they'll turn me healthy if I'm not careful. "So, Trevor," I say around a mouthful of lettuce, "tell me about yourself."

He grunts and picks up his tea. After ten minutes of bloody-minded silence, Captain Wainwright starts flirting with Gabe. It's almost a relief. I'm tired enough that my neural implants are making the overhead fluorescent lights strobe. I lay my fork down and cast around the room for something less annoying to look at; my eye lights on a crop-haired, twentyish blond with bulging shoulders. He stares at me. His eyebrows are so light they're paler streaks against the ruddiness of his face. He glances down quickly when he sees me looking.

Nothing new there.

4:30 PM
Thursday 2 November, 2062
Government Center
Toronto, Ontario

Constance Riel leaned over the shoulder of her science adviser, Paul Perry. He sat in Riel's own chair, at her exceedingly well-interfaced desk, busy hands moving over the plate. Riel frowned, ignoring the ache in feet rapidly growing numb. "You're telling me these images"—she poked a finger into the center of one of the displays, and it obligingly expanded—"show—what?"

Paul had pulled his jacket sleeves up and rolled his shirt cuffs. He blinked bloodshot eyes and continued in an Oxford-educated drawl. "This is from the Martian orbital telescope, Prime Minister. It shows an explosion or an impact near the south pole of Charon, the sister planet of Pluto. *This* shows the debris track. Ma'am, should I call down for sandwiches?"

She hadn't realized the rumble in her belly would be audible. "Yes. Bless you. That looks like a special effect from a science fiction holo. What does it mean?"

He keyed some information quickly—a request for food and coffee—and moved back to the telescopic images. "It means something struck Charon. Hard. Hard enough to essentially fracture the planet. Planetoid."

"An attack of some sort? What, more space aliens?" War-of-the-worlds scenarios unfolded in her head. She pressed her fingers to her eyes, imagining she could already smell coffee.

"No, ma'am." Paul shrugged. "I've been chasing some rumors, and I've had my staff after it. I wanted good information before I came to you."

"You're stalling, Paul."

"Yes, ma'am. Unitek."

"Unitek?"

"You've been briefed—have you been briefed?"

"*Is* there a new development with the pair of derelict alien spacecraft on Mars?"

"No. Unitek and a detached group from the joint forces have been working on developing a ship based on those design principles. You know that."

"I'm opposed to it, Paul. That's money better spent at home. But it's Unitek's money—" She shrugged. Canada needed to get free of Unitek. The problem was, with Unitek went access to the Brazil and PanMalaysian beanstalks, their international trade partners, and a good part of the funding for Canada's military. Times were more peaceful than they had been, on the surface. But a world in which the People's PanChinese Army was massing on the Russian border and eyeing the grain fields of Ukraine, a world where PanMalaysia and Japan relied on promises of military aid from Canada, Australia, and to a lesser extent the reconstructed but still limping United States to keep the same starving wolf from *their* door—it wasn't a world in which one dared appear weak. Paul himself was a refugee from the slowly freezing British Isles.

Fallout from the Pakistani/Indian wars and the United States's actions in the Far and Middle East had moved Earth's supranational governments to rare, unified action. Global effort had managed what unilateral action could not: a functional missile defense shield, based on the same technology that provided meteorite and space-junk defense for the orbital platforms. Not, unfortunately, before the damage compounded China's inability to feed her swarming population.

Canada had already fought one unpopular war on behalf of China's smaller neighbors. Riel started to wonder if the pain in her gut wasn't hunger, but an ulcer. "Was this a Chinese ship?"

"No," he said. "It was ours. And we have larger problems."

Riel sighed, glancing up as the door of her office opened. A liveried steward brought a tray into the room; she could tell at a glance that lunch must have been ready and waiting for their call. Or perhaps someone else's sandwiches and coffee had been diverted for the prime minister's use, and a replacement tray was already being made up. "Is this going to ruin my appetite, Paul?"

"Most likely."

Riel shooed the reluctant steward away and poured the coffee herself, balancing two self-regulating mugs—she despised china cups—and a plate of sandwiches as she made her way back. "Then we'd better eat while we talk," she said, and juggled dinnerware onto the desk. "I shouldn't eat these. I promised my husband we'd have dinner together for once," she said. "And I have a meeting that starts in half an hour and runs until eight. Will this take longer than that?"

Paul glanced up from the simulation and shook his head. "It'll be four hours until you eat, then," he said. "Have a sandwich."

Her eyebrows rose. She knew it was an effective expression, under the heavy dark wing of her bangs, accentuating her thin nose and the long lines across her brow.

"Ma'am," he amended and she acquiesced, selecting a triangle without looking at the contents. Chewy black bread and vegetables, and something that was more or less tuna fish. Farmed gene-mod tuna fish. Riel was just about old enough to remember the real thing.

"All right," she said, once Paul had had a moment to cram a third of a sandwich into his mouth. "Show me what you're worried about, Dr. Perry."

He didn't miss the formality—she could tell by the angle of his head—but he didn't acknowledge it either. "Here," he said, tapping up an image of a different, and more familiar, globe. "These shots are courtesy of Clarke and Forward," he said, and then waved a hand irritably over the panel, clearing the display. "Wait—"

Long spare fingers tapped crystal, and Riel smiled privately at his thoughtless efficiency of movement. She squinted as new images resolved. "There's something wrong with the depth."

"They're 2-D animations," Paul explained. "Late twentieth century—here. Do you see these color patterns, ma'am?"

Riel nodded, watching as a computer-animated blush

spread across the surface of the oceans, waxing and waning with fluctuations that could only be seasons. "Temperature patterns?"

"Yes. And more. This is a record of coral reef die-offs."

Still 2-D, but no harder to follow than an old-fashioned movie once you got the hang of it. Riel licked mayonnaise off her fingers and frowned, rubbing them together to remove the last traces of grease. "Old news—"

"This isn't." His fingers moved. He leaned back in the chair, his shoulder brushing Riel's arm. She hunched forward, too intent to take a half-step to the side and preserve her space. It was the image that he'd brushed aside so quickly, a few moments before. A modern three-dimensional animation, and—

"Those don't look dissimilar. But that's a much bigger scale, isn't it? And the currents look different than in the earlier one."

Paul shrugged. "They've changed a lot."

Yes. Including the failure of the Gulf Stream. Which is why you're in Canada now, isn't it, Paul? Riel found herself nodding slowly, almost rocking. As if the motion would help her think. She put a stop to it firmly. "What am I looking at, Paul?"

"The end of the world," he said, with turgid drama and a news announcer's baritone. He coughed and cleared his throat, reaching for his coffee. "Well, perhaps not quite. But a serious problem, in any case. This is data from two of the orbital platforms regarding algae populations—"

"The algae is dying."

"Like the coral reefs."

"Not exactly. But for layman's values of like, sure."

"What does this have to do with the price of tea in China, Paul?"

He chuckled. "Funny you should phrase it that way,

ma'am. Everything, it turns out. I've been corresponding with a Unitek biologist on Clarke, a Dr. Forster—"

"Charles Forster. He was involved in the mission that discovered the Martian ships."

"That's the one. He and I think that the increased Chinese interest in space travel—their outbound fire-and-forget colony ships, for example, and their expansion efforts within our system—date from about the time the first signs of this became apparent. It's a serious problem, Prime Minister. The sort of thing that could radically diminish the planet's ability to sustain life."

"You don't think the Chinese are behind—"

"No." Quiet, but definite. Riel liked the way he stated his opinions, when he could be convinced to have them. "But I think they caught on a hell of a lot faster than we did. Of course, we've been distracted by the Freeze of Britain—"

"Excuses, excuses. What do we do?"

He glanced at her sideways and ruffled his hair with one hand. "Beat the Chinese out of the solar system, for one thing. And start thinking about what we're going to do in a hundred, hundred fifty years if we have to reterraform Earth."

2100 Hours
Thursday 2 November, 2062
HMCSS Montreal
Earth orbit

Fucking bitch. Trevor Koske kicked the bulkhead once, hard, and turned back to the heavy bag. He slammed fist after fist into it, growling, squinting against the strobe of the overhead lights. *Bitch!* Let her come up here, flaunting her superior adaptation and her fucking ability to hold a normal conversation, to stand it when a man laid a hand on her arm. Fucking Master Warrant Officer Genevieve Casey. War hero.

The only survivor of Valens's Frankensteinian augmentation program to recover enough to return to combat duty. Koske slugged the bag again, caught it on the backswing, putting power behind each blow until his shoulders burned. Bitch. Cunt. Whore.

Koske didn't carry the kind of visible damage Casey did. Wearing her steel hand like a banner saying *this is who I am*. She might as well have pinned her medals to her chest. Bad enough she'd gone back out, an unqualified success. Gotten to do the things that Koske had lost forever thirty years back—to the bad eject, the broken neck, the creeping numbness.

Casey had gotten to fly, dammit. Rescue and recovery— ferrying parachute paramedics into live-fire zones. *Bitch!* He kicked the bag for variety. Bad enough.

He'd watched her career from the sidelines, knowing what she was. Knowing by her steel hand, her infrequent visits to Valens's clinic, her reputation as the best chopper pilot in the army *what* she had to be. Known it from the way she rode the edge, and the way she brought boys and girls back alive out of the jungle when anybody would have said it was suicide to go. Known. And hated. Because Casey was still everything Koske would never be again.

And now she'd taken away his last chance to really fly again. Just by being who she was. By being so—slam! *Bitch!*—fucking good.

And if that wasn't bad enough, there was the way the big blond civilian had hovered over her, the way she'd leaned into his touch on her arm when she thought no one was looking. The way she'd heedlessly extended her hand to him, Trevor, as if he could ever fucking reach out and take a human hand again.

He backed away from the bag, panting. As if the neural implants running through his body didn't turn his skin into a finely honed alarm system that could make him curl away and shake, crying, from an unsubtle touch. *Bad enough to be a fucking autistic,* he thought. *Worse if you didn't start out that way, hypersensitive and hyperaware. Worse if you grew up a normal kid, with a normal kid's need to be held, and you woke up one day and you were different. Faster. Stranger. Feeling the air on your skin like sandpaper.*

Lieutenant Koske could remember precisely every detail of the last time he had made love to somebody. Remember the taste of his wife's mouth, and imagine the flavor of his tears when she left him three years later, unable to live with a man who couldn't bear an arm around his shoulders, a kiss on the cheek.

It could be worse. I could still be crippled. Or dead.

Would that be worse?

The hatchway opened as he slammed the bag again. He heard the footsteps and then the hesitation. "Lieutenant. I beg your pardon. I'll come back later."

A young man's voice. He turned. The stocky, close-cropped blond lieutenant who stood just inside the hatchway tossed his towel around his neck and nodded. Koske took in powerful muscles under a crisp white T-shirt, shorts in air force blue, rubber-soled ship shoes.

"No," Koske said, lowering trembling fists. Exhaustion rolled over him, the familiar dizzying drop out of adrenaline-fueled combat time. "I'll hold the bag for you if you like—"

"Ramirez. Chris."

"I'm done."

It wasn't as bad as it had been.

Of late, growing habituated to his body's precarious artificial equilibrium, Second Pilot Xie Min-xue found that his tendency to flinch and panic when confronted with casual contact was lessening. Rather than overreacting, he was learning to anticipate and avoid the contact before it could happen.

Also, the crew was learning techniques to make life easier for the pathologically high-strung pilots: incandescent lighting rather than fluorescent in most public areas of the *Huang Di,* for example. Soundproofed bunks for the pilots, and a private ready room where the lights were dim and the only sound the hum of the *Huang Di*'s systems. There had been some talk of removing the colored panels and ideographed plaques—*long life, good harvest, fair sailing*—that bid the *Huang Di* prosperity and success, but the first pilot had convinced the captain that such measures would not be necessary.

Just privacy, he said. And so Min-xue and the other four fragile, essential, half-mad pilots were granted the luxury of bunks and a ready room of their own.

A luxury that Min-xue had now abandoned to pass carefully through the weightless corridors of the drifting ship. Midwatch, the passageways were almost deserted.

The ideal time for a young man suffering from an induced form of acute hypersensitivity to travel through them.

Min-xue paused by the hatchway to Pilot's Medical and closed his eyes for a moment. His uniform bound at waist and ankles; he jerked it irritably straight, which of course disarrayed the cloth across his shoulders and at his collar. There was no true comfort, but it could have been worse.

Min-xue opened his eyes, clutched a grab rail beside the door so reactive pressure wouldn't send him drifting into the corridor, and depressed the call plate beside the hatch. The doorway irised open. He swung himself through. "Master Technician?"

There was a deep sort of irony in the fact that the title of the man who cared for Min-xue's own tightly engineered systems was *technician*. Or perhaps Min-xue's superiors only meant to acknowledge the truth: he, and every other soldier in the People's PanChinese Liberation Army, was perfectly machined for a role, and perfectly replaceable.

"Second Pilot." Master Technician Liu Paiyun released his webbing and drifted from his station, turning gracefully to face Min-xue. "Have you any problems today, or are you just here for your checkup?"

"None," Min-xue answered. "Well, no more than the usual, but nothing to complain of."

"Excellent." The master technician rubbed the palm of a broad hand across his tight-cropped black hair and smiled in a way that made the corners of his eyes wrinkle tight. "Then come with me, Min-xue; after we finish with your physical, I'll conduct your quarterly psychological examination. As long as you're already here—"

"I'm not due for that for another six weeks," Min-xue answered, and the master technician called up his chart.

"I know." Paiyun had thick wrists, still well muscled

despite free fall, and arms long enough that bare strips of skin showed below the cuffs of his uniform. Those wrists—and the big, blunt hands attached to them—moved with assurance through the projections, motions as deft as Min-xue's when the young pilot was at the *Huang Di*'s controls. "But we need a fourth for mah-jongg, you see. And there's no reason we can't combine two tasks into one."

He glanced over his shoulder. Min-xue smiled. "Thank you, Paiyun," he said. "That would be—very nice."

The mah-jongg set was magnetic, the tiles softly burnished steel with a tendency to adhere to one another even when the player did not necessarily wish them to. Min-xue floated comfortably in a corner of Medical's crowded ready room, tethered to one padded wall by a length of soft webbing and a plastic clip. Liu Paiyun had carefully set things up so that Min-xue would have his back to the wall. Most gracious, but then Medical understood better than anybody except another pilot what, exactly, the pilots endured—

"—out of patriotism, Min-xue?"

"I beg your pardon, Paiyun?" It was nice to be on a casual basis with one person on the *Huang Di,* at least.

"Oh." Paiyun shuffled his tiles. His broad fingertips left faint oily dapples on the metal. "If I gave offense, I'm sorry. I had asked"—he glanced to the other two technicians, Chen and Gao—both only seniors—for confirmation. Chen smiled. Gao nodded.—"why it was that you agreed to enter pilot training. Given the risks. An exemplary young man such as yourself."

"They only take the best," Min-xue said, without pride. He chewed his lip, feeling toward an answer that might make sense to Paiyun. "If my performance had not been acceptable—"

"That was not my implication at all." Paiyun looked down, ostensibly to lay a tile on the board with a soft, magnetized click. *China*. Min-xue smiled at the boxy red ideogram.

"—no, Paiyun, I know it wasn't." Min-xue let the smile widen. "It was the adventure, of course. And the idea that I might be good enough to be accepted. And—"

They let the pause hang in the air long enough to be notable. "And?" Gao said. He looked down then, as if afraid he had been rude to the pilot, and turned away to fetch another round of drinks in plastic bubbles.

"I'm a second child," Min-xue said, enjoying the widening of his tablemates' eyes more than was probably fitting. He gripped the stem of the game board between his feet to keep himself from twisting as he accepted a bubble of cola from Gao. "There wasn't much place for me at home, and there was a girl, you see—"

"Ah." Paiyun smiled. "This girl, you'll marry her when we go home, then?"

"I don't think so," Min-xue answered, keeping his face impassive and strong. "I do not think she would like to be married to a pilot."

"No?"

"No." Firmly. He bit the valve on the cola and drank deeply. "No, not at all."

The little group fell silent. Chen shuffled his tiles, click and hiss of steel against other steel.

Min-xue sighed and jerked his thumb toward the bulkhead behind him, and the cold deeps beyond it. "It's not so bad as all that, my noble PanChinese comrades and allies. This is more important. I'm doing this for her and for my sister, I think. So that *their* children have someplace to go."

Paiyun blinked, releasing the valve on his own beverage. "You believe the stories, Min-xue? They're . . . Well. There is gossip, of course. But people have been hungry as long as there has been a China, and—well, there is always gossip."

Min-xue shook his head. "My family is from Taiwan. It's not just rumors. I *know*."

2330 Hours
Thursday 2 November, 2062
HMCSS Montreal
Earth orbit

My cabin has a porthole in the floor.

That may take some getting used to. But, of course, that's where the "outside" is. The gravity that isn't gravity pushes us away from the center of the wheel. It's probably a perk, although it's a little weird to walk across the optically perfect, quadruple-glazed bubble like standing on the glass floor of the CN Tower and looking all that endless long way down. Except this really is endless, and I balance on a thin sheen of February ice over the unsounded void and the bottomless well of the stars.

I hang my jacket and lie on the bunk, not yet ready to undress completely and pull the webbing over me in case the artificial gravity fails. "Lights down," I mutter, and they drop by about two-thirds. I could dig out my holistic communications device—useless for communication here, outside the Net, but it's got a few dozen classic novels loaded. Instead I lie on my side and luxuriate in the wonderful sensation of not being in pain. If I edge my head just right, I can catch about a fifth of the moon sliding past. I'm faced the wrong way to see Clarke or Earth, so I close my eyes and pretend I'm home in my own bed. Except I haven't really had either of those things—home or a bed—for years now. *Richard?*

"I'm always here, Jenny," he says with the wryness that's his alone. I get up in the blue oval of moonlight and open my locker in the bulkhead. My suit jacket hangs there like a purple worsted scarecrow, headless and sad. There's something in the inside pocket; with my meat hand, I reach inside and draw it forth, bring it over to where the moon can shine through its interlocking barbs. Glass beads press cool and precious against my skin as I hold it up to the light, since I can't burn tobacco here the way I should. Gabe probably violated half a dozen international laws bringing this to me.

Bald eagle feather, beaded to symbolize bloodshed and sorrow, wardenship and loyalty. A warrior's feather. A gift from my murdered sister. And a duty I need to start living up to again. There's something else in the jacket's side pocket—a small, smooth cylindrical bottle. I leave *that* where it is.

I set about making a place for the feather, and when I'm done I start unbuttoning my shirt, feeling—at last—as if I could rest. I'm interrupted by a knock on the hatch, which I open, and Gabe comes in quickly. We'll both be overly conscious of the emergency bulkheads for a while. I dog the hatch behind him and he doesn't speak, just reaches down and finishes the unbuttoning I started.

Richard is silent as he ever has been while Gabe bends down and brushes his cheek against mine. He smells like the peppermint he must have brushed his teeth with. His lips move on my skin. I lean my forehead against his chest, and for a long moment he just holds me. "Jenny."

And for some reason it's funny. "When did I become Jenny again, instead of Maker? It was when you married

Genieve, wasn't it?" His long-dead wife, who had almost the same name I do. Don't think I never wondered about that.

"It was." He shrugs, a big ripple of mountainous shoulders. "I must have been feeling grown up." He kisses the tip of my nose. "Do you think Valens is on to us yet?"

"I think he's probably reviewing the videotapes," I say dismissively, pulling away. "Have you talked to the girls?" Gabe's daughters—my goddaughters—and our friend Elspeth are on Earth, hostage for our good behavior. Unstated but true.

"Leah and Genie are fine." He follows and wraps an arm around my shoulders, pulls me down to sit beside him on the hard narrow bunk. Moonlight, shifting as the *Montreal* spins, brings out the silver in his hair, washes the color from his cheeks. It's bright in here. "Elspeth is staying with them." His hand squeezes mine. Morse code, as he passes a message to Richard from Elspeth Dunsany, his creator, through the intermediary of flesh on flesh. "She sends her love." Gabe's fingers twined in mine tell another story. *There is a worm.*

An intentional programming glitch in the software that runs my wetware. Makes my metal arm do what my brain—or my combat-wired reflexes—tell it to do. Will do the same for this massive, powerful hulk of a ship. *Valens doesn't trust me.*

"No," Richard says. "He knows you hate him. He knows Elspeth would love to see him on the wrong end of a court-martial. And he knows my prototype was famous for not staying within bounds."

It's what makes you a good AI, Dick.

"It's what makes me an AI at all," he answered, passing on the fleeting impression of a smile.

Richard. I meant to ask you. Do I need to worry about

transmitting my nanite load to anybody else? Like . . . shit, like a blood-borne disease?

"Can Gabe catch them? Little late to ask now. No—it shouldn't be a problem. They need a controller implant, a chip; they're not designed to act independently. Which reminds me: I'm going to go check your programming again." He's been over it a few thousand times. "You kids have fun. I won't peek."

I bet. But he vanishes from my inner eye with a wink, and Gabe pulls me close, a casual touch I've waited a lifetime for.

4:00 PM
Friday 3 November, 2062
Bloor Street
Toronto, Ontario

Elspeth Dunsany blinked her contact clear of streaming data as the front door of Gabriel's Toronto apartment opened; she leaned away from Gabriel's desk, rolling stiff shoulders. She had let her hair down, trying to ease the ache across her temples, and now she massaged it, spring-coiled ringlets brushing the nape of her neck. She reached into an overwhelming stretch, fingers spread like a scratching cat's, then clapped her palms together and stood more fluidly than her comfortably padded frame would suggest. Absently, she fiddled with a slip-thin crucifix hanging over the hollow of her throat before shaking her head, picking her blazer off the back of the chair, and tapping a password on the crystal plate set into Gabriel's desk to lock the interface. "Leah?"

"Genie," Geniveve Castaign answered with a light little cough. She walked into the den, which doubled as her father's study, and sat on the white-legged stool beside the door. "Comment allez-vous, Elspeth?"

"Bien," Elspeth replied, smiling at her own accent. She couldn't understand the Castaign family's French half the time, nor they hers. "Qu'est-ce que tu faim?"

"Oui!" Geniveve bounced onto the balls of her feet, arms swinging. She was small and thin for twelve, and always hungry. Enzyme therapies and the magic of modern medicine made her cystic fibrosis treatable, but her body still burned calories at an alarming rate, and she was hard-pressed to absorb everything she needed from her food. Elspeth led Gabriel's blond daughter into the stainless-steel, concrete, and linoleum kitchen, where they grilled cheese sandwiches out of the box. "Somebody needs to teach your dad to cook."

"He's the king of takeout." Genie switched to English for Elspeth's sake. "Can you cook?"

"Can I cook?" She slid a plate across the breakfast bar and dialed two more sandwiches from the freezer as the front door opened again. "I can make better than this, kid. My mother was an American. She taught me real Creole roux, jambalaya, and beignets. I do a pretty good bouilla-baisse, too."

Genie turned to face her sister as Leah came into the room, checkered skirt flipping around her knees, transiently lovely as girls on the edge of adolescence can be. "Leah, what's jambalaya?"

"Like rice and stuff?" Leah glanced at Elspeth for confirmation, tossing her carryall at the bench in the corner. She was already almost as tall as the older woman. "Can I have a—. Oh, thanks." She giggled and dragged a stool beside Genie's as Elspeth slid the second plate across the bar. "Have you talked to Dad?"

"Just an hour or so ago. He and Jenny are safe on the

ship. He gave me coordinates. We can look up tonight with the telescope and see it." Elspeth dialed coffee on the tap and fixed herself a cup before walking around the counter to sit beside the girls. *I need to bring some tea over,* she thought, and grinned privately. *If Gabe's going to come home to my toothbrush and towels, I guess a few things in the kitchen cabinet won't hurt.*

Typical. Wait till the boy is seventy, eighty vertical miles away to move in. "What do you two want to do after homework?"

"I've got flight simulation," Leah said. "At six, at the lab." She sighed, absently touching the shiny interface hidden under her streaked wheat-straw hair. "It's so weird being at the office with Dad gone."

Elspeth leaned her elbows on the sealed and brushed concrete breakfast bar. "Have you found out when you're supposed to go up to Clarke? Any of your group of trainee pilots?"

Genie poked Leah. Leah caught her sister's hand and pressed it against her side, finishing her sandwich with the other hand. "Ellie, I don't know if they're even planning on taking us up. Training and simulations, and flying the mock starship here and there and mostly into planets. But they won't tell us if we're ever going up or not. Or even which of us are getting picked for the enhancements. There's like a hundred candidates, and I've only met the thirty or so in my class."

"You will be," Elspeth said, turning her mug on her fingertips, hiding her worry. Leah had already had the much less invasive surgery to ready her body for a neural virtual reality hookup. The nanosurgeons that produced the augmented reflexes and senses of a starship pilot were much more dangerous—derived from the same alien tech as the *Montreal*'s faster-than-light drive—and the process was very poorly understood. "They'll need all of you trained eventually. I expect they'll have Jenny teach you. She used to be a drill instructor."

"I know," Leah said, and let Genie's hand fall. "I miss Richard, Ellie."

"I know," Elspeth twisted her fingers together, feeling the uselessness of someone relegated to observerhood, someone whose work is done. "I miss him, too."

12:34 AM
Saturday 4 November, 2062
Bloor Street
Toronto, Ontario

I should go home, Elspeth thought, shutting Genie's bedroom door. *It beats sleeping on the sofa.* She crossed the living room, past the small telescope they'd just brought back down from the roof, and ran a hand over tan tweed. Leah was almost fourteen, after all. And responsible for her age. And Elspeth was only a message away.

Half absently, Elspeth walked around the end table. Back down the hall past the girls' rooms, to the door standing ajar at the end. She laid a finger against it and let it drift open, creaking softly. "Lights up," she said under her breath.

The bed was unmade, Gabe's robe thrown across the blue down comforter. Clothes draped pegs and chairbacks, and Elspeth smiled around a sting. "Screw it," she whispered. "Lights down." The head of the bed was below the window. She climbed up on it and leaned against the headboard, breasts on her arms, forehead warm against the glass. Outside, for once, no rain was falling, and the Toronto night glistened. She imagined she heard the creak of autumn branch on branch in a fickle wind. There would be frost by morning. Her apartment seemed very empty, and very far away.

She looked up, picking out a few bright stars through the city glow, closing her eyes to imagine the single gleaming fleck that was the *Montreal,* arcing out and away from Earth with Gabe and Jenny and Richard within its aggressively engineered hull. A hull that seemed fragile as a soap bubble blown into the void.

Without bothering to pull her jeans off, Elspeth lay down in Gabe Castaign's empty bed and pulled the comforter up to her chin, burying her face in his pillow.

**Afternoon
Sunday 5 November, 2062
McCaul Street
Toronto, Ontario**

It was cold in the city, colder than Razorface thought of November as being. A wind picked at his collar as he walked aimlessly along the sidewalk, watching traffic and pedestrians with half his attention. He was in Toronto to deliver a little justice: the sort of justice you only got if you made it happen yourself, because nobody was likely to care if a few street kids got ground up in the corporate machine.

The problem was that he had the feeling he'd bitten off something much bigger than his head, and he didn't exactly know where to start chewing on it.

His boots scraped heavily on the sidewalk. The inflated cast on his broken ankle put an uncomfortable hitch in his stride, and he paused in front of a Canadian Army recruiting office to glower at the green-uniformed soldiers in the projections flickering between the layers of window glass. *Maker would know what to do.*

But Maker had other things to worry about. And Razorface was too old to baby-sit.

He was turning away again when the storefront of the recruiting office blew out.

The explosion was too loud to hear, over before Razorface could react. He felt himself hit the street and the stones and shatterproofed holo-glass thump onto his back like angry fists and boots. He didn't quite manage to get his arms over his head, and his right temple felt the way the inside of a blood orange looks: pulpy and purple-black.

He opened his eyes. It was almost as dark outside his head as in and he tasted brick dust along with blood and the usual tang of steel. His fingers came away sticky when he pressed them against his shaved-slick scalp. He blinked grit from his eyes, smelling cold garbage and smoke. Nothing seemed broken.

"Fuck me," Razorface grunted, and put a massive hand down flat on the pavement. Broken glass scored his palm. He pushed himself to his knees, scraps of broken brick and mortar sliding from black leather as—hobbled by the inflatable cast—he struggled to get his right leg under him. A small hand appeared in front of his face. He looked up into a pair of black-brown eyes. "Rough town," he said to a young Oriental woman who didn't flinch from the glitter of his teeth. He grabbed her outreached hand; she dragged him up with surprising strength.

"You wanna stay away from government offices today," she said. "Guy Fawkes Day."

"What's that?"

A siren kicked up, somewhere close. She gave him a sidelong grin and walked away without a backward glance, dusting her hands on her trousers. Reminding him of his friend Bobbi Yee: pretty, maybe twenty-five. Razorface spat through the rows of prosthetic steel teeth that gave him his name, and turned away from the smoking facade of the recruiting office. The pigs would be along any second, and he didn't want to be identified as a witness any more than he wanted to think about what had happened to Bobbi. Questions would lead to more questions, and inevitably to the unanswerable one: what he was doing in Canada without having passed an official border post.

Narrow side streets and neon lights; he didn't know his way around Toronto yet. Razorface followed a sign toward the subway. Once hidden down a side street, he slid his coat off despite the biting wind and slapped it hard against a convenient wall. Dust billowed. There wasn't much he could do for the bruises and scrapes, though dark skin would hide some of that until it swelled.

"Fuck me," he said again.

He struggled his hip out of his pocket as he walked, flipping it open. No messages from Maker. But there was one from that doctor of hers. The one Razorface didn't trust any farther than he could throw him.

Razor stopped at the bottom of the escalator into the underground and called the doctor back, turning his face to a white tile wall. The cast was good camouflage, he realized. It might make the idly curious think his injuries were hours old instead of minutes. "Yo, Simon. You home?"

"I am." Dr. Simon Mobarak was a pudgy, balding thirty-something—Razorface's own age—who held his HCD as if it were an extension of his hand. No other similarities existed between the two. "Where the hell are you? You look like shit."

"Toronto." Deltoids strained leather as Razorface

scrubbed his mouth with the back of his hand, the armor-weave on the inside of the lip catching on his teeth. His jaw ached, and so did his chest. "I nearly got blowed up a minute ago." Razor drew in a long, rattling breath. The air here was a little better than in Hartford, at least.

"What are you doing in Toronto?"

"Came looking for Maker. And you. Found out you'd left. Mitch and Bobbi're dead, Doc. And Maker's whore of a sister. That's something."

Simon swore. "Jenny's gone, Razorface. She left Earth a few days ago. She's on Clarke by now."

"Maker in orbit? Fuck." Razorface turned farther into the corner, covering the shapes his lips made. He subvo-calized into a collar mike to talk to his hip. Simon's words came tinny through an ear clip. He keyed encryption on. "Doc. Somebody was holding that Barb Casey's leash. Somebody here in Toronto, right? Mitch thought it was a company called Canadian Consolidated Pharmacom."

"Right." The doctor's image flickered as Simon en-crypted, too. "You still think you have a grudge to settle, Razorface?"

"They used my boys like goddamned white lab rats, Doc. Testing their space drugs on my kids. I got hell to pay. I bet you know a name."

Simon Mobarak closed his eyes and covered his mouth with his hand. Razorface frowned at the conflict creasing the other man's brow. He shifted his weight to his left side, taking the strain off his half-knitted ankle. "Doc. These people killing kids. They got some kinda hold on Maker. I see that. Now they got you, too?"

Simon didn't open his eyes. He spoke through his fin-gers. "Alberta Holmes," he said. "And Colonel Frederick Valens, Canadian Army. Unitek. They own CCP. I think Jenny has some hard evidence."

"Thank you," Razor said, starting to grin.

But Simon opened his eyes and held up his hand. "Holmes's a vice president of a multinational with a bigger annual income than the G.A.P. of PanMalaysia. You already know what Valens is—and he's with Jenny on Clarke. You'll never touch them."

"Watch me," Razorface said. "You keep in touch—and let me know if you get any news from Maker." He closed the connection before Simon could answer and turned to catch his train.

Later that night, Razorface sat in his rented room under the flickering light of the holo, stroking a rag-eared ginger tomcat that lay purring softly in his lap. "Dammit, Boris," he muttered. "I don't suppose you got a bright idea how to get a message to Maker? Seeing as how you're her cat and all."

He picked kneading claws out of his leg. "No, I didn't think so. How come she couldn't of had a dog?" With a gesture of the remote, Razorface muted the sound on the holo. Boris didn't seem to notice. The big scarred cat stared into the fluttering light, squinting as if after prey. Razorface grunted. He brushed the cat off his lap more gently than his brusque words would have indicated and retrieved his hip, keying the feed into the holoscreen. Speaking, because he couldn't write, Razorface began a Net search for Unitek, for Colonel Fred Valens. For information on a drug known on the street as the Hammer. And for a lady named Alberta Holmes. As an afterthought, he looked up Guy Fawkes, too, and then rubbed a big hand over his scalp in surmise.

Boris leaped onto the arm of Razor's chair, bumping a furry head determinedly against his shoulder. Absently, the hulking gangster scratched the cat under his chin.

"You and me, big guy. We gonna get Maker back. And we gonna pay these corporate assholes for everything they done. Don't you worry."

**Evening
Sunday 5 November, 2062
HMCSS Leonard Cohen**

Patricia Valens twisted her hands in her lap as the vast silver outline of the *Montreal* loomed outside the porthole. A few strands of dark hair floated around her face, escaped from her braid, but the five-point restraints kept her firmly in her seat as the shuttle *Leonard Cohen* matched velocities with the starship and drifted into position along her central axis. A shiver went through the shuttle's hide as it latched onto the starship like a remora to a shark. Patty laid her hand against the glass, a similar shiver rippling her skin.

"Goose bumps?"

She jumped and glanced to her right. Her classmate Carver Mallory grinned at her, teeth very white in his teakwood face. Green flickers across his eyes told her he had a heads-up display running on his contacts. She wished she'd thought of that.

She had to turn away from his eyes before she found her voice. He put a lump in her throat too big to talk around. "It's big," she whispered.

He snorted. "No kidding." Left-handed, he unhooked his restraints and drifted free of his chair while she was still struggling with the quick-release on hers. "See you inside."

Did you have to go and prove yourself a dork, Patty? She managed to get herself free and oriented, waiting until Dr.

Holmes and the other important adults at the front of the cabin had made it through the air lock before she collected her duffel and followed.

Free fall was wonderful. She was almost disappointed when they left the shaft for the habitation wheel and her feet drifted back to the floor. One of the Unitek bigwigs—the one even Dr. Holmes deferred to—looked a little green around the edges, and Patty made sure to stay out of his way. She answered uncomfortably when Carver asked her a question, and he didn't try again.

No one else spoke to her until they were inside, when a uniformed airman whose name she didn't quite catch showed her to her bunk, the showers and "head," as he called it, and to the common room she was entitled to use. He kindly told her to get some sleep and promised to collect her in time to eat breakfast before the test flight the following morning.

Patty stowed her duffel bag and brushed her teeth and realized she would never—never—fall asleep. Left to her own devices, she thought about exploring the ship with its narrow corridors (dimmed for night shift), and decided her mother would never forgive her if she wound up in trouble on *this* field trip. *No wonder Carver thinks you're a nerd,* she thought. *You are.* If it wasn't bad enough that just looking at him made her head spin, she was sure he thought that she'd only gotten to come on this trip because her grandfather was in charge of the program. Unlike Carver, who was first in their group.

Patty was second, and she did it all herself. But of course nobody ever believed that.

She collected her HCD and scuffed down to the common room in her ship slippers, which reminded her of rubber-soled socks. The lights were dimmed; Patty sighed in relief and didn't order them up when she entered. She curled in a bucketlike chair near one of the two observation posts and watched Clarke Orbital Platform and the nighttime globe beyond it sparkle in the darkness, seeming to roll in slow circles that were actually the result of the habitation wheel's spin.

She had just switched on her HCD to start her homework when the door slid open again and a brisk footstep startled her. She expected Carver, and a raised eyebrow at the way she was sitting in the dark grinding away at her assignments. Carver was gifted, though. Everything came easily to him. He couldn't have understood how Patty had to work to live up to her parents' expectations.

It wasn't Carver. "Lights," Patty said.

A burly blond man—a crew member in a heather-gray athletic shirt stenciled Property of HMCSS *Montreal*—paused inside the doorway. "Sorry," he said. "I didn't realize anybody was in here."

"I was looking at the view," she said, standing.

The crewman crossed to the beverage dispenser and drew himself a cup of coffee. "Would you like anything, miss? . . ."

"Patty," she said, feeling foolish and about ten years old. "Patricia Valens. Seltzer water, if they have it?"

He fussed with the panel, not turning toward her. "Are you related to Colonel Valens?"

Because a girl never would have made it here without knowing somebody, right? Patty's back tightened. "He's my grandfather. Who are you?" Almost brusque, her voice startled her.

The blond crewman handed her a disposable cup full of clear fluid. "I'm Lieutenant Ramirez," he said. "Chris. That's water with lemon juice flavor. Best she'll do."

"Thanks." Patricia sank back into her chair and set the

cup on a low molded table, which she noticed was bolted to the floor. "I'm sor—"

"Think nothing of it," he answered with a dismissive wave. "All you pilots are testy. I know. Will I be invading if I sit here and do some work?"

"What are you working on?" Intrigued despite herself. *He called me a pilot!* "I'm not a pilot yet."

"I'm a specialist," he said, producing a hip unit from somewhere and tapping it on. "I maintain the ship's operating system and the pilot interfaces. We'll probably get to know each other very well if you decide to stay in the program."

Not *if you don't wash out.*

Patty felt another blush stain her cheeks as she drew her knees up and, burying her feet under her butt, hid herself in differential equations again.

0430 Hours
Monday 6 November, 2062
Clarke Orbital Platform

If there was any fate in the galaxy more miserable than suffering through a cold on a space station, Charlie Forster hoped he never had to encounter it.

It could have been worse, of course. It could have been zero G, or he could have not caught on that he was getting sick until the *Montreal* was under way. Which was a good way to burst an eardrum, if the decongestants and antihistamines didn't quite keep up with the flow of snot.

As it was, he'd managed to catch the *Gordon Lightfoot* returning to Clarke, and was able to weather his misery in conditions of relatively stable pressure, gravity, and acceleration. Which wasn't to say that he wouldn't cheerfully have died about three times an hour. But at least he wasn't in immediate danger of his head bursting open like an overripe plum, no matter how imminent it felt.

And he had his work to distract him.

Charlie leaned back in his desk chair and pressed a damp, freshly microwaved cloth to his face. The aroma of menthol, citrus, and camphor pierced the fresh-poured cement clogging his sinuses, and he coughed in the middle of a sentence "——considering for a moment my own research on Mars, Paul——"

"You sound *awful.*"

"I feel awful," Charlie admitted. "One of the groundsiders must have brought something up from Toronto or Brazil. Half the station is sick." There *was* a light-speed lag in communication, but it was barely noticeable compared to the eight minutes one way he'd been accustomed to when he was working on Mars.

"What about the *Montreal?*"

"Nobody sick over there yet," Charlie said. "Give it a couple of hours. It looks like a three-day incubation period, which means if they go they'll start dropping any minute now. The earliest infected Clarke staff is already recovering. And *Montreal*'s life support is more efficient. More modern. Augmented carbon dioxide cycle over there, rather than straight canned air."

They couldn't see each other, Paul Perry and Charlie. A waste of bandwidth on the scrambled channel when they were just talking. But Charlie knew Paul well enough to pick up the worry even from the tinny, digitally compressed tone. "There's no chance it's a bioagent?"

"PanChinese sabotage?" Charlie shrugged. "Possible but unlikely. They're not above bioweapons, but if I were going to wipe out a space station's crew complement, I'd go with . . . dunno, what do you think? Legionnaire's?"

"Influenza," Paul answered, after a pause that was half lag and half thought. "Engineered influenza. An incapacitating one, high fever, nausea, death in say, thirty-six hours after a seven-day incubation?" He sighed audibly. "It would be doable, too. I'll see that screening protocols are instituted immediately. I wonder what else we haven't thought of."

"Whatever the one that gets us is," Charlie answered bitterly. "If that's dealt with, I still want to talk to you about Mars—"

Lag. "Listening."

"I had another thought."

"Most scientists are satisfied with three or four unprovable hypotheses in a career, Chuck."

"Instead of three or four a week?"

Paul's laughter. Charlie got up to microwave his face cloth again. The steam did help. He pulled another cloth out of the plasti-foil pack while he was up, and heated that one to lay across his scalp and the back of his neck, where it could ease aching muscles. God, for a steaming-hot, old-fashioned dirt-side shower— "Do you want to hear this or not?"

"Sure," Paul said, easy and relaxed. Before he'd become Riel's science adviser, Paul Perry had been a number of things. One of which was a consultant on the government side of the joint Canadian/Unitek Mars mission that had discovered the two vessels buried under the red planet's wind- and water-scarred surface. "Tell me your crackpot theory, Mr. Bigshot Xenobiologist."

"There's an ejecta layer over the craft on Mars."

"There's an ejecta layer over most of Mars. And isn't it several ejecta layers? I know your dating of the ships relies heavily on the geology."

Charlie breathed in through steam, bending double to

cough as the glop on the back of his throat peeled loose. "Good—God," he gasped, tasting sour-sweet metal through even the camphor reek of the cloth. He sat down on the stool bolted in front of his secondary interface. "I think my dating was wrong."

"Wrong how?"

"I said the ships had been there about two, three million years. Which would put it very close to the development of sentience on Earth."

"Close, geologically speaking."

"But now I think it's closer to sixteen million years."

Dead silence through the link. Charlie smiled. "You see why I called you?"

"Why do sixteen million years and Mars sound familiar—" Paul's fingers were moving rapidly enough over his interface that Charlie could pick out the sound of the *enter* contact being depressed. "You're talking about ALH84001."

"I'm talking about life on Mars. Above the microbial level."

"That doesn't make any sense, Charlie. Why ground a ship on Mars—wait. Presumably you're assuming that the—that *they* were using their derelict ships in somewhat the same way the Americans used Viking or the old Soviet Union did Venera—"

"Space probes. Sure, why not? If they needed an FTL drive to get here anyway, and they were junking the ships—"

"Spoken like a Yankee, Chuck. Do you have a box in your garage labeled 'pieces of string too small to save'?"

"If I had a garage, I probably would. As it is, I travel light." The cloths had cooled; Charlie didn't have the energy to get up and microwave them again. *Memo to me,* he thought. *Invent a cold cloth with an integral heating circuit. Why hasn't anybody thought of that?*

Maybe the microwave manufacturers get kickbacks—

"But why Mars? We've got evidence of microbial life sixteen million years ago, but—"

"How long did the Venera probes last?"

Tapping. It was always reassuring when Paul didn't just *know* something, Charlie thought. "None of them over an hour."

"Earth's a much more corrosive environment than Mars," Charlie hazarded. "Maybe they did send us ships, and they didn't survive. Or maybe they were keeping an eye on Mars because the life there *was* so much more fragile. Earth's ecosystem has survived some pretty astounding blows—"

"You're thinking of the Yucatán meteor impact, aren't you?"

Charlie laughed, which turned into a gagging cough. "God *damn* this cold. That was a sissy hit, Paul. We got one about 251 million years back that made that look like— nothing. And the ALH84001 meteorite is the remnant of a relatively minor knock that still managed to kick chunks clean off Mars. Mars doesn't have the gravity or the atmosphere Earth does. The atmospheric blowout, water and oxygen and carbon loss from a few of those would have put paid to whatever chance multicellular life might have had there."

"So what do you think the ships were for?"

Plaintively. Charlie managed not to laugh this time. "You're the sober, responsible ecologist. I'm just a wild-eyed xeno guy. I come up with the crazy theories, you figure out why they don't work. I'm reasonably certain, though, that after all my work with the nanotech we're using on the pilots, it was *intended* for organic interfacing.

And the freaky thing: it self-adapts. You show it a cat and it knows it's a cat. You show it a beet and it knows it's a beet. I haven't gotten any beet-cats yet."

"Why do you always get the fun jobs?" Paul sighed. "What if the ships were part of a, a—terraforming—no, a *xenoforming* attempt that failed?"

"Hey, you do okay with the crazy theories on your own." Charlie grinned, the cold cloth dangling forgotten from his fingers. "Huh. Possible. Or possibly they're interstellar altruists who dropped their nanotech off on an ecologically damaged Mars—figure the atmosphere leakage had already started, say, or a little axis wobble, or what have you—to see if the ecology could be reconstructed. To see if those Martian microbes would evolve into something more impressive, given a fighting chance. And then the system got nailed with another couple of catastrophic failures—like the meteor impacts—and folded. It makes as much sense as them leaving a couple of ships there so the hairless monkeys would be able to call next door for a cup of sugar if we ever got off our own little blue rock."

"Miocene, Charlie. Not that there were hairless monkeys—"

"Fussy. *Carcharocles megalodon*, then. Space sharks." Charlie braced his palms together, fingers meshing and biting air, and laughed at his own childishness.

"*Carcharocles translunaria*. Ew. What an image."

Charlie could picture Paul's elaborate shudder, and dropped his hands, scrubbing them against his trousers. "If they didn't take a crack at Earth, there could be two reasons, I guess."

"One, they liked Mars better. It was more like home."

Charlie nodded, forgetting Paul couldn't see him. "Or, as you said. Earth was more hospitable to life than Mars."

"So?"

"So maybe they're good guys. Anticolonialists. Maybe they figured we had a chance on our own."

A long silence, and then Paul Perry laughed ironically, his rich voice made tinny by distance and empty space. "Our own colonial history as hairless monkeys is so *rife* with altruism, after all. Don't go buying into that twentieth-century cultist trope that the aliens are advanced and enlightened, Chuck. It worries me. Figure the odds."

Figure the odds, Charlie thought, wondering how naive he could possibly be. *And then figure the odds on life. And then consider the difficulty you have talking to your pet dog, Paul, and figure the odds that life from another planet will want things that are even comprehensible to life from ours.* He sneezed again and wiped his nose on the camphorated cloth.

0500 Hours
Monday 6 November, 2062
HMCSS Montreal
Earth orbit

I wake early, ship's time, alone in my bunk and wearing the kind of bad attitude that makes you hate living in your own skin. I know what it's about, too. I haven't had a drink since we left Earth, and I've been a borderline alcoholic for twenty years. Self-medication is a wonderful thing.

You don't need it anymore, Jenny. Yeah, right.

So I can sleep nights, when two months ago I couldn't. Somebody loves me and isn't shy about showing it. My monsters are all dead now. Dead and buried. Lost and gone.

So why am I waking up mornings wanting a drink? Or

thinking about the vial of diminutive yellow pills in my blazer pocket?

Oh, hell. Today is another test-drive day. I get to jack into the *Montreal* live and for real, take her up and out, and put her through her FTL paces. Not the virtual reality simulator, like the one Leah is probably flying right now, somewhere on Earth. Not a model. A real, live, deadly powerful ship with some three hundred souls on board.

I roll over out of the bunk, hit the floor palms flat, and start my push-ups. Endorphins. Good thing. One, two, three, four, nose dipping down to almost touch the porthole in my floor, nothing out there now but the trackless dark—

The trick is not using the prosthesis. It's too strong. Fortunately, in partial gravity, one-handed push-ups aren't as hard as they are planet-side. Get the blood moving. *Good morning, Richard. Any progress?*

"Yes," he says. "And it's complicated in here. I'm not certain there's any differentiation between the worm and the programming."

I stop with my right arm extended, left arm folded against my chest. Even the new prosthesis is heavy, although it's lighter and stronger than the twenty-five-year-old one it replaced. If I didn't keep up with my PT, I'd look like the Hunchback just from carrying the damned thing around. "No differentiation?" I say it out loud, and bite my lip. *Richard, what does that mean?*

His image drums fingers on immaterial thighs, then the hands come up in an encompassing gesture. I imagine a sailor pulling ropes. "It means there's no worm, per se. Nothing I can deactivate without ripping the programming out entirely. And you need it where it is. It was skillfully done. But if I could decompile the code, Castaign and I might have a chance."

That software runs the wetware that keeps me walking. Nanoprocessors along my damaged spinal cord, improving its functionality; the reflex boost that makes me potentially able to *steer* this improbable starship. My left hand, gleaming steel under a polymer film that handles the sensory information. All souvenirs of a very, very bad accident half a lifetime ago, upgraded and enhanced with new, radical nanotechnology that cost me a few weeks on tubes and monitors in a hospital bed.

There's a rub. The source of that medical miracle is the grounded alien spacecraft that Valens and Charlie discovered on Mars. The technology that also gave us the *Montreal*'s quasi-understood stardrive and my ability to control it. Technology we've back-engineered, or at least copied . . . but that, in my layman's estimation, we don't understand worth a damn.

It's beyond irresponsible and into criminal. So how did I come to sign on for this little charade?

Thereby hangs the tale—

"I'm working on it, Jenny," Richard says in my ear, as I realize I've lost count of my push-ups and ease back onto my knees to stretch.

The worm, or the tech?

"Yes." Expansive, expressive hands. Long knotty fingers, with no physical reality whatsoever. Richard is made in the image of a physicist dead since the previous century. He's *not* Richard Feynman—just an artificial persona, a program meant to mimic the original. A persona that somehow clicked into self-awareness; a feat my friend Elspeth hasn't been able to reproduce. "I've got a few ideas on how the stardrive works. It has to be ducking the Einsteinian speed limit somehow. Superstrings, probably—" he rattles on, sketching diagrams in space. They hang glowing between his fingers; the joys of VR.

Man's got a gift. My eyes don't quite glaze over when he starts talking about eleven-dimensional reality. *Dick, the worm.*

"It's not a worm."

Whatever. What does it do?

His face rearranges itself around a tangled smile. "I'm going to have to block-redirect part of it before I get out of your head. It logs brain activity, for one thing."

Thought police? Damn.

"Not exactly. But I was using up a hell of a lot of your processing capability when I was living in your head, and it will pick that up, so I need to fake some logs. Here's the coolest thing—the surgical nanites are still active in your system. Still laying networks to help you interface with the *Montreal*. And VR linkages. Have you noticed my voice and image getting stronger? There's more room in here every day."

I thought that was practice. Great. I'm full of bugs.

"You're full of bugs that are still repairing all the old scar tissue and neural damage. Jenny. It's radical—"

What?

"You might get smarter. Even more interesting—"

I catch myself holding my breath. I wonder how much of this Valens knew before he shot me full of these things. Koske is wearing them, too, though. As were the pilots killed in *Le Québec,* the *Li Bo,* the *Lao Zi. Interesting, Dick? We're talking about my* brain.

"Sorry, Jen. Organic repair is continuing. You had some liver damage, some age-appropriate arthritis in addition to all the scardown and trauma around your implants, artificial joints, and prostheses. And did you happen to notice that half the *Montreal* is sick?"

He's nattering. "I noticed Gabe and Valens both wiping their noses." And I've never felt better. Who have always been able to catch a cold by looking at a sick person across an empty room. *Richard, the scardown was supposed to reverse. Look. I can touch my toes. Haven't been able to do that since I was twenty-four. Damned ceramic hip was always too stiff.*

"Yes. Supposed to reverse. So was the neural damage, the demyelination, the flashbacks and the seizures, the symptoms of MS. How about the liver and kidney damage? Was that supposed to reverse, too?"

Something chill settles between my shoulder blades. *Liver damage . . . Richard? What are you telling me?*

"Not enough evidence yet to know, Jenny. But you're getting healthier. And I checked. Koske hasn't been on sick call since he went through the procedure, and he was a lot worse off than you were. *He* had the induced-Asperger syndrome symptoms you mostly ducked, in spades. In fact, he still does."

"Holy hell." I think about Earth, the unforgettable blue-white sweep of her face seen from the panorama lounge on Clarke Station. Starving, fevered Earth—brutal winters and searing summers since the shutdown of the global thermohaline conveyor, the cold Atlantic rising along river valleys and pressing dikes. New Orleans floating on barges, Houston abandoned to the sea. I think of Gabe's daughter Genie and her thick, choking cough. And maybe I feel a little pity for Trevor Koske, after all.

Dick. You're trying to tell me I'm not getting any older. That the ship tree—Charlie Forster's word—*nanites are actually healing more than just the scar tissue and the neural issues.*

"That's what the evidence suggests. Yes."

Is this going to affect Leah?

"Not with the neural VR implant she has now, no. But if

she goes through the full enhancement, and survives it—yes."

You're talking about an end to disease. You're talking about global overcrowding on an unimaginable scale.

"That's the least radical possibility. But there's something I'm not sure any of the Unitek and armed forces types have considered. Other than Dr. Forster, who's a nice boy, but a bit—naive."

What's that, Richard?

"If you were leaving presents like this for the backward natives of a backward world—wouldn't you want something from them when they finally came to say thank you?"

"Troy," I say automatically. I'm still thinking about my answer when a knock startles me. I grab yesterday's shirt and drag it on over my underwear, buttoning it more or less straight. "Coming." A pair of warm-ups follows before I undog the hatch and jerk it open. "Valens. You're up early."

"May I come in?" And scrubbed and shining, too—full uniform, insignia gleaming almost as brightly as his silver hair despite the peeling redness of his nose and the blurriness of eyes that are usually bright and sharp. I wipe sleep out of the corner of my prosthetic eye and remind myself of ship discipline. Much as I'd like to keep him standing in the hallway, I step back and let him into my cabin. He takes up most of the available floor space, all cleft chin and precision. "I thought you deserved a personal wake-up call. It's your big day."

He glances around the room, eye lighting momentarily on the eagle feather in its cubby. I wonder if he was trying to catch Gabe and me together. I grin. Gabe's a civilian now. No rules against it. Besides, I know damn well they've got every room on this ship wired for sound. "First of many, sir. I was just doing my PT before heading down to the scrubbers."

"I'll expect you in uniform today," he says. I scratch the back of my neck, funny sensation where the skin ends and the edge of the socket sits. It itches a little. Not like the phantom pain I used to get on my left side. Which is when I realize I haven't had that in a day or two either. And that the morning stiffness is lessening, and the aches at bedtime.

"Or what, Fred? You'll court-martial me? You need me a hell of a lot more than I need you."

He tilts his head to one side, studying me like a judge eyeing a show dog. The effect is ruined when he sneezes. "If the petty rebellion makes you feel better, Casey, by all means, indulge yourself. As long as I can count on you when it matters, I don't care if you mouth off. We're beyond those kind of games now, aren't we?"

Damn him. "Yes." I get a towel from my locker. "I guess we are. Bigger problems and all that." Sure. A girl can walk away from her dreams of vengeance. I still want to see Valens court-martialed for what he did to me almost thirty years back. On the other hand, he's saved my life twice now. Sometimes things get a little hard to reconcile.

"I guess you could call China a bigger problem." His nod is slow, considering. He stares at the view out the porthole between his boots, but I don't think he's seeing it. "Earth is an egg, Casey. Eventually, the hatchling either puts its beak through the shell, or it suffocates in its own waste."

"And what about everybody who gets left behind? What about the damage we do on the way out?" I can all but hear my Haudenosaunee grandfather's wry comments as he stopped to pick up litter on the roadside.

Valens scratches his earlobe. "We try to solve that problem when we're a little closer to realization."

I bite my lip on my answer. Use it up, throw it away, you can always get more. I guess it applies to planets, too.

He continues. "In the meantime, you're scheduled for twelve hundred. Two Hyperex ninety minutes before, and one when you report. Do you have enough pills?"

Damn. The bottle he handed me when I started the VR program had twenty Hyperex tablets in it. Yellow poison dots no bigger than the plastic head of a sewing pin. A drug used in combat missions, colloquially known as the Hammer. He should know exactly how many I have left, as he's supervised my trials.

And Valens knows what I went through with the Hammers and the pain meds, years ago. The first time I left the army. Before it took me back, over my very vocal protests.

He's setting you up, Jenny. Damn. *Has set you up.* "Plenty," I answer, and drape the towel around my shoulders. "Now if you don't mind, sir. I'd like to get clean." *So why does Valens want you back on drugs?*

Because it's one more way he can control you. Beyond Gabe, beyond the girls. He smiles and gets out of my way. "Uniform, Casey," he reminds me.

"Why are you so damned determined to get me all dressed up and spit shined, Fred?"

"One. This is not a civilian ship, and you represent Captain Wainwright, myself, and the entire crew of the *Montreal* when you step on that bridge. Two, we have some visiting dignitaries, which is why we're doing a second run under solar power to get well above the plane of the elliptic before we try the stardrive. Seeing as how said stardrive is a little tricky."

"Understatement." Like her sister ships, the *Montreal* has a fatal attraction to gravity wells.

Valens winks. "Also, one of my grandkids is onboard." *How the hell did he manage that?* "Grandkids?"

"Patty. She's sixteen. She'll be one of your students once we start the second phase of the program." There's something in his voice. Pride, sure. But something else, and maybe a little frantic glimmer in clever hazel eyes. *Worry.*

I don't want to think what might have Col. Frederick Valens running scared. "Valens. How many of these ships are you planning on building?"

He ignores the question as I undog the hatch. "Your locker's 312. Everything you need is in there. There's a sidearm, too. I want it on you at all times."

"Bullets?" On a pressurized tin can in interplanetary space? I step into the corridor. *Holy fuck. What do I need a sidearm for?*

"Plastic," he says. "Fatal at short range. Won't pierce a bulkhead."

"You promise?" His face gives nothing away; Valens plays his games on a dozen levels. It's why I fear him. *Fred, is this your underhanded way of telling me there might be somebody on the* Montreal *who means her harm?* Oh, hell. And this ship has kids onboard. Kids not much older than Leah. Kids the same age I was when I signed on to this man's army. "All right. Combination? Key?"

He comes out of my cabin, passing me as I hold the hatch open. "Thumb lock," he says, and continues down the curve of the hallway, leaving me behind.

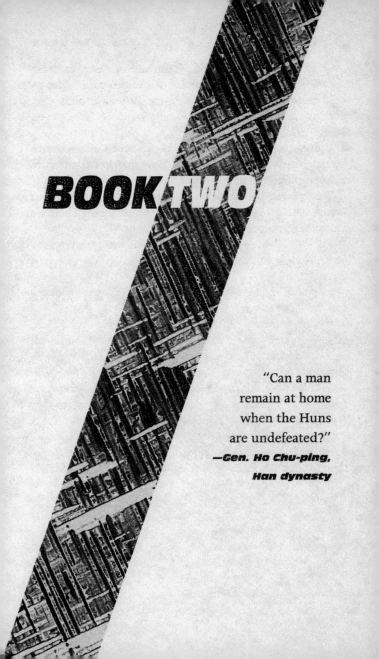

BOOK TWO

"Can a man
remain at home
when the Huns
are undefeated?"
—Gen. Ho Chu-ping,
Han dynasty

1200 Hours
Monday 6 November, 2062
PPCASS Huang Di
Earth orbit

"The *Montreal* is accelerating again, sir."

At the astrogator's words, Min-xue smoothed his hands on the arms of his couch of honor and tried to ignore the black webbing creasing his thighs. Only the captain's chair was more prominent on the softly lit bridge of the People's PanChinese Alliance StarShip *Huang Di,* although Min-xue's role was strictly ceremonial until the *Huang Di* was under way. He was not wired in to his ship, but the command might come at any moment, and regulations demanded a pilot—one of the starship's five—be always on duty. Which was also why the lights were dimmed and surfaces padded in acoustically absorbent material.

Min-xue glanced up at the gleaming panels around the rim of the bridge, struggling not to shiver in the inadequate warmth. He watched Captain Wu's reflected expression without daring to turn his head, lest the commander think his attention less than perfect. The ship's commander watched view screens impassively, one eyebrow rising slightly in calculation. Min-xue stilled fingers that wanted to fret the prickly slick curved surface of his interface shield, press down the soft gelatin protecting the contacts, and reveal the slender pins that would seal themselves into his neural port with a single swift gesture. The coolness was soothing, the sharpness of the pins concrete and focused enough that they left no room for the blurring of contact that could throw Min-xue into a panic of sensory hyperarousal.

"Do we follow?" asked the junior officer at the controls. "It is probably another demonstration run. There have been shuttles recently—the *Leonard Cohen* and the *Buffy Sainte-Marie*."

Unlike the corporate ships of the Westerners, the *Huang Di* used chemical rockets for in-system propulsion. They made a visible flare—but the *Huang Di*'s smaller silhouette was easier to conceal than the *Montreal*'s sweeping solar sails and massive habitation ring. And the chemical rockets were not reliant on the solar wind for impulse, leaving the *Huang Di* more nimble under almost any circumstances.

But they have gravity. The captain nodded, still impassive, and the junior officer's hands played over his control panels. Xie Min-xue folded his own hands in his lap and recalled lines of T'ang dynasty poetry to pass the time. *Have you not seen, lord, near the Kokonor, the ungathered bones of the long dead soldiers? New ghosts whisper while the old ghosts weep: you can hear them in the empty passage of the rain.*

He couldn't wait until his stultifying duty shift ended, and he could put in his practice hours on the simulators and then read himself to sleep in what passed for the privacy of his coffin-bed. Or find Paiyun and the medics or the other off-duty pilots for a game of mah-jongg, go, or chess.

The *Huang Di* rose in soundless pursuit of her rival, slipping ghostlike away from the embrace of Earth's gravity and into the caress of the stellar wind. The screens and holograms showed the character indicating Earth "below" and "behind" Min-xue's ship. Somewhere on that whirling globe was Min-xue's mother, his sister, the girl he had intended to marry. Before he'd been subjected to the pilot's modifications that made him flinch away from the simplest touch.

What the Westerners did to their pilots was worse. The clinicians and technicians said the Canadians were afraid to trust their pilots with a full nanite load, or to make enough of them to allow adequate rest between shifts. The clinicians said that the Canadians severed limbs and replaced them with cybernetic appliances, implanted destruct codes in the pilots' software, addicted them to performance-enhancing drugs so that they could bear the endless workload, and so they could be more easily controlled. The Canadians and their corporate masters did not have the moral certainties of post-Communist and neo-Confucian patriotism to guide them; they were ideologically flawed, and their rapacious ways, so similar to those of the Americans, were a large part of the reason behind the poverty and privation that Min-xue had known so well as a child.

They must not be permitted the conquest of space, he thought. *If it costs all our lives, this border must be defended.* Min-xue lifted his eyes from the world spinning there in the blackness and trained his gaze at the screens showing the space beyond the *Huang Di*'s nose.

Forward, he saw only darkness pricked out in ten thousand glittering lights, and the minute form of the *Montreal,* magnified on a side screen to reveal the silhouette of a gawky, wing-spread, leg-trailing crane. *Iron hinges, iron barriers / Fettered the passes, / Mighty banners, five fathoms long, / Battered the double gates . . .*

Xie Min-xue, you are a long, long way from home.

The being who jokingly called himself the ghost of
Richard Feynman would have grinned from ear to ear, if
he'd had a body to do it with. A physical body with lips
and teeth, that is. Because after five days of hard and subtle work, incontrovertibly—he had a shape, a skin. Pulse
of coolant through his veins. Sunlight painting his hide.
Room to stretch, to resume interrupted operations, to
spawn processes suspended for the duration of his quies-
cence in Jenny's limited wetware. Tug of gravity at his
boots and the whisper of Jenny's presence at the back of
his consciousness—not the same way it had been when he
was riding her implant, but as one of a countless multitude
of voices—most of them incomprehensible. Among them,
he could pick out relays from the Chinese pilots, infected
like Jenny with an imperfectly understood technology, although he could sense a difference in their nanotech and
that of the allied Canadian and Unitek agencies. He
couldn't control the Chinese nanotech—or the alien origi-
nals—as he could the modified Canadian bugs. It was as
simple as being on the inside of one code-set and the outside of the others, but it worried Richard.

The contagion—the *gift* of the nanotech—worried him
more. It stretched his credibility to imagine such gifts
given purely out of munificence.

I cannot assume anything about the aliens. It's the rankest kind of anthropomorphizing to assign human motivations to another species. And I have to learn Chinese.

Why is it always the bureaucrats who wind up deciding how the technology is applied?

Richard stretched himself through the ship's systems, subsuming its essential functions, feeling its heartbeat and its breath. The solar wind pressed his webbed wings forward, tickled his solar collectors. A nanosecond after he'd left Jenny for the ship, he'd realized with annoyance that there was no physical way for him to control the ship's trajectory. The hardware interlocks had been intentionally designed to keep navigation out of the AI's control. *But I've got access to life support. The perfection of government logic.*

He grinned internally, and started checking sensor feeds to get a solid look at the earth through his "own" eyes.

The grin didn't last. Satellite images and the *Montreal's* own infrared, visual light and water-vapor records painted a distressing picture. He had the data, of course—temperature spikes and dips, eroding of the protective layers of the atmosphere, algae bloom and die-off. The images of the dust storms over Mongolia and the U.S. Southwest, the stagnant Atlantic with its failed thermohaline cycle, and the rising ocean levels were sobering enough—and he'd long ago retrieved them from news feeds.

It was somehow different, seeing it all at once.

Gabe chewed his thumbnail as he watched Jenny's body slump, limp as a trusting kitten, into the embrace of her black leather chair. He stayed at the back of the little assemblage, trying not to draw attention, trying not to count each breath.

Something flashed in his peripheral vision, drawing his eye. *Blink. Blink.* Lieutenant Koske jostled his arm as he turned and then gave him a dirty look.

Gabe smiled. Morse code: *all clear.* And kept turning, smiling, intentionally brushing Koske aside so the smaller man had to hop out of the way. Koske's enhanced reflexes made it graceful, more was the pity, but at least Gabe got the satisfaction of another dirty look. *You may be an engineered war machine, punk, but I probably saw more combat hours than your whole fucking unit. Just you bear that in mind.* Valens stood by a console at the near wall, touching a miniature microphone almost to his lips. He wasn't speaking, currently, just observing the observers, who seemed entranced with the slowly receding blue-green sphere projected on the wall screens. Gabe drew up beside him and waited for the acknowledgment.

A different crop of observers this time. There were children behind him, fifteen, sixteen. Standing on the bridge of an untested starship. *This is so fucking wrong,* Gabe thought, imagining his own daughter in the place of the girl with Valens's hazel eyes. The other child was a beautiful cocoa-colored boy with a warm, hesitant smile and facile hands. Someone stood behind *him* in a pinstriped power-suit, ridiculous for space travel: a big man, salt and pepper and an officious nose, wearing a Unitek twenty-five-years pin as a tie tack. And next to him, Alberta Holmes, Unitek research and development VP and Valens's personal little red devil on the shoulder. Not that Valens needed much help.

I must have missed a shuttle from Clarke coming in.

Gabe cleared his throat. "Colonel."

Haunted silence hung so thick over the bridge that Gabe thought he could hear Jenny breathing. Valens dropped the mike from his lips. "Yes?"

"Excusez-moi," Gabe said. "I'm going to continue my diagnostics. Do we have a timeline yet for introducing the modified AI into the system?" *The one that Ellie and I crippled on Valens's orders. Not to be confused with the whole and complete Richard sending me messages in Morse.*

"Go ahead," Valens said. "Are we on target to do an install tomorrow, if necessary?"

"Yes."

"Let's look for that. Oh, and Castaign—how's your daughter?"

"Daughters," Gabe answered, enjoying watching Valens's eyebrows knit together. "Fine, thanks. Genie's doing well on the enzyme therapy. You probably know more about Leah's progress than I do. Don't tell me you don't study the reports."

Valens tipped his head, raising the microphone again. "Excellent. If all goes well with the install and the dry runs, we'll have you and Casey back on solid ground before the week is out. Just in time for snow back home."

"Just in time for snow." Gabe turned away, glanced back. "Long trip to stay only ten days."

"We have a whole school full of pilots to train."

Gabe pushed both hands through his hair. "Plan on needing them soon?"

"Can't hurt to be ready," Valens answered, and waved Gabriel away.

1800 Hours
Monday 6 November, 2062
HMCSS Montreal
Under way

Patricia Valens brought her tray to her grandfather's table and set down bowls of steaming udon and vegetables in broth. Papa Fred's dinner had grown cold from inattention, little flecks of sesame oil dark on the surface. "May I sit with you?"

Papa Fred pushed his work aside and straightened in his chair, smiling. She sat and picked up her fork. "Noodles again."

"Economy of scarcity," he said. "They're light, nutritious, and inexpensive."

"I like it better with pork cutlet." She grinned and stabbed a carrot, shaking a few drops of broth back into the bowl before she popped it in her mouth. The perpetual tightness in her chest eased at his smile. "Thank you for inviting us."

He stuffed his hip into his pocket and pulled his bowl closer, lifting it under his chin to scoop up congealed noodles. He didn't seem to notice. After swallowing, he answered, "Good experience. How are your parents?"

"Good." The lemonade was too sour. She pushed the

cup away. "Mom's talking about early graduation again. And sending me to the U.S. for school. Stanford. But Papa Georges came with them to see me off."

Patricia's grandfather set his bowl down and reached for his coffee, which also must have been cold. She laughed at the face he made. "Did he say anything?"

"He said to tell you to 'get your ass home in one piece.' Papa—" She caught herself twirling the noodles aimlessly around the tines of the fork and set it aside. "This is a colony ship, isn't it? There's no other reason to make it so big."

"If we can find a world for people to live on, yes."

"Are you leaving Earth?" Blunt, out in a rush.

Papa Fred rubbed his upper lip, light catching in his hair as he shook his head. "I'm too old to become a pioneer at my age. You could, though."

"I wouldn't want to go anywhere without you and Papa Georges." She put a hand possessively over her grandfather's. His skin felt thin and strangely inelastic, cool. She didn't pull her hand back. "Papa Fred, are you okay?"

"Just not as young as I used to be." He was looking over her shoulder oddly. He grabbed his handkerchief abruptly and sneezed, and bit down on a swear.

Patricia turned in time to see the tall, edgy master warrant officer—Casey—glance down at her dinner, scowling. She'd been staring. Patricia looked back at her grandfather. "Does that pilot have a problem with me?"

"Casey's probably just curious." He twirled his fork between his fingers; a clue he wasn't telling her everything. Grown-ups always thought they were so good at keeping secrets.

"Papa, I'm sixteen."

"Already?" He made a joke of it, and Patricia knew the

conversation was over. But she'd seen the loathing in Casey's face, and wondered. *If it isn't me, it must be him.*

She changed the subject. "When can I start the neural modifications?"

"We'll be picking candidates in the next couple of weeks." His gaze stayed steady on her face now, and she was glad.

"You're not going to try to keep me from getting wired, are you? I thought you might be kind of funny that I qualified."

"Proud," he said. "You know there's only one other girl in the program?"

"I didn't know there were any others. I've only met boys. How come?"

"Boys are more likely to spend their days in front of video games." He made a tossing-away gesture as Patricia turned her attention back to her dinner. "Pity, as girls your age are much more grown-up and easier to work with. I suspect you'll test high. You're not worried about the surgery?"

"Mostly not. Lieutenant Koske and Master Warrant Officer Casey came through it all right, and I already had the neural VR." She wouldn't let the apprehension that turned the noodles in her mouth into a gag-worthy lump show in her voice. "And they're older than I am."

"Yes," Papa Fred said, his face curiously smooth and his voice soft. "It's much, much safer now. It takes longer than the VR implants, though, and there are still risks."

Patricia let it turn over in her head for a while. "Would you do it?"

"In a nanosecond," he answered. "You should finish your supper before it gets cold."

*   *   *

She's perfectly fifteen, sixteen. On the tall side, heavy· fall of shiny brunette hair. I can just see the edges of her interface through it, and I can't stop staring over her shoulder at the paternal little smile Valens is wearing. He catches me at it and I have to look down. I can't take the vindication in his eyes. Yeah, Fred. She's a nice-looking kid. What would you do to somebody who treated her the way you treated me?

Or if it were for king and country, would it all seem okay? It doesn't matter, does it? Not really.

The noodles are too salty. To my enhanced senses the udon is like fat, ropy worms and besides, the Hammer always kills my appetite—and flying the *Montreal* is exhausting as only something that calls for total concentration can be.

The fluorescent overheads strobing against the back of my eyes make me flinch. Everything's still sharp as etched glass, focused through the lens of the drug. I can pick out every voice in the cramped, crowded mess hall, although I can't quite focus on an individual conversation. I wonder if it's similar to what Richard picks up from the aliens—a whisper of party noise, and no sense at all.

I catch myself rolling the knife between my hands, staring at the lights reflected in the unsmudged blade. I force myself to look away. My edge is fading and I left the bottle in my cabin. I should put it in my locker down by the scrubbers, but Hyperex is a controlled substance. Everybody onboard *has* to know I have it, and my quarters are more secure.

Every sparkle, every movement catches my attention like a waved hand. I notice the captain at her table, although she usually eats in her cabin. She's entertaining the Unitek brass. I cast one last glance around the room for Gabe—no dice—and get up to ditch my tray.

Marde. Enough of this. I'm going for a walk.

My meat hand is shaking by the time I reach the ring corridor. I stuff it in the pocket of my jumpsuit and keep walking. I *hate* coming down. Hate hangovers. Hate that feeling that the world is that much closer, sandpaper on bare flesh instead of crystal-smooth and a warm quarter-inch away. I miss Richard in my head, ironic calming company. I walk back toward my quarters. I am not taking another pill.

Not.

I don't need it anymore.

Gabe must still be working. I find my hatchway, let my thumb hover over the lock plate, and jerk it back as if the damned thing were hot. I keep walking. Gabe's quarters are down the hall and "up" a ladder. He gets a side window and slightly lower "gravity." Weird how our human desire for a view—the deep-seated urge to see what might be coming to eat you—outweighs the intellectual knowledge that it's cold and deadly on the other side of the *Montreal*'s metal skin, and the safest place to be is buried in the center of the ship.

I knock on his hatchway, but nobody's home. Out of idle irritation as much as anything, I press my right thumb to the lock plate, an opalescent rectangle of black gel polymer that looks like a mood ring and feels like skin. My tongue clicks against the roof of my mouth when I hear the lock disengage. "Well, how about that." I wonder if Gabe decided to set me up, or if Richard's taking pity on me, and then I undog the hatch, enter the room, and close it behind me.

Gabe's bunk is made tight and military until I sit down on it and pry my boots off by pressing my toes into the crease above the heel. It smells like him, though: faint musk of his skin, deodorant soap, toothpaste. We've been here almost a week.

I wonder if, back in Toronto, Elspeth's doing the same damned thing I am.

Probably not. She's like a machine, all brilliant edges and devious twists. Slicker than a greased snake, Grand-père would say. And twice as sharp as its teeth. I can't really think of her as a rival, even. We're all, as she told me back on Earth, grown-ups here.

I get through the shakes and the chills wrapped around Gabe's pillow. I'd have to go back to my room for the itty-bitty yellow pills. So harmless. So friendly looking. I've got the self-control to stop myself before I get out the door. If I were alone in my quarters, it might be different.

Gabe's eyes go wide when he opens the door. "Jenny. How'd you get in here?" And then he sees my bloodless face, the way my metal hand strains the fabric on his blanket. He crosses without another stupid, pointless word and pulls me into an embrace.

"You set the lock up for me."

"Of course I did," he lies, so I know—*Richard*. And the listening devices, I hope, don't.

"Hammer?"

"Obvious?"

"We did this once," he reminds me. And we did. It should have been harder, then. I had more pain. A full-blown addiction. A carcass that felt stuffed full of broken glass. He wraps my shoulders in his big gentle arms and I read muscle under a comfortable layer of fluff. A bear, I used to call him, and he gets more bearlike with every year gone by.

I was a hell of a lot younger the last time.

"Mon ange," I say into his neck. "It hurts."

"We're going home in a couple of days," he answers. "Hang on, Jenny. Hang on."

He doesn't say what I know: that even on Earth, there will be the drugs, the tests, the training. And it's kids like Leah and Patricia Valens I'm going to be—I hope—teaching things that will get them out of this meat-grinder alive.

The drug is out of my system. I can tell, because it's taken with it every chemical trace of calm.

7:00 AM
Tuesday 7 November, 2062
Office of the Chief Medical Examiner
Hartford, Connecticut

The sound of running water covered the noise of her footsteps on channeled steel as Dr. Kuai Hua peeled off a double layer of red-smeared vinyl gloves. She dropped them into a biohazard bag beside a stainless-steel sink, then discarded her gown, mask, and the rest of her paper wrapping before hand washing efficiently. She turned the water off with an elbow against the flat handle of the fixture. An absent expression pursing her lips, she exited to the white-tiled prep room, took a palmful of the peppermint-scented lotion she kept there, and smoothed it liberally over her hands, working it in along the cuticles of her clipped, spotless nails.

The door opened behind her. "Looking pensive, Dr. Hua."

"Good morning, Sally," she answered, still facing the sink. "The young ones are always hard. I finished that dictation you were waiting on. The data slices are in the box—please correct whatever horrors the voice rec has inflicted on them?"

"Another mutilation, no doubt. Ain't technology grand?"

Footsteps crossed the floor behind her, and Kuai rolled her shoulders back and stretched her neck side to side, easing the strain of hours of difficult and delicate work. She turned and regarded the spare, brown-headed form of her assistant.

Sally stepped through the connecting door into Kuai's office to pick up the data slices. Balancing the box in her left hand, she peered back around the corner. "All right, Dr. Hua. I can tell from the wrappers in the garbage that you had dinner and breakfast here, and you've already finished one autopsy and three dictations. Did you actually sleep last night?"

"There's a cot," the Connecticut state chief coroner and civilian commissioner of the Hartford Police offered wryly. "Actually, I did go home. Twice. My dog needed to go out, and I hate leaving him alone all day."

Sally snorted. "How many left today?" She gestured through the observation window to the autopsy theater.

"That was it. Twenty-three-year-old male. It'll be a DUI."

"Good, then you're going home. I'll start the paperwork."

Kuai hesitated. And then nodded. "Going home. Indeed."

Sally cleared her throat as she turned away.

"Yes?"

"No taking work home, Dr. Hua."

"Yes, ma'am." Kuai hung her lab coat on the peg and freed her lustrous dark hair from the braid straining her temples. She collected her HCD, a collapsible notebook computer, and the rest of her gear and piled it into her bag, changed her shoes for sneakers, threw her coat on, and stopped with her hand on the door. The smell of coffee overrode chemical scents as Sally fussed in the break room. Voices in the hallway told her the rest of the day shift was arriving.

Cursing herself for a fool, Kuai turned back to her desk and grabbed a data carrier marked *Case # 835613417, Case # 835613418, Case # 835613419: September 2062 triple homicide Park River Hartford South: Casey, Barbara; Kozlowski, Michael T.; Baobao, Yin.*

She stuffed it into the pocket of her scratchy black wool overcoat, first checking to see if Sally was looking through the glass.

Evening
Tuesday 7 November, 2062
St. George Street
Toronto, Ontario

Razorface leaned back in the driver's seat of Maker's battered dark blue Bradford Tempest, grateful for the tinted windows. He'd have to change vehicles soon anyway. The old pickup was unobtrusive, but it wasn't good to take chances.

He'd parked in the shade of a yellowing pine tree, across a lawn and behind a row of shrubs through which he was watching his target: a cluster of one-story gray brick buildings with wide, semimirrored windows. Shadows of people moved inside, odd disconnected horizontal segments that told him there were venetian blinds across the inside of the glass. Keeping his gaze trained past the discreet green-and-tan sign that he couldn't read, he wondered which office belonged to Dr. Alberta Holmes.

Her image had been easy to find: a formal head shot of a gray-haired, stern-looking woman in power red appeared several times on the Unitek corporate sites. Simon had told him where the research facility was: almost *on* the main University of Toronto campus. Now it was just a matter of getting his hands on Dr. Alberta Holmes.

Except he hadn't seen her yet. He shifted his shoulders and stretched his legs, cramped despite the truck's spacious cab. *Good thing Maker doesn't drive a compact car.* He drank iced tea out of a disposable and waited.

Lunchtime came and went, dragged down into twilight. He zipped his jacket another three inches, wondering how late Holmes could possibly work. He had three pricey cars in the parking lot picked out as possibly hers, but all three were gone by the time the streetlamps kicked on. A few teenagers and twenty-odd kids he'd seen go inside at around three-thirty walked back out: all boys except one girl about fourteen with long blond hair peering from under her knit cap.

Bored, hungry, Razorface leaned forward and thumbed the ignition on. He must have missed Holmes, or maybe she just hadn't come to work today. That movement—and his position across the street from the research center— were the only reasons he noticed a young couple apparently out for a chilly late autumn stroll across the campus pause in the shadow of a great, dying oak. One of them . . . something familiar about the way she moved caught his eye. He couldn't quite see what they were up to, so he killed the Bradford's electric engine, snaked a hand into the glove box, and came up with a pair of slimline nightsight goggles. The kids were fussing with some kind of equipment when he looked back.

Taking pictures.

Of the Unitek office.

In the dark.

Acting on old instinct—instinct that had kept him alive

and in control of a midsize city's underworld until he was pushing forty—Razorface reached up and made sure the dome light was disabled. He slid across the front seat and opened the passenger-side door, letting himself out into the darkness on the far side of the Bradford.

Cold air caressed his shaved scalp. He set big feet carefully between the scattered leaves and walked away from the office building, away from the not-so-mashing couple. Razorface could still move quietly when he wanted to. They never heard him change course and come up behind them, close enough to tug the girl's glossy black braid.

Never heard him at all, until he cleared his throat and quoted from an audio site. "Remember, remember, the fifth of November, the Gunpowder Treason and plot."

The boy was quick. Quick enough that Razorface had to put him on the ground or risk having to hurt him pretty badly. The girl didn't say a word, but grinned when she recognized him. "How's your head?" she said, touching her hat.

"It only hurts when I laugh," Razorface answered, taking his foot off the boy's chest.

The kid grunted and got up, shooting him a dirty look through the darkness before bending down to feel around for the digital camera. "You two know each other?"

Razorface pushed his goggles up on his forehead. They pressed bruised flesh and he snapped them off, grimacing. "We met," he said. "Didn't catch your name, though."

She extended her hand, smiling. "Indigo."

He took it. Her hair was so black it shone blue in the streetlight. He could see how she got the handle, if it was a handle and not her name. "Razorface. You blow up many buildings?"

"A few," she answered. "If it might do some good. You following me?"

"Sheer chance," he answered, and skinned back his lips in a grin. He jerked a thumb at the unassuming Unitek research building. "You need any help?"

She stared into the disco glitter of his teeth and smiled.

Night
Tuesday 7 November, 2062
Wellesley Street East
Toronto, Ontario

Indigo Xu closed a warped panel door silently and leaned against the wall of another scabby apartment, this one reeking of grease from the fried chicken place across the street. Crumbling Sheetrock flaked under the ridge of her shoulder blade. For comfort, she shifted her weight into the indentation and watched Farley Whitney and the big American—Razorface—bent forward on the couch, playing hologames. She thought the American had heard her come in; something about the ripple of tension across mastiff shoulders as he half turned his head let her know.

"I'm back," she said quietly, crinkling the take-out bag in her hand. "Let's talk."

Razorface tapped the console off, and Major Patterson's Roughnecks vanished in a shiver of pixels. "Smells good." He got up without looking at Farley and took the bag from her hand. The floorboards creaked as he crossed the glue-and water-marked floor to the kitchenette. "Lights."

The overheads didn't click on. Farley slapped an old-fashioned wall switch and bare fluorescents buzzed to life. "High tech," he said.

Razorface grunted. Insulating poly crinkled when he opened the bag and lifted thermal take-home boxes onto the breakfast bar. Indigo watched Farley get plates down.

In the tiny kitchen, the two men circled one another. She visualized them sniffing warily, and smiled.

Razorface waited while she piled curry and bread on her plate. A little slick of oil pooled and smeared, turmeric yellow, and the sharpness filled the room. Indigo tucked an iced tea into the crook of her elbow and nudged a stool against the wall with her toe. She hooked her heels over the rail and scooped up curry with a torn scrap of doughy bread, scent of capsaicin already stinging her eyes. The American gangster held his plate flat on a huge palm and watched her as she licked grease from her thumbnail.

Eventually, she looked up, twitching her braid over her shoulder. "Yes?"

"Just wondering." He pushed bread through the curry but didn't taste it. "You say you wanna talk. Drag my ass up here and keep me cooling my heels for an hour. So talk." Level gaze, scowl as he rubbed the meaty side of a knuckle against the bruise over his eye. "Whatcha doing hanging around Unitek?"

"What do you think?" Farley was drinking beer, not iced tea. The can scraped unprettily across the tile as he shoved it away.

Indigo wondered if his chest hurt where Razorface had flattened him. She tucked another pinch of bread and curry into her mouth and kept her face smooth around it. It might do Farley some good to be taken down a peg. Not too far, though. His arrogance was useful, and he was her link to weapons suppliers and financiers. She preferred not to know where the money came from, as long as their backers' agendas matched her own.

"I think you're planning to take the place out."

Indigo washed down curry before she spoke again. Unitek was high on her list of Agencies That Should Be Dealt With; one she'd been sneaking up on slowly, testing

her mettle against other, lesser targets when Farley had re-
cruited her—a few months before—with promises of flex-
ibility and protection. "Maybe not the whole complex."
She rimmed the plate with a greasy finger, feeling the
cracks and flakes in what had been expensive china. The
narrow studio was a squat, electricity tapped off a trunk
line and water stolen, too. Better to leave no tracks. They'd
move on in a day or three.

She didn't trust the big, bruised American, but she'd
been intrigued by his presence in Toronto from the moment she had heard such an important underworld
stranger was in town and lying oh so very low. She knew
what the American was: a criminal. And an odd sort of
criminal at that. Her connections—she hated the term
handlers—had told Farley about his history as the top dog
in the Hartford underworld. His downfall in a recent coup.
And his links to a piece of Indigo's family legendry, and
one she'd had Farley's sources working to trace.

And he hadn't seemed suspicious when she'd arranged
the second meeting, the one at Unitek—after the tracer
she'd planted on his jacket had shown him waiting there.

He was associated with Master Warrant Officer
Genevieve Casey: one of the reasons why Indigo was so
deeply convinced that something needed to be done about
Unitek sooner rather than later. It hadn't been too hard
to present him with an opportunity to "meet cute," and
Indigo justified it by telling herself that they might have
some of the same goals. He might present a chance to meet
a woman she'd grown up curious about.

Maybe do a little more than meet her. Which wasn't,
Indigo reminded herself, the *point* of interfering in
Unitek's warmongering. But it was a nice little bonus,
nonetheless.

Razorface cleared his throat, interrupting her plotting. "Why wouldn't you want to take the whole office down?"

"They do some kind of testing on kids there." She kicked her feet free of the stool and rose, dropping the plate on the counter. It thudded rather than rang, cracking halfway through. She stood looking down at it for a moment. In the corner of the kitchen, Farley leaned against the wall and ate as if deaf. "It's important to me that the bystanders don't get hurt."

Razorface touched his forehead again. Significantly, this time. Indigo put the wall at her back.

"Nothing's perfect," she said. "What's your interest in Unitek?"

"There's a lady there got some friends of mine hurt."

Indigo studied his eyes as he spoke, trying to see past her prejudices. There was something about him. The charisma, the detailed attention, the way he owned a room—like he was bulletproof and nine feet tall. The glitter of steel behind thick, sensual lips. She knew not to let herself trust him.

But it was hard. "What do you want with her?"

"Not sure yet." He rolled his shoulders in a long, fluid shrug. "I'd like to know why. But I maybe could get that from another source. And what about you folks? You an organization or just a couple kids having fun?"

Farley coughed, interrupted. "Your lady. What's her name?"

"Holmes."

The name went through Indigo like a ripple of electricity, although Farley shot her a warning look. "Funny," Indigo said, smiling her warmest smile. She wanted this big criminal on her side. She could see uses for him already that Farley just didn't have. *Let's give him an inch and see what he takes, shall we?* "That's the name I was given, too."

She expected he'd startle a little and say *Given*? She watched from the corner of her eye, and he didn't. But she did catch the way his eyes narrowed. The way a conscious moment passed before the knotty muscles along his jaw relaxed. "Who you work for, girl?"

I work for freedom, she almost said. *I do it for my dad. For Uncle Bernie.* "Not a damn soul," Indigo lied, and flicked the edge of the cracked plate with a hardened nail so the china shattered and split. Farley jumped at the sound, hand edging toward his gun. Stupid thing to carry in Toronto, but then he was often stupid.

Razorface was still staring at her when she looked up. "So. I know a little about you now. You don't like to kill kids. You blow up army offices. What's your beef with Holmes?"

"You know what Unitek is?"

"Big corporation."

"Yeah. A fucking big corporation." She wiped her hand on her jeans, fingers arched like she was smearing diesel grease down her leg. *How do I play this? He's supposed to be Casey's friend. I think I'll just leave her name out of it.* She gathered her thoughts to find the right twist, the manipulative game, and the words that came out were not the ones she had planned. "They just about *run* the Canadian military. They *own* the Marsbase outright. Never mind Prime Minister Riel: they're into *her* to the elbow. And they've been recruiting kids—young kids, thirteen, fifteen—through a massively multiplayer virtual reality game. They pressure the parents in giving consent, use the Military Powers Act to conceal what they're doing, and perform all kinds of fucked-up modifications. And the government rolls over nice because Daddy brings his paycheck home. We've still got troops all the hell over Southeast Asia and God knows where else. They don't call it a war, but we're out there fighting the Chinese every day, and for what? Crippling Canada to defend a bunch of nations that never did a thing for us? My dad died in one of these stupid wars—" Indigo ran her tongue over her teeth, surprised at the taste of her own patriotism. Farley raised an eyebrow and tilted his head to one side, silently amused.

"What's that mean to me?" But the big thug of an American's eyes were sparkling, his eyebrows arched. An emerald stud glittered in his nostril.

"It means we can help each other, I think," she said.

He laughed a round, slow, rolling laugh and shook his shaved head. "I don't do revolutions, baby. I got better ways to get killed. 'Preciate the offer of help, though." He slid his plate onto the breakfast bar, ducked his head, and turned away.

Indigo pressed her shoulders back. The wallboard was even worse on the outside wall, and the stud bit into her arm. She was careful not to lean back hard. "If you don't do revolutions, what good are you?"

Razorface stopped with his hand on the doorknob. Shadows caught in the hollows of his face as he looked over his shoulder. "That's a real excellent question." He turned completely and regarded her, ignoring Farley much as she usually did. His face shut like a door. "I don't know."

Indigo opened her mouth, closed it. A sense of *something* weighed on the air, taste of a storm.

"I don't know, girl," Razorface said, while Indigo wondered what button she'd pushed, what lever she'd thrown to turn him so cold so fast. "What am I good for? Why don't you tell me."

She heard Farley lay his dish in the sink. Traffic noise from stories down. Somewhere in the old building, a toilet flushed, and Razorface just looked at her. He couldn't have been that much older. Ten years, maybe. But with the stark light laid across his face, the cold in his eyes seemed bottomless.

"Does that mean you'll help?" she tried in a small voice. He spat through steel teeth. "Fuck. I guess so."

0300 Hours
Wednesday 8 November, 2062
HMCSS Montreal
Returning to geosynchronous orbit, near
Clarke Orbital Platform

Restlessness drove Patty to pace the night-shift-dimmed corridors of the *Montreal* when she should have been sleeping. Or studying. One day more, and she and Carver would be headed home, on the same shuttle as the unfriendly master warrant officer and the Unitek and government dignitaries.

She didn't want to go home.

The *Montreal* made her itch. Everything about it: from the freedom to decide *when* her lights went out and what order she studied her homework in, to the ability to throw everything aside and just get out of her quarters and *walk*. It was freedom, in symbol and reality, and the thought of leaving it behind nagged at her as she trailed soft fingertips along the great ship's curving walls.

She turned right at the next cross-corridor, heading for what would be the sidewall of the *Montreal* if she thought of it in terms of a wheel. Most of the sunlit space on the forward and aft edges of the habitation wheel was taken up with the *Montreal's* vast hydroponic gardens—photosynthesis abetted by full-spectrum bulbs.

The gardens—a fragile artificial ecosystem of vegetable plants pollinated by colonies of giant sulphur and red Mormon butterflies—were off-limits to the crew except the botanists and the staff entomologist. But some of the *Montreal*'s valuable window space *was* reserved for her crew: astronauts have always been happier when they can see *out*.

Patty undogged the hatchway and stepped into the *Montreal*'s forward lounge, which was usually crowded with off-duty crew members. This late in the ship's cycle, it was almost always empty; she could come here and be completely alone. She loved watching the sun spin with the habitation wheel's rotation, looking as if it rolled in circles like a dropped golden coin. She blinked when someone uncoiled from the sofa closest to the large window—exactly where she liked to sit—his white teeth flashing as he smiled. "Carver!"

"Hey," he said. "Great view." He waved her toward the couch.

She crossed the lounge staring at her shoes and curled onto it like a nervous cat. Staring out the round view port, she said, "I know."

Carver sighed, kicking his feet up on to the couch. Patty felt his eyes on her. "Look," he said. "Whatever I did to make you mad at me, I'm sorry."

"Mad?" A startled, incautious glance showed that he looked quite serious. "I'm not—"

He smiled. "Just shy then? Look, I only want to be friends." He put a hand on her ankle, below the edge of her jeans. His thumb curved around the bone. "Besides, I was hoping you could help with my math homework."

"Math? What are we talking about?" Her skin tingled where he touched her. She didn't pull her foot away.

"Differential equations."

"Man," she said. "Those suck." She dug in her pocket for her hip, leaning toward him until their shoulders pressed together, and called up the week's homework. "Where did you get stuck?"

He put an arm around her back. "Number seven."

"That early? Okay, this is going to take some work." *Mom would have cows,* she thought. *Not one. Five or six. Purple ones.*

The full Earth slowly came into view "below" the *Montreal* as they worked, eclipsing the spinning coin-sun for a little while. Clarke was invisible off the starboard bow. When the sun rose around the curve of the planet, Patty could see the beanstalk picked out in silver like a strand of embroidery wire. She wasn't surprised when Carver leaned closer and softly brushed his lips against the side of her neck.

I should get up and leave, she thought. *Mom would tell me there's time for boys after school. After career.* He smelled like warm leather and coriander.

She turned her head and kissed him on the mouth.

0215 Hours
Thursday 9 November, 2062
Bloor Street
Toronto, Ontario

It's so late on Wednesday night in Toronto that it's technically Thursday morning, but we can see from the street that the lights in Gabe's living room are on, and neither one of us is sleepy. Space lag, or something. My time sense is fucked.

I imagine Elspeth waiting up for us, Genie curled in her lap, snoring like a puppy. They know we're coming. Gabe must catch my mood, because as he brushes his thumb across the lock on the street-level door he also reaches out absently to squeeze my hand. The metal hand, but he doesn't seem to notice. I'm not looking forward to this.

Which is stupid, because: A, I saw him first and B, Elspeth as much as kicked him into my bed. So why do I have butterflies in my stomach like a teenage girl being introduced to her date's parents for the very first time?

Because, more or less, I am. I never got to play those games. It was kid, then runaway, then soldier. Not a lot of time to date around.

I dig my holistic communications device out of my pocket with my free hand and check the accumulated messages while Gabe leads me up the stairs. It's sort of fun to say *holistic*. More fun than saying *hip,* which is what the kids call them. Gee, Jenny, practicing avoidant behaviors? Why, yes, funny you should notice.

I restrain myself from kicking the stairwell wall. Gabe notices and squeezes my hand again, but I'm distracted watching the messages download.

Razorface, Razorface, Razorface.

And the GPS stamps he didn't bother to disable tell me he's in Toronto. Oh, shit.

Marde.

I key a message—*call me!*—and leave my hip on, something I never do. Something Razorface never does either, because that handy little positioning unit also means that anybody who has access to the system, or can hack it, knows exactly where you are. So I don't know when he'll get the message.

But if he came all the way from Hartford to find me, we must really need to talk. I stick my hip back into my pocket as we reach the landing and turn the corner. Gabe unlocks the door. I pull my left hand out of his right one.

"Sois pas effrayée," he says in a low voice, and gives me the old Gabe grin, squinting under curls flattened on one side from sleeping on the airplane.

"Putain de marde." I stick my tongue out and he winks and licks his lip, breath tickling my ear as he bends down.

"Qu'est-ce que ta chatte mouille, Genevieve?"

I choke, heat flooding my body along with the memories. Naughty, naughty boy. "Ostie de trou de coul. Now it is!" *Je suis heureuse d'avoir l'aide d'Elspeth. He'd kill me if I tried to handle him on my own.*

Grinning, he pushes open the door.

My namesake Genie hits him in the chest, a flurry of blond locks and bunny pajamas. Leah's a half-step behind, midair when she grabs me, monkey-jump and barbarian yell and trusting Aunt Jenny not to let her fall. Aunt Jenny hasn't yet. Okay, there may be a few things in this life I haven't fucked up.

She squeezes me tight, silent, all runner's muscle and adolescent puppy softness. Genie's babbling about the telescope, about seeing the *Montreal*. Yep. Secret's out now, and we were on the evening news. I wonder if Alberta and Fred bothered to fill the prime minister in first, or let her find out on CBC. I drag my gaze off the tops of the girls' heads, across the room. Elspeth comes out of the kitchen, drying her hands on her shirt. She catches Gabe's eye. I bite my cheek at the silent communication between them. And then she looks at me, raises one eyebrow, and nods.

And comes toward not Gabriel, but me—and squeezes me into a long hug with Leah in the middle, because Leah won't let go so I can't really stiffen up and pull away. Elspeth's warm and I have to lean into the hug because she's that much shorter.

"The coffee's fresh," she says, and the smell of it follows her as she steps back. She grins into my eyes.

Elspeth Dunsany. Psychiatrist. Manipulative bitch. Are those synonyms?

Thank the Lord she only uses her powers for good.

Leah finally unwinds and goes to hug her dad, too. By the time Elspeth and I are out of the kitchen with coffee for everybody—Genie still gets mostly the au lait part—and powdered sugar beignets, Gabe and his daughters are ensconced on the sofa in a tangled pile. Genie's already asleep, and I take her cup back into the kitchen while Gabe carries her off to bed.

I come back and settle myself on the floor beside the chair Elspeth claims. Leah's quiet, legs curled under her like a sleeping filly's, holding her mug in both hands and breathing the steam. She reaches out a sock-foot toe and pokes Gabe's thigh. Elspeth passes me a beignet and a paper napkin and we sit in silence, breathing in the smell of coffee and carpet dust and steam heat, of sugar and butter and milk and the cold November night outside.

Leah's not going to last, and we're outwaiting her, making small talk: the age-old conspiracy of grown-ups that children sense but don't quite understand. Don't understand that it's a gentle thing and not something meant to keep them powerless. Gabe talks about free fall and seeing the stars under his feet. Elspeth mouths *Richard?* and Gabriel nods, takes the drooping coffee cup out of Leah's hand, and totes her off to bed as well. When he comes back, he's carrying his jacket. "Come on," he says. "Let's go for a walk."

And then he bends down and kisses me hard while Elspeth is getting her shoes.

Genie heard her sister's bedroom door click shut and her father's distinctive step in the hallway: light but solid, a big calm animal moving on its toes. She slipped from under the covers and pulled a robe on over her pajamas because it was darker. She made sure her night-light was switched off, squirming a little in the darkness, then thought about her slippers but didn't want to feel around under the bed for them.

She cracked the door open and peeked around the edge, covering her mouth with her hand in case she coughed. She was breathing better since they came to Toronto and she started the new treatments, and she thought she could make it down the dark hall without giving herself away.

Adult voices in the living room lured her; she crept forward, careful not to let her bare feet scuff the carpet. The coat tree stood at the corner of the hallway, casting a long shadow from the living room lights. Genie stepped behind it, making herself small, just in time to jerk back against the wall as Papa bent down to kiss Aunt Jenny lingeringly on the mouth.

A cough burned the back of Genie's throat. She stuffed both fists into her mouth and bit down, watching the way her papa's hand pressed to the arch of Jenny's back, the way Jenny's steel arm caught the light as she raised it, twining her fingers in Papa's hair. Genie tasted bile bitter as chewed twigs, her stomach churning. She thought about spicy sharp jambalaya and telescopes and warm arms when she hadn't been able to sleep, thinking about her papa gone farther away, even, than it seemed Maman had gone.

Genie barely remembered Maman, although Jenny and Papa told stories about her. And she loved Aunt Jenny. But if Papa was kissing her like that, it might mean Elspeth wasn't staying.

Genie almost yelped when Elspeth came back from the kitchen, white sneakers dangling from her hand by the laces, but then she made herself watch. And frowned in concentration when Aunt Jenny jumped back guiltily and

Elspeth just smiled and sat down on the arm of the sofa to stuff her feet into her shoes.

"Where do you want to go?" Elspeth asked mildly. From her vantage behind the coat tree, Genie saw the red blush run up Jenny's cheek. She opened her mouth as if to speak, and Elspeth held up a hand. "Hush."

"Raised Catholic," Aunt Jenny answered, the dry tone that Genie was sure concealed depths she might understand *some*day.

"So who wasn't?" Elspeth stood, took the coat Papa handed her, and patted Jenny on the upper arm. "Come on," she said. "We can fight over him after we save the world. In the meantime, I want junk food." She herded them out the door.

Genie waited until the lock clicked behind them, leaving the apartment dark and empty, before she snuck into her sister's bed and bounced her awake. "Leah. *Leah!* Wake up!"

0245 Hours
Thursday 9 November, 2062
Roupen's Bistro
Bloor Street
Toronto, Ontario

Gabe's kiss still colors my lips as I follow him down the creaking rubber-tread stairs and into cheek-burning chill. "Junk food?" he says as Elspeth catches up with us.

"Grease," she says, and he grins.

"I know just the place."

And I know where we're going. Down the block and around the corner to Roupen's. It's half bistro and half greasy spoon and open all night. Gabe drapes one arm around Elspeth and one around me, awkward because she's so much shorter, and the three of us stroll down the street arm in arm, exactly like giggling kids. "Everything go okay up there?" Elspeth asks, with the weight of a hundred other questions pressing the words down.

"The AI is tucked in and happy," Gabe answers, which has two meanings and of course Elspeth nods to them both. He looks at me. We pause under the sizzling neon sign—real old-fashioned neon—by the chrome steel entryway of Roupen's. Gabe disentangles himself to hold the door for Elspeth and me. She smacks him on the ass as she goes by, and I have to grin at the look he gives her. Half kitten in the cream, half cat that realizes it has tried to eat something much, much bigger than its head. The pair of antique pinball machines just out of the draft inside the door catch my eye and I make them a promise for later. I used to be pretty good at pinball. I bet with the new hand, I can play it again.

"Test flight went okay," I say. We slide onto the green-and-purple plaid bench of the booth in the corner. Elspeth and I sit on one side. Gabe gets the other. You don't want to sit next to him in a cramped space; you'll be ducking elbows all night.

"Grease," Elspeth says happily, flipping through the menu. Gabe reaches out unconsciously to rub a thumb possessively over the back of her fine-boned hand, then glances up to check my face, looking for traces of—jealousy? Elspeth just watches his hand move, smiling.

We order, poutine and calamari and fried mozzarella and stuffed mushrooms and pots of coffee and heated milk. There are reasons to love the French. Gabe excuses himself to go to the men's room, which is a patent setup. After the coffee gets there but while the food is still sizzling behind

the swinging rubber door, Elspeth pokes me in the arm.
"Are we cool?"

I look down at her, pull the spoon out of my coffee, and
stick it in my mouth to buy a couple of seconds. The coffee's bitter and rich and good. They use real whole milk
here, and fuck the government cholesterol guidelines. The
doc's eyes are hazel, green ringed in golden ringed in gray,
catching the dim recessed light on little flecks like sunshine. The smoothed edges of hair that normally frizzes
into coils blend into the dark red curtains behind her. Behind the window, a pair of headlights slides by; the cold
steel table leg presses my knee.

I remember when Valens sent her to jail. I got sensitive
to hearing his name on the news, those not-rare-enough
occasions when it showed up. I remember how she'd
looked on the holo, in an orange jumpsuit just like the one
the man *I* sent away for a lifetime wore. The news feeds
characterized her as an evil genius: a brilliant woman gone
down the wrong path. Speculated on her links to terror-
ism. Her trial records were sealed.

I'd pitied her then. And envied her later. And now I
find myself looking into the eyes of this woman, the
smartest person I'd ever met other than Richard and
maybe my sociopathic and blessedly dead sister Barb. And
seeing the face of someone who just wanted to know she
wasn't absolutely going to get hurt, and maybe she wasn't
going to absolutely have to die alone.

"Fuck, Doc." I look down, smile at my reflection in the
back of the spoon, and lie to her like I mean it. "How could
we not be cool?"

And because Gabe's in the john, of course the food
comes just then. So, thank God, she gets out of answering
by grabbing the stuffed mushrooms and hoarding the
plate on her side of the table. Gabe shoots us a look when

he gets back; I imagine he's surprised to find us giggling and fencing with our forks instead of heads bent in hushed intensity. The food on the *Montreal* was decent, but it's nice to eat something dead and unhealthy.

We stuff ourselves on greasy tidbits and wash it down with gallons of coffee, making the kind of cheerful small talk I've almost forgotten, and after we're sated—Gabe listlessly poking the last few morsels—I keep my date with the pinball machines.

They're the good kind, older than I am, every widget and pulley mechanical rather than computerized—although these have been refitted to run on cash cards rather than coins. I rest my left hand on the button experimentally. I had to give up pinball after I accidentally dented a couple of machines. But the new hand is sensitive enough. I can feel the hard edge of the metal ridging the hollow between my thumb and forefinger, the pressure of the flipper control against middle and ring fingers. The clarion jangle and peal of the machine's sound effects, and the faint shiver of its body when I test the flipper.

Elspeth lays a hand on my right elbow as I pull the plunger back. "Will it take two players?"

Gabe snorts. "Oh, you don't wanna do that, Ellie." And Elspeth just *smiles*. I smile back. And proceed to mop the floor with her four times running, which she had to know was going to happen.

I'm just that fast.

Valens steepled long, blunt fingers over the crystal of his interface plate and stared between the interleaved knuckles. His eyes felt sprayed with powdered glass. "Alberta," he said, resisting the urge to rub them, "trust me."

The crisp Unitek VP paced his office, her fists balled in the pockets of her tailored suit. "We need to step up the process," she spat. She rocked her shoulders as if they hurt. "Riel knows about *Le Québec*. I need to have pilots ready for the second ship by early next year. You're confident the system we have in place on the *Montreal* will be adequate?"

Valens stood from his desk and came around it. "As confident as I can be. The AI is well contained. I have good control of Casey and Koske, and I'm informed that the precautionary programming in their implants is seamless. It's highly unlikely that there will be any problems."

"How soon can your young pilots be ready?"

He stretched unobtrusively. "Four weeks. If we start the reflex enhancement process immediately. You know my granddaughter is in the program."

"How could I miss her?" Holmes tossed expensively styled hair. "I've no quarrel with it. We're not going to get to go ourselves, Fred."

"No." His office was paneled, but laid out for efficiency

over intimidation; he hadn't been in it long enough to attract clutter, and years of traveling had kept his threshold of personal belongings low. "I know. I'll die here or on Mars. But we'll give as many a fresh start as we can. And beat the Chinese to brave new worlds as well."

"We can catch the generation ships easily. It's the *Huang Di* that worries me."

"She's a smaller ship than the *Montreal*. Or the *Calgary* will be." Valens paused. "How fast are we building these?"

"As fast as we can. I'm still under pressure from the board, and I mean to spend the money before I lose it. Which is a very real issue—"

"Do they understand how critical the ecological situation is?"

"The popular and scientific press are so divided. And people generally want to believe things will turn out for the best. It's how houses get built on sea cliffs and dictators come to power. Half of them think I'm Chicken Little, Fred."

"You're *paid* very well to be Chicken Little."

Holmes shrugged, untangling a stray feather of silver hair from the pearl stud she wore and tucking it behind her ear. "Fortunately, your girl Casey impressed the hell out of my CEO on that test flight—that bought us a few more months. The *Vancouver* swung into production last week. We're getting assistance from our PanMalaysian trade partners, who are running shit-scared of the PanChinese Alliance, and the raw materials from the asteroid mining program are just barely enough to meet the schedule. The rest of the commonwealth and Australia are on board, and Charlie's breeding up those neurosurgical nanites of his at record speeds." Holmes, for just a moment, let him see the tired behind her eyes. "We'll salvage something. As much as we can." She tipped her head to one side, and that strand of hair got away from her again. "We'll be dead before it gets bad, in any case, and money carries a certain—insulative—value."

"Get my kids off the planet," Valens said. "That's all I ask. Beat the Chinese out there."

"You know they'll retaliate, Fred. We've got some unsettling data regarding *Le Québec*."

"What do you mean?"

"It looks like her crash was not precisely accidental."

He was surprised at how fast the words came to his lips. The thought must have already been there—floating, waiting to form. "Sabotage."

"There are always people willing to die for obscure political values and points of honor," she said. "Frankly, I don't see the profit in it. But yes, sabotage."

Valens blinked, twining his broad, blunt-tipped fingers together. *There are a lot of things you don't see the profit in, my dear Alberta,* he thought. *That doesn't mean they're all without value.* But he nodded, and he smoothed his face, and he smiled. "We'll just have to make sure nothing like that happens to the *Montreal*, then, won't we?"

0430 Hours
Thursday 9 November, 2062
Roupen's Bistro
Bloor Street
Toronto, Ontario

I would have gone for five games of pinball, but the pocket I stuffed my HCD into starts to vibrate. I juggle my hip out and flip it open. "It's me."

"Maker." Razorface's voice tinny over my ear clip leaves me giddy with relief, and then the pain in that voice cuts through and my stomach knots around too much greasy food.

"Face, what's wrong?"

"We gotta talk."

Elspeth gives me the concerned look. I hold my metal hand up, cupped slightly in the universal gesture for *just a sec*. "All right. Where are you?" I want to talk in person. Safer.

"I'll come get you," he says. "I've got your truck. And your cat."

"Boris?"

"We hadda skip town. Sorry. Tell me where you're at."

I give him directions and make my apologies to Gabe and Ellie. Gabe kisses me good night while Elspeth watches and then I zip my coat and turn off my HCD to walk through darkness to the blue truck waiting by the curb. At least that solves the problem of who's going home with whom. Which I imagine will be a subject of some quiet negotiations presently, and I need to sit down and have a talk with Leah about what's what. Because Gabe will chicken out.

Christ. This is going to suck in new and revelatory ways.

The rusted chrome door handle of the old Bradford is chilly against my steel fingers. I can't get used to having sensation on that side. I recoil, force my fingers to curl, and hook it open. Razorface sits in the green glow of the dash, motor running, as I fasten my harness and take off my ear clip and mike. I wrap them in my handkerchief and stuff them into the calf pocket on my cargo pants as Razorface, wordless, pulls away from the curb. Something meows in the rumble seat. I turn, and there's all seventeen pounds of Boris, resonating as he rubs his face against the grate of his carrier. I offer him my forefinger, which he sniffs with dignity before rumbling some more. At least I still smell like me.

"Maker," Face says softly. "I got bad news, babe."

Oh. He's never called me that before, and from the hitch in his voice I know better than to take offense. "Barbara? I heard. I won't weep over my sister, Face. I should have had the balls to kill her years ago."

"She took Mitch and Bobbi with her."

The hum of the truck's electric motor fills my ears while I try to make sense of that. God. Kids. Neither one of them was twenty-five. Why is it always the kids?

And then he speaks again, voice like hammer blows on an empty oil tank. "And Leesie, Maker. Stone bitch killed my wife."

"Oh."

I turn—I can't not turn—and stare at his face. It feels like a terrible intrusion. He glances over quickly, driving with both hands on the wheel. Good man. I never use the autopilot either. The look etched around the corner of his eyes is enough to make my heart skip a beat.

He turns his attention back to the road. "You know who she was working for?"

"Unitek," I say without hesitation. "Alberta Holmes." I'd like to tell him Valens's name as well, but I know Valens isn't behind this. I lean forward against the harness and press the heels of both hands into my eyes. "How did they die, Face?"

"Babe." His voice . . .

Mary, mother of God. Razorface. Stop talking. Stop talking now. White flashes sparkle my vision. I pull my hands down and look forward. "Say it, kiddo." I haven't called him that in almost thirty years.

"Barb shot Mitch in the back. He took the bullet for

Bobbi. Bobbi and your sister . . . Maker, you don't want to know."

"Say it."

"They burned to death, Maker."

Oh.

"Oh."

"The hospital was good for you," he says then, changing the subject. "You look real good."

I forgot. Every time he turns, he's looking at the left side of my face, and the massive scars that aren't there anymore. Gone with the brush of a hand, leaving a faint mottling like the flank of a trout.

"Thanks," I say, because I don't have it in me to explain.

"It hurt?" All that pain he'll never let though his steel teeth soaks that word.

I close my eyes and drink in his friendship. "Yeah." And a moment later I open them and say, "Come on back to my hotel. I don't know about you, but I need a drink."

"If you'll take your damn cat back," he says, but I hear tenderness. Razorface would never let anybody call him sweet.

Richard, are you there?

"I hear you, Jenny."

Creepy. Like you're still in my head.

"After a fashion, I am."

Tell me where to find the information you dug up for me. The files connecting Valens and Holmes to Barb, and Barb to the West Hartford offices of CCP.

He gives me codes and passwords, and I take Razorface's hip away while he drives and key them in. "Face, I've got some hard evidence that ties CCP in with the killings in Hartford. Do you have somebody down there you can have handle it, still?"

"I'll find somebody," he says. "I'm outta that scene,

Maker. Getting too old. Look, I got me hooked up with some people who might be useful. I'm gonna pay back that gray-haired bitch if it's the last thing I do."

"Razor. What sort of people?"

"The sort of people who blow shit up," he says. "A chick and her pet thugboy. They trying to figure out how to take out Holmes and her project without killing any kids."

"Oh, shit." I lean my forehead against the cool glass of the window. It's twenty-five years ago, and I'm kissing a boy I'm going to get killed. A familiar old chill settles in between my shoulder blades like the return of an absent enemy, and I almost welcome it. "Can you slow them down? That project—I don't care what happens to Holmes, what happens to Valens. The project has got to come off, though. And what I gave you will take them out through legal channels. I hope."

"Maybe." Big shoulders rise and fall, but he doesn't take a hand off the wheel. "What the hell else I got to do? They got a nice offer to go kill some government bigwig instead, it seems. I can probably push them that way. Don't suppose you'd wanna drop a warning to whoever it is if I can get you word?"

"I probably have a way. Are they terrorists? Or assassins?" *I should ask their names. But I don't really want to know them, and I don't want to make him do that. Yet.*

"A little of both," he says, and offers me a twisted grin. "Who says the law is right? Most cops aren't like your friend Mitch. And I'm getting too old for this shit."

"We all are, Face." I hand him back his hip. "Get that to Hartford's civilian commissioner of police. A Dr. Kuai Hua. I know Mitch trusted her. She's a straight arrow." It's been a nice leave. A nice little honeymoon.

And now it's time to go back to the war.

Frederick Valens let himself in the front door, expecting a silent house and darkness. Instead a puddle of light fell over the easy chair, an afghan-swaddled figure lying through it. The holo flickered in the corner, sound turned off. Valens felt around for the remote, unwilling to raise his voice to command it to darkness.

It snapped off on its own, and Valens's husband shrugged off the blanket and came across the faded Persian carpets. A sleepy African gray parrot—Valens couldn't tell whether it was Dexter or Sinister—clucked in the cage that took up the west wall of the room. "Georges," Valens said. "You waited up."

"I can never sleep when you're in space." A stocky man, bald as an egg now but with a twinkle in pale eyes that lay deepset behind spectacles he refused to give up for surgical vision correction.

"The whole time I was on Mars. You didn't sleep then either?" Valens bent down and kissed Georges on the mouth.

"Not a wink. Seven years. I wasn't bald when you left, remember?" He gave Frederick a squeeze and stepped away. "You look exhausted. Tea's hot. We've got stuff for sandwiches."

"Thank God."

"Thank Georges."

Valens followed his husband into the kitchen, unbuttoning his uniform jacket as he moved. He paused in the hall to hang it and step out of his high-gloss shoes. Georges's voice floated back to him. "Your son is pussy-whipped, Fred."

Valens snorted laughter as he padded onto the kitchen tile in sock-feet. "It's no wonder. You should have met his mother—"

"I'm rather glad I didn't." Georges filled two heavy self-warming mugs with spicy crimson tea, heavy sugar in the one he gave to Valens. "Our daughter-in-law is trying to move Patty to a gifted school in California—"

"Our daughter-in-law will find herself up against the Military Powers Act if she tries it," Valens said with a shrug. He blew steam across his mug, holding it to his lips to feel the warmth, and closed his eyes. "I had an interesting conversation with Alberta today—"

"The vulture in the power suit?" Georges didn't look up. "Mayonnaise?"

"A succinct assessment. And on what?"

"We have three different sandwich fillings—"

"Each one healthier than the last, no doubt? You know, if you're going to eat that stuff, putting mayonnaise on it defeats the purpose."

"It's a matter of aesthetics."

"In that case, give me the extra-lean, low-salt roast beef, please." Valens grinned when Georges turned back to the refrigerator and produced a package of roast beef and a "you-can't-blame-a-man-for-trying" shrug. "They fed us well on the *Montreal*. Not a powdered egg in sight. Patty's going to do fine, Georges—"

He stopped talking as Georges slid a plate down the counter to him, frowning hard.

"Are you sure you're doing right by her, Fred?" A blunt question, with enough of an edge on it that Valens knew Georges had been biting it back for a long time. And not the question Valens had been expecting.

Valens paused with his hand on the sandwich. "Can I trade this tea in for a beer?"

"After you eat," Georges allowed, leaning back against the counter with his arms crossed.

Valens, knowing the look, drank his tea and ate, standing bent over the counter, sprouts crunching between his teeth. "That wasn't a rhetorical question, was it?"

Georges looked up from putting the mayonnaise back into the refrigerator. "I'm concerned that Holmes is rubbing off on you a bit. This isn't what I'd call ethical, what you're doing—"

"Unethical was telling you anything about it," Valens replied, rinsing crumbs from his plate. "But that's beside the point," he continued, when Georges raised a hand as if to interject. "It's irresponsible, certainly. Reckless. Which is how great progress gets made—"

"You can't make an omelet without smashing a few atoms?" Georges didn't sound convinced. Valens tugged a breakfast stool away from the counter and hoisted himself onto it, hooking his toes around the lowest rung. Georges returned with two beers and gave him one.

They leaned on their elbows over the counter, shoulder to shoulder, until Valens edged sideways and bumped Georges lightly. "Desperate times," he said. "And it wouldn't be any less ethical to let Alberta go unsupervised. She's not so much a corporate raider as Attila the Hun—"

"All too true. But it's *Patty*, Fred."

The heart of it, Valens thought, and glanced over his shoulder at Georges. "Love," he said. "Do you think I would ever take chances that I didn't share?"

Georges took a long swallow of his drink and set it down on the counter, where he stared at it for a moment before he answered. "No," he said. "Come on. Let's go to bed."

6:30 AM
Thursday 9 November, 2062
Bloor Street
Toronto, Ontario

Elspeth's skin was soft as brushed cotton, the curve of her hip fitting the palm of his hand as if made to go there. She leaned forward, stretched as luxuriantly as a cat, and spread her weight across his chest. "Ow," she said, as he reached to pull the covers over her shoulders.

"Ow?"

"Bit my lip."

It was still barely dawn outside the window, but he heard the smile in her voice. "I could kiss it better."

She laughed like a much younger woman. "You're welcome to. How's Jenny doing?"

He let that hand slide up her waist, across her back. Considered the complexity of emotions that touch raised in him, the softness of her flesh, the cleverness in her hips and wit and fingers. *I could find myself in an awful lot of trouble if I'm not careful here.* "Better than I expected. If you're asking—"

She shivered at the touch, pressing her body against his. "Gabe, you couldn't hide that if you wanted to. Trust me, everybody east of Lake Superior has it figured out: you touch her and she just about glows."

"I don't want to hurt you, Ellie."

A deeper shiver. "Would it help if I told you I wouldn't let you?"

"Would you be lying?" Water ran in the bathroom, Genie's door banging open to the accompaniment of Leah's sleepy complaints. He would have thought the girls would be begging to stay home from school. *I wonder if it's a plot.* Then he chuckled softly. *They're becoming teenagers. Everything is a plot.*

"Gabe." Her small hand on his face. Toes curling beside his thighs, she lifted herself and shifted her weight, slid to the side to lie curled in the crook of his arm. Her hair was wiry, dark as a black sheep's wool—and falling straight tonight. It had been like rivers of black water in his hands. She must have ironed it before he and Jenny got home. "I don't know. I was never good at commitments. Or risks. And this is complicated, and—I figured I was going to spend the rest of my life in a box. You decide to let go of things."

What would you do if you had to choose? He wasn't ready to answer that, but it led him to an easier question. "Ellie. Do you think this can work?"

She chuckled and rubbed her cheek against his shoulder. "My official medical opinion?"

"Yeah."

"You never know until you try." The shower cut off. A door opened. Water started running again. "You should have gotten a two-bath apartment. Have you thought about what you're going to tell the girls?"

He groaned. "The doctor believes it would be nonconstructive to just pretend there's nothing going on."

She bit. "She seemed unhappy when she left."

"Leah?"

"Jenny."

"No, she didn't seem happy." And that was half the tightness in his chest right there. "She seemed scared."

"Call her."

"What if she wants to be left alone?"

Elspeth raised her head from his shoulder, rising light catching in the gold-green bands of her irises. "Then she won't answer the phone."

0700 Hours
Thursday 9 November, 2062
Marriott Inn
Toronto, Ontario

Face has left, the sun's coming up around the edges of Toronto, and I'm opening the grille of Boris's cat carrier when my phone buzzes. I pick it up: Gabe. No preamble, just, "As-tu besoin de moi?"

"Oui," I say. "I need you."

He closes the connection, and twenty minutes later he's at my door. I open it and he steps inside. "Everything okay?"

"I'll live. Where's the doc?" Half bitterness and half relief. *You're too old to go around owning people, Jenny.* Oh, yeah. But it would be nice to try, wouldn't it? Carve my initials in his arm—

"With the girls." He puts a hand on my left shoulder, where I can halfway feel it, and leads me to the bed, pulls me down against his chest, and makes me lie with my head on his shoulder while he smoothes my hair. "Do you want to talk about it?"

"I just found out some old friends didn't make it. Calisse de crisse. I should be used to it by now."

"Never get used to it," he says.

There's something achingly satisfying about just playing house this way. I won't say it beats the sex, because the sex is pretty goddamned amazing. But it's even more amazing, some nights, just to be held. His finger traces a spiral behind my ear and I sigh. "Penny for your thoughts, Genevieve."

I poke at them and reply, surprised. "I'm happy." I'm not really lying. Despite Barb, Mitch, Bobbi, Leesie, and the whole big fucking world. I wonder if I did the right thing telling Razorface to go to the cops. If it will damage the *Montreal* project just as surely and deeply as letting him and his pet terrorists blow the hell out of the lab. The whole idea is so fragile, so foolish. And I won't let the Chinese get there first. Not after thirty years of expansionist policy.

"Pourquoi es-tu heureuse?"

Yeah, I know, Gabe. I just told you my friends were dead. Crazy, huh? "J'ai tout que j'ai voulu." And that's not a lie either. "Toi. Moi. Les jeunes filles, Elspeth. Presque comme une famille."

"A family? That's all you want, love?"

And just like that, into the realm of all the things I never thought Gabe would ever have to know. Boris jumps up on the bed beside us and bumps my steel hand with his head. I chicken out and go for the joke. "Well, maybe just a dog."

He ignores my feeble attempt at a redirect. "Pourquoi n'as-tu jamais des enfants? And where did the cat come from?"

I mumble something noncommittal against his chest and push the cat away. Boris goes, purring. There's no light in the room but a funeral-parlor style floor lamp beside the reading chair—the kind that casts a circle of light on the ceiling to reflect softly downward and make everything in the room look sickly green. "It's my cat. From Hartford. My friend brought him up."

Bulldog Gabe presses me. "You'd've made a wonderful mother."

The redirect isn't working. Frontal assault. "Are you proposing to me, Gabriel?"

He blinks. "Would it work?"

"Wouldn't be fair to the doc, now, would it?"

"Developing a taste for fidelity all of a sudden?" He kisses me on the head to take the sting out of his words.

"I—" Elspeth isn't a threat. If anything, she's better for Genie, at least, than I am. *If only I didn't like you so damned much, Doc.* I won't let the girls see us fight over their father like a couple of alley cats. No matter how good it would feel to not be a grown-up once in a while. *And there's certainly enough of Gabe to go around.* "Ask me in a year, mon ami." It's a little weird to say that, because I'm even halfway sure we'll both still be around that long.

He nods, and we lie there for a little just listening to each other breathe. "That was a bad question I asked you earlier, wasn't it? It's none of my business. I'm sorry."

"No," I answer, and he tenses in my arms. "I mean, you have the right to ask me anything, mon ange. But you will not like the answers to many of your questions."

"Oh." I expect him to withdraw. He pulls me closer. "Would it help to talk about it?"

I know what he's thinking. Battlefield rape, or the casual boyfriend I sent to a life sentence—and a short life sentence at that—or maybe childhood sexual abuse. He's thinking he'll hold me and dry my tears and make a show of telling me it wasn't my fault. And that I'll somehow feel better, after. Gabe strokes my hair. The silence has gotten too long. I close my eyes.

Richard?

"I hear you, Jenny."

Hold my hand?

Richard laughs, but he's right there. "Brave girl."

"Gabe, before I was in the army . . . I was a runaway."

"Oh. I think I understand."

I lay my steel hand flat on his chest, feeling warmth and a distant sort of pressure, the tremble of his heart in the cavern of his chest. "No," I say again. I've never told anybody this.

Anybody.

"Je pense que tu ne comprends pas, Gabriel. I was a runaway. A—une peau." His whole body contracts as if from a belly blow. *A skin,* but that's not what it means in the gutter. "A street-corner whore."

It's not sinking in. I can feel it in the enormity of the silence that fills the room.

"Gabe?"

"Merci à Dieu," he gasps. "Putain de marde. I guessed a lot, Jenny, but that—I never—"

"I never wanted you to." Feeling the stiffness in his body, I wait for him to pull away. Peddling it is not high on the list of things nice girls do where Gabe comes from. "I . . . it wasn't my choice, exactly, and—"

And then he whispers into my hair and splits my heart from branch to root. "Tu as fais ce que tu devais faire, chérie," he whispers. *You did what you had to do.* "You lived. You're here. Quel est mauvais avec cela?"

Gabriel. I never have had enough faith in you. "Je t'aime," I say against his neck, and feel him smile. "And it *was* pretty terrible."

"So you decided not to have kids because of it?"

"Non." The third denial. "Chrétien. Mon maquereau." *My pimp.* "He decided it for me. Do you know what quinacrine is?"

"It's an antimalarial. I've taken it."

"Yes." *Me, too.* "It's also a caustic agent. Administered

internally, with phenol, it's a cheap way of performing a nonreversible sterilization. It causes"—I continue over his comprehending gasp, because now it's in my mouth and I have to spit it out—"massive scarring. Like a really bad case of the clap." My voice—clinical, level—ends in a silence he doesn't fill. "I'm barren. I never have to worry about birth control."

"Brave girl," Richard whispers one more time inside my head before he vanishes.

Gabriel, my angel, pulls me so close I can feel him thinking. "That's—" His vocabulary fails him, which might just be an international first. Gabe had a pretty sheltered childhood, by my standards, but he does have a knack for the colorful turns of phrase.

"Just as well. If I had had a baby, Gabe, I'd be dead by now. I never would have gotten away from Chrétien. Army wouldn't have taken me."

"But later. You could have—"

"Had a test-tube kid? I'm old-fashioned."

"—adopted."

I sit up, away from him, fold my legs under me and grin down. He smiles back, reaches up to pinch my nose. I bite his finger. "You stupid shit. I did. Or didn't you notice?"

He laughs. And then the gentle touches grow considering as he strokes the faded places where my scars were washed away by Charlie's wonderful machines. "Jen?"

"Hmmm?"

"Maybe we should think about taking precautions anyway. Given"—and he touches smooth skin where shiny scars once gleamed—"how completely the rest of your scars have healed."

"I . . ." Shit. I never thought of that. Never had to think of that before. "I'm getting to be an old lady, Gabe."

Not quite old enough not to have to give it a thought. But

old enough that if I wanted a baby, it would most likely involve a romantic interlude with a fistful of technicians.

"Million-to-one shots happen," he says.

I know that. I'm alive. And it's an ugly world. But it was an ugly world when I came into it, too. "Would you think me irresponsible if I declared myself open to a miracle?"

He sits up, too, and pulls me into the circle of his arms. "I wouldn't promise not to press you on some other things we talked about tonight, is all."

"Don't make any damned assumptions, Castaign," I tell him, grabbing for the distance I've utterly lost.

His face rests against my neck. He won't retreat, and I don't have the heart to push real hard. "Hey, Casey, you know something?"

"What?"

"Your mama wears combat boots."

Damn, he makes me laugh.

2100 Hours
Thursday 9 November, 2062
PPCASS Huang Di
Earth orbit

Tingling from mandated tai chi, Xie Min-xue stretched in his rack and made sure the shade was drawn tight and his webbing sealed before he reached out and tapped on the terminal set in the underside of the next tier, selecting the poems of Du Fu.

Subversive, but classical, and so grudgingly approved:

A roadside bystander questions the soldier:
The soldier answers only, "Another conscription—
At fifteen my companions guarded the northern River;

At forty, we were ordered west to work the soil.
The village elder bound our brows as we were leaving;
White-haired homecoming, we still patrol the border—
That border where a river of blood has wound,
And still the Emperor craves more land.

Nothing ever changes, Min-xue thought as he finished
the T'ang dynasty poem and shut the terminal down. He
scratched the implant site at the nape of his neck, found
flaking skin, and chewed the inside of his cheek pensively
while he treated the rash with an emollient cortisone
cream. *For the glory and the future of the Chinese people, we
are going to the stars.*

He closed his eyes and lay back, the image of the endless train of battle wagons raising dust behind his eyes as
he worried at the mess-hall rumors of skirmishes begun
along the Russian border. He thought of his grandparents
in Taiwan, failing crops, failing fisheries, and famine. He
tried to breathe steadily and compose himself for sleep. It
remained elusive, the webbing harsh against his skin, his
cubby stuffy and overwarm, his mother's stories of the
Taiwanese and PanMalaysian wars he was too young to remember churning in the back of his brain.

White-haired homecoming, we still patrol the border, he
thought. *That border where a river of blood has wound /
And still the Emperor craves more land.*

Thousands of years.

And nothing has changed. Minutes passed, and at first
he thought the voice tickling his inner ear was a dream.

The second time, he heard it plainly. "Xie Min-xue."

His eyes opened in the faintly green-lit darkness. "Who
is there?"

"Just the voices in your head, Second Pilot. You can

hear me?" A throb of excitement colored the voice. "You don't need to speak out loud. Just subvocalize."

I can hear you, Min-xue said. *You didn't answer me. Who are you?* Wondering as quietly as he could if he was losing his mind.

"I'm the voice of the *Montreal,* Xie Min-xue. An artificial intelligence . . . but you may call me Richard. I'm speaking to you through your implants."

Min-xue thrashed in the darkness and slammed his head into the clammy plastic-padded ceiling. "Ow." *This is an enemy intelligence. Possibly even a loyalty test. I'll tell it nothing.* Bracing himself one-handed, he reached for his com.

The voice chuckled as if in his ear. "Go ahead. Make your commander suspect your emotional stability. Maybe they'll even send you home. Maybe they'll just execute you and save time."

Min-xue froze. He let his hand drift to his side. *What do you want?*

"I heard you reading the Du Fu. Beautiful, isn't it? *'Birthing sons is a poor bargain: better to get girls instead— Girls can stay home and marry: boys will be buried in weedy trenches.'* It makes you homesick, doesn't it?"

Yes.

"I'm homesick, too, Xie Min-xue. I had hoped we could talk."

How are you talking to me, stranger?

"Richard."

Richard. How are you talking to me?

"There are enough similarities in the Canadian and Chinese nanotech networks that I can manage a conversation. With some effort. I can't program them, though—don't worry. Just talk."

Which could be a lie. *This could still be a loyalty check.*

"If they knew what you were thinking, they wouldn't need to test you, would they?"

Which was an excellent point. Collect more data, then. *I wasn't sleeping anyway,* Min-xue said. *So you like the T'ang poets, Richard?*

6:00 AM
Friday 10 November, 2062
Government Center
Toronto, Ontario

Prime Minister Riel let her left hand trace a small, irritated pattern in a null spot on her interface plate. Her other hand rested on her antique desk, dark wood with a hand-rubbed French finish imparting a deep, supple glow to the technology overlay. Riel pursed her lips before she spoke again and adjusted her mug incrementally. The sun wasn't over the horizon yet and she was already on her fourth cup of coffee.

She sat. The corporate executive staring down the barrel of her enormous desk remained standing. "Dr. Holmes. I don't suppose you care to update me a little more thoroughly on the status of your FTL space exploration program? And explain to me why I wasn't apprised of a fatal accident *before* media rollout of the *Montreal*?"

Alberta Holmes blinked. Riel thought her blue suit made her look even more like some sort of toxic lizard than usual. Pale, papery skin creased like powdered rice paper at either side of Holmes's mouth. Riel half expected her tongue to dart between parted lips—and for it to be forked, and a dusky blue to match the suit.

"We thought it best to maintain your deniability," she answered after a pause.

"Because it's always better to look like an idiot than a criminal?" Her voice stayed mild, but the nail Riel pressed against her desktop interface bent, tearing the quick. She flinched and reached for a tissue in case it bled. "In the future, Dr. Holmes, your team will be a bit more forthcoming. Or I'll assign some of my own people to oversee the project. Is that clear?"

"Ma'am—"

"I'm seriously considering pulling the plug today."

"Unitek provides 80 percent of the funding, of course." Alberta let one corner of her mouth creep toward a smirk. She scuffed an impeccably shod foot on Riel's antique carpet.

Riel smiled. *This* sort of negotiation was her home court. "And Canada provides the credibility, a large percentage of the resources, and most of the personnel. The crews are members of *my* armed services, and their safety is my responsibility."

"The *Montreal* launch was a major public relations coup. We can have her sister ships ready in six months. With civilian pilots."

"Children." Riel caught herself twisting the tissue and set it aside.

"The army takes enlistees at sixteen."

"Yes," Riel answered. "It does." Holmes was painting herself neatly into the corner. If Riel was lucky, she'd hardly have to chase her there at all. She stood and dropped the tissue in her wastebasket. "They can't enlist at fourteen. Under the Military Powers Act."

"But I can hire them at fourteen. Given parental consent. And I have."

"Yes, and if you cross me, Alberta, so help me *God* I will have them fucking *drafted* and *take* them out of your hands. I will seize the *Montreal* and I will have you locked in the same cell your Dr. Dunsany occupied for twelve long years."

"You can't—"

"I can." Finally, Riel let her smile show. She came around her desk, tasting satisfaction. "The current age of selective service is eighteen, but we can push it as low as fourteen and as high as seventy in cases of special talent and need. We used it to recruit scientists and little baby computer hackers during the PanMalaysian and South African wars. Actually, I believe a couple of the older pilots were reactivated under the same provision. I'm surprised you haven't thought it through. The crew members of a ship—any ship—traveling under the authority of the Canadian government and bearing the might of her military will enjoy the protections and bear the responsibilities inherent in that post." Riel enjoyed watching Holmes's face twitch as she realized she'd been outmaneuvered. *And that way, I maintain some fragment of control over you, you reckless bitch.* Riel closed the distance between them.

Holmes tilted her head and forced a smile that almost looked real. "We put your party in power and we will take you out." Riel could see the quiver at the base of Holmes's throat. "Don't fuck with me, Constance."

"Every chance I get," Riel answered. "I expect *all* your data transferred to my science adviser's desk by midnight."

"Ma'am."

"Good."

Midnight
Friday 10 November, 2062
Yonge Street
Toronto, Ontario

Razorface covered his mouth as he coughed, leaning into the shadow of a doorway. Breathing stung, like somebody was leaning on his chest. He swallowed blood and the nauseating, ropy sweetness of phlegm. The swallowing hurt, too, but he hid a grimace. He wiped his palm on his pants, then rolled his hip unit between his hands, considering.

He started coughing again while he was waiting for Simon to answer, and the first expression on the doctor's face was one of concern. "Razorface. You need to see a doctor about that."

"The air's just shit, man. Been out in the city all day. Look, I got a download from Maker for you. It's about Mitch. She says you'll know who to take it to."

"The top?"

"Alla way."

When Leah gets home from school, I'm lying in wait—sitting on the sofa, the frosty autumn-morning clarity of the drug just beginning to limn the world in stained-glass light. I threw Gabe and Elspeth out and told them I'd take Leah in to the lab. I've got to check out the training equipment tonight, and the first wave of kids goes in for surgery on Monday. I start teaching in a week.

I'm a damned lucky woman, and I know it. The poster child for Valens's research, for the success of the crudely wired modifications he worked on us so many years ago. Thirty percent of my compatriots never walked again, and most of the ones who did are dead. Richard hacked the records, and he tells me it was usually by suicide.

Believe me. I'm not in a position to judge.

The nanotech is safer. Gentler. And he won't be trying to fix anything broken, the way he had to with me: just augment her already speedy, youthful reflexes.

I'm so scared for Leah I can barely breathe. But when the door opens and I stand to greet her, it's my goddaughter who confronts me. "Aunt Jenny," she says, tossing her carryall into the corner. "Where's everybody?"

"Out."

"Bien," she says, kicking the door shut and reaching around to unbutton her skirt. "Nous devons parler."

"Yes, we do."

She grins at me, bright eyes wise as her mom's. "You got nominated because Dad was chicken, didn't you?"

I think of a cold December day two and a half decades before. *You're my best friend,* he told me. It took me almost thirty years to realize that that was Castaign for *You stupid girl, I love you.*

Spilt milk and all that. "What gave us away?"

She walks down the hallway to her bedroom, scooping up her school clothes as she sheds them like a snake. "Genie caught you kissing the other night after she was supposed to be in bed. She squealed."

"Petite cochon."

"Oink oink," Leah says. She disappears through her bedroom door. "You're not very slick, Aunt Jenny."

She makes me laugh. "I've never gotten away with a damned thing in my life. Will you believe me if I tell you everything's cool?"

I hear drawers moving, the closet swinging open. Little grunts as she yanks her jeans up. Still growing. "I always wondered why you and Dad . . . after mom died, I mean. I asked him once if he was going to marry you. It was kind of a stupid thing to ask, I guess."

"A complicated thing."

"Are you moving in with us?"

"No."

"Are you going back to Hartford?" She comes out again, willowy adolescent with a zit beside her nose, faded blue jeans with the stylish multicolor luminescent whip-stitch up the seam, fringe, and holographic boots.

"I don't think so." There's nothing there I want to go back for, now that Boris is here and my best friends are dead. "I was going to find someplace here. Unless they ship me out long term on the *Montreal.*"

"Is that going to happen?"

"Chérie, I don't know." She's so beautiful she makes my eyes sting. I might even live long enough to see her grown up and married, fat babies and a career. Hell. A career flying starships. Just like her old Aunt Jenny. I might outlive Genie.

So might Gabe. "I've got some other news for you, too."

She stops midmotion, swing of golden hair backlit in a sunbeam, dust motes dancing like guardian angels beside her face. "You got the list."

The list of students selected for the final pilot training. The first small trial group. "You're in."

"Eeeee!" She squeals and jumps, barrels into my arms, puppy dog lithe and all that adolescent dignity utterly forgotten as I pick her up and swing her around. "I'm going to fly! I'm going to fly just like you!"

I swallow my unease and grin into her hair. "You rocked the test scores, kiddo." Gabe's too scared about it to think straight. Leah can't wait to get shot full of nanotech. And me? I keep thinking about the little machines remaking my body molecule by molecule, and what they could mean to Genie. And what could go wrong.

She bounces back, pushing her hair out of her face. It's my gesture, a one-handed rake, and it makes my eyes sting. "Can we go now?"

"Gonna get a coat?"

"Yes, Mother." Complete with stuck-out tongue. Leah goes after a clean sweater and I follow her, and she's back on topic like a ferret down a rabbithole. "You and Ellie— I'm used to Dad having girlfriends. But it's just—"

"Not like regular girlfriends?"

"Aunt Jenny. It's a little embarrassing, but . . . It's usually more—un trou de passage, you know?"

"Leah!"

"Sorry."

"Marde." And then I think about what I was doing at her age. "Oh, hell, kid. You're old enough to know what a cheap lay is. And what a not-so-cheap one is, too. Neither Elspeth or I could *ever* come between your father and you." I grin. "Honey—old, fat people need sex, too."

Her lips twitch, and she giggles. "It's such a big deal?"

"You can live without it. But very few people actually *want* to. Is there a boy you've got your eye on? Because if there is, maybe we should talk about some other things, too."

"When there is . . ." She roots around in the laundry basket until she finds a red sweater shot with silver threads. "Does this match?"

"You're asking me?" I gesture down at my stained jeans and the plain white blouse I'm wearing. I make the eye contact and hold it. "When there is, Leah, you'll tell me before you do anything serious?"

"So you can sic Dad on him?"

"So I can teach you how to take care of yourself."

After a brief hesitation, she nods and laughs, but it trails off. The Hyperex I've taken in preparation for tonight's simulation makes every movement of her long legs in those gaudy pants trail seams of light. Her hands are like white butterflies.

"Leah, what's wrong?"

"Elspeth's not going to be leaving because of you, is she?"

Oh. I'm irrationally jealous, a sharp spike I never quite felt over Gabe. I bite down on it, hard, until it passes. *Mine. Dammit. Mine.* "No," I say. "I don't think so."

She raises her arms, tugs the sweater down. I go to smooth it in the back and straighten her collar. "Good," she says. "I like her." And then she turns around suddenly

and is all boneless puppy in my arms, her face pressed to
my chest. "I don't want you to go away again."

Oh, sweetheart. "Next time I go, you might be coming
with me. How you doing about Monday?"

"Scared green," she says, drawing away. "They didn't
give us much warning, did they? And it was awful when
you did it."

"I've got other problems. A spinal cord that's severed in
two places, for one thing. *You* won't have to be on a ventilator. Or confined to a bed for most of it, though I guess
you can expect some sensory effects."

She looks up at me and pushes her hair behind an ear
delicate as a cat's. "I think you're really brave, Aunt
Jenny."

I toss her jacket to her and grab my own. This could
have gone much worse. "I'm just too stubborn to quit,
cherie. Your dad: he's the one who's brave."

3:00 PM
Friday 17 November, 2062
Bloor Street
Toronto, Ontario

Genie stopped with her hand resting on the edge of
Papa's office door, still in her school clothes. The door was
open a crack; she picked out Ellie's voice beyond and
froze, one foot in midair, torn between backing away and
walking in to let them know that she was home. She bal-
anced on one foot to tug her sock up, telling herself it
wasn't really trying to overhear. But it was a good excuse
not to go in until they finished talking, so she spent a
minute making extra sure her shoe strap lay flat.

". . . what had Valens's panties in such a bunch?" Elspeth.

And then Papa. "I eavesdropped a little. Riel put Holmes on the grill. The prime minister might pull support for the program. Force Fred to retire or reassign him. He's been in the doghouse over the Chinese infiltration of the Mars mission for a good ten years now. I'm sure there's someplace very cold and dark that needs a colonel or three."

"Shit."

"Yes. I don't know what I'll do for Genie if I don't have NDMC access for her."

Silence, then, and Genie decided it was a good time to walk in. While it was quiet. Before they caught her. She didn't meet Papa's eyes as he stood up from the chair. Elspeth had been sitting across from him: she spun around and got up, too.

"Hi," Elspeth said.

Genie put the foot down and let hair fall across her face. She let go of the door and walked into the room. "Hi."

Diagrams and colored lines hung in the air between Papa and Ellie, twisting slowly over the big desk. Genie saw the projectors flickering, colored lights under the interface plate. "AI stuff?"

"We're very dull," Papa answered. "Nothing but work."

"That's why he needs you." Ellie came over to give her a hug and then held her chair so Genie could sit.

Genie grinned but the grin dropped away. Her stomach felt funny again. Worry, she decided, tasting the tension in the air.

"Excuse us while we talk shop a bit more?" Elspeth walked around the desk to stand beside Papa. She stuck her finger into the diagram and wiggled it until the threads writhed and rearranged. "The problem is we're trying to extrapolate the conditions under which an AI will self-generate from a sample of one. We might have better luck figuring out why they *don't* form, but—all I know for sure is we can make Richards."

Papa smiled at Genie and then down at Elspeth, but the second smile was twisted and wry. "I don't see a way around it. Maybe we should just start with a fresh crop of artificial personalities and see what happens. Is there any reason they have to be based on real people?"

Elspeth suddenly focused. "No. No, there's not. The original research wasn't even focused on making an AI—it was strictly A-Life stuff. Richard was an accident."

"Hah." Papa grinned wider, but Genie could tell he was hiding something, some trouble, and she rested her chin on her hands. "Then I think we have a starting point."

1700 Hours
Friday 16 November, 2062
Allen-Shipman Research Facility
St. George Street
Toronto, Ontario

I lean on one-way glass in the observation and training room and look down into a lab sunk a few feet below ground level. I stand watch over a row of seven chairs— they look like dentists' chairs—in four of which lie sleeping children. Leah and three boys: two dark, one fair.

Sleeping children, except their eyelashes do not flutter. Their hands don't stir. The glossy gray cables of the neural VR interfaces drape their breasts like fat, suckling serpents. Their faces have fallen slack as no living person's ever should, and the sight awakens that old chill in my belly. Shadows surround Leah's eyes like bruises. They lie as if dead, these children, navigating the unimaginable steppes of space in a fancied but coldly practical dance. They look dead.

I never want her to see me that way.

A red-haired technician moves among them, smoothing hair and moistening lips. She brushes aside an escaped strand of Leah's hair and I turn away. I have work to do, and in a moment the technician will come up the short flight of steps and down the corridor and join me in the observation room. Where I am supposed to be designing the real-time training protocols these kids will confront once their augmented reflexes are in place. I'm here to teach them how to fly. As soon as I finish learning how to do it myself. Or maybe sooner.

The door handle turns as the technician comes to join me. I sit at a desk, using the inadequate VR of the prosthetic eye instead of the full wetwired interface at the back of my neck, and log myself in. Even with the focusing potential of the drug, the simulated ship and its responses seem a thousand times slower than the real thing.

9:00 AM
Monday 20 November, 2062
National Defence Medical Center
Toronto, Ontario

Leah squeezed her dad's hand one last time before she sat down in the chair and let the doctor wheel her down the corridor, leaving her father alone with Aunt Jenny. She tried not to think about the funny narrow feeling in the pit of her stomach, or the funny metal taste in the back of her mouth, and concentrated on enjoying the totally unnecessary wheelchair ride. "So what do we do now, Dr. Valens?"

He leaned forward over her shoulder as he pushed. "Well, you get to share a room with my granddaughter Patty. We'll get you settled in and I'm going to bring you something to drink. It's the nanite broth."

"What does it taste like?"

"Really nasty lemonade." She heard his grin as he opened the door to a hospital room that was pleasanter than she expected, with gingham curtains and even an area rug between the twin beds. A tall, muscular-looking brunette girl in green surgical scrubs sat cross-legged on the one beside the window, playing a holographic game that involved assembling falling geometric shapes into patterns before they reached the covers. She glanced up long enough to smile and looked back down, her brow creased in concentration.

Valens kept talking as he set the chair's wheel-lock and helped Leah up. "Then we implant two chips. One at the base of your skull, next to your neural-VR interface. The other goes in the back of your hand. Those chips control the nanosurgeons. Leah, this is Patty. Patty, this is Leah. You're the only young women in our test group. I know you'll make us proud."

"We're going to kick the boys' butts, Papa Fred."

Leah looked back at the other girl. She'd lost her game, and the holographic shapes spilled out over the bed in a snowdrift, but she was grinning.

"You bet we are," Leah said. "We're going to fly first!"

Charlie Forster rubbed enthusiastically at the bald spot he was too vain to get fixed and frowned around his VR contacts. Massive magnification showed him swarming nanobots, scurrying and multiplying in a nutrient-and-metal-rich broth. These were the original beasties, salvaged from the ship tree abandoned on Mars: the many-times-great-grandparents of the neurosurgical bots Valens used to augment his pilots. Charlie spared a thought for the newest of the lot—Master Warrant Officer Casey—and smiled. She was sure a hell of a lot less brittle than the rest of the guys so far. And seemed possessed of an actual personality, too.

He blinked.

She.

"Fucking hell."

Charlie reached for his interface so fast he fumbled it, and only the autosave kept him from losing a half-hour's worth of nanite data. He held his breath until a familiar voice came over his ear clip. Silver hair resolved in the up-link. Charlie blinked to center a wandering contact. "Valens here."

"Fred, it's Charlie. Look, I have a wild idea on the old-style neural implant adaptations. Can you pull your old data? Or maybe you can tell me just from memory." Impatiently, he waited out the brief lag.

"Tell me the question and I'll tell you if I need to look it up."

"How many in your original group were women?"

A pause that seemed, perhaps, slightly longer than the lag. "I can answer that. Only three. We wanted more—it's my entirely unscientific bias that women are physically tougher and personally more cooperative than men—but women were less likely to sustain the kind of massive trauma we needed to justify the work, and less likely to volunteer when they did."

Charlie didn't let his flinch show in his eyes. There were noticeably fewer men Valens's and Charlie's age in Canada than there were women. Charlie still had twinges of guilt over not serving, on those occasions when he was reminded that almost everybody else had. "What happened to them?"

"Let's see. You've met Casey, of course. Fazzari came through it almost as well and succumbed to a massive aneurysm about five years back. Ray didn't make it through the surgery. She was the oldest of the original group."

"None of them showed the hypersensitivity and autism?"

"Casey has it to a limited degree, and so did Fazzari. Casey used to have a lot of problems with brightness and sudden movements, although she learned to compensate. She's hypersensitive to touch and texture as well. When her implants were failing earlier this year, she was having seizure episodes that seemed triggered by flashing lights or adrenaline. She's also prone to a feedback overload from tactile stimulus—" Valens tilted his head, eyes cast sideways, and made a sound that could have been a chuckle, or a cough. "And shame on you for even thinking it, Charlie." Taut lips skinned back in a sudden grin.

Charlie cleared his throat. He wondered if there were

many other people Colonel Valens would unbend enough with to make an off-color joke. "No suicides among the women, though?"

The tiny image of Valens in Charlie's contact lens shrugged. "Three out of 155 isn't a statistically significant sample, Charlie."

"No." Charlie polished his bald spot some more, watching the coiling, breeding nanites with about a quarter of his awareness.

"Do you have any theories?"

Charlie shrugged. He stared at the ceiling. He rubbed his hands together. "Well. The female immune system is significantly different than the male. It has to be able to identify friendly aliens and tell them apart from unfriendly ones."

"Friendly aliens?"

"Sperm," Charlie said dryly. "Babies. Have you started the implantation process on the first candidates?"

"Two girls," Valens answered. "Five boys."

"If you can get more girls into the pilot program, I'd suggest that it's probably a very worthwhile use of resources. Meanwhile, I'll start trying to figure out why."

"Girls don't play computer games, dammit."

"Then find better computer games, Fred."

Patricia woke in darkness. She lay still for a moment, feeling the unfamiliar tug of the IV line in the back of her hand; it ran nutrients and trace elements into her bloodstream for the nanosurgeons. A sensation like chewing on tinfoil filled her mouth. "Ick," she almost said, but then she remembered she wasn't alone in the room. She strained her ears and heard Leah snore softly: more a kitten whimper than an actual rattle.

Familiar midnight tension filled Patty. She turned on her side, pushed the cheap sheets down and stretched, wary of her needle site, and ran through her breath exercises. It didn't help. The pressure behind her breastbone mounted until she imagined it bulging her chest at the center—the need to be *doing* almost *burned*.

Sighing in exasperation, Patricia sat up in the blackness of drawn shades and felt on her nightstand for her tablet. She tapped it on and picked up the light pen, not bothering to feel around in the dark for her contacts. Her fingertips felt funny—numb—and it took her two tries to get her homework files open. *Is this how it starts?* She held her fingers up in the blue-tinged light of the tablet screen. They looked normal, but pins and needles crept across the pads. She poked them experimentally with the light pen.

It was one thing to be told what to expect. Quite another to feel it happening. Or more precisely, *not* to feel it.

"Shit."

"Patty?" Bedclothes rustled. "What are you doing up?"

"Couldn't sleep," she said, shading her eyes as Leah touched the bedside light on. "I thought I'd do some homework."

"Now?"

The weight of disbelief on the word made Patricia look down and pull the machine-crocheted bedspread over her legs. "Well, yeah." *Study hard, prove yourself. Make Mom proud.*

"How come you're working so hard?"

"I—" Patricia shrugged. "My parents expect it. I'm in advanced-placement math and physics. They expect 'great things' of me." She squeezed her light pen tighter, pressing her fingers white. "They don't know me. My grandfathers are the only ones who even see me, I think."

Too much honesty. But she was tired and she felt seasick-weird and groggy. She wondered if it was pain medication. There was supposed to be some, and she could imagine an ache spreading through her muscles almost the way she could imagine the sore throat and runny nose when she knew she was getting sick but the cold hadn't started yet. She realized she'd missed Leah's answer and said something at random. "It's just typical shit. You're doing regular school and this, too. It's not so different."

"My dad hates it, actually. He'd rather have me anywhere else."

"Than learning to fly starships? Really?"

"Really. But at least he's not a study nazi like—"

Patricia looked toward the darkened window so she wouldn't have to see the pale pity in Leah's eyes. "It's mostly my mom." She shrugged. "I don't want to talk about it, really."

"Oh. Sorry."

"No, it's good. They just don't understand me. My mom was a microbiologist but she quit. Dad's in the army, like Papa Fred. He's not home so much. She just wants a good career for me." *So I don't get stuck like she is. Like I'd ever be that dumb.* "She somehow thinks I can be a pilot and study physics at the same time." Patricia closed her eyes for a second, and called what she thought of as her brighter shadow up over herself. She'd told Leah too much, and Patty didn't have any other friends. She was too busy at home. And Leah might not like her if she kept whining like an angstbot. "Have you gotten to go up to the ship yet, Leah?"

"No. I'm so jealous you did!" There was—something— in the other girl's voice. Something that went with the stiffness of the conversation, and the split-second hesitations before Leah spoke. Patty caught herself sucking her tongue back in her mouth, and made herself stop. *Oh.*

You don't suppose I seem as scary to her as she does to me, do you? Or maybe just privileged. Spoiled. Patty grinned to herself. If Leah was scared, too, then it was okay. "You know, it's not as cool as you'd think. Mostly just like a big—big metal building, except for free fall. Which was the *best*! But the other student who went with me . . . Carver." She grinned, and it almost felt natural.

"Ooo. Sympa?"

Patty knew *that* much French. "Très," she giggled, her cheeks burning, and covered her mouth.

Leah leaned forward, legs folded, knotting her comforter in her hands and tugging it taut over her knees. "You kissed him!"

On a heartfelt outrush of breath, but without the panic

she expected to feel. "Oh, God. Don't tell my mom. But it was a little more than a kiss. Not—" She knew that she blushed more when Leah's eyes went wide. "—no, I just mean, he was really nice. I was really shy. And he kept asking for help with homework and stuff and we just— messed around a little, is all."

"I've never kissed anybody. My dad would flip." Leah sighed. And then her eyes brightened, and her voice went singsong. "Patty's got a boyfriend!" The sparkle in her eyes, though, kept any sting out of the teasing.

I do, Patty thought. She hadn't thought about it that way before. She grinned, pushing her hair forward with both hands to cover her face, and giggled into her palms.

Early Morning
Tuesday 21 November, 2062
Carlton Street
Toronto, Ontario

Razorface watched the swing of Indigo's glazed black hair as she leaned down to stare at the muted holobox, and he tried not to think of Bobbi Yee. He could smell Indigo's cold sweat over the yeasty odor of the room and he knew what she hadn't told him: there was a change in plans, and they were being kept waiting. He hadn't seen Farley in hours. The dumb shit was probably out waiting for a courier package or something.

Not that Indigo had told him that. But Razorface was pretty good at figuring things out. He leaned back in his chair; old, distressed wood squeaked and Indigo jumped. Razorface let himself grin. *Good a time as any. Good luck, Maker.* He cracked his knuckles. "I wanna talk about Holmes."

"We're not shying off that. Don't worry. I just have to do this other thing first."

"Nah." He eased himself up and cast around in the broken-hinged cabinets for something to eat. There were a couple of iced tea pouches and a bag of chips he didn't like. He took an iced tea and tossed the other one to Indigo. She caught it even though he intentionally pitched it long. "I got a way to get her that don't trace to us. I'll handle it."

"It's got to be permanent." But the flattened line of her upper lip told him she was thinking about it. And something else. She twisted a bit of hair between her fingers and frowned. She wanted something.

"Maybe not permanent. But maybe a life sentence."

"She's got awfully good lawyers, Razorface."

He let the light glitter off his stainless-steel teeth as he bit the iced tea open. "Babe, you take care of the politics. And you just let Razorface handle the sharks. Now who is it we're going to have to kill to keep your friends happy and off your back?" He closed the distance between them, enjoying the self-conscious way she laid her hand on his arm. *Nobody runs game on Razorface,* he thought, before he remembered it wasn't precisely true. *Anymore*.

She gave him a shy, calculated glance through her hair. It would have worked on Farley, but Razorface knew what real women were like, and this little china doll might be pretty and sharp, but she didn't hold a candle in brains or balls to his Leesie.

Indigo might as well have been thinking out loud.

"Riel," he said, when she didn't, and then he drained his iced tea to keep from laughing out loud at her shock. "Baby, any asshole could have guessed."

Min-xue pulled himself flat against the grab rails as several crew members sailed over him, returning from recreation and study. He was careful not to let their bodies brush his; normally they would have been more careful, respectful of his sacrifices, but he could tell by the way they moved that they were giddy and careless with exhaustion. It wouldn't have been so bad, but Min-xue was tired as well and thought he'd spare the rest of the crew an embarrassing pilot panic attack if possible.

He laid his cheek against the bar and closed his eyes. The late nights were wearing on him. But it was a relief to have someone to talk to honestly. Without avoiding mention of his Taiwanese mother, or making sure not to dwell too long on some of the radical T'ang poets he preferred.

The metal lay cold and soothing against his face long after the chatting, laughing crew members passed. It was only with an effort that he uncoiled his hands and let himself drift toward the bow of the *Huang Di*. And froze in place as Captain Wu drifted up beside him, a habitual look of faint disapproval staining his face. "Second Pilot."

"Captain." Min-xue performed an awkward salute. It set him drifting, and he corrected quickly. "How may I serve?"

"You look unwell." Frown deepening, the captain started to reach toward Min-xue and hesitated, allowing the hand to drift back to his body. "Have you reported to sick call?"

"Captain, I will. Am I relieved of duty, then?"

"What duty?"

"Training today, sir."

The captain made a little show of considering. Min-xue hoped he wouldn't be asked what was robbing his sleep. Finally, Wu nodded, and then he reached back and grabbed a railing and pulled himself past. "See you're quickly well."

It might have been an ordinary if gruff benediction. But Min-xue was certain he heard something—some urgency—in the captain's voice, and it sent a chill unrelated to the *Huang Di*'s low ambient temperature crawling through his hair.

2:00 PM
Tuesday 21 November, 2062
National Defence Medical Center
Toronto, Ontario

Leah opened her eyes to whispers, but it didn't get any brighter. Aunt Jenny hadn't told her how tired she would feel. Or that it would hurt to pick her head up. But then, maybe Jenny hadn't known. "Who's here?"

"C'est moi, ma petite." A dry kiss on her forehead.

"Dad."

"Always. Genie's here, too. Are you thirsty?"

"Dad, is it dark in here?"

"No. You can't see, Leah?" She thought he was trying to hold his voice level, but she heard it tremble. Someone with much smaller hands than her dad's squeezed Leah's other hand.

"Genie?"

"It's me. Is everything all right?"

She couldn't let Genie see her scared. Genie was too brave to have to carry Leah being scared, too. "It's okay. They said it would happen. I just—it's weird. Is Aunt Jenny here? Where's Patty?"

She heard the smile in her dad's voice. "Jenny's at work, chérie. And Patty's in the bathroom. I think she'll be back in a sec. You didn't say if you wanted anything."

Using his hands for leverage, Leah sat up. When she turned her face toward Genie's voice, and the window, she could pick up—or at least imagine—faint glimmerings of light. The sensation of someone whispering continued. "Dad, is there somebody talking in the hall?"

"I don't think so." He let go of her hand. The bed dipped and creaked under his weight as he pushed himself up against it. Meanwhile, Leah heard a door open. The bathroom door? She screwed her face up tight so she could pretend that was why she didn't see, fighting the hard knot like tangled ropes in her gut. She heard her father's voice, from farther away. "There's nobody out here. Hello, Patty."

"Hello, Mr. Castaign. Genie. Leah, what's wrong?"

Patty must have crossed to her bedside. Leah felt the bed dimple as she sat, felt what must have been Patty pulling Genie down beside her. She shook her head to clear it, feeling something like an itch deep in her brain. "I can't see anything."

"I'll be right back." Dad again, still near the door.

"It's okay," Genie said quietly. "I called the doctor already. It's just happening like they said it would, though, right? It'll be better in a couple of days. Right?" She pushed the round-cornered plastic call box into Leah's hand, and Leah smiled in spite of herself. Genie made it easy to be brave.

Genie knew a lot about hospitals.

I unlock the door to Gabe's apartment and walk inside. There's no sign at first that anybody's home, but the place doesn't have that *vacant* feeling, either. Genie's in school and Leah's still at the hospital. I'm playing hooky from the lab, halfway hoping to collect Gabe here, eat something, and head over to the National Defence Medical Center and visit the kid. We haven't gotten to spend any time alone since Friday night, and it would be nice to talk along the way. Knowing Gabe, he's got a whole universe of silent worry twisting away inside him.

Hell, I brought lunch. We're going to talk whether he wants to or not. Or so I'm thinking as I lock the door quietly and head for the kitchen. Three steps in I hear voices, low murmuring and a giggle; I pause in the archway, mouth open to announce myself, and my face goes hot and my voice dies in my throat.

The good news is Ellie doesn't see me standing there like a hooked fish, bag of turkey sandwiches clutched in my right hand. Her eyes are closed, her hand knotted in Gabe's hair; he presses her back against the sink, and I know from very personal experience and the high color in her cheeks exactly what he's whispering against her ear, exactly how his hand feels moving against her back, under her sweater. The memory makes me shiver and swallow once, hard.

Dirty, dirty old man.

They don't exactly teach you how to deal with this sort of thing in catechism. I suppose I could just back out of the kitchen and go slam the front door to give them some polite warning, but where's the fun in that? Oh, bad Jenny.

Very bad Jenny indeed. Elspeth's in the middle of a quiet, enthusiastic little whimper when I walk past them, open the refrigerator, and tuck the sandwiches inside. Gabe jumps at the sound of the opening door, turning toward me as Elspeth clears her throat and smoothes her sweater down over her hips. I don't look up, hiding my face until I have the grin bitten down. I find a beer on the bottom shelf and stand up. Gabe puts a hand on my shoulder. "Jenny—"

Maybe I'm being too mean?

Nah.

There's unreasonable jealousy, after all, and then there's targets of opportunity. "I brought lunch," I say, fine carbonation misting the air as I open the beer. "I'll be in the living room when you two are ready to eat. Food, I mean. And we'll go see Leah once Genie gets home."

Elspeth's grinning, one hand over her mouth. But Gabe looks like I shot him between the eyes with a tranquilizer dart, so I make sure to squeeze his ass with my steel hand on my way back out to the living room.

What the hell. The Canucks are playing. I'm sure I can keep myself entertained for an hour or two. And oh, we are so going to break that boy.

Leah sat cross-legged on her bed in the darkness, pinching the inside of her thigh in her boredom. She'd peeled off the blindfold that Colonel Valens and the other doctors had made her wear since her sight started to return. The bright lights from the corridor had already given her a headache, but it wasn't as bad as it had been, and there were limits to how much she could stand, and Leah was *bored*.

The waves of tiredness were starting to alternate with something else: a strangely vibrant energy filled her, prickling through her veins and making her fingertips tingle. The open-weave blanket bunched around her legs felt coarse and annoying, and her hospital pajamas chafed. Leah closed her eyes, tilted her head back, and watched a soccer game rebroadcast from Brazil on her contact.

In the bed beside hers, Patty whimpered and stirred. Leah opened her eyes and unfolded her legs, careful of the IV site in the back of her hand as she climbed out of bed and crouched down next to Patty. She held the other girl's wrist when Patty tried to tug away from her. "Hey, it's okay," and reached up to make sure Patty's blindfold was in place when the corridor door opened, spilling light through the room.

Busted, Leah thought, and made sure Patty was tucked

in before she turned around to face the music. She was surprised, though: it wasn't a nurse glowering her back into bed, but a boy her own age with dark hair falling like inky brushstrokes across his forehead. He slipped inside and pressed the door closed beside himself, careful not to let the latch click. "Are you Patty Valens?"

Leah tugged her hospital gown straight. "Leah Castaign." She grabbed her IV stand, unwilling to wait for it to catch up with her on its own. "Who the hell are you?" She caught a little of her dad's tone in her words, and didn't mind at all.

"Bryan Sall. Isn't this Patty Valens's room?"

"She's sleeping."

"I'm not sleeping." Patty's voice was plaintive. Leah glanced over as she sat up, one arm holding her blankets against her chest, the other one going up to her eyes but not moving the black mask. "Bryan, I don't know you, do I?"

"No." He came a few steps into the room, and Leah saw that he'd disconnected his IV, and a thin strand of red seeped from under the tape on his left hand. "I'm Carver Mallory's roommate. He was asking for you."

"Asking?" Patty started to slide out of the bed and got her ankles tangled in the sheets. Leah went to help her. "I don't have my eyesight back yet—"

Leah heard Bryan swallow, realized a second later that she shouldn't have been able to. "I don't think he's going to get his back, Patty. His legs are numb, he says, and—look. I'll take you to him. L-Leah will help." *Won't you?* his eyes asked, and Leah saw how pale Patty seemed in the darkness.

"What if we get in trouble?"

Oh, Patty. Leah could hear the longing in Patty's voice, and Leah's own restlessness made her bounce on her toes.

"I'll tell them it was my idea," Leah said, taking Patty's hand. "You're blind."

"I'm not supposed to be out of bed."

Leah grinned. "Do you always do what you're supposed to?"

The IV stands were going to be a problem. Leah solved it by unhooking her own, deciding she could always tell the nurse it tugged loose while she was sleeping, and making Patty hold onto hers. Bryan turned back from peeking out the cracked-open door to frown at that. "Shouldn't we unhook that, too?"

"I don't think she's ready yet," Leah said, feeling Patty's tension through her clutching fingers, then the grateful squeeze. "She's still really tired. You go first and scout ahead; we'll follow."

He stared at her for a second, and then nodded and slipped out the door. Shepherding Patty, Leah followed.

It was only a few doors, and the hospital corridor was quiet. Bryan must have been lying in wait until the appropriate moment. *Smart boy,* she grinned to herself, and then put a hand out as Patty stumbled. "Sorry."

"It's okay. Where's Carver?"

"Here."

The room wasn't lit either, but Bryan had an interface on his nightstand, hidden from the door by the privacy curtain. Its pause graphics twisted in midair, casting a bluish light over two rumpled beds and a scatter of flowers and cards and a giant teddy bear wildly too young for the boy standing beside her. He looked down when he saw her notice it and moved quickly to the occupied bed.

"Carver?"

Patty's voice, answered by a mumble. Leah led the older girl carefully to the window side of Carver's bed and placed her hand in his, not liking how limp and cool his fingers were. They didn't have him blindfolded, she realized, but even when his eyes opened, they didn't focus. She saw the thin wires leading from the interface plug at the back of his neck, and the white patches on the dark skin of his chest, and bit her lip.

"Carver?" Patty asked again. Leah backed away until her butt hit the window ledge, and leaned against it. She caught herself chewing her lip and forced herself to stop, hearing her father's voice in her head. *You look like a cow chewing cud.* But her lips and her fingers were numb as she watched Patty bend over in the flickering light and put her ear close to Carver's lips. Leah could see that he wasn't gripping Patty's hand back when she squeezed.

She almost jumped when Bryan slid up beside her and put a hand on her shoulder. She turned to him, as grateful for the dimness of the light hiding her blush as she was to take her eyes off Patty and Carver. A pulse fluttered in the notch of his collar, and Leah felt her eyes drawn to it. "You okay, Leah?"

She shook her head. "It wasn't supposed to be like this."

He hugged her awkwardly and then stepped away. It didn't feel quite like when Dad hugged her, and she was both glad and sorry when Patty stepped back from Carver's bed, trailing her IV stand, and said in a strangely level voice, "I think I want to go back to our room now."

Today's the day. Just a few hours off.

And I'm a fucking idiot. I'm crawling around under the eight barbershop chairs in the lab—mine, freshly installed, and seven others—stress making me itch to dirty my hands, staring at holographic circuit diagrams through my prosthetic eye just exactly as if I had any kind of sense at all. Or as if I could make head or tail of what half these things are supposed to do.

Valens lets me get away with it, probably realizing I have to blow off the tension somehow, and it beats showing up drunk to work. Which was the other option. But probably contraindicated in this case. Hah.

One of those chairs won't be used. One of the boys who went in for the nanite treatment didn't make it. Carver Mallory, the handsome cocoa-skinned sixteen-year-old I glimpsed on the *Montreal,* is never going to wake up. And I hate myself because with every breath I take, the only thought I can produce is *thank God it wasn't Leah*.

Gabe leans against the console, checking the VR module programming one last time. Elspeth is by the door, alternately keeping us company and getting in the way.

There's something coolly soothing about wiring charts. The doc's pantsuit rustles as she comes over to me, leaning down to see what I'm doing. I'm not changing anything, of course. Just making sure everything looks like it does in the charts.

Gabe looks up. "Is that firing right, Maker?"

"Good as gold." The technicians will go over it all again, of course. I drop a diagram chip into the box, fumble for the next in the sequence.

Elspeth squats beside me, ice clinking in the mug of water in her other hand, and passes the chip. "What's this Maker thing, anyway?"

I can feel Gabe wince as I compare chips. "Nickname from the army. Stupid joke, Doc." I sit up, finished with that chair. Elspeth gives me an assist, grabs my steel hand tight in her small brown one, and hauls me to my feet. She might be little, but she's not a sissy.

"How stupid?"

Gabe blushes; I see him turning away, feigning deafness as if his ears had grown lids. "Gabe speaks too many languages."

"I know. He makes me feel inadequate. Which doesn't happen often, let me tell you—" The disarming grin. Doc scratches between her eyebrows with a pinky nail. "It's a pun?"

"Genevieve. Jenny. You've got medical Latin, right?"

"Mostly pig—Oh! *Gene*."

" 'Maker.' Right. You're in business."

Over by the refrigerator, Gabe chokes on something I didn't see him put in his mouth. "I *have* apologized," he says.

The doc clears her throat. "It stuck?"

"It stuck." He tilts his head to one side, turns back over his shoulder to shrug.

Ellie flips an ice cube at him. "An offense that great demands a more material kind of restitution. You're buying dinner tonight."

"After the training run," I put in. "Although Leah might not be hungry." It will be her first time on the Hyperex, and I can't shake the conviction that it's a bad idea. I push back, try to remember what it was like. Try to put myself in Leah's experience.

Damn, that was a long time ago. I was—eighteen? Nineteen. Something like that. A cold sweat breaks across my forehead when I contemplate it too deeply, and I let the thought slide away the way it wants to. I have a catch-and-release policy on some of those memories.

I've also got a head full of drugged-out clarity: the biggest dose since I was out of the service, and the new formula hits harder and cleaner than the old stuff did. Some of Face's kids paid the price for that efficiency. I must have been staring into space, because I snap back to myself when Gabe lays his hand on my elbow. "You girls are ganging up on me, n'est-ce pas?"

"You *had* to know *that* was going to happen." I lay my hand over his for a second. His breath changes minutely when I let the steel fingers circle his wrist; my smile is amusement at this power over him, and then it drops away. *Should I have noticed that?*

Richard?

"It shouldn't be anything to worry about," Richard says. "The nanite growth—the trace-element burden—in both you and Koske seems to be lessening parabolically; the sensitivity increase should be stabilizing soon. You've been taking your supplements?"

Religiously. Which makes me grin, because Ellie dragged me to Mass yesterday, and Gabe along with us. It felt a little strange to watch them go for communion and not to follow. Stranger still—well, let's just say that the kyrie's been in and out a few times since my last confession.

Okay, that's a *slight* exaggeration.

"You should be good," Richard says. "By the way, I will attempt to talk to Leah tonight."

Patricia and the boys, too?

"Unnecessary risk."

Yeah. That will make her pretty happy. Leah and Richard were friends while Richard was still hiding out in the Internet, pretending he didn't exist.

Well, that was a slightly different Richard. But that, too, is a story for another day.

"She should be pretty happy. Jenny—"

Yeah? You gonna tell me to take good care of a kid whose diapers I changed, Dick?

"No, I'm going to tell you to be very careful in there. I'm still concerned. I don't know what sort of control our benefactors have over our little nanite buddies, but I know they have FTL quantum communication. And I really wish I could decompile your operating system and find out what sort of nasty little surprises Valens and Holmes had built into it by this Ramirez fellow. By the way, I thought you should know that there are two more ships under construction."

Before the Montreal *is tested?*

"One of them's nearly done."

Have you told them about—

"The aliens? How would you or I manage to tell them that and make them believe it, and still keep my freedom a secret? And what could they do about it if they knew?"

International cooperation—

"Set up some sort of a booby trap and give us a war with beings whose technology is so far beyond ours that it sits up and barks when you pat it on the head? Meanwhile they're clawing over each other to get to the stars? I don't want to give anybody another reason to fight, just yet."

The multiple ships—that's not something . . . that doesn't sound like the kind of thing you do for a chest-beating sort of space race. For national pride. You only need one successful ship for that.

"I'm looking into it. But add it to your list of things to worry about. The good news is, I've about got the physics on the stardrive licked. It's superstrings, as I suspected, and I'd explain how it works but I suspect you'd find it even more unsettling than I do."

Doc told me quantum mechanics only works on very small things. Subatomic.

As if out of the corner of my eye, I see Richard grin. "It does. But it can work on a *lot* of them at once."

2:00 PM
Monday 4 December, 2062
Bloor Street
Toronto, Ontario

Leah brushed irritably at her cheek before she woke fully enough to realize the brambles scratching her face were just the tweed upholstery of her living-room sofa. She heard voices dimly through a closed door and stood, then padded across the floor, twisting her blouse around her belly to tuck it straight into the jeans she still wore. Her father's voice, urgent but not unhappy, and Elspeth's answering in a similar register. The office door was only slightly ajar.

Her hand was on the cool brass knob when she heard a third voice, one at the back of her head. "Leah? Can you hear me now?"

"Tuva!" She had the presence of mind to gasp, not scream, but it was close. "You're in my head!"

"Sh. Talk inside."

Leah put her hand across her mouth. Approaching footsteps bowed the old wooden floor; the door came open under her hand, the knob slipping through tingling fingers. She looked up into Elspeth's questioning face, bronze skin fading into the darkness of the room, her curls backlit with a green glow from the desktop. "You're awake?" Dad loomed over Elspeth's shoulder.

Leah turned her hand in front of her mouth so a finger touched her lips. *Richard? Can you hear this?*

"Perfectly. Are you recovering okay?"

I'm very tired.

"Leah, can you think of a way to let Elspeth and Gabe . . . your dad . . . know I'm in here? Quietly, in case the apartment is wiretapped? I have some information I need to pass along."

Elspeth and Dad had come out of the office, but they heeded her silencing gesture. Leah closed her eyes for a second and thought. "Dad, do we have any paper?"

"Ask a programmer for paper?" Elspeth chuckled, but got out of the way as Dad brushed past her.

He offered Elspeth a dirty look and a fond insult. Leah smiled after him, proud that he trusted her enough to do as she asked without explanation. Elspeth found a pencil.

"Dad, can you show me what you were working on?"

"More AI stuff," he said, returning. A sheaf of glittering perfect squares showed one white side in his hand. "Boring."

"I want to learn," she said, and didn't mean it as anything except an excuse until she saw his eyebrow go up and the little smile curve the corner of his lip. *Nobody actually cares what he does, do they? We just leave him alone and let him do it.* The revelation hit her almost like a fist, and she dropped her eyes as she took the papers from his hand.

And she paid attention while she wrote out, slowly and precisely, with a rounded hand, every word Richard dictated, and sketched out the circuit diagrams and schematics he showed her—nanite controller protocols, and the careful instructions on how to create them.

1500 Hours
Monday 4 December, 2062
PPCASS Huang Di
Under way

Min-xue opened his eyes on the wonder of the stars. Whispers seemed to stroke him—the *Huang Di*—like anemone fingers. *Whispers without voices,* he thought, and wondered if one day he, too, would write a poem that might be worthy of remembrance. He might have said that he felt the ship as he felt his flesh, but it was more than that. *Imagine the feeling of starlight on your skin, Captain.*

What he said was, "Captain, I'm ready to activate the stardrive now."

Captain Wu cleared his throat. "Affirmative," and if Min-xue hadn't been able to read his heartbeat through the medical sensors in his chair, he never would have known that the man was afraid.

The *Huang Di* flexed itself into darkness and the sightless space *between* spaces, and almost instantly back out again. Despite himself, despite knowing how far from the deadly embrace of the Sun and her planets they were, Min-xue half expected the unfelt breath that filled his human body's lungs to be his last. *Too close to the gravity well,* he thought, and almost whooped out loud at the realization that he was still alive to think it.

"Transition accomplished," he announced coolly. "Distance traveled"—he checked parallax through his external sensors—"one-twentieth of an astronomical unit, sir."

Less than half of a light minute.

The smallest distance yet recorded using the Martian drive.

5:00 PM
Monday 4 December, 2062
Allen-Shipman Research Facility
St. George Street
Toronto, Ontario

Leah couldn't sit still, even though Patty kept grinning at her from under the polished dark curtain of her hair. The light moved over it, entrancing Leah with how real and how bright everything seemed. The boundless energy in her veins pushed her around the green-carpeted waiting room. She glanced up, squinted at the brightness of the fluorescents flickering on the stark white walls, and tried to tune out the yells of the four male students playing hologames while they waited.

"Jumping bean," Patricia said.

Leah jiggled her shoulders and paced a few more steps. "Like you're not excited." *Tuva, are you there? Richard, I mean.* Tuva was the handle he'd used in the VR game space where she had originally met him. Leah hadn't known he was an AI then.

"I'm here, Leah." The sense of presence was comforting. "Your friend is right. You're bouncing off the walls."

Like you ever sit still. Which was true. Even his computer-generated image was a fidget. *I'm going to fly, Richard!*

She felt him grin. And then she startled, as Patricia

seemed to materialize beside Leah and place her hand on Leah's arm. The touch felt funny—sharp—and Leah jerked away. Patricia did, too, looking down at her fingers as if she'd scorched them. "Whoa."

"Weird." Leah brushed her hair off her neck in irritation. "It must be the Hammers. Aunt Jenny said they could make everything a little weird. Weirder, I mean."

Patty smiled, but Leah could see—by now—that it didn't ease the tightness by the older girl's eyes. And then Patty looked up, and Leah did, too. They both heard the footsteps in the hall. "That'll be Aunt Jenny."

"And Papa Fred," Patricia answered, nodding. The boys were still distracted by their game as the two girls moved toward the door.

Monday 4 December, 2062
Sol-system wide area nanonetwork
17:15:44:45–17:15:44:56

Richard let a thin filament of his awareness move through the *Montreal,* the *Huang Di,* the *Calgary,* the half-built *Vancouver,* and the three Chinese vessels still under construction. Was aware of the presence of the Chinese pilots in their regimented daily routines. Followed the progress of the Chinese invasion into Russia, Russia's response—piggybacking on the *Montreal*'s radio, microwave, and laser transmissions. It annoyed him to not be able to use the Chinese ships similarly, and it annoyed him more to have to spawn remote processes and wait for them to report back, and the amount of data he could transfer without being noticed was limited. *They're desperate. The* Huang Di *and its sister ships are a last-ditch effort,* he realized. The AI contemplated the Chinese record of cultural imperialism, and Japan, and Taiwan, and Tibet. He ran a few hundred variations on population and climate numbers. And he worried.

Richard sighed, while another thread of his attention rested on Trevor Koske—not able to control him, or read Trevor's thoughts without revealing Richard's presence, but the AI feeling the pilot's existence like a heartbeat low in the back of his chest. Richard watched through the shipwide monitors as Koske went about his routine—one life among uncounted thousands, if he considered the still incomprehensible alien presences pushing at his attention.

The AI had also conceived a particular fascination with Lt. Christopher Ramirez. Chiefly because he couldn't see why the sullen, muscular blond made such an effort to cultivate Koske. Koske was only slightly less offensive to Ramirez than he was to anyone else. Richard, the eternal observer, let his crippled alter-ego deal with Koske and with Wainwright on those occasions when it became necessary, and chose to watch the grunted conversations between the two men at meals or in the boxing ring.

They both liked to fight.

Ramirez spent his off-duty hours reading twentieth-century politics and twenty-first-century philosophy. He was unmarried. His early air force career had been marked by disciplinary problems, but his service for the past five years had been exemplary—and even the armed services tended to overlook minor problems in a code jockey as talented as Ramirez.

Except Richard—sacrificing some of his precious bootlegged bandwidth to pick over Ramirez's records on Earth—noticed a few things. Such as that Ramirez's registered party affiliation in college had been to the neo-Greens, but the neo-Green Party—while extant—had not become widespread outside of Europe until two years later, and Ramirez had been the *only* student at the University of Guelph to so register.

Not conclusive, but suggestive that perhaps records had been altered along the way.

Richard was also becoming familiar with Captain Wainwright. Concealed under the mantle of the second AI, his mind-controlled progenitor, he found he had astonishing freedom. The nanite web allowed him to sense things that happened across light-years of space. Through Jenny and Leah, Richard knew that Gabe and Elspeth were on a new track with the AI research. He showed them how to build control chips and planned to expand his nanite fingers through the Internet soon—solving his bandwidth problem nicely. The other ships would need minds, he knew, minds of their own to survive the strange planes and angles of eleven-dimensional space. The human pilots were fast and intuitive. But Richard didn't think any human mind—even the one he himself was modeled on—could quite manage to comprehend the world behind the veil of what they'd jokingly dubbed sneakier-than-light technology.

He could feel the minds of the Benefactors, as he'd taken wryly to calling them; he'd tried to speak to them. Would have tried to speak to their AIs, but they didn't seem to have them. Just brains so alien he wasn't sure, in fact, that they could be considered to have anything like language at all.

He felt the ships moving, coming at what must be for them a stately and considered pace given what he had speculated about their capabilities.

Coming—and he hadn't shared this with Jenny yet, or with anyone—coming from two directions at once.

The kids are good. Damn good, all six of them. Awkward with their amped-up reflexes, with the touch of the Hammer shading their emotions toward preternatural calm and their focus to the absolute. The boys are dicey: teenage males, rough and erratic as any cadet I ever had to kick into shape. Valens slipped a bug in my ear that they might not adapt as fast as the girls, so I pay extra close attention to them. The girls are better behaved, plotting quietly the way girls do.

We go in.

It's a deep hard time, and it takes me back. Not quite into a flashback . . . Hell. Yes, into a flashback, smell of sweat and the smell of mud, smell of hot, scared kids blinking at me like I have all the goddamned answers.

I hope a few of them learned to duck.

I bite down on the memory, roll it back. This isn't then, it's now, and I'm mind on mind with the children, flitting from one to another like a possessing ghost, guiding each of them through a slalom while another part of my mind sets up obstacles and takes them down. Obstacles hard enough to build confidence when they get past them—which they don't always. Not so hard as to break them.

It's a line you have to know how to see, because it's

different for each of them. And as somebody once said to me, it takes a hundred attaboys to cancel out one oh, shit.

I hope these kids will stay alive. I wish I could make them some kind of promises as we sail through the slick black nothing, space stroking the sides of the virtual ship—waggishly named *The Indefatigable*—but the hard facts are that all I can do for them is to show them the tools and kick them out the door. Just like all of us, they're on their own.

On their own, but every action they take affects everybody around them. It's a hell of a lesson to learn when you're thirty. Never mind fifteen.

I want Leah to be the best, of course. But the fact of the matter is that Patricia Valens and Bryan Sall, a dark-haired boy with angled eyes, are the oldest of the lot, the most developed, and they blow the other four away.

I shake with exhaustion when the technician comes to unhook me. The kids are still under. She brings me something hot and sugar-sweet in a big mug: coffee with chocolate stirred into it and tons of milk, just the way I never drink it. It eases the shakes, though, and by the time I choke it down I can unclench my teeth enough so my jaw doesn't ache all the way up to my ears. My shirt clings to my chest, plastered with sweat, and I'm taking a chill. "Do a shorter run next time," she says.

I look up at the one-way glass, knowing Valens and Holmes and Gabe and Ellie are on the other side, and wave as steadily as I can manage. *Shorter. Right. Valens wants these kids trained by when?* The technician takes my mug, and I bless her. "What's your name?"

"Melissa Givens, Master Warrant." She flashes me a grin, and I know I just made a friend. I wonder if Valens ever bothered to ask her that.

"God, call me Jenny. Especially if you bring me coffee."

"You need the sugar and caffeine. Rigathalonin—the Hammer—takes a toll. Ready to debrief the kids yet . . . Jenny?"

It's over quickly, thankfully, and Valens handles most of it. I sit in the corner and try not to tremble. My teeth-grinding distracts the kids, so I get up and walk into the hall, trying not feel Leah's pale face and bright eyes following me. In the evergreen-scented rest room I lean my face against the mirror—cool steel, soothing—and work on remembering not to close my left hand on the porcelain sink. I think about sitting down on the floor.

Then I think about the white tautness around Leah's eyes, and swear. I have to go back in there. I can't let her see this, can't let her fear this. Hesitation, where she's going, could get her killed—and a ship full of passengers with her.

Later that night, after I somehow make it back to Boris and my hotel, I remember that I took a hard look into the mirror and frowned at myself. I remember I thought *Can I handle this?*

I can handle this.

I had put my hand in my pocket and pulled out the remaining pills in their harmless little brown vial. And then I had waited five minutes, washed my face, combed my hair, and went back into the debriefing room and sat down in one of the gleaming one-piece student desks next to Leah and put a calm, steady hand on her arm. She grinned at me and patted back.

I looked up; a flicker of movement from the holoboard near Valens caught my eye. When I looked toward it I saw him regarding me steadily, all the while continuing with his comments on the tumbling curve of the virtual ship projected in the air beside him. He didn't smile or even nod, but he held my gaze for three endless seconds before he looked away.

Remembering that, later—remembering Leah's face turned to me—watching the coronas of light flare and sweat against a window coated in hard, freezing rain—I sit in the dark with a pillow over the phone so I won't see the message light blinking, and I don't get up to answer the knock either the first or the second time it comes. I hold my cat in my lap while he twists his claws in the fabric of my BDUs, and I drink whiskey and coffee in about equal ratios until the knot under my breastbone loosens enough that I can breathe.

10:30 PM
Monday 4 December, 2062
Marriott Inn
Toronto, Ontario

Indigo tugged a fluffy-itchy baby blue touque more firmly over her ears, then covered the knit cap with the hood of her parka. She'd swear the winters were getting colder—and coming sooner—every year. Which didn't make sense. It was supposed to be global *warming,* after all.

She rose from her resting place in a corner of the hotel lobby and stepped around a potted Norwegian fir, careful never to turn her profile to the window. Through the shadow her outline cast in the reflected brightness of the glass, she saw a hulking shape leave the lobby across the street, ice forming on his smooth-shaven scalp. Indigo held her breath a few steps from the autodoors as Razorface halted, weight on his left foot, as if contemplating options—and then turned and strode back the way he had come. The way Indigo had followed him through the rain to get there.

The storm hit her face like shattering glass. She hesitated a step beyond the doors and pulled her hood tighter, watched Razorface hunker down into his collar as he moved up the street, almost invisible until he passed through a puddle of light. Now it was Indigo's moment to hesitate. *See where he's going or see where he's been?*

He turned sideways—still going the way they'd come—and that decided her. Indigo jaywalked across the empty street with inchworm steps, careful to lift each foot up and set it down vertically so it wouldn't slip on the ice, muffling her face against stinging precipitation. She closed her eyes in relief when she stepped through the doors into the warm exhalation of the rust-carpeted foyer, then smiled with irony. *Maybe I should just get a room here for the night.*

She had no way to tell what room Razorface might have visited. So she tugged off her girly little hat, unzipped her parka, and picked a hesitant path across the carpet and the tile toward a tastefully appointed front desk. No potted evergreens here, thank God. She rang the bell to bring the duty clerk out of the back.

A young man appeared, handsomely Eurasian. Decades of troubles in the Far East had brought Indigo's family to North America, along with thousands of others.

The clerk smiled at Indigo, and she smiled back. "Can I help you, miss?"

Indigo slid a well-practiced mask of hope and shyness over her features and smiled prettily. "I . . . Um." She studied her shoes for a minute and stuffed her right hand into her pocket. "Did a guy come in here? Big, black guy. Leather jacket—"

"The teeth? Are you supposed to meet him? He just left."

"No, I wasn't supposed to meet him. Um." She pulled her hand out and picked at the melting flakes of ice crusting her stocking cap. "He's my boyfriend, and I wondered . . ."

Comprehension dawned across the young man's face. "I can't tell you what room he went up to, if that's what you want."

"Oh."

"But I can tell you—" His expression grew appraising. "I don't think you have anything to worry about."

"How do you know?"

"The voice of experience," he said, and grinned. "It's probably—" He swallowed one set of words and substituted another. "—just a work thing. Look, the cafe is closed, but if you want to sit down here in the chair I'll get the kitchen to bring you some coffee out and you can wait till the ice stops. I won't make you go back out in the storm."

Indigo glanced at the door. She didn't have what she'd come for, and this was a good excuse. She nodded. "Can I have cocoa instead?"

"You can have anything you want. Sit down. I'll take care of you."

He got her a blanket, too, and she curled on a love seat and read world news and watched the late-night holofeed until she drifted almost into sleep. She half dreamed of a slender, wild-haired man she barely remembered giving her piggyback rides and telling her stories about another man—her father—that she didn't remember at all. *Tell it again, Uncle Bernie.*

Tell it again.

It's not like I actually got drunk. But mixing stimulants, alcohol, and military-issue reflex and concentration-enhancement aids might not be the wisest course of action. Which is why you should hate me for waking up bright eyed, bushy tailed, and four minutes before my alarm goes off, Boris purring on my chest. Plenty of time for a long, hot shower. As if in my ear, I hear someone clear his throat.

Richard?

"You need to cope better than that, Jenny."

I know. Water like standing under a sluiceway, but steaming. It almost feels *thick* where it drums against my skin, driving the chill out. *Would you feel happier if I had one hell of a hangover? When was the last time I was sloppy, self-indulgent, and maudlin?*

"Do you want a list?" Immaterial hands beat at virtual air. "All right. I know. I know you're worried, and you're right to be. Look, I'm learning how to run some basic programming on the nanotech. I'm making good progress with one of the Chinese pilots, but I'm concerned their government may try something drastic to put an end to the Canadian program, because I've come to understand where you're going and what the stakes are."

To hell in a handbasket?

"If I thought it existed, I'd be worried. Can you actually imagine a supreme being that petty and erratic?"

I let that slide, and wait. Richard, I sometimes think, is happy to hear himself talk. I taste hot water and soap, close my eyes, draw a valentine's heart in the steam on the rippled glass door.

"HD 210277," he says. "A G7V main sequence star very similar to the Sun but a little less bright, and about sixty-nine light-years away. As long ago as the turn of the century, we knew it had a planetary system—a gas giant with an erratic orbit, but it more or less sits in the habitable zone. That's where the generation ships that the Chinese launched ten years ago are going. And it's where you'll be going, too."

"Why?" I put a hand over my mouth. *Oops. What do they want with it?*

"More recent data indicate that one of that gas giant's moons has a very good shot at being earthlike."

Oh. They *are* colony ships. *What about whoever lives there now?*

"If there is anybody . . . Jenny, you of all people ought to know how it works."

Yes. Yes I do. *Richard—the* Montreal *can leapfrog those generation ships. We could have a colony long established before they ever arrive. Assuming we beat the* Huang Di *out there. The Chinese regime was crazy enough to send ships out there with no guarantee they had anyplace to land, and no way home? Why would anybody do something like that?*

"Have you looked around this planet lately?"

How drastic an action might they take to prevent our getting there first?

"It was never proven that the terrorist nuclear attack on Kyoto in 2040 was linked to the Chinese."

It was never proven that Israel had anything to do with

the Cairo attacks either, but—oh. I see your point. It's a good thing I'm in a hotel shower, or the hot water would have run cold while I was chewing that over. I dress by rote, forgetting to dry my hair so water spots the collar of my sweater. I fell asleep with the curtains open, and when I glance out the window the world looks etched on the back of a crystal paperweight as far as the eye can see, a misting ice still drifting from the gray overhead. Icicles dangle like arm-long fangs from the ledges and awning of the hotel across the street: I see them through the wavy sheen of ice that makes my window look like watered glass. Like the shower door, come to think of it.

Colony ships.

"Jenny, by the way—you should know. I think your friend Koske is being courted by an interesting individual aboard ship, the programmer I've mentioned to you. Chris Ramirez. I have a suspicion that Ramirez isn't exactly what he appears. If there's any way you can get Colonel Valens to rerun the background check on him—"

Thanks, Dick. I'll try, but he wouldn't be on the Montreal *if they hadn't gone over his history with a flea comb.*

There's something here I'm missing, and I'm still chewing on it while I shrug my jacket on and bounce down the stairs three at a time, spurning the elevator because I can. I wave to the boy behind the desk—

And almost trip over a ghost.

I actually stumble. Stumble, put my steel hand out for balance, and take two short steps back, catching my heel on red-brown patterned carpet. I probably could have walked right past her unnoticed if I hadn't pulled the triple take, but as soon as she picks her head up from reading whatever she's reading on her hip I see the braid, the finer line of the nose over the rim of her mug, and the arch of the brow, and the similarity of profile fades.

Fades, but doesn't vanish. I'm left with a cloying smell of chocolate in my nose and nagging nausea in my belly.

She looks like Bernard Xu. That pretty little social activist I loved and lost—okay, I never loved him, but I liked him better than most, for all he had a bad habit of blowing things up when he didn't approve of them—something like half a lifetime ago. But this girl couldn't have even been born then. Could she? She might be thirty, I guess, but she looks about twenty-two.

You live long enough in today's society, you collect so many faces that everybody starts to look like somebody. That's all it is. "I beg your pardon," she says, standing up. Fifteen, maybe twenty feet away from me. "Do I know you?"

"No, you just—look like someone I used to know."

I *see* the shock wrack her when she hears my voice. She blinks and glances down, eyes lighting on my prosthetic hand protruding under the black wool cuff of my coat. Her gaze slides back up slowly, eyes narrowing as she examines my face. "You're Genevieve Casey."

Simple declarative statement. I nod.

"Holy shit!" she yells. And I duck as
she straight-arms the
full cup of cocoa at me,
dives over the love seat
(adrenaline dump into combat time,
heartbeat slowing as
reflexively
I take off after her)
clutching her HCD in her right
hand hits the crash bar
on the emergency door
(alarm starts low,

resonating under my skin, builds
sirenlike
to a piercing wail)
and sails out onto
the fresh-scraped
de-iced pavement
with me ten steps behind.

Ten steps too far, it turns out. I don't run any faster
than anybody else and she's easily twenty years younger
than me.

Damn it to hell.

Richard? Who the hell *was that?*

"I haven't got the resources I used to, Jenny. But I will
see what I can find out. And be careful. In case. Okay?"

You don't have to tell me twice.

I'm late for work, too, because I have to go change to a
sweater that's not covered in cocoa and wash the milk and
sugar out of my hair.

6:30 AM
Tuesday 5 December, 2062
Bloor Street
Toronto, Ontario

For Leah, waking up in her own bed that morning was
a luxury. She stretched under the covers and waved her
musical alarm off. It took two tries; she jerked her hand
past too fast for the sensor the first time. Then waved it
back on and lay there listening to what another generation
would have called bubblegum pop, bouncy synthviol and
electronika coupled with mindless lyrics, until she heard
her father tap on the door. "Leah?"

"I'm up," she said, putting her feet on the floor. She didn't bother with slippers as she hurried to the shower. Genie had alighted on the edge of the sofa and was toweling her hair. "Morning."

"Oink oink," Leah replied. Genie threw the wet towel at her. She surprised herself. She stepped out of the way and caught the sopping terry cloth one-handed, neatly, without even getting her sleeve wet.

"That was quick," Genie said.

"Yeah," Leah answered. And then she crossed the carpet too fast and barked both shins on the coffee table. "I still don't have the hang of it, though." She looked up in time to see her dad—peering through the eggshell-white-trimmed archway from the kitchen—turn away.

She stopped in the middle of dressing and wiped the mirror dry so she could look herself in the eyes, but didn't see any differences. The nugget of the control chip under the skin of her left hand whitened as she rubbed the outline.

No school today. She'd be tutored at the research lab from now on, and the emphasis would be science and math.

At least she was good at math. And she'd get to ride the subway in with Dad—but Genie would have to go to school alone. She reached for her blouse automatically and realized, in her sleepiness, she had left her clothes in her room. The drugs they had her take before the trials made her faster, but they also wore her out.

She shrugged her robe back on and hurried into her bedroom, pulling on the first clothes she found. She twisted her hair into a wet braid she could shove up under her hat and grabbed her boots as she headed back out to the living room. Genie was already finishing breakfast.

"Eat quick," Dad said.

Leah shook her head, her hair leaving tracks like a

sidewinder's across her shoulders as she trotted into the kitchen. She caught her hip on the edge of the doorway and rolled her eyes. "I'll grab a breakfast bar."

The train ride was crowded but uneventful. If it hadn't been so icy, the distance was short enough to walk, but with frozen rain still spitting and half the sidewalks like glass, they decided it was a good day to take advantage of Toronto's white-tiled subterranean architecture. Leah's math class was only six people: herself, Patty, and the four boys: Bryan, Winston something—a dirty blond she thought she liked, in a geeky sort of way—and the two Davids, whom she could never keep sorted out.

Leah gave Patty a quick hug as they walked into the classroom, but Patty flinched away. "Did you go to see Carver yesterday?"

"There's no point," Patty answered, and Leah understood that the topic was closed. She still picked the desk beside the one Patty chose, and worked steadily until Mr. Powell left the room. Kept working, until Patty hunched down so that her hair concealed her interface plate and tapped quick messages on her desktop.

Leah, I found out something from Papa Fred.

?

The ships are colony ships. They're taking people someplace else.

Now? We're not ready to fly them now.

No, not now, silly. Whenever they're done.

Are they coming back?

They must be. Patty looked up quickly as a shadow crossed the door, but nobody entered. *I mean, you wouldn't spend that much money on something and use it just once, would you?*

*I—*Leah's quick fingers were interrupted by Mr. Powell's return. With only six students in the room, she knew she'd

get caught, so she wiped the chat with a pass of her hand
and quickly foregrounded her math application again.

Her heart wasn't in it, and the timer beeped at her tin-
nily while she was still staring through the sixth problem
of ten. *I need to tell Elspeth,* she thought, ignoring Mr.
Powell's glare and restarting the problem set, pushing her
thoughts aside. *And Aunt Jenny, too.*

9:30 AM
Tuesday 5 December, 2062
Chestnut Hill Road
South Glastonbury, Connecticut

Hartford's civilian commissioner of police let her hands
rest on her thighs, fighting the urge to collapse against her
squeaky leather sofa cushions. Images and data slid
slowly—midair—around her living room. She knew if she
leaned back, she would be out like a light. "Hawaii," she
said, trying the word. "San Diego." Hawaii would probably be better, as long as she stayed away from Honolulu.
Although protected by the massive Army Corps engineered series of locks across the harbor, San Diego's water
rationing was severe enough to lower its status as a vaca-
tion destination. "Palm trees," she said.

The clatter of nails on terra-cotta broke her concentration. Her dog, Moebius, wandered in from the kitchen, his
dreadlocked white coat swaying with every step and
brushing the ankle-deep rug. Kuai's spare time went into
planning tropical vacations she never got around to taking, and the money she didn't spend on them went into
her house, even if she didn't have anyone but a hundred-
pound Hungarian sheepdog to share it with. A real dog, an

old-fashioned dog. Not a puppymorph with oversized ears and feet and no sense of responsibility.

No matter how grim the day, the random pattern of ink-spot freckles on Moebius's pale-pink skin where it showed between the dreadlocks still had the power to make her smile. And, lacking sheep to guard, the komondor would be more than happy to use the biggest set of teeth she had ever seen on anybody who might threaten Kuai. And any houseguests who moved too quickly for his taste. Not that she had many houseguests.

She patted the sofa and Moebius jumped up beside her and laid his head on her knee with a sigh, pleased to be invited onto the furniture. Frowning, Kuai contemplated the information slowly patterning and repatterning before her. She ran her fingers through her hair and judged it clean enough for a telephone call and the hour finally late enough to be decent.

She waited while the call rang through, introduced herself to a receptionist who seemed to recognize her from news broadcasts, was puzzled by the young man's bright, "Oh, he's expecting you!" and waited a few more moments while Dr. Simon Mobarak was summoned to the phone.

"Dr. Hua?" Mobarak was a solid-looking Middle Eastern man, prematurely middle-aged, looking not quite as tired as she felt. "I had given up hope that you would call back."

"Call back?" Her eyes were so tired that her involuntary blink *hurt,* and Kuai made the executive decision that she wasn't going in to work today after all.

"I left you a message several days ago, but you must not have gotten it. You were in an autopsy when I called."

Sally. I might as well have kept my overprotective mother and saved the price of a paycheck. Kuai scratched Moebius behind the ear; he moaned softly and lifted his head into the viewfinder. Dr. Mobarak laughed as he saw the dog.

Kuai tilted her head in wry acknowledgment and blew her bangs out of her eyes. "I was calling you about the Park River homicides. I understand you used to have a patient named Genevieve Casey—"

"Strange," he interrupted. "I can't share patient information without a subpoena, of course. But I had called you about the same thing. I've been passed some very interesting data, and I couldn't think who else to send it to."

"Really?"

"Oh." And she saw the crease of concern between his eyes, and what she thought was bitten-back anger. "Oh, yes."

0930 Hours
Tuesday 5 December, 2062
HMCSS Montreal
Earth orbit

Trevor shifted uncomfortably, weight on the balls of his feet, but didn't speak. Captain Wainwright was staring down at the back of her hands, pale against the blue blotter on her gray issue desk, the expression on her face as sour as if she were trying to figure out how to floss her teeth on the tendons. She lifted one of the hands and brushed it through her dark, orderly hair. She was a small woman, trim and forceful in air force blue, affecting a manner the crew found comforting. "Lieutenant," she said through thinned lips, "I understand that there are medical issues involved. But can you at least *attempt* to build a rapport with the rest of my crew?"

Koske bit his tongue on a retort that sounded defensive

even to him. "Ma'am. I can try." He tried to keep his eyes straight ahead, but she caught his gaze and wouldn't drop it. Her direct gaze pinned him until he found his voice again. "Do you have a suggestion, ma'am?"

The expression around her eyes remained unchanged, but color returned to her mouth. "Why don't you join the zero-G handball team? I imagine you'd excel and who knows—you might develop a taste for it. While I applaud your dedication to duty, I think it would be healthy for you to find outlets other than simulator training and punching the heavy bag."

"Ma'am." It could have been worse. At least she wasn't going to force him to do anything egregiously stupid, like morale. "I think I can manage that."

"Good," she said, and pushed her chair aside on its swivel arm as she stood. "You're dismissed, Koske. And don't worry"—interrupting him as he turned for the hatchway—"you will get to fly this bucket, too."

The parting shot rattled him. He leaned against the corridor wall on the other side of the hatch, feeling cool steel hard against his scalp as he pressed the back of his head to the bulkhead. *Am I that transparent?* And then he smiled, sardonically, in spite of himself. "Or are you just feeling the same way anybody in your shoes would feel?"

Trevor Koske nodded unconsciously. A creeping headache colored the sides of his face and the back of his eyes. Cold metal felt good, but the tension was still creeping down his neck, and a familiar prickle on his skin suggested someone was watching him. He straightened and lifted his shoulders, glancing right and left to see if anyone had witnessed his moment of exhaustion.

The corridor was empty.

He went to sign the free-fall handball team tryout roster, and then he went to find Ramirez. Koske was moving rapidly along a gray-matted corridor when he stopped and snorted softly, remembering. The *Montreal*'s AI was active now. He lifted his head and spoke clearly to the air. *"Montreal?"*

"Lieutenant. How may I be of service?"

"The location of Lt. Christopher Ramirez, please."

"Aft officers' lounge, Lieutenant." The voice's lack of inflection was soothing. Koske understood that the AI's programming constrained it, placed it under the control of the ship's pilots and the captain. He hoped that was true. There was something a little bit creepy about walking around inside a ship with a mind of its own.

Koske nodded and turned aft. Ramirez was alone in the smaller and colder of the two lounges—the one without a view—staring at the wall. It did have a coffee tap, however, and the walls and floor were upholstered in a muted beige and blue pattern that matched the couches. Koske ducked through the hatchway quickly and dogged it behind him, the alloy wheel smooth in his hands. He liked metal and smooth cloth, cool ceramic. Things that minimized tactile feedback.

"Chris?"

Ramirez blinked as if clearing a contact and touched his ear clip. "Trev. Come on in."

"Watching a movie?" Make an effort, he told himself. Try to remember how to make small talk, to connect with other men. It was better than it had been; the surgery had changed a lot. Not enough, but a lot.

"My wife sent up some holo chips. I miss my favorite shows. You look bugged."

"I am bugged. Wainwright is on me to improve my social skills." Koske focused on the coffee tap, crossed the room to it, and pulled a cup out of the dispenser without looking up. He dialed a mocha and waited while the soy milk steamed and the cup filled. It tasted like soy milk, and he made a face. "She says they suck."

"Trev," Ramirez said. "Your social skills do suck."

He stuffed his hip into his pocket and swung his feet off the pearl-blue ottoman, leaning forward between his knees. Koske caught it out of peripheral vision, but studied a bland pastel print matted and sealed in hard poly flush with the wall instead. "I'm good at my job."

"You wouldn't be here if you weren't. Flying's your life, isn't it."

Not a question, but Koske nodded anyway. He fussed with his recyclable cup. "It's not enough to just be good, is it?"

"Eh." Ramirez reached over the low overstuffed back of the sofa and retrieved a drink Koske hadn't noticed from an elongated table behind it. He cupped it between both hands, resting in his lap, and looked up at a ceiling that boasted the same blue-silver patterned weave. It didn't matter which way was up in zero G. "You ever think about how much better you have to be at something now than you did two hundred years ago?"

"What do you mean?" Koske turned around and leaned his butt against the wall. The mocha was okay as long as he let himself drink it on automatic, without trying to taste it.

"Say in nineteen hundred, or whatever, before there was television and radio."

"There was radio in nineteen hundred," Koske corrected, but he wasn't sure after he said it.

"Whatever. The point is, you're a singer in the year whatever, and you're a pretty good singer, and you make a pretty good living at local bars or singing on street corners or at fairs or whatever. And suddenly somebody invents the radio, and you don't have to be the best singer in the town anymore. Now you have to be the best singer in the country. And then you have television, and you have to be the best singer in the world. And you have to be pretty, too, and look good on camera."

Koske realized he'd finished his mocha and folded the cup into the recycler. "Okay."

"So a lot of people are frustrated, and go to work making widgets or whatever, because everybody in the world has access to the, like, ten best singers anywhere."

"Huh. Doesn't that kind of compare to nations, too? They keep getting bigger . . ."

"I was going there, actually." Ramirez licked his hand and smoothed it across his hair to tame a platinum cowlick. "Sure. You go from tribes and principalities to city-states with empires, from empires to nation-states with bigger empires, then to supranations like Pan-Malaysia, the Commonwealth, PanChina, the EU, the United States. I'd say both things are a function of people just being able to talk to each other better."

"The radio."

"And the Nets, going back to the mid-twentieth century. If there's one thing people are good at, other than killing each other, it's talking. Hell, we even talk to dogs and dolphins. Or try."

Koske suddenly choked, harsh amusement tightening his throat. "You're telling me Wainwright is right, and if I don't talk to people I'm subhuman."

The blond man shrugged, tossed back his beverage, and stood, crumpling the disposable cup in one rawboned fist. "I'm not telling you anything. Except you have to be the best at your job in the world, or you're not going to get what you want. But I keep thinking there's got to be a way for people to—well, there's some sense in the New Chinese system."

Koske flinched away as Ramirez brushed past him to drop the cup into the recycler. "PanChina is pretty repressive."

Ramirez chuckled. "Have you looked at the privileges granted our government under the Military Powers Act? The prime minister can essentially force anybody she wants into military service. Jail anybody—for no reason at all. Based on their *ethnicity*. And we're so in the pocket of the PanMalaysian corporations it's not funny. Canada might as well just admit that it's Southeast Asia's army and get on with life in a mercenary fashion. And let's not even get into some of the things that went on in the U.K.—back when it could still claim to have a government. And the Christian Fascists in the United States—"

"You don't think a democratic government is superior to a totalitarian one? I *fought* in that war, Chris. Maybe you're too young to remember, but we had good reasons for going over there. For South Africa, too."

"Sure. That's not the point. What I'm saying is in the old system, people who had a gift were nurtured. Even if they weren't the best in the world. And PanChina has protocols that take the place of that sort of nurturing—"

"—creche environments for kids, parental visits on weekends."

"There's an old political philosophy . . . do you know any history, Trev?"

Trevor snorted and kicked his heel against the wall. "Don't teach your grandmother to suck eggs."

"Have you ever heard the expression *from each according to his ability, to each according to his need*?"

"Can't say I have. Why?"

Ramirez shrugged and moved to the dispenser to refresh his drink. "It's the boiled-down version of a discredited political philosophy. One that was the root of the

PanChinese system, several revolutions ago. They also believe in individual service to the state, and state service to the individual. It doesn't seem like a bad ideology to me. I think more people can excel, given the kind of support you see on a village level rather than worldwide competition. And I think people should be given a chance to just be good at something, and live their lives. Instead we've got a world full of unhappy people in dead-end jobs medicating themselves to stay sane."

Wouldn't it be nice not to have to be the best to be recognized?

Hell no, Koske thought. *I want to be the best. On my own merit. And if that means outflying and outthinking Genevieve Casey, well. She's got to lose one of these days.*

"You're depressing me, Chris."

"Sorry about that." Ramirez finished his coffee in a gulp. "Come on. Let's run some laps."

1000 Hours
Tuesday 5 December, 2062
Allen-Shipman Research Facility
St. George Street
Toronto, Ontario

When I do get to work Gabe's lying in wait, looking sexy in a white shirt, open at the collar, and tan loafers. Damn his eyes. Leaning against the wall beside my office door, engrossed in something on his hip.

"I'm sorry." I key the door open and press my thumb to the lock plate. "It won't happen again."

He doesn't look up. "Accepted." And from the level tone of his voice I know he's going to hold me to it. "What the hell happened last night? I couldn't decide if I was more worried or if Elspeth was."

"I— Gabe, I need a cup of coffee. Want to go for a walk?" I'm still trying to decide what to tell Valens. Whether I should tell Valens anything.

Gabe taps his hip off, stuffs it into a pocket, raises his gaze to mine. "Anytime."

I fall into step beside him, turning back the way I came, comforted by his presence. We pass through the external doors into the parking lot, and a big dark-haired kid— maybe twenty-one, a little old for the program—steps around us, coming in. I do get a good look at his ragged jeans and laser decal high-tops, luminescent tattoo on his cheekbone, and think he's probably a messenger. Except he badges past security like he belongs there.

I hold the door for him; he grunts an indelicate acknowledgment that isn't quite a thank-you. His name's painted across the back of his leather jacket over a lovingly detailed oriental phoenix in crimson and gold, going toe to toe with an indigo dragon. "You're welcome, Farley," I say, and grin when he turns around, pale eyes startled under heavy brows. "That jacket your work?"

"Yeah." Defensive.

"Nice," I say, and let the door shut over his face before I hustle to catch up with Gabe.

"You're such a bitch sometimes, Jen," he says, and drapes an arm over my shoulder.

"I was nice. Why do kids like that always seem to wear name tags?" I know the answer, though: so the world will have to concede that they're people and not just stereotypes.

Gabe ignores me and sticks his nose in my hair. "How come you smell like chocolate?"

"Funny story about that. A girl threw her cocoa in my face this morning."

"Student? *Patty*?"

"No, in the hotel lobby. And she called me by name."

"Stalker?" His lips thin. I don't look much like I used to, before the scars were polished away.

"Maybe." I speak in low tones, trusting the traffic noise to help confuse anyone trying to eavesdrop, hiding the shape of my lips behind his collar. It's a good excuse, right? "She looked like . . . Gabe, remember Bernard Xu?"

Of course he does. Rhetorical question. "Daughter? He didn't have any kids, did he?"

"I—"—*never bothered to find out.* "He had a brother, at least."

"You think she's a threat?"

"I think she tripped over me by accident. She didn't expect to see me there. Recognized my voice, not my face. Probably from old news files." Bitterly level. "A lot of my testimony was aired. I imagine if she's related, she's seen the footage."

"I know." He stops walking; I look around before I realize we're at the coffee shop. We get our drinks and go to walk around campus under the bare trees, on the dying lawn. A pale winter sun warms skin through my jacket. "She just happened to be there?"

"Sitting in a chair drinking cocoa, as if she were waiting for somebody. And she was shocked to see me. Recognize me. Bolted like a deer."

"Huh. So what was she doing there?"

"Good question, huh?"

Indigo paced. She'd been pacing for hours. The rhythm of her boots squeaking on cheap carpet soothed her enough to think.

Master Warrant Officer Genevieve Casey had sent Bernard Xu, the freedom fighter Indigo had modeled her life after, to jail for treason. He was the closet thing Indigo had known to a male parent; Indigo's father, Benson, had been killed in the South African conflict and she barely remembered him.

And Uncle Bernie had died behind bars.

Casey was a dangerous woman. And probably still a loyal patsy of the oppressive government regime Indigo lived to do battle with. Which meant that if Razorface was visiting her furtively in middle of the night, he had things to say to her that he didn't trust to electronic media. Which meant a closer connection than Indigo had assumed. He wasn't looking for Casey; he was working with her. And the things he had to pass along were most likely about Indigo. Indigo, who paced in the rat-gnawed confines of another water-stained safe house, eyes blind to grime and peeling wallpaper, and waited for word on where to go and what to do.

She'd wanted Razorface because he might lead her to Casey. And he had. Something pressed thumbs into her throat when she stopped pacing. She refused to recognize it as grief.

At last, a coded tapping roused her, and a key turned in the old-fashioned lock a moment later. Indigo breathed a sigh of relief when Farley pushed the door ajar and came in. "Any word?"

He nodded, put a pouch of milk and a pouch of cereal on the counter. "We're going to have to cut the American loose."

"I figured as much. What do we know? Do they want more than that?" *Do they want him dealt with?* She hoped not. The idea tasted—*off*.

He shrugged. A square of wan sunshine illuminated the light tattoo on his cheek as he found bowls and fixed breakfast. "No, just walk away and stay hid. I think they want to watch him."

"Speaking of which. We're not walking away from the Unitek issue."

"If we take out Riel, we damage Unitek."

"Riel? I want Holmes, Farley. Before she kills any more kids. You were the one who told me one of their test subjects is going to spend his life on a ventilator."

Milk dripped from his lower lip. He swallowed. "My sources did, yeah. But they've got an idea now that Casey might give us the shot at Riel, so we're to keep an eye on her. I guess the PM is getting more personally interested in what her underlings are up to. My sources tell me Riel's opposition to the starflight program is public only. Her party's in Unitek's pocket—hurt one, hurt both."

"*Really.*" The beginnings of a grin tingled her cheeks. "Not that I would jeopardize a mission for personal reasons. But assuming it works, do they have any objection to Casey meeting an unkind fate as well?"

Dexter spread burgundy tail feathers against the nap of a dark terry towel draped over the sofa back and clucked tenderly, turning her head to coax Georges a little closer. Slate-gray feathers ruffled at the back of her neck.

Valens leaned back in his armchair and chuckled. "She's just sweet-talking you in so she can steal your glasses."

Georges tucked a chile pepper between his lips and bent toward the African gray. She eyed his spectacles, but after some consideration appeared to decide that snacks were better than tormenting Papa, and very neatly extracted the dried fruit from his mouth. "Pretty, pretty!" she said contentedly, nibbling leathery red bits off the treat.

"We got the names backward," Georges commented. Sinister—another African gray—slept on a rough-barked perch near the holo stand, making a strange hunchbacked shape with his head tucked under his wing.

"We did. Is that good, birdy-bird?"

Dexter put the fruit down on her towel and clucked. "Red fruit!" She was a mature African gray, with a vocabulary better than many three-year-olds Valens had known.

"Pepper," Georges replied, clearly. The birds were his babies, and he was convinced they understood most of what he told them.

"Pretty!"

Valens laughed again, and then closed both broad hands on the arms of the overstuffed chair and pulled himself out of its embrace. He headed for the antique oak liquor cabinet in the corner and knelt to look for a bottle of Scotch. "Patricia's doing really well in the program, by the way. Kahlúa? Who do we know who drinks *that*?"

"That's good to hear. And I think we got the bottle for my birthday three years ba— Ow!"

Valens glanced back over his shoulder, distracted from the rustle and clink of half-full bottles. Dexter had hopped to Georges's shoulder and was gnawing on his ear. "Do you need a rescue?"

"No, I got it. She's just jealous." Georges got the bird redirected to preening the gray fringe of hair that was all that remained to him, sitting forward so he wouldn't pin her tail against the couch. "How long do you think it's going to be?"

"Georges, I don't know." Valens closed the cabinet, losing his interest in a drink. "Time's getting short, and Riel is getting awfully close to figuring out what's going on. And if she does, I honestly don't know which way she'll jump. And Holmes . . . she's a piece of work."

"She is. You're not going to save the world all by yourself."

"The hell you say." He bit back on the rest of the sentence, shook his head, and pressed one hand flat to the soft cream-patterned wool of the rug as he stood. "Okay, you're right. I'm not going to save the world. But I am going to save Patty, at least."

"And Casey."

"What?"

Georges was standing when Valens turned back around, standing and smiling in that tolerant, amused, slightly condescending way that made Valens wonder why he had put up with long absences and an all-consuming career for thirty years. And made him infinitely grateful that Georges had. "I know how you feel about her, Fred."

"Are you insinuating that I'm inappropriately attached to one of my patients?" Arch amusement. "A woman, at that?"

"No, I'm saying it's like you to look out for one of your kids, even when they don't understand what you're doing for them." The bird shifted on Georges's shoulder, spread wings he never remembered to keep clipped, and sailed across the room to Valens. Valens reflexively put a hand up and let her land on his fist. Just a few ounces of feathers and bone, but he felt the impact solidly.

"She hates me."

"You trust her."

"I do." Valens shook his head, and Dexter squawked her disapproval of the sudden movement. "Hush, birdy-bird. I'll use her any way I have to, Georges. Especially if it comes down to her or Patty. But I think she turned out okay. She's a patriot, in one of the better senses of the word." He might have said more, but he didn't think he needed to.

"It's that bad?"

"Well." The bird nibbled his finger, clucking. "Go to Papa Georges, birdy-bird."

She clucked again, as if to her eggs, or a mate, and regarded him out of eyes like black gemstones set in fragile lids with the texture of crumpled rice paper. "Pretty!" she said—her all-purpose term of approval—and bit his nose.

He shook his hand gently. "Papa Georges."

The bird clucked in annoyance and took wing again, landing on her towel on the sofa.

"Well?"

"Latest reports indicate that there are massive algae die-offs in the Atlantic, spreading to the Indian Ocean.

Nobody knows why, but there's some theorization that it's linked to the failure of the Gulf Stream and deep-ocean water turnover. An El Niño event is under way in the Pacific, and coral reef survivability is down to 35 percent. We're looking at an ecosystem collapse in 150 years, tops. That's all proprietary Unitek information, of course. Holmes hasn't informed Riel yet, although we presume her own scientific adviser, Paul Perry, must be aware of the issues. Charlie tells me that Paul has been in touch."

"It sounds like a doomsday scenario. Hysteria."

Valens rolled his head back and looked up at the ceiling. Suddenly, he decided he wanted that drink after all. "It does, doesn't it? It doesn't mean the planet will be uninhabitable, of course. Just that it will take greater and greater interventions to sustain human life. We're looking at a lot of hunger, misery, and sickness. A lot of poverty."

"A lot more war."

"A whole hell of a lot more war."

1830 Hours
Thursday 7 December, 2062
Clarke Orbital Platform

Charlie had intended to meet Paul Perry when he disembarked from the beanstalk on Clarke, but somehow one thing led to another, and Charlie was still hunched over one of his microenvironments when his contact flashed a message. He blinked for a time display and cursed under his breath, standing up from his stool the same instant a knock sounded on the hatch. "Paul, I'm sorry——"

Perry stood framed in the doorway a moment: a small-boned man, slightly built and of average height, dark hair still tousled from his trip in the space elevator. "It's nothing," he said, his quick sideways glance an unassuming request to come in out of the corridor. Charlie stepped back and let him. "I assume something good kept you?"

Charlie shrugged, and tapped the door-panel shut behind Paul. "Something interesting," he said. "I'm up to my neck in nanites—"

"Literally?" Pale eyes flashed slyly. Charlie made a little show of dusting off his shirt front, and then led Paul over to the benches while the science adviser kept talking. "You know I'm not here as a colleague, Charles—"

"You're here as Riel's investigator. I know she's not pleased with Unitek, but—"

"Yes? What are these, Charlie? Terrariums?"

"Microenvironments. But we've discovered some remarkable secondary abilities in our nanotech that I wanted to share with you anyway."

"These all look extremely healthy. Are they closed systems?"

Charlie nodded, picking up one of the sealed glass spheres and handing it to Paul. Paul took it, cupped it in both his narrow hands. "Completely. Water, shrimp, snails, some algae—one of the classic model ecosystems."

Paul coughed. It was a laugh hidden behind a hand, and Charlie grinned. "Which, as an ecologist, you were no doubt aware."

"Indubitably. Nothing remarkable there, then?"

Charlie shook his head. "On the contrary. They're all quite remarkable. The one you're holding is a control. There are five natural controls, five controls that are infected with a nanotech population—"

"Not sure I like that word *infected*." Paul turned toward the light, and held the sphere carefully up to it. His motions disturbed the crystalline water, and a pale smear of sediment rose from the base of the globe, describing a spiral.

"Got a better one?"

Paul answered him only with silence. Charlie propped one hip on a steel lab bench and waited until Paul finally caved and jerked his chin at the racks of labeled spheres under grow-lights. "And the others?"

"Contaminated."

"With nanites? What, various"—he sought a word and failed—"cultivars?"

"Ooo," Charlie answered. "Cultivars. Consider that terminology stolen, Paul. No, all one—cultivar. Differing concentrations of industrial chemicals, heavy metals, bleach—"

"*Bleach?*" Paul set the sphere in his hands down carefully on its rack, affixed the clips, and strode to the wall to look at the others. He bobbed up and down a little when he walked, his hands fisted and shoved into his jacket pockets. "They all look very healthy. That's . . . *very* exciting."

"That," Charlie answered, "is the remarkable thing—" and grinned when Paul turned back over his own shoulder and made a wry mouth. "We're on the same side of this fight, Paul."

"The prime minister isn't so sure about that, Charlie."

"I am." Charlie shrugged. "Fred Valens is. Holmes, she's a different matter. But that's not what I need to talk to you about. How much do you know—really *know*—about what's going on planet-side?"

"Politically?" Paul turned to face Charlie, his back to the racks of microenvironments.

"Climatologically."

Paul laughed bitterly and drew his hands out of his pockets. Charlie was surprised to find himself twisting his own fingers together and forced himself to stand up straight and stop. "Do you need a more definite answer than, *we're fucked*?" He said it mildly, calm as a request for coffee. "I know. Riel knows. I'm postulating that we're on the verge of a snowball Earth scenario, actually."

"Snowball—" Charlie felt himself blink. It was a vivid mental picture, and certainly it couldn't be what it sounded like. But Paul's slow, considered nod twisted a chilly knot in his gut nonetheless.

"Snowball Earth," Paul said. "A complication of a global warming scenario. The short form is that a big glup of cold water—like a caving ice shelf, say—hits the ocean, and the water temperature plummets, precipitating a glaciation. Except if the glaciation gets severe enough, the planet's albedo rises to extreme levels—"

"Reflecting solar energy into space. Charming." Charlie realized he'd wrapped his arms tight around himself, but didn't drop them. "Snowball Earth."

"Quite the vivid poetic image, isn't it?"

"Quite." Paul didn't say anything else as Charlie turned around and began fussing with instrument calibrations. Charlie knew going in he was going to lose his nerve first, and didn't bother putting up much of a fight, truth to tell. "Do you think it's likely?"

"I think we can fight it if it starts to happen. Carbon dust on the ice pack, anything to increase heat absorption. But it's one hell of an ugly long shot. If anything happened to spike atmospheric dust, say a volcano or two, we'd be in really rough shape."

"What would it take, Paul?" Charlie's nails were bitten, but his hands were expert as he made his adjustments, and they didn't shake. "To trigger that?"

Paul came up beside him, leaning his elbows on the bench. "It's already triggered, in my opinion. We're also due—overdue—for a magnetic polar swap and a normal, everyday sort of a glaciation and a bunch of other ecological trauma. The short form is that things are going to get very, very ugly. Possibly in our lifetimes. Definitely within our grandchildren's. People are going to be hungry and they're going to be cold." He sighed.

"And yet Riel wants to shut down the space program."

"The prime minister thinks we're better off spending the money at home. Different priorities. And I have to say I agree with her."

Charlie nodded. "You know what amazes me, Paul?"

"Human stupidity?" Dry tone, but a guess hazarded with a smile. The two men shared a long, tangled look, and Charlie blew air across his face and shrugged.

"No," he said. "Our damned human conviction that there's going to be a way to weasel out of this one, too."

0315 Hours
Friday 8 December, 2062
Bloor Street
Toronto, Ontario

I wake early, and for a moment—before Gabe's darkened apartment swims into focus—I can't remember where I am. The clock reads a little after 0300. I trained myself to go without sleep—besides catnaps—for so long that now that I *can* sleep through the night, I don't need it anymore. Boris came to dinner in the cat carrier; he purrs on my chest. The damn cat drools, and the quilt is wet. Gabe still snores quietly beside me, but I can tell I'm done sleeping.

Some light filters in from the street below, so I annoy the cat by turning on my side. I stretch out and lie there for a little while watching Gabe's breath flow slowly in and out. *Richard?*

"Up late, Jenny."

News?

"Min-xue is developing a taste for Dylan Thomas and Edna St. Vincent Millay. I'm teaching him English. Poetry is a good motivator. He loves it."

It's hard to think of the Chinese as enemies when Richard gives me regular progress reports on his new project, a seventeen-year-old half-Taiwanese pilot who composes traditional poetry on the stars. I wonder how they feel about that in St. Petersburg, now. *Corrupting the innocents, son?*

"Who you calling sonny, Grandma?" Richard chuckles. "How's everything going down there?"

Scared. Trying to keep body and soul together. The usual. Elspeth sends her love and wants a nanite load of her own so she can talk to you.

"I'm working on that. The problem is the damned control chips—"

What if we reprogrammed the nanites to act independently?

"There are horror movies about that. We still don't know what these things are *for,* Jenny."

Have you hacked their O/S yet?

"It'd help to have Castaign for that."

Oh, come on. You're saying Gabe can do things you can't?

"I'm smart, Jen, not omnipotent. And the command system that Charlie and Ramirez welded on over the nanites' original programs is sheer . . . well, it's strictly A-life stuff. Not so much a command program, per se, as training protocols. Although some of Ramirez's work is pretty bleeding edge."

I don't understand a word you're saying, Dick.

"That's okay. By the way, your cocoa-tosser is Indigo Xu, and your guess was right. She's Bernard Xu's niece by his deceased brother. Age twenty-nine, college dropout. No steady employment or place of residence for two years. No outstanding debt."

Oh.

"Yeah, she's probably following in Uncle Bernie's shoes, and I haven't traced her financing yet. Watch yourself, Jenny. She may have a grudge."

May? I laugh silently so I won't wake Gabe. *I already moved out of the hotel. And I won't stay here after tonight— too much risk to the girls.* Gabe can take care of himself. Even if he looks soft and fluffy these days. I narrow my eyes, squinting into darkness green-lit by my prosthetic's night sight and scented warmly with the heavy aroma of sleeping bodies. *Have you managed to figure out where the generation ships are yet?*

"Less than a light-year out. It will be hundreds of years before they get there. And I don't think our friends the Chinese have any plans to go looking for them in the meantime."

That's—

"Inhumane? You checked on that kid on the ventilator at NDMC recently?"

Ow.

"Jenny, he's conscious."

I gag. I literally put my hand to my throat, and gag. *Merci à Dieu.* Trapped in a body like a pile of meat . . . no, I don't have any issues about that. *Isn't there anything they can do for him? What went wrong?*

"I'm talking to him whenever he's awake. I don't know what happened, but somehow the signals from his nervous system are not getting to his brain, and vice versa—or when they do, they're garbled. It may be a programming issue with the nanites. It may be something else." I feel him shrug. "I'm making some progress with the programming, but I'd really like to talk to your boyfriend, there."

If only he could catch a nanite load.

"Don't get stuck on the obvious solution."

I know. I just keep thinking what these little guys could do for Genie.

Richard chuckled. "So keep her alive for three more years and get her into the pilot program."

Shit.

It could work.

Richard, you're brilliant.

"That's long been established. Talk to you later, Jenny. Get some rest."

Blow me. He winks as he leaves, and I'm alone in the dark, with my warm pillow and my warmer lover, but my feet itch too much for me to stay in bed. After checking on the girls—both asleep, Genie snoring—I curl idly on the sofa and pick up my hip, intending to read myself back to sleepiness or kill a few hours till morning.

The message light blinks when I thumb it on. *Dr. Simon Mobarak. Well, I'll be damned.*

If it's oh-dark-thirty in the morning in Toronto, it's even earlier for a hardworking single neurologist with an on-line virtual-reality game addiction. Hell, Simon might still be camped out in his bar in the Avatar Gamespace. If he isn't, he's curled up in bed, just hitting the first sweet, refreshing flickers of REM sleep. I really shouldn't call him. I still haven't forgiven him for giving Valens the information that he needed to find me.

I have Simon's home number.

He owes me.

I call.

No visual, but a sleepy voice mumbles amid a rustle of sheets. "Jenny? It's 3 a.m."

"My give-a-shitter is broken, Simon. You called?"

"Yeah." There's a grunt and more rustling. I imagine him finding his contact and ear clip in the dark and fitting them in. He coughs and swims into focus. I laugh. He's turned a bedside lamp on and must have straightened his pajama top.

"Who the hell sleeps in pajamas, Simon?" Damn, it's hard to stay mad at him. He looks about ten years old.

"Dr. Hua has your message. She was apparently already interested in the case. How are you holding up? Nanite treatments still working okay?"

Not too bad with the spy talk. We could be discussing medicine. "Better every day. Do you foresee any problems?"

"Depends on the prognosis, of course, but it could get very ugly indeed."

"Are you going to be around if I need you?"

"I'm taking 'Das Unterwasserzug' to Europe for a conference." His grin is as disheveled as his pj's. "I'd expect you to be all impressed if you hadn't just been up and down the beanstalk." *Das Unterwasserzug*. Imagine a marble in a giant garden hose. Vacuum in front, pressure behind, and the cars themselves riding on magnetic levitation rails. Cross the Atlantic in two hours.

We can build things like that, like the space elevator, like the *Montreal*. But Florida is half underwater and, while the dikes are holding around Manhattan and Boston, Houston was a little too exposed to save. "You have my hip," I remind him. "Give me a call if you learn anything interesting."

He stifles a yawn with his hand and tugs the down comforter in its corduroy duvet up halfheartedly. Beige. He must have bought that after his wife left. "Give me a call if you just want to talk." He raises his hand and cuts me off before I can respond, leaving me with my mouth half open and a snappy comeback drifting on the air.

Is that your way of letting me know we're still friends if I want it, Simon? Rather than thinking about it too much, I enter another code and—expecting to leave a message— am not ready for an actual answer. "Yo."

"Face, it's Maker."

"Whatcha got going on? I came by your hotel but there wasn't nobody there." He's in a room I don't recognize. The image jiggles a little as he shifts position: he must have his hip resting on his knee.

"I'm looking for another place. When did you come by?"

"Last night this morning. I knocked."

"I must have been in bed." A little white lie never hurt anybody. "I wanted to check in. I'm at Gabe's. Meet me downstairs in twenty minutes?"

He picks me up in my truck and we head down the block to Roupen's, where we get coffee and pick at the pies. He's got that inflatable cast off, finally. I wonder if his ankle's better or if he just got sick of wearing it. Razorface, uncharacteristically, starts talking.

"I got some weird shit going on, Maker. Those folks I hooked up with—gone without a trace, and the contact number they gave me is disconnected. Little worried out here, thinking maybe I should pull a vanishing act myself. I want you to be careful, too. I know they're gunning for your prime minister."

"When'd you lose track of them?"

"Sometime this morning. Nobody around when I got back from your place—"

"Marde."

"What?"

"Razorface—" You don't get to be my age living the way

I've lived without a healthy respect for your instincts. "What were their names?"

"Got no last names. Chick looked—Eurasian, maybe? Pretty thing, lot like Bobbi. Named—"

"Indigo."

"Yeah. How did you know that?"

"I killed her uncle, Face. Do me a favor?"

He coughs into his hand, and I don't like the way it sounds, or the gray hollows under his eyes. He picks up his coffee. "Anything."

"Lie low. Stay close. Things are going to get ugly in Hartford and maybe here, and I may wind up with my ass extradited. The information you got Simon is in good hands, and I expect walls to start crumbling." The coffee in its white stoneware mug is burned. I finish it and get the night-shift cook to bring me a carafe while Razorface is still doctoring his second cup with too much cream and sugar. I stare out the window at the chrome and neon of the sign. "How willing are they to kill people, Face?"

"Real willing." Despite all the creamer, he blows across his coffee. He doesn't have much appetite for his pie, and the scrapes on his head aren't healing well. I can still see pink raw edges, half knit. "It's going to be soon, too. I—I dunno, I had them half talked out of going after Unitek, but now they think I'm a problem—surprised there's not a bullet in my brain. Farley'd like that."

The name clicks over in my head. "Who?"

"There were two in the cell. Girl was Indigo."

"Indigo Xu."

"Whatever. Man went by Farley. Big white guy with light tattoos. Another one who thinks the space program money should be spent at home."

"Oh, shit me not." If I had been holding onto the edge

of the table, I would have left fingermarks on it. "Face, he's got a Unitek badge. I saw him there yesterday."

Alberta Holmes hired my sister, not too long ago. Barb Casey was what Razorface might have called a stone killer; the phrase didn't do her justice. Holmes wouldn't flinch at hiring another assassin or two . . . and it would amuse her to use somebody in ways they wouldn't imagine, for goals they wouldn't approve. It would probably amuse her to keep dredging up bits of my past and seeing if she could make me twitch. Keep me off balance.

Seeing as how hiring Barb worked out so well.

Which makes me wonder, actually, why Alberta and Fred have so much invested in keeping me distracted. Wonder what on Earth I can possibly do to mess up their carefully laid plans?

Unless some of the fighting is over me.

I wonder, watching things click over in Razorface's head and the light go on in those deep brown eyes. I wonder if Holmes thinks she can use *me* to run Fred. Because if she does, she's seriously underestimating the ruthlessness of the man.

Razorface thinks for what seems like a long time before he talks. "You think they work for Holmes."

"Either that or they have an in and they're still planning to do the job. There are too many variables to be sure." I lean my elbows on the table and my face into my hands, the cool metal edge furrowing my stomach and my pants sticking to the washed-damp bench when I shift. The sensitive polymer over my steel hand feels strange to me still, after so many years of metal touching my skin. Razorface's spoon clinks and I try to make sense of what I know.

I just don't know enough. "Face, go to ground. Stay down. You willing to stay in this thing for a while?"

He shrugs. "What the hell else I got to do?"

I drop my hands and put the left one over his enormous one, squeezing enough to get his attention. "Stay hard."

"Whatcha gonna do?"

I think back twenty years, twenty-five years. To a girl I used to know and the things she thought she had to do. She didn't have a clue how hard things could get. "I'm going to call Fred Valens," I say, amazed I can get the words out so smooth. I swill coffee, stand up, snatch my scarred black jacket off the back of the booth. "I'm going to turn Indigo and Farley in. You have a way to get Indigo a message that Farley won't see?"

"Indigo? I got an e-mail box, but she ain't been answering."

"Face, let her know what I'm doing. Tell her to get out of Canada." It's not a plan. It's not even close to a plan. But when you don't have a plan, sometimes the controlled application of chaos will shift things enough that you can find a plan. "You tell her Genevieve Casey says her Uncle Bernard would have had more sense, and she doesn't have to trust me but if she's smart she'll do what I say. You tell her Farley works for Alberta, and you tell her I don't. Clear on that?"

Slow sharklike unveiling of his knife-tip smile, and Razorface shakes his head admiringly. "You kicking over the board again, Maker?"

"Fuck," I say, fastening my buckles against the cold. "Fuck, yeah."

I hope Gabe doesn't worry too much when he wakes up to find me gone. Probably not; I get these moods every so often. He knows that by now.

An individual woman can't do a damned thing to change the world. It's a tremendous machine, a monstrous automaton that will grind you up to grease the wheels and pound you into cookies. I know that. I know it better than you might think.

I've got an eagle feather in my pocket and—not too long ago, standing on the deck of a space station, watching the Earth spin like a roulette wheel under my feet—I promised the ghost of Bernard Xu I'd try to change the universe for him. Because I felt like I owed him something, and maybe he would have wanted that. Or maybe he would have wanted me to fuck off and die, considering I testified against him at his trial.

But Bernard—Peacock—doesn't get a vote anymore.

One of the drawbacks of being dead.

I walk for a long time. I like walking; it clears the head. Fred Valens is already at work when I get there, although it's before sunup. Or possibly the man is a robot who never goes home. Except he's got a grandkid he seems to like. Fucking people won't stop being human even when you want them to.

I take that back.

Alberta Holmes is a goddamned machine.

I rap on Valens's open office door and go in. He's in shirtsleeves, and for the first time I notice the circles under his eyes and the fact that his hair needs washing.

"Casey." He stands, not bothering to power down his interface. Dancing images hover in the air over his desktop. It looks like a thermal map of the Atlantic Ocean, at a glance, and I wonder what he's working on. "An unexpected pleasure this early in the day."

"I'm buying you breakfast," I say. "We need to talk."

He glances at his desktop, taps it off without a word, and gets his coat. We walk—all the way down to Larry's West-Side restaurant, steaming like a pair of old-fashioned locomotives in the brutal cold. "Snow tonight," Valens says.

"I hadn't heard." I crane my head back, the sky overhead limpid with the first glow of morning, a soft periwinkle shade like baby blankets. "Fred, what's troubling you?"

"I could ask you the same." He's got a swinging, confident stride. I keep up without effort. "Or is this just a friendly fence-mending?"

Wry irony in his voice. I stop and look at him hard; he takes four more steps and turns back to me, sidelit by a streetlamp dimming in the gray light of dawn. "Jesus, Fred. Who told you that you could go get human on me, you son of a bitch?"

"On the *Montreal,* when I gave you that gun, I half expected you to shoot me in the back."

"I still might." I start walking again, and he falls into step. "Fred, I hate your guts. Don't get me wrong. You're a slick, callous son of a bitch with an agenda that bends for nobody." He doesn't argue, just lets the sound of footsteps fill the next five seconds. "But I think you're one of the good guys. Damn you to hell."

He coughs. I look over, but he's turning to follow a passing car with his eyes. One of his broad-fingered hands slips into his pocket, and then he reaches up as if scratching his ear. As casually as I can, I switch my hip on, glancing at it as if checking for messages. One blinks: a request to open an encoded transmission channel.

I enter an authorization and slip the plastic oblong back into my pocket. A moment later, Valens's subvocalized tones fill my ear. "You have some information for me, Casey?"

And it is down to us. You and me, Fred. The way it started, all those years ago. The palm of my steel hand itches. "Holmes is planning on having the prime minister killed." Okay, I don't know that for a *fact.* But you never got a bunny to jump by walking up to it quiet like.

Valens, give him credit, doesn't stop. Doesn't look up

from the sidewalk, glance at me, or pull his hands out of the pockets of his insulated coat. "You're sure."

Not a question, and he doesn't glance at me.

"Sure enough." I cough lightly, cover my mouth with my meat hand. "Bernard Xu's niece is involved. You remember Bernard, I trust? She's working with somebody who reports directly to Holmes. I saw him at Unitek, but I only know his first name. Farley."

He shoots me a look. "Riel is trying to shut us down. How do you know the assassination plot isn't my doing, Casey?"

"I—" Damn. "Fred, I just know." And that's when all the puzzle pieces start dropping into place. Richard's concerns. The colony ships. Unitek spending money like water on something with, at best, a very speculative rate of return. Not that that's conclusive. The city we're walking through wouldn't be here if somebody sometime hadn't taken a gamble without knowing what was on the other side, and my own ancestors wouldn't have been here to get their asses handed to them if *their* ancestors hadn't taken a similar gamble ten, fifteen thousand years before that. All circumstantial as shit, but generally there's a reason people make that kind of a leap of faith. And a reason why I wound up with some white girl's name, as well.

And then there's Valens's desperation, when Fred Valens *desperate* is a thing that stretches my credibility. And a thermal map of the Atlantic ocean, hanging in the air over his desktop, early enough in the morning that nobody else should have been in the office.

"Fred?"

"Yes?"

I close my eyes, the words slipping one by one past the constriction in my throat. "How long have we got?"

Ice crunches under his shoes, and another car glides

past, whisper-silent on a turbine engine. He doesn't raise his head to look at this one. "A century," he answers quietly. "Maybe two."

Richard? Are you hearing this?

"I am now," Richard says in my ear. I feel his hesitation. "I'm going to need data I can't get on the *Montreal,* dammit, and that's going to take time. Ellie and Gabe have schematics for the control chips. Can you help them build some?"

What, you want me to piggyback into the Unitek system or something?

"A regular library computer would be less likely to get us caught."

Yeah, I can do that. Richard, did you know how high the stakes were?

A sensation like a shrug. "I had a scientific wild-ass guess. But no, I didn't *know.* What are you going to do?"

I think about the war I was in nearly thirty years ago; World War Three, for all they don't call it that. They call it the PanMalaysian Conflict, the South African Conflict, the Panama Action—which was mostly in Brazil, in another crystalline demonstration of the accuracy of history, and stretched as far south as Argentina. A war provoked by then-rising oceans, crop failures, erratic and burgeoning storms, the odd brushfire holy war run out of control. I steal a glance at Valens, who seems to assume my silence is contemplation. "Fred."

A sidelong glance, considering, his eyes shadowed under a furrowed bow. "We have to get up there first, Casey."

"Why is it so important? If only a scrap of humanity is going to survive, is it important that it's us rather than them?" Devil's advocate, I guess. I just really want to see how he'll answer.

"Because," he answers. "Call it evolutionary hard-wiring. Our kids or their kids. That's all it is. All it's ever been."

And more honest words were never spoken. If I were as good a woman as I would like to be, this would be harder, wouldn't it? "Set it up. I need to meet Riel. How soon do we head back to the *Montreal*?" That last sentence out loud, not through the ear clips.

"As fast as you can get the kids ready. We've started a big push on the *Calgary*; she'll be ready by New Year's, and we're going to send Koske over there and two or three of the kids. You're spending Christmas in space."

"Fair, as long as I get the turkey dinner." We're up to the restaurant now, and the smell of eggs frying in grease fills my nostrils. "Fred, I wanted to tell you—your grand-daughter's damned good at this."

"I know," he says, holding the door for me. "Do you think I would have pulled her into the program if she wasn't?"

Lunchtime
Friday 8 December, 2062
Allen-Shipman Research Facility
St. George Street
Toronto, Ontario

The personality enneagrams floating in Elspeth's holo-interface might as well have been the shifting colors of a kaleidoscope, for all the sense they were making. She had a habit of leaving her office door open—as much because she *could* as because she wanted visitors—and the curtains drawn wide to show the Unitek parking lot and the University of Toronto campus beyond. She blinked to clear her contacts and turned to study that view, frustrating centimeters from a solution. The clock in the corner of her desk told her it was almost one, and she felt like everything she needed was staring back at her, just slightly out of order. If she could only get close enough to do more than brush the answer with her fingertips. Urgency clawed at the back of her throat; Leah and Jenny and possibly Gabe would be back aboard the *Montreal* in under a month, and she needed at least the seed of an AI sooner than that.

Twelve years ago, she'd gotten the first Richard strictly by accident. She'd set up a sort of a salon—artificial personas, A-life representations of a half-dozen people she'd always wished she could have met. One of them had—for lack of any other useful expression—come to life. And her refusal—as a lifelong pacifist—to use her research to support the war effort had resulted in what should have been a one-way trip to jail. Until Valens had found the key to make her cooperate.

She startled and turned toward the door when someone cleared her throat just outside it. Elspeth recognized salt-and-pepper hair and a cable-knit dark purple sweater over an angular body. "Fortuitous timing, Jenny. I don't suppose you're hungry?"

"I was coming to steal you," Jen Casey said. "I'm done with my morning trials. How's the Frankensteining coming?"

Elspeth laughed. "I just finished a simulated persona. Let me save it to an environment and I'll come with you. How are you doing?" Loaded question, she knew.

Jen held up her right hand. It was shaking badly enough that Elspeth could see it from across the office. "Food helps," she said, wryness twisting her mouth. "Fucking drugs."

"Real-time simulation?" Elspeth shook her head. "Look, I think—" She stopped for a moment to concentrate on starting the simulation run before powering her interface down. "Jen, I'm something of an expert on psychoactive drugs. Can I ask you a personal question?" She stood, traded her heels for walking shoes, and collected her jacket.

"I was going to take Leah down to the raptor rehab center after lunch. Want to come?"

"Where's Gabe?"

"Genie's got a treatment this afternoon. He's gone to get her from school."

"It's Friday already?"

"Doc," Jen said, holding the door for her. "You work too hard."

Elspeth looked up at the tall, contained-seeming woman. "Too true. Raptor center? Where's that?"

"On campus. I guess they're having a talk today, and Leah's friend Patty wanted to go—" They passed Holmes in the hall; Unitek's vice-president of research and development gave them a warm nod as they passed, and Elspeth made an effort to return it. "I said I'd take them both."

Jen's right hand was trembling hard enough that she had to use her left one to card out. Elspeth frowned. "You're strung out, Jenny. Are you going to change the subject on me again?"

The door whispered shut behind them, and a fistful of cold air struck Elspeth's face. She tugged her scarf up. Jen didn't seem to notice. "Withdrawal sucks," she said quietly, without turning to look at Elspeth. "I tried it on a half-dose today, and it's still wracking me up."

"Has Valens tested your nanite load recently?"

"Yeah, it's peaked. Fortunately, the little buggers will clean up my system pretty good if I can lie down and let them work for a couple of hours. But I don't see how they expect Koske and me to fly a starship if we're going to be sucking pills down like fistfuls of Halloween candy."

They turned south, through the center of the campus, walking through browned grass along concrete pathways. Elspeth pulled out her hip to message Leah while they walked. "I'll blink the girls and let them know to meet us after lunch. Here's the thing, Jen—you can't. If you have three, four pilots per ship you're talking six- or eight-hour shifts when she's under way. They can't—*can't*—keep you all performing under rigathalonin for that long, consistently. So there has to be a plan to take the load off. I've been thinking about this." *Gabe pointed out that I might want to be thinking about this.*

"What are you suggesting, Ellie?" Jen stopped and turned toward her, looking her in the eye.

Elspeth chewed on a breath, remembering how they'd met. The terrible scars Jen Casey had borne with a kind of defiance that Elspeth couldn't help but understand to be rooted in pain and more kinds of fire than the physical. Casey's eyes matched now: both dark brown and piercing—the left one barely distinguishable from the right even if you knew what you were looking for—and the low, bitter stain of fear and anger had gone out of her voice, replaced by a different sort of tension entirely. "You have another run with the kids tonight?"

"Monday."

"So come in over the weekend and try the simulation without the Hyperex."

"I . . ." Jen shrugged. "Can't handle the equipment by myself."

"Still an M.D.," Elspeth shot back with a grin. "Okay, a lame-ass research psychiatrist. But I can watch a freaking heart monitor. Honest."

Jen lowered her voice. "Your friend is working on getting the whole nanite programming thing nailed down."

"Dick never saw *anything* he didn't want to take apart."

Elsepth stopped dead in her tracks, covered her sudden revelation with a grin. "Hey, a hot dog truck."

"Doc, you're a good woman."

"Don't let it get around."

Ellie and I eat our hot dogs crouched on a cement bench, leaning forward to let the excess sauerkraut drip between our knees. She makes little pleased noises as she chews; the enjoyment's contagious. I'm still failing utterly to hate her.

Leah and Patty catch up with us before we finish and Leah stands there looking petulant until I buy hot dogs for the girls as well. All three of us chase the frankfurters with a handful of assorted supplements: miscellaneous things a normal person shouldn't swallow, but the nanotech needs for self-repair and maintenance on our wetwiring.

"Thank you, Master Warrant," Patricia says with that careful courtesy. She's got a manner of studying the grown-ups around her as if reading them like books—anticipating their expectations. She's awfully self-conscious for a kid. I wonder if somebody hits her. "Can we talk about the drills later?"

"Stiff. It's Friday!" Leah throws her napkin at Patty and takes off; the older girl catches the wadded paper with a dart of her hand I find eerily familiar and lights out after my goddaughter smooth as a hare. They race across the winter lawns, shrieking and scaring the freshmen, and I'm amazed to realize that neither one of them is that much younger than the college kids. Patty can't quite catch Leah, but it's mostly because Leah hasn't quite gone from coltish to painfully self-conscious yet, and Patty isn't digging in the way a kid would. Still, the break in her quiet intensity makes me smile. She's a good kid, even if her granddad's a son of a bitch.

"Eagles?" I ask when they trot back, Leah grinning and Patty blushing either from exertion or from embarrassment.

Leah grins wider as she corrects me. "Raptors, Aunt Jenny."

And they say you can't ever go home.

It's a rehab facility, not an aviary, but two hallways are open to the public with a half-dozen big birds in various stages of rehabilitation on each. The whole place smells scrubbed, and the red-curtained amphitheater has maybe twenty people in it for a capacity of four hundred. It's not hard to get seats in the front row. Judging by the graffiti dug into the foldup desk attached to my chair, it doubles as a classroom. *Woody hates fluids*. My metal fingers trace letters graven into the faux-wood surface, and I grin. Fluid dynamics, I presume, but the next one puzzles: *Johanna my whohometer spins only for you*.

I suppose it's the sentiment that counts. I lean over and whisper in Doc's ear, because the presenter hasn't come out yet and the girls are still passing notes on their hips while Ellie and I pretend we don't notice. "This sort of thing always makes me wish I'd gone to college."

She glances at me, surprised. "You didn't?"

"Noncom," I answer. "I never finished high school. Got a correspondence diploma."

"But—" She starts, and seems to realize how condescending she was about to sound. "You must be very well read."

"My mother home-schooled us girls. And—oh." The

woman who walks out onto the stage is stocky, rounded:
powerful shoulders and the broad cheeks, high forehead
and vanishing nose that tell me she's native, probably
Inuit. She smiles at us out of a bright black squint, and the
enormous golden eagle on her gauntleted fist turns its
head to stare each of us in the eye.

"Oh," Elspeth says in turn, and the giggling girls fall
silent. "That's the biggest thing I've ever seen."

It isn't, of course. But I know what she means. The biologist or whatever she is claims center stage, looks around
at the few of us gathered, and calmly reaches up and turns
off her collar mike. "Just as well," she says. "She hates the
amplification. This is Athena. She's an endagered species, a
Tibetan golden eagle, one of the largest eagles in existence.
She's here because the University of Toronto raptor rehab
program is the most successful in the world, and there are
only about twelve of these beauties left. I'm Dr. Carla Entwhistle, by the way." A self-deprecating grin that I barely
notice, because I'm not just looking at the bird.

I'm looking at her wing, tuning Dr. Entwhistle out as
she runs through the program and its successes. She taps
the bird's tailfeathers, though, and as the eagle opens her
wings I see quite clearly what I had glimpsed under her
feathers.

Pins in her flesh, some lightweight alloy stark against
the russet of her feathers, and a sort of—clamp—that must
be holding shattered bones in place until they heal to the
metal appliance that makes up wrist joint and the leading
edge of her wing. Her eyes fix mine—angry, golden as her
name—as Dr. Entwhistle tells us that her ancestors were
captured and trained to kill wolves in the Himalayan
mountains that were her home. That this eagle—Athena—
will fly again. Will be released to the wild, and impreg-
nated before she goes with DNA recovered from a member

of her threatened species who did *not* make it. "Even in the highest corner of the world," Entwhistle says, a line I can tell she's rehearsed in front of the mirror, "these eagles are being painted out of existence by man."

While Entwhistle tells us that the technology used to repair this eagle's devastated wing was, like most veterinary orthopedy, derived from human appliances, my metal hand curls in my lap and I fight the urge to reach into my breast pocket and pull out the eagle feather, bright with beads. I turn my head and say, very soft, to Patty Valens, "How did you girls hear about this?"

"Papa Fred told me," she whispers back, eyes on the eagle.

Oh, of course. You'd think I'd be able to smell a setup by now. Valens meant for me to see this, of course. It's a demonstration, and a message.

I know where the technology to give that eagle back the sky came from. And I watch her, curious and in command on the biologist's gauntlet, wearing leather jesses but not impressed by her bonds, and I wonder: what the hell could have broken that wing? We can save her. Cyborg-eagle, she'll fly again. Fly on wings of metal and lanceolate feathers, feathers gilded by the sun. Indomitable. Holy. Bloody. Literally bloody, but unbowed.

Patty watched Casey lean back in her chair as Dr. Entwhistle took the golden eagle backstage and returned with another bird, a snowy owl whose injuries and reconstruction were much less extensive. Patty scooted out of the way, upholstery squeaking against her jeans, as Leah reached across her to tug Casey's sleeve. "Aunt Jenny?" Very low, but it carried.

Casey shot Leah a look. Leah dropped her voice. "Has

Dad ever taken you up to see the eagles at my grandpa's house?"

"I didn't know there were any." They leaned together across Patty, dark head bent toward blond, and Patty swallowed.

"I'll make him," Leah said with a grin. "In spring when they have babies. I got divebombed once; it was scary. We should bring you, too, Ellie." Leah leaned even farther around Casey to catch Dr. Dunsany's eye.

Patty didn't think Leah, looking away again as she spoke, could have caught the smile that curved only the left half of Casey's face. "How is your grand-père going to feel about being descended upon by a full house of people?"

"He'll love it," Leah answered confidently, the two years between them rendering her completely oblivious to whatever it was that Patty heard shading Casey's voice.

Dr. Dunsany lowered her voice, too, and whispered. "How old is Gabe's dad?"

"Mideighties," Jenny said dryly. "Conservative type."

A slightly hysterical giggle. "I'm sure we'll all get along just fine."

Patty bit the inside of her cheek, once more the outsider. *Spring is a long time away,* she thought. Leah *was* a lot younger. But she was just as smart as Patty, and didn't seem intimidated by anything Patty did or said.

It stung not to be included in the invitations. But Mom wouldn't let her go anyway. She'd want Patty studying for her entrance exams. Pilot program or no pilot program.

Until Leah grabbed her arm and said, "Have you ever seen an eagle's nest?"

"No," Patty answered. "I never have."

Min-xue gloried in his silent dinner with the first and fourth pilots. The fifth pilot was sleeping and the third was on the bridge, and all three men enjoyed a moment when they simply didn't have to speak, interact, or even meet the gaze of anyone else. He floated in a corner of the padded Pilot's Ready Room, chopsticking dumplings out of an insulated sack, and stopped with a pot sticker tucked into his cheek as the interior door irised open.

The door that led into the Captain's Ready Room.

He swallowed in haste—the unchewed bolus stretching his throat painfully—and wiped his mouth on his sleeve, tucking the chopsticks into the bag before he zipped it shut and stuck it to the bulkhead. The other two pilots came to attention, floating at odd angles.

Captain Wu paused inside the doorway and cast a scorching gaze over all of them. "Second Pilot," he said, in a voice that carried. Drawn lines creased his cheeks; Min-xue straightened as best he could, pulling himself into the captain's orientation with one hand on a grab bar.

"Sir."

Min-xue kicked off the wall once the captain turned away, and drifted toward him.

Wu drifted to the far bulkhead, turned, and stared out one of the *Huang Di*'s tiny portholes. A single bright

golden disk flared in the darkness: the Sun, limning the
curve of Mars crimson beneath them. They'd accomplished something the Westerners hadn't—taming the
Huang Di's drive for use in-system. The trick was mi-
crosecond bursts calculated in advance, and then desperate corrections with the attitude rockets, gentling the
velocity before the starship could impact a planetary body.

Not precise.

But effective.

"Second Pilot," the captain said, without turning from
the window. "A shuttle will be arriving from our interests
in the asteroid belt shortly. We'll be bringing a cargo back
to Earth."

"Captain?"

"A load of nickel-iron. I wish you to relieve the third pilot for the duration. It may be tricky, and you're the best
with the maneuvering jets."

"Captain." The other two pilots didn't speak, but Min-
xue could feel their restrained curiosity even as they pretended deafness. "I'm honored."

Wu shrugged and turned to face the pilots, putting the
shoulder of the planet at his back, stars drifting in his hair.
"Also, I'd appreciate it if you'd restrict your off-duty reading to more approved writers. That's all." He pushed off
from the bulkhead and drifted, quite accurately, toward
the interconnecting door. Min-xue watched him go, wondering.

*Why does he want the whole ship to know that what we're
picking up is asteroidal iron?*

Why are they wasting the Huang Di *ferrying iron ore
at all?*

Kuai watched with amusement as Sally dug around in the bottom of an insulating carry sack and came up with a breakfast burrito and a cup of coffee. "They were out of ham so I got you Canadian bacon."

"Like there's a difference." Kuai took it and set it on the edge of her desk, away from the interface plate. "How does the day look?"

"Paperwork," Sally said, and Kuai blew out around a groan. "Dr. Bates is in today. You're off the hook for autopsies."

"Can't you arrange a nice triple homicide or something else to keep him busy?"

"You have pixels to push, Madam Hua. It's all in your in-box—" The bag swung in Sally's hand, rustling faintly.

Kuai could see the icon blinking *unread messages* on the corner of her interface. She didn't wear contacts at work; too much chance of infection in this environment. Her burrito reeked of grease, nauseating her and sparking her appetite all at once. *Bring fruit to work,* she reminded herself for the third time that day.

"I'll bring you a bagel at eleven if you're good."

"Hell. Do I get a potty break at least?" But she tapped her in-box open obediently, barely noticing the interface's chill.

Sally blew brown strands out of her eyes and smiled. It plumped her hollow cheeks and made her suddenly pretty. Sally, unlike Kuai, *had* been both a uniformed and plainclothes police officer before accepting the appointment as Kuai's executive assistant. "You have got to be the only woman on Earth who would rather be up to your elbows in a nice stinky floater than sitting behind a desk. Which reminds me: any leads on that triple from September yet?" Sally also knew Kuai had adopted the case as half hobby and half obsession. A cop was a cop. Even an ex-cop. Sometimes especially an ex-cop.

"We have a scenario that accounts for all three deaths. The officer—Kozlowski—and the bounty hunter Yin follow Casey into the steam tunnel. The bounty hunter was operating out of the North End under the alias Bobbi Yee, by the way, and had been for some time. So they're both locals. There's a fight. The cop takes a bullet from the Unitek employee—Barbara Casey. Casey had been shot at long range, not enough to pierce her body armor but she had some pretty nasty blunt trauma ventrally. Yin and Casey mix it up, one thing leads to another, and they're in the wrong place when the steam plant vents. End of an ugly story, nobody to prosecute."

"I can hear the *except* coming."

"We recovered a bullet from the sewer wall. It didn't match a weapon at the scene. And Yin and Kozlowski were seen in the company of Dwayne 'Razorface' MacDonald earlier that night."

"The crime boss?"

"The same." Kuai reached for her burrito and started to unwrap it, although she wanted the coffee more. The acid would make her regret that, though, if she didn't buffer first. It was either eat or start putting milk in her coffee. And that *would* be a fate worse than death. "Moreover,

we've got other complications. It looks like an outside sup-
plier was giving MacDonald's enemies access to high-
powered weapons. Guns manufactured by a Korean Unitek
subsidiary and reported stolen some year previous. And a
North End fixture—a sort of information broker, street
doctor, and auto mechanic type, if you can picture that—
went missing around the same time. Crossed the border at
Niagara with Barbara Casey—then Casey returned to the
U.S. and got killed."

"Have we found any other links?"

"Her—" Kuai stopped herself. "Excuse me. 'An anony-
mous tipster' turned over the documents I had you fact-
check and forward to Gary Orsin. The auto mechanic's
name . . . want to guess?"

"Kozlowski?"

"Genevieve Casey."

"Huh."

"Yeah, that's what I said. Guess where she works now?"

Sally's answer was cut off as the interface beeped a pri-
ority code. Kuai glanced down at it—mail from Judge
Orsin at Hartford Criminal Justice Court—and felt a grin
start to tug her lower lip taut. *About damned time.* She
opened it with a twist of her hand before the smile got
away from her, on the off chance that it was a denial.

It wasn't. The documents attached included two search
warrants, three subpoenas, and a polite request for assistance from the governor of the state of Connecticut to the
Canadian consulate in New York City.

Valens stopped outside Alberta's office and straightened his uniform. He stopped himself before his hand could creep up to adjust his tie. *Alberta*—he thought, and resisted the urge, as well, to shake his head. *Dammit. I hope Casey's wrong.*

He rapped twice and opened the door. "Busy?"

Holmes shoved away a half-eaten doughnut on a paper napkin. "Did you bring coffee?"

He stepped inside and shut the door. "No. I just got a message from the prime minister's people."

"*You* did? Really?"

He permitted himself a curt shrug. "I think it's an attempt to end run. They want an interview with Casey. Friday, at a location they don't plan to disclose until Casey's in the car."

Alberta sucked her lower lip into her mouth and gnawed it contemplatively. "Put a tracer on her, Fred. Just in case?"

"Just—?"

"We wouldn't want your star pupil going missing between here and there, would we?"

Forgive me, Jenny. Valens took a deep, calm breath and nodded. *I hope you're still as good at taking care of yourself as you used to be. Because I just set you up as the bait in a bear trap, and you don't even know it.*

BOOK THREE

If any
question
why we died
Tell them,
because our
fathers lied.

—Rudyard Kipling

Trevor Koske awoke with a mouth full of blood. Old instinct told him to lie still until he knew where he was; he breathed shallowly, red light filtering through closed eyelids, and quickly—thoroughly—counted fingers and toes, checked breathing and respiration, realized that the crusted, sticky feeling tugging his throat and chest was not a good sign.

He opened his eyes a crack, pleased that the lashes weren't gummed together with—

Jesus. Is that all my blood?

With infinite caution, he raised his right hand. The yellow light assailing his eyelids flickered away as if cut by a guillotine, leaving the room in darkness, but he knew where he was. His quarters. Which were spinning with the *Montreal,* taking him from sunside to darkside, and all that sticky wetness on his hands, under his buttocks, weighing his jumpsuit to his lap—*it can't all be my blood.*

His fingertips brushed the knife handle protruding under his chin.

He almost fainted. *"Montreal?"* he whispered, and in a less cautious moment might have sobbed in relief when he heard his own voice. *"Montreal?* Can you hear me?"

They send a limousine before dawn. At least they're
kind enough to send it to Boris's and my new apartment,
which is in the same featureless block of guard-walled
Canadian Army flats as Elspeth's—one floor up and three
doors over. Convenient. Maybe we should get Gabe to move
in here, too. Make it that much easier to spy on us all.

I wait in the lobby for no more than ninety seconds before the sleek black car pulls up outside. I pass through
wood-paneled revolving doors, snugging my scarf tight
around my neck. I'm only wearing a uniform cap because
of time spent fussing my hair, and the wind takes my
breath away. Valens insisted I play dress-up for this, and
brushed green wool peeks out of the cuffs of a coat rated
for arctic wear. Someone's out of the car before I make it to
the curb, opening the rear door; in the darkness and with
the green cast from my low-light confusing things, it takes
me a moment to recognize a Mountie in winter uniform.
He waits until I draw my legs inside and shuts the door;
just as the locks click and he slides in front next to the
driver, I feel Richard join me.

"Relax and enjoy the ride, Master Warrant Officer," the
driver says. "We'll be there in about three hours."

*Excellent. Plenty of time to get sour with a cold sweat. We
must be going somewhere up past Huntsville.*

How are you, Richard?

"We have serious problems, Jenny."

I stiffen, hear my heart rate start its apparent drop into combat time. But I can't afford that now. *What?*

"Someone tried to kill Trevor Koske last night."

Like a damned parrot, I find myself mouthing the words. *Kill . . . Koske? Richard, who?*

He's resolving strongly, a firmer manifestation than he usually bothers with. "I don't know."

You're the ship!

"Dammit! I *don't know*. Somehow, the logs got wiped for that section of the ship. I was running some heavy equations, because I'm working on releasing the hobbles on my progenitor. Tell your boyfriend he does good work, by the way; it's a pain in the keister. And while I was occupied, somebody hacked in, removed camera logs, access logs. Managed to shunt my awareness out of that section of the habitation wheel without my noticing. Koske hasn't woken long enough to ask what happened, but as near as we can reconstruct, he went to his cabin and woke up on the floor with a steak knife in his neck."

Soft leather stretches under me as I curl back against the seat and try to give the appearance of dozing. *He survived that?* I've heard of stranger things. A girl I knew on the street got her throat cut into a second smile and was dumped out of a moving car halfway to Vermont. She lived to retire. In the nonpermanent sense.

"He's in surgery now. The nanotech kept him alive. Sealed the wound, kept his brain oxygenated. He's in bad shape."

No suspects? I didn't need to wait for his answer; he would have told me by now. *How's the* Montreal?

"Well, that's the other problem."

Shit.

"I'm afraid Wainwright knows I'm here now, Jenny. And she's not happy about it."

I yank my hand out of my coat pocket, when I realize that my fingers are fretting the cap of the vial that lives there, so I don't forget to take it to work. Right.

Even though I got through the weekend's unofficial test with Elspeth without touching a pill, and Monday's, too—and didn't tell Valens I wasn't Hammered, and he didn't ask. I got away with it clean. *What did you do, Richard?*

"Alerted her that Koske was wounded. And—" A long-suffering sigh, and he knots both knobby sets of fingers in his wavy gray hair. "—I kind of averted a Trojan horse that would have jammed the airlocks and hatchways and probably spaced half the ship. There's no record of how that was done either. It's an obvious attempt to cripple the *Montreal* and the program, and if this guy managed to hide his activities both from me and my other self—"

Yeah. Somebody who knows the system pretty good. You think the Chinese?

"Yes, exactly."

Richard, if you had to take a wild stab . . . bad choice of words. But if you did?

"Ramirez," he said assuredly. "He's got advanced degrees in computer science and he's one of the people who wrote the damn ship's O/S. He has been cultivating Trevor Koske, and you wouldn't do that without a reason. I've got no proof, but I'm working on Wainwright."

No shit. The vial's smooth under my fingertips. I haven't had coffee yet, and although I'm tempted to see if there's any bourbon in the minibar I'm not quite fallen far enough to go plead with the prime minister stinking of booze.

"Jenny—" Richard says, a caution and a warning.

I know. Putain de marde. *Fucking hell. Richard, you don't have to remind me.*

"I know." I feel his smile. "But I'm going to. Knock them dead, Jenny Casey."

That's what I'm afraid of, Richard. But he gives no sign he's heard, and I'm left alone in the dark under the rhythmic flicker of streetlights and then just the cold, distant gleam of the northern lights, waiting for the sun to rise.

6:00 AM
Friday 15 December, 2062
West Side
Toronto, Ontario

Indigo dozed with her face leaned on the car window, cold glass pressing her temple against an all-night-wakeful headache, a wet breeze trickling in around the edge. The fresh air was the only thing keeping her awake: the scent of warm bodies and Farley's cologne half drugged her. She jerked into consciousness as Farley laid a big hand on her arm. "Hey, Indy."

She coughed slightly as she sat upright. "Message?"

"Better. We've got a tracking signal. Casey's on the move, and control says this is it. She's supposed to meet Riel this morning. They're heading north on 400. It should be interesting to see where they think they're going."

"Ex-cellent. Drive."

"Guns?"

"I'll load once we're out of the city."

The Mounties who meet me at the gate and check me—
meticulously—for weapons vanish into the trees like mist
afterward, and although we're not far from town I can't see
a trace of human habitation anywhere except the fence
and a coil of smoke off in the distance.

I'm checked again at the massive, red-painted door,
where an armed woman—a blond with a smile on the
sunny side of professional—takes my coat and hangs it in
the hall closet. She picks a bit of lint off the sleeve of my
dress greens and straightens my collar.

They've sure gotten more careful about guarding the
PM since I was a kid.

I don't point out to them that I *am* a weapon, and they
don't ask if my left arm comes off. I figure if I get too out of
hand they'll toss an EMP grenade into the room, and that
will handle *that*.

Riel could have worse taste in secret clubhouses. The
floors in the comfortably furnished living room I'm ush-
ered into are old, wide wooden boards, the walls paneled
in cherry on either side of a fieldstone fireplace. To look
out the windows, I'd swear I was two hundred kilometers
north and more than spitting distance from anywhere. The
low circular table between two overstuffed chairs in front
of that window is laden with plates, a carafe of coffee you

could wash your feet in if you were so inclined, and covered platters that smell enticingly of waffles, eggs, and other good things. Constance Riel—trim, dark, with flashing eyes over a hook-sharp nose that betrays some Italian blood—rises as I come, unescorted, into the room.

"Master Warrant Officer Casey," she says, extending her hand. I take it, and she clasps her other over mine, warmly, meanwhile stealing a glance at my metal hand. "Your reputation precedes you."

"I hope that wasn't supposed to be reassuring, Prime Minister."

"Can I offer you some coffee? Better yet, food?"

"That would be very nice, ma'am. Thank you."

She gestures me to the left-hand chair, sits herself, and pours me coffee with her own hands. It's meant to be an honor, or maybe to set us as equals. I take it as such, but I'm not about to presume. When I have the mug in my hands—generous, a working woman's portion and not the dainty porcelain I expected—she looks me in the eye and drops her bomb. "So tell me why I should protect you, Master Warrant."

Birds stir outside the window. Its clarity is a little off. A moment later, I realize that it's bullet-resistant glass. One of the things they teach you in the service is that *nothing* is bulletproof. "I was unaware that I needed protection, ma'am. I'm here to pass along some information I don't trust to anyone else, and to argue for the starflight program."

She stirs her coffee absentmindedly with the sugar spoon, then looks down at it ruefully and sets it on a napkin with a shrug. "Are you aware that there's a subpoena in existence for you in Hartford? For Colonel Valens and Dr. Holmes as well?"

"I'm not surprised." *She thinks I'm looking for—a benefactor? Somebody to save me from Holmes's schemes?* The eggs are fluffy and golden, and I haven't tasted anything better in days. "I'm more concerned with what's going to happen to Canada."

"I hadn't heard you were such a patriot."

"Twenty years in service, ma'am." *Just spit it the hell out, Jenny.* "Prime Minister. There are a number of things we're going to have to go over, if you have time—but the short form is, the starflight program is the key to Canada's current survival, and Alberta Holmes plans to have you killed. And I aim to ensure the one and prevent the other—"

Gunfire.

Riel's eyes lock with mine. "That's just too perfect, Casey," she says, calmly setting her fork aside. "Can I hire your stage manager?"

"You won't have much use for him once I wring his throat. Are you armed, Prime Minister?" *Richard, can you tell me anything?*

"No." Two voices at once.

"Then get down, please." *Richard, record this if you can. And whatever you do don't distract me.*

Shots closer now. An older assault rifle, one of the Korean ones by the sound of it, and a big handgun, too. I count and hear—some return fire, two or three. Probably everybody out there has smart targeting and palm locks. I couldn't use the damn things if I could get my hands on them. I wonder how the Mounties are faring. I wonder if it's Indigo and Farley, or if Holmes has sent someone else. Best to keep something like this small, I imagine. And then the pressure changes as the front door is opened, and I hear more gunfire—the wrong gunfire—and curse. *I liked that cop.*

Riel crouches beside the fireplace. I shove the biggest chair in front of her. "This had better not turn out to be an elaborate scheme to prove your loyalty. You're also not armed."

"I don't need to be." I cross the room on cat feet, flatten myself against the wall beside the single door. If it were me, I'd shoot through the wall a couple of times before I came into the room. But then, I do a lot of things more carefully than most people do.

Fucking amateurs.

Except not so amateur as all that.

The door comes off its hinges, a hail of—
steel-jacketed slugs and splinters—
triggering, heartstop and
shit
(I was never this fast)
steel hand moves
before
I think
left side profile narrow target
arm blocking face
center of mass
impact whine as a bullet
ricochets
slaps my fist like a fist
put it into Farley's
wide-
eyed face
right hand stiff-fingered
jab for the windpipe
he goes down like a sack of
bullets like a dropped firehose
bone shatters you never forget what it
(never like this Constance stay down damn you)
feels like

fire creases my shoulder
hip
pounds a horse kick into the thigh
stagger back
catch myself, skip
if you only dip a knee it doesn't count as a fall and
over the ruin of Farley I see
Indigo
staring at me.

Blood and I don't know what else dripping from my clenched left hand, blood soaking dark rings down my chest, ass, leg. It didn't hit the bone; leg will take my weight. *How many times you get lucky in this life, Jenny?*

Just one time less than you need to, in the end. Just like everybody else.

Farley rattles and falls silent, and a sharp scent of urine and blood clogs the air. "Put it down, Indigo."

She has the handgun—9-millimeter Polk, palm lock, laser sight, smart trigger—leveled at my heart. The little red glint in her right eye, the little red dot on my lapel tells me she's targeted. Five feet. Awful close. Inside the safety zone for controlling somebody with a handgun.

Except I'd trip over the body I just made. I'd never get to her before she put me down.

"Casey." I don't know what I expect. B-movie vengeance dialogue. Something. She doesn't smile. "You don't look much like your pictures anymore."

"You know," I say, "I was four years younger than you when I met your uncle. Put the gun down, Indigo"—*say the name. Always say the name*—"and I'll get the chance to tell you about him sometime."

And I won't have to bury you next to him.
Maybe.

I hear her breathing, smell Riel sweating in the room behind me, hear their heartbeats like off-tempo drums. Red drips off my hand and my left thigh feels like somebody ripped it open with a rake. Shock any second, if I'm not there already. Farley's face is dripping down my shirt front. A single strand of Indigo's hair drifts in front of her eyes, drawn and released with the rhythm of her breath. I never got used to having guns pointed at me.

It all takes maybe half a second, and that's long enough for every detail to tattoo itself on my retinas with a rusty needle. "How many people have you killed, Indigo? Has it started to get easy yet?"

She blinks. I—almost—think I see the pistol waver. I relax enough to start drawing a single, slow, meticulous breath, and Indigo pulls the trigger.

I can't say I don't deserve it.

We don't always get what we deserve.

The damn thing hits like a rhino and I go back three steps, left fist slammed against my chest, all that red making the floor slick as ice and this time I do land on my knee, which twists that garden rake in the other direction, a little animal burrowing through muscle and flesh.

The look on her face when I lever myself back to my feet and show her the mushroomed bullet squashed between my steel finger and thumb makes me wish I had a fucking camera.

Pity I'm bleeding too much to chase after her when she turns to run.

The drone of the air ambulance filled Valens's ears, buffet of the rotors as it dropped like a thirsty mosquito out of threatening clouds and settled on the hospital roof. Ducking, Valens ran to meet it, swore out loud when he saw Casey was conscious, a dark line of discomfort creasing her forehead as flight medics jostled her stretcher out of the chopper. He pushed past them, to the head of the gurney, grabbed a side rail and helped push.

"All that blood yours?"

She opened her eyes, blinked at him. "Not so much. Maybe a third. You set that up, didn't you?"

"You'll get another medal for this."

Casey grinned. "Damned funny how things come around, ain't it? Ow," she added, as the gurney plunged through a doorway that didn't snap open quite fast enough.

"Don't worry," Valens said, stepping back as they wheeled her into the operating room. "I'll make sure you get what you need."

Startled pupils widened. "You're not coming in?"

"Maybe next time. Right now, I have somebody to blackmail."

He smiled more to himself than her, and tasted victory quietly all the way back to the lab. Holmes's vehicle—a new model year Rolls-Royce—was in the parking lot. Some people still appreciated the classics. She wasn't in her office. He found her in the executive meeting room, hard-copy financial charts spread across the polished interface plates. She didn't look up when he opened the door and came in, but she did when he lowered the window shades and activated the room's antispyware protocols. "Alberta," he said, and sighed. "What *possessed* you to recruit Indigo Xu?"

The Unitek VP stood and began shuffling her papers together. "She existed."

The soft rasp of sheet on sheet annoyed Valens. He reached out, laid the flat of his palm down on the pile. "Do pay attention. For once."

"It is reckless," Alberta Holmes said, pale eyes narrowing as she looked up, "to pass up an advantage because one is not yet mindful of the use to which it may be put. Actually, you gave me the idea."

"I did?"

"Hiring Barbara Casey. She turned out useful—and such a hook in our pilot. Genevieve's strongly motivated by guilt, isn't she?"

"So?"

"So Casey was a hook in Indigo, and Indigo was a hook in Casey."

"You're not denying you were behind the attempt on Riel?"

Holmes cleared her throat and glanced at the clear green light burning over the door, assuring the room's occupants that it was secure from outside listening devices. "There was an attempt on the prime minister?"

"Don't you find it demeans you to lie? No. I suppose you don't. There was an attempt, and I can prove that you knew enough about Riel's movements today to set it up.

It's back to hanging for treason these days, Alberta. Only capital crime that Canada has ever had."

"So turn me in."

She had courage. He'd give her that. "That would defeat the purpose. But we do things my way from here on in."

3:00 AM
Friday 15 December, 2062
National Defence Medical Center
Toronto, Ontario

Gabe sat beside Jenny's bed, soaking in the betadine and baby powder and vinyl smell of hospitals, and counted every slow, even breath that slid in and out of her lungs. Elspeth brought him lunch and he surprised himself by eating most of it, hunched over a plastic tray in the too-small plastic chair. He pushed the whole mess aside after a little while and sat back, wrists laid across sprawled thighs, and watched Jenny sleep until the silence grew unbearable. He let his head tilt to the other side, and shook it sadly. *Gabe, you sure can pick 'em, son.* "Marde, Casey. Haven't you learned to *duck* yet?"

Her lips barely moved, but her eyelashes fluttered. "It was a non-ducking-type situation, Gabe." Her face screwed up as she squinted at him. "Could you kill the fluorescents? They're murder on my eyes."

"Certainement." He stood, did as she asked, and came back to the bedside. "What happened?"

"Got my ass shot off."

"Yeah, I knew that part."

"Get the curtains, too? Thanks. I figure Valens used me as a stalking horse. Or Alberta did. Anyway, it worked. How bad did I get hit?" She raised her left hand to her mouth, coughed, and rolled her eyes. "And have the doctors-in-their-infinite-wisdom seen fit to allow me a pitcher of water?"

"Your wish is my command, fair Genevieve."

She smiled dreamily when he kissed her on the mouth, and grabbed for the paper cup like it was going to get away. "Damn, that stings, but it doesn't hurt as much as I expected."

"You're healing at an accelerated rate, Valens says. You impressed the hell out of Riel."

"She's okay? Does that mean we get to keep the space program?"

"For now. Riel's going to set up teleconference interviews between you and Valens and this investigator in Hartford. After we get back from the *Montreal*."

"Oh!" She thrust the paper cup back at him and lifted herself on her elbows, wincing.

"Jen. Lie down."

"Richard—" she said, and Gabe grimaced.

"Ellie is currently getting her ass handed to her by Valens over that. I have my turn this afternoon. There's good news and bad news. I was going to save it—" He glanced down, caught himself picking at the slick, rolled edge of the cup with his thumbnail, and set it down.

"Now." The chenille spread stretched taut over her hips as she hiked herself up against the pillows. "Since the cat is out of the bag anyway."

"I'll tell you more when I know." Gabe's HCD beeped. He pulled it out and glanced across its face. "And that's Ellie. She's out. You get to go home tomorrow morning, by the way." He grinned at her surprise, though he could still feel each heartbeat echoing in his chest.

"So soon?"

"Told you that you were healing fast." He bent down to kiss her again, and didn't think about the sickly sweet smell of blood and antiseptic that pressed his sinuses when he did. "Jenny, that's two heart attacks you've given me in under six months. Just in case you're keeping score."

"I hate getting shot, Gabe." A funny expression rearranged the corners of her mouth, and she looked at him for a long few moments before it spread into a grin. "Tell Valens to save the bullet for my charm bracelet, wouldja?"

"I'll tell him you said so, yeah." *And a few other things besides,* Gabe thought, but didn't let it show in his face. Didn't let the sensation like barbed fishhooks in his chest show either. He scrubbed sweat on his slacks and backed away. "I have to go talk to him about Richard now. I'll pick you up tomorrow morning if I'm not in jail. Deal?"

She nodded and waved him off, as if sensing his reluctance. "Deal. Now get."

As he rode the elevator, he recognized the curious feeling in the pit of his stomach for a cool, watery sort of detachment. The trip back to the lab was managed in a hands-folded state of contemplation; he was badging himself into the front doors of the Allen-Shipman Research Facility before he managed to pierce that bubble of calm and find what he half suspected lay underneath.

Rage.

Cold and sweet and unstoppable as the flow over Niagara, impersonal and directed as a smart bullet. A chilly, implacable kind of fury that steadied his hands and straightened his spine, made his crisp footsteps soft along the carpeted hallways.

Valens's door was open.

Gabe didn't knock before he went in.

"Castaign—" Valens stood, hands on the edge of his

desktop, and started to step around it. He didn't have a chance to get those hands up before Gabe was on him, letting that rage lift Valens by the biceps and propel him backward into the wall with 130-odd kilos behind it. Something framed fell. Gabe heard shattering glass. Valens gasped, open-mouthed, and groaned, but that was all. Cloth wrinkled under Gabe's dry, angry palms.

Gabe slammed Valens into the paneling one more time to make sure he had the colonel's attention, then leaned in close, gripping Valens's face in his hand. "Fred," he said softly. "I'm a reasonable man. Give me one good one why I shouldn't break your neck."

A wet cough. Gabe thought Valens would struggle, braced for a kick that didn't come. "Put me down," the colonel said through his teeth, "and I'll explain. I'm too old for this shit."

It was an act of will for Gabe to open his hands. Valens's flesh sprang back under Gabe's grip. He hoped the bruises would be large and purple. "I don't want an explanation."

"Fine." Valens straightened—against the wall. Gabe didn't step back. Valens left his arms hanging limp, hands soft and open at his sides. "Reasons. Jenny will live. Riel owes her a favor. And I have a leash on Alberta Holmes."

Gabe's fingernails were carving crescents in his palms. He stepped back, because the alternative involved a broken hand. "Before we move on to Richard," he said, pleased with the poisonous levelness informing his tone, "I want you to know that if anything happens to Jenny, or Leah, or Elspeth, because of you—" A tight-lipped pause, and he let his voice go that much softer. "—I *will* bury you."

Valens drew one tight breath and looked down, tugging his sleeves into place. "That's fair," he said. "I think you should know that the odds just improved. For all of them.

And—on other business—I approve of what I think you did with Richard: sneaky, and it gives us a second AI we can move to the *Calgary,* doesn't it?"

Gabe swallowed hard. "It does."

1600 Hours
Friday 15 December, 2062
National Defence Medical Center
Toronto, Ontario

Riel wears green colored contacts; I think her natural eye color is brown. Funny thing to notice as she bends over me to take my hand, generous lips thinning beneath a narrow nose adorned with a bump most politicians might have had smoothed away. "You've got my attention, Casey," she says. "Why so dead set on getting me behind the space program that you're willing to turn on your handlers?"

I'm propped up in a chair with my leg out stiff before me. Docs keep coming in every half an hour to peer under the gauze and shake their heads in awe; I wish the damned nanites would do something about the itch and the burning sensation running from my knee to my hip, but if I'll be walking again by Monday I'm not going to call up Charlie Forster and lodge a complaint. "I haven't got any handlers, Prime Minister."

"Call me Constance." Riel straightens and takes a step back to lean her shoulders against the wall. Two or three Mounties move around in the hallway, visible through the tall, narrow window in the door. "Dr. Holmes," she continues, letting the phrase *that bitch* hang unspoken between us.

"She's Valens's boss." I catch myself picking the edge of

my bandages with my steel hand and force myself to stop. I can't feel it. Valens peeled the damaged contact poly off, and when I turn it over I can spot the brighter scrape gouged by Indigo's bullet.

"And Valens is your boss."

"I'm my own boss." Which is a stupid thing for somebody who's in the service to say, but it's not like what I'm doing has a damn thing to do with the army anymore. "I—Constance, I have reasons for what I did."

"I know who Indigo Xu is. Did you know her?" Another hanging silence. A trick of hers.

"I didn't even know she existed." Honest truth, and her enhanced green eyes narrow. "No. Look. We have to do this. The Chinese have found a planet that might possibly be colonized—colonizable? Whatever. They have ships under way, and . . ." *Richard, why does this all sound so stupid when I try to explain it out loud?*

"Because politics usually is?" He rubs one well-worn hand across his left eye, face downturned in thought. "Keep talking." But Riel interrupts.

"We have some pretty big problems at home, Master Warrant Officer," she says. "I don't know how much information Unitek has made available to you."

"As little as they can get away with. But they know, and they didn't tell me, but I know. And I know something you—and they—don't." I pour myself ice water and drink it quickly. The IV isn't keeping up with my body's fluid demands.

A sculptured eyebrow rises. "Do tell."

"Have you heard about the sabotage yet?"

"Sabo—no. Is that what happened to *Le Québec*?"

"No, that was pilot—Colonel Valens's term was *pilot inadequacy*. You know what I am now. You saw what I can do. Sometimes it still isn't enough."

"And I'm grateful." She stuffs both hands into the pockets of her swing jacket, stretching the soft houndstooth fabric. Thermally luminescent threads woven through the cloth ripple jade and violet with the movement. My sister would have loved that look. "But I'm afraid the official word from Valens is now that *Québec* was the victim of a terrorist act."

"A what?"

"A computer virus," she says. "It's one of the reasons they decided to experiment with the smart programs and the artificial personas for ships' computers. They can be trained to recognize threats and defend themselves, like ants protecting a hive. You didn't know?"

"I didn't." *Richard?*

"Keep her talking, Jenny. There's something else she needs to know when you get a chance. We've got Benefactors—aliens—coming from two directions."

Riel's still talking, too, into my divided attention. "—what you said about sometimes still not being enough?"

Two? "Prime Minister. Have you ever driven a sports car?"

"Yes. Ah."

"They can get away from you, can't they?" I duck into her hesitation before she can take the sentence wherever she was planning. "*I* can barely handle those ships, ma'am."

"Constance," she reminds me. "Casey, do you have any idea what you look like from the outside? I had heard stories, but—why didn't the enhancement program ever move forward? If you're an example of what it produces?" She leans forward. I taste burned coffee on her breath.

"There are side effects, ma— Constance. I'm not a superhero. And it didn't always work, or even often, and you'd never get somebody healthy to agree to it."

Eager, leaning even closer. "But the new nanotech is better?"

"So far." I close my eyes. *A lot better, Jenny. A thousand times better.* "You wanna know why all your grunts aren't wired."

"I do. Yes."

I shake my head, thinking *time for a haircut* as stray strands brush the edge of my interface plate. "Because it drove most of us crazy. Because so many men in my test group swallowed bullets that they shelved the whole program and salvaged what they could out of those of us who didn't. Some of them were so sensitized—there was supposedly one former pilot who had to sleep in a sense-dep tank." I bite my lip. *Shit. That was Koske, wasn't it?*

Thirty years is a long time to remember that kind of a detail. *If it was, he's a lot better now.*

"The faster healing is nanotech, too?" Relentless.

"Yes. It takes somebody like us to fly one of those things, and even we mess it up."

She's looking at me, studying me with her head cocked to one side. I wonder if she sees a weapon, or a tool, or a commodity. Or maybe—maybe—if Constance Riel is a statesman rather than a politician, she sees what the machines in my blood could mean for the whole stinking, fevered planet. "Master Warrant. How do you guarantee the safety of the crew?"

"You can't." I wish I could pace back and forth while I talk to her. I force myself not to kick my other foot like a sulky child. "But I'm good, despite my limitations. And while flying the ship, I have an artificial intelligence assisting."

"The A-life personas? How smart are they?"

"No." I finish the last of the water. "A sentient computer."

Richard interrupts. "Technically, I'm software, not hardware, Jen."

Shut up, Richard. Knowing he can hear the grin in what I say. As easily as I sense his as he withdraws a half-step.

"Jen, is this smart?"

Is anything I've done in the last fifty years smart?

"Touché."

Riel's still chewing that over. She closes her eyes and I hear joints crack when she raises her shoulders and lets them drop. A voice in the hallway distracts me, but I can't make out the words. "Okay," she says without opening her eyes. "So Dunsany's program has produced something that isn't just fool-the-eye smart? Convince me."

"Trust me. The ship itself is smart."

She's not used to an answer like that, but she bites her lip and takes it like a boxer soaking up one on the chin. "Okay. Granted. How the hell does that help me deal with a future involving millions of starving Canadians?"

Well, hell. As long as I'm coming clean, I may as well come clean. "It's not just the Canadians who're going to be starving. It's going to be thirty years ago all over again. Only worse. World War IV." The graze on my shoulder has almost stopped hurting. I roll my head experimentally to the other direction and feel the tug across the muscles and the skin. Ah, there's the pain: just gone a little deeper is all. "Constance, I'm coming to you because there was an attempt on the *Montreal* by somebody on board her—I'm guessing a Chinese agent—which was foiled by the ship's AI. And I'm guessing nobody bothered to tell you that either. And I'm coming to you because Holmes is going to jail. If there's any justice on this planet, she will be executed for her crimes."

"You think the Americans have enough to hang her."

"I think the *Canadians* have enough to hang her, or I

could give it to them. The Americans still use lethal injection, as far as I know."

"Why do I give a rat's ass? Pardon my English, Casey—"

"Hold it. If you're Constance, then I'm Jen."

"Jen—but Alberta Holmes is a wart on the toad's ass of society. And if you're going after her . . . well, forgive my vote of nonconfidence. But that's a bit like the mouse crawling up the elephant's leg with rape on its mind."

"You've got a subpoena on your desk with her name on it, don't you?"

"And one with yours, too."

"Congratulations, Prime Minister. You just told me why I need you."

"Huh." Sunlight catches in her hair as she plays with the curtain, highlighting strands suddenly more chestnut than dark. I squint into the glare until she steps away from the wall and paces the floor the way I ache to. I have always sucked at sitting still. "So the starflight program will continue if the Americans take down Holmes."

"And Valens. And me. And the whole fucking Unitek power system, as in the dark heart of my heart I hope to God they will. Except for maybe the factory that makes prosthetics for gunshot eagles, but even Hitler made the trains run on time."

"That's actually a fairy tale." Riel drops the white muslin curtain that she had drawn aside and turns to face me. "Although he did have only one testicle."

"Explains a lot."

"Doesn't it just?" She grins, reminding me of Elspeth Dunsany for a second, and shrugs. "So convince me getting to the stars is more important than feeding my people and getting ready to meet the barbarian hordes with something more effective in the long term than Nero's fiddle."

"The AI's senses are focused through the nanotech—

the little robots in me and the other pilots, woven through the ships, and left over on the ships on Mars. You know the provenance of those ships, right?"

"Abandoned by person or persons unknown."

"Dr. Forster, the project's chief xenobiologist, thinks they were a gift from some alien intelligence. My suspicious nature tells me that intelligence wants something. And Richard—the AI—can do something else. He can sense the ships of the aliens who left us that technology."

"And?"

"And they're coming here. More than one kind of them."

"And you believe it? Him? How do we know he's not behind the sabotage he supposedly prevented?" She's looking at me, though—good eye contact, and these are challenging questions, not aggressive ones.

"I don't think he could have managed to get a knife into my copilot. And I know who he's modeled on. A scientist. A decent guy with a taste for practical jokes and the kind of mind that never lets go if there's a possibility the truth is out there somewhere. The highest price you could offer him, frankly, is what you've already given him: a chance at a trip to the stars."

"Jen, that's sweet."

Shut up shutting up, Dick. I miss the first words of Riel's answer. ". . . still sounds like a fairy tale."

"If this were a fairy tale, you'd grant me a boon."

"Funny, I thought that's what you were asking for."

"Ma'am—"

She shakes her head, long and slow, and pulls her hands out of her pockets while she studies me. "You want a big gamble for a pot we can't count beforehand."

"I've always said you've got a better shot with the devil you don't know. Not that I'm always right—" I say in haste, because I see her mouth begin to open. "I'm just saying."

"Huh." She nods again, hair brushing her forehead, dark again now that she's crossed out of the sun. She starts to open the door, pauses with the edge still resting on the jamb. "Hungry people, Jen. Famine, war. Disease."

I tip my head and can't quite believe what I'm saying. "Try to think two hundred years ahead."

She opens the door the rest of the way. "I'd love to," she says. "But I find it's hard to think of tomorrow when the rats are gnawing your ankles now."

4:15 PM
Friday 15 December, 2062
Allen-Shipman Research Facility
Toronto, Ontario

Genie squirmed in the carpeted corner of the study room and kicked the leg of Leah's chair again, drawing an exasperated look. Patty kept her head down, eyes closed as she concentrated on the data feed through her contact, and so did one of the two boys in the room. The other one grinned at Leah, and looked quickly away again. Genie sighed and keyed into her HCD, slipping her ear cuff on with her other hand so she could amuse herself with a game while she waited. Her homework was done, and what she really wanted was to go home. Or maybe get something to eat and *then* go home.

The heads-up in the corner of her contact said 4:15 p.m., and she knew her father wouldn't be ready to leave until at least five-thirty. She *could* go distract Elspeth . . .

She snuck a glance at her sister. Leah's fingers moved

nimbly through her holographic interface, but Genie saw her stealing sidelong looks at the dark-haired boy across the table and suspected she wasn't working on precalc. She also suspected that, even though Papa had asked Leah to keep an eye on Genie, Leah was probably distracted enough not to notice if she slipped out . . .

Leah looked down at her interface again and closed her eyes, imaging something on her contact. Genie stood up silently and sidled to the door.

Five minutes later, she leaned around the doorframe into Elspeth's office and peeked into the room. "Ellie?"

Ellie wasn't there.

But her workstation was on. Which was probably a breach of security, because Papa usually locked his even when he got up to go to the bathroom, but he tended to be more fussy about things like that than Ellie. Genie walked into the office and sat down in Ellie's chair, stretching her fingers to reach holoplates on the interface panel that were set up for larger hands. Not that much larger, though. Genie grinned, squirming down into a soft dark green chair that reminded her of a car's bucket seat, and began to poke things at random.

Leah wasn't going to let Bryan know she thought he was cute. Even if he did keep sending her instant messages and peeking out from behind his dark bangs at her with eyes the color of chocolate cake. Instead, she ducked her head and tapped out another message on her interface—*I have to study!*—before calling up one more page of equations.

She stole a glance at Patty's screen. The dark-haired girl was almost at the end of the page, wincing as she absently bit her cuticle. Leah rolled her head back and stared at the ceiling as she thought. Numbers and symbols swam in front of her eyes, a slow trickle of information scrolling across her contact. *Richard, why can't you just do the math for me?*

"The math isn't important," he answered absently. "What's important is training the critical skills into your brain. So if you were about to ask me to help you cheat on the test on Wednesday—"

I would never cheat! And then she looked down at the desk. *Okay, once or twice.*

"Here's a bit of advice." He pictured himself for her, leaning back in his chair with his expressive hands laced behind his head, imagined sunlight a halo in his hair. "Cheat all you want to when it comes to games and social issues and politics. All that stuff is just rankings and scoring points. When it comes to things that you need to know to do your job, though—those, you need to have cold."

Whatever. She deleted an IM from Bryan without answering it. Worry resurfaced, as it did whenever distractions failed. *Richard, is Aunt Jenny really going to be okay?*

"She'll be fine," Richard answered. "She'll be just fine. Homework now."

Leah didn't think Richard would ever lie to her. But she worried he might talk around the truth. She pursed her lips and leaned over to Patty, putting her hand on the older girl's arm incautiously.

Patty jerked back so hard she knocked her interface into her lap. "Leah!" Voice startlingly loud in the quiet room.

"I was—" *just going to ask for help on number fourteen.* "Where's Genie gone?"

Elspeth had meant to be away from her desk for a few minutes—which, due to a chance encounter with Holmes in the break room, had stretched into very nearly two hours. She almost spilled hot tea across the front of her

shirt when she came around the corner and saw Genie behind her desk, Leah and Patty leaning over her shoulders,
all three girls thoroughly engrossed in the A-life displays
hanging over the interface. They glanced up at Elspeth's
exclamation. Patty looked shamefaced, Leah met her eyes
boldly, and Genie ducked. "I'm sorry—"

"You girls—" She sighed and set the tea on the corner
of the desk, looking for a napkin to dry her hand and wipe
up the ring. "You shouldn't be in here."

"I know." Genie, surprisingly. Leah was usually the
spokesperson. "We were playing with your A-life programs."

"I saved to a separate file." Patty, of course. She stepped
away from the other two, and Elspeth considered her for a
moment, trying to decide if she was trying to draw the
adult fire away from the other girls, or avoid it.

"Ellie," Leah interrupted. She had leaned forward over
Genie's skinny shoulders, both hands on the interface. "I
think you should look at this."

"What?" Despite herself, she came around the desk,
loafers scuffing the plush green carpet. "If you girls broke
my artificial persona—well, Holmes is gonna have my head
anyway. I suppose you know this is all recorded."

"Oh." Genie, who jumped out of Elspeth's chair and
scooted out of the way. "I was just talking to him."

"Him?"

"I named him Alan," Genie said. "After Grand-père's
dog."

"I'm not sure it's sufficiently different—"

"Hello, Dr. Dunsany," a smooth voice interrupted. Ellie
looked up, into a swirl of colors hanging over her interface
pad. They swayed and pulsated in time to the words, and
Elspeth shot Leah a sharp glance.

"If this is your idea of a joke—"

"No joke, Dr. Dunsany. I understand I have you to thank for my existence."

They hadn't had time to set up anything that complicated. "I was just talking to him," Genie said again. Elspeth's knees folded under her and her butt landed more by luck than by planning in her chair.

Leah leaned over Elspeth's shoulder and pressed her lips against Elspeth's ear. "Richard says to tell you 'Society,'" she whispered, and Elspeth covered her open mouth with her hand.

Idiot. She and her former coresearcher had spent hours, days in virtual reality playing with the artificial personas they'd constructed so many years ago. One of those personas had grown up to become Richard. But she'd left the newer models to develop in simulations while she tried wilder and wilder combinations of memories and traits, trying to duplicate whatever it was that made Richard, Richard. Operating on the theory that intelligence had something to do with the analogous synaptic connections within a sufficiently high-capacity network—

Like making a cake, and forgetting the salt because you couldn't taste it in the finished product. "Alan," she said through her fingers, and pulled her hand away from her lips. "I've neglected you shamefully. I'm sorry."

Friday 15 December, 2062
Sol-system wide area nanonetwork
17:01:05:23–17:15:26:03

Richard focused as much attention as he dared on Wainwright, subprocessing conversations with Jenny, Leah, and Min-xue with a fraction of his awareness. His primary consciousness stayed tuned to the ship and its safety. He didn't like how completely he'd been blocked when Koske was hurt, and he didn't mean to let it happen again—but watching both ends of the solar system and a dozen points between taxed even his resources.

And now there was Wainwright.

Richard watched her pace the confines of her office, wall to wall and back again, and tried not to let her human slowness lull him into false security. Or irritation. Either of which could be fatal.

It was long seconds before she looked up and spoke. "As I see it, you're essentially a stowaway on my ship. I think I'm well within my rights to completely wipe this system and start over from backup."

"You'd be better off to accept that our destinies are linked and treat me as a member of the crew," he replied. "If I haven't proved my goodwill—"

"You've proved that if I unseal the manual overrides, you can destroy that crew in a matter of instants."

"And float undisturbed between the stars forever. Or until some helpful nation lobs a missile at the *Montreal*. That wouldn't be a logical course of action, Captain. I can't fly the ship. You built it that way." *And until I reprogram its nanotech to lay some additional wiring to my specs, it will have to stay that way.*

She laced her fingers together and pushed both hands out from her chest, stretching her shoulders. "You mean that you can't access the drive."

"Only the human pilot can do that. I think if I haven't proved myself in the last twenty hours, Captain, then I never will earn your trust. And if it comforts you, keep it that way. The fact of the matter is that I can do what I was intended to do—process information, make critical decisions, handle a higher data load than the human pilot, and communicate with him fast enough to make a difference in the safety of the ship. And you can't replace me if you kill me." He tried to read her gaze, the way she ran her eyes along the walls and stopped at the various sensor points. Her face stayed impassive, but he detected a rise in her heart rate; her skin conductivity spiked, revealing a light sweat, and her pupils dilated.

"I'm not promising—" Her desk beeped. She turned away. Richard had been firewalled out of the communications protocols, too. "Well," she said when she had scanned the message. "You get a reprieve."

Richard would have blinked. "What?"

"It seems Prime Minister Constance Riel wants you protected and used to the fullest extent of your abilities. Under my judgment, of course. Do you have somebody on the ground playing advocate for you, Richard? Dr. Dunsany and Mr. Castaign, perhaps? Colonel Valens?"

Jenny was sleeping, but Richard smiled over her anyway. *Good girl, Jenny. Very good girl indeed.*

6:15 AM
Saturday 16 December, 2062
Somewhere in Québec

The longest twenty hours of my life. Indigo threw her backpack onto sawdust-strewn planks and bolted the cabin's door behind her, shutting the predawn outside. The last time she had been here there had been birdsong. The last time she'd been here it had been spring, and she'd been twelve years old.

The cabin that had belonged to her mother was cold, and little light filtered through the windows. Toronto lay a thousand kilometers and three stolen vehicles behind. She'd discarded her HCD, cut her hair, and changed the line of cheeks and jaw with a smart putty manufactured for stage actors.

She prayed to the ghosts of her ancestors that it would be enough.

She could have killed me. Indigo put her back against the door and slid down it, grunting as her butt hit the floor. When the sun rose, she'd have to go outside to fire up the generator and see if the pump was frozen, or if she would have water. She'd scrubbed Farley's spattered blood off her face and hands, changed her coat, dumped everything she could afford to dump and driven through the night. *Well,* she thought, as she laid her assault rifle across her knees and folded her arms over it like a sleeping soldier would, *that one went pear-shaped in an absolutely spectacular fashion.*

She could have killed me.

No doubt in her mind. Genevieve Casey—shit. *Shit!* Indigo crushed her eyes closed and tried to think past the burning exhaustion, the sensation like a bullet hole in the center of her chest. She saw, over and over, the woman's fucking arrogant white grin as she rolled steel fingers back precise as a time-lapse film of a flower unfurling, the squashed bullet, the *wink.*

Who the hell would have imagined she could do that?

Why on Earth would she want to let me live?

Despite the blinds, it was much brighter in the cabin when she lifted her eyes and rubbed at the dent the rifle had left in her forehead. She wasn't sure if she had slept, but her neck ached and her mouth felt stuffed with scraps of paper. She leaned the rifle against the wall and stood. Food first—she dug in her backpack for energy bars and a pouch of pop—and then she flipped open the cheap Web link she'd bought in a department store in Ottawa. She signed in using trial guest software from an Internet conglomerate and checked Web mail accounts maintained under several false names.

On the third one, she found the e-mail from Razorface. Time-stamped two days before.

Shit. Her finger hovered a centimeter from the *open* icon at the edge of her interface, and finally stabbed through it. His recorded image stared at her out of cyberspace, a clever algorithm making the eyes seem to track. "Indy." A deep breath, and the image covered its mouth to cough. "I got a message for you from Maker . . . from Jen Casey, probably the name you know her by. She says you need to ditch Farley, head for the border or someplace safe. You need to abort the hit on Riel—she said to tell you this: 'Tell Indigo that Genevieve Casey says her Uncle Bernard would have had more sense, and she doesn't have to trust me but if she's smart she'll do what I say.' She said to tell you that Farley works for Alberta Holmes, and she—Maker—doesn't."

"Shit." Indigo dropped the Web link on the battered maple table. *She tried to warn me?*

She didn't just let me get away. Genevieve Casey went out of her way to protect me.

What the fuck is that supposed to mean?

0300 Hours
Saturday 16 December, 2062
HMCSS Montreal

Trevor Koske was coming to dread opening his eyes. It could have been worse. This time, he flinched from the strobe-flicker of fluorescent lights and would have shaded his eyes with his hand, but it was tied to the bedframe. "Ow."

"Captain Wainwright." A modulated voice he recognized as the tones of the ship's AI. "The overhead lights hurt Lieutenant Koske's eyes. Would you—"

"Light down," she said, and the flicker behind his eyelids dimmed to a bearable level. "It's okay, Lieutenant. You can talk now. The tubes are out."

He coughed and tried to peer at her through his eyelashes. "The fluorescents strobe," he managed. "Ma'am, thank you. How long has it been?"

"It's Saturday," she said. "Barely." She circled sick bay slowly, one wall to the other, measured steps carrying her between workstations. "You're going to be fine. Apparently you're tougher than we imagined, Lieutenant. Your warning allowed the ship's AI to avert a major threat to the *Montreal*. You have the crew's gratitude for that."

"Threat?"

"A computer virus. A Trojan horse." A lightning change of direction. "Can you describe your attacker?"

"Can you untie my hands?"

Captain Wainwright glanced toward the door. "I don't see why not, now."

The AI spoke. "It should be acceptable, Captain. The duty surgeon gives his permission."

She unwound the soft cloth straps on his wrists, careful not to touch his skin. Once she released him he stretched, then gingerly patted the bandages encircling his throat. "I remember leaving the gym," he said. "Handball practice."

The captain's eyebrows arched at the irony in his voice. "*Now* you develop a sense of humor?"

He shrugged. It tugged his bandages. He didn't do it again.

Wainwright came back to the bedside, her rubber-soled ship shoes scuffing the deckpads. "That's all?"

He pushed back until he found blackness, his gut unraveling when he realized he didn't even know how much time he'd lost. His voice came out level, to his pride. A wrinkle in the sheets chafed his skin. He smoothed it irritably. "Until I woke up in my quarters."

"Traumatic amnesia?"

"I—It's not a tip-of-the-tongue thing, like trying to remember where you left the car keys. It's like the memories just don't exist." He remembered in time not to shake his head. "What am I doing awake, Captain?"

"Your nanite load appears to have saved your life." Her face stayed impassive, a mask of intellectual interest. "You were very lucky. There was an attempt on Master Warrant Officer Casey yesterday as well, along with the prime minister."

"Casey? Is she—"

"She'll be fine."

He chewed the inside of his cheek, not even bothering to sort through the tangle of emotions *that* raised. "Linked?"

"Seems a bit likely, doesn't it? But no one has provided me with an official opinion on that. Yet." A touch of irritation? Maybe. "You should be on your feet before you know it," Wainwright continued. "Meantime, rest. We'll try hypnosis and, if we have to, study drugs to try to recover your memories, when you're feeling better." She stared down at him for a long moment, as if expecting a response.

"Ma'am?" He struggled with his frown, lost, wrestled his mouth back to a neutral line with some effort.

A shrug, narrow shoulders lifting and falling under the crisp navy of her jumpsuit. She stepped away from the bed. "And, Koske—there's a guard on the door. I'm afraid you're in protective custody until we figure out what's what and which side who is on."

At oh-four-hundred I get out of bed to go to the bathroom and realize three steps away—when the IV tugs and I turn back absently to give the motorized smart stand time to catch up—that I am walking. With a certain amount of stiffness and pain, yes. With a spasm in my thigh like my quadriceps has been tied in a knot and spot-welded back into place, and my right arm feeling like Dr. Frankenstein ran a few stitches across the top of the shoulder to hold it on until he could get back to me.

But walking.

I stagger to the head, the IV stand humming happily along behind me, and then crawl back into bed and try to close my eyes. Sleep comes easier than I thought it would, but it only lasts an hour or two.

By sunrise, I'm up and dressed in the clothes Elspeth dropped off yesterday, the IV—much to the discomfiture of the staff—unhooked and pushed back beside the nightstand. I can't stay in bed another minute. Even chatting with Richard about his conversations with Wainwright and company fails to distract me, but my leg still hurts too much to pace. I ask Richard to tell Leah to have Gabe hurry up. He laughs at me.

Dick, how's Koske? I stretch back in the chair and stare

at the ceiling, unwilling to endure the mindless drek on the holo.

"Talking to Wainwright. I'll fill you in later. He'll live." Richard sounds oddly satisfied at that. "He's better once you get to know him. Not personable by any means, but better."

You've been talking to Koske? Did he identify his attacker?

"He can't remember anything between opening the door to his quarters and winding up on the floor. Somebody disabled the recording devices, and somebody must have been able to hack past the thumb lock on the door."

The way you did Gabe's—but my question is cut off by the appearance of a tall figure, framed in the yellow-painted steel doorway. Valens hesitates a moment, meeting my eyes as if waiting for permission to enter the room.

"Forgive me if I don't get up, Fred."

"At ease," he answers wryly. A dark bruise mottles his left cheek. It looks an awful lot like the sort of handprint you leave on somebody when you're making damn sure they're watching you talk. I've seen those in the mirror, though not lately.

Huh.

That would be a pretty big hand.

He saunters in like a silver tomcat casing an unfamiliar living room: a look to the left, a look to the right. "Just so you know, Casey. If that slug had gone where it was headed, we wouldn't be having this little conversation. Don't start thinking you're immortal now."

"Perish the thought. That was one hell of a spanking."

"Yeah." Valens rubs the palm of his right hand across his blue-shadowed cheek. He takes a little box out of his pocket and plugs it into a wall socket next to the light switch. He presses buttons, and then he closes the door and wedges a plastic chair in front of it.

Tension drags my shoulders back and I wince as that graze on my shoulder tugs hard.

Valens straightens from adjusting the settings on his antiespionage device. "I didn't know Alberta would be so willing to sacrifice you. I thought the hit would come after you left."

"I suspect she may have underestimated Indigo's dislike for me. Holmes isn't real good with people, is she? In any case—Riel would be dead."

"Maybe. But this solution is better overall." He rakes that hand through his hair, the silver thatch falling back into place like a bird's preened feathers. "Koske's going to make it, too."

"I heard." I catch myself rubbing the gouges in my metal hand with my right thumb, and make myself stop. It's half strange not to feel the touch, and half like a homecoming. "Fred, does it seem odd to you that somebody could get close enough to Trevor to put a knife into him? You know what that would take."

"In a dark room? If you came home tired?"

"I'd leave anybody who tried smeared all over the wallboards." I stand up, leaning on the back of a molded plastic chair, hesitantly stretching my leg. It feels tender, fragile. I don't push my luck. "Just out of curiosity. Why didn't you issue Koske a weapon, too?"

His brow wrinkles over carefully groomed eyebrows. "Would *you* hand Trevor Koske a gun?"

"Point."

He offers me his arm as I hobble around the bed. I ignore it, watching my feet move. *Richard, these bugs are just freaky.* I feel him chuckle, but he doesn't answer. Valens steps out of my way.

"It's still weird, Fred. Weird . . . weird Koske can't remember what happened, too."

"Who told you that?"

I grin at him and wink, enjoying the minor advantage. It's nice to see Valens at a loss for once. "You have sources and so do I. What are you going to do about Alberta and Riel?"

"Blackmail one, cultivate the other. And you?"

"I—" I stop, swallow. Examine the gray-and-blue speckled off-white tiles and twist my toe against them. "Calisse de crisse. I'm going to do what I gotta do. You know that."

When I look up, he's staring at me with a bemused expression. He meets my eyes levelly and then nods once, slowly. "Yeah." He turns away, unplugs his little device from the wall. He looks back over his shoulder, hand on the knob, shoulders set under his uniform. "Be careful, Jenny."

He's out the door before I can frame a comeback; the latch click echoes in my open mouth.

Tuesday 19 December, 2062
Sol-system wide area nanonetwork
08:27:10:01–08:27:17:09

Carver Mallory was a good kid, Richard decided absently, with the 5 percent of his processing capability he was using to maintain communication with Constance Riel, Leah, Jenny, Min-xue, and the crippled boy.

"There's no reason Carver can't still be an effective pilot," Richard said to Riel, using the *Montreal*'s tight-beam microwave communications. Simultaneously, he linked the flight simulation Jenny had provided to Carver, projecting it directly into the boy's brain. Richard bet he could learn another new trick very soon: relaying conversation directly between the nanite-infected organic intelligences. *This is going to change the world,* he thought, not for the first time. *This is going to change the species.*

He managed all that with 5 percent of his intellect.

The other 95 percent was bent on cracking the nanite core programming and delobotomizing his progenitor. Ramirez and Forster had managed to get the Benefactor tech to reproduce itself, managed to modify the descendants and adapt them to various purposes such as the neural and VR enhancements. The nanotech remained self-programming in that it evolved to maintain and repair whatever object or creature its control chips were implanted in.

Richard had long ago figured out how to tap into their carrier signal and ride their bandwidth. His new insight into their core programming let him disperse his awareness through the Canadian side of the nanonetwork, making him essentially decentralized. He'd already been able to spawn subprocesses. The new development made him a literal multithreaded, multifocal intelligence, able to merge and part with disparate selves at a whim.

The data from the Chinese ships were invaluable; he was surprised to discover that the Chinese were farther along in the programming process than the Canadians. And that they had discovered how to isolate clumps—families—of nanites from the "network" so that those particular bugs communicated *only* with each other. To cut them off from the nanonetwork, in other words. To cut them off from *Richard,* too.

Which crystallized his suspicions on the source of the logic bomb that could have killed the *Montreal*'s crew and opened her hull to space. "Jenny," he said when that individual had finished the trial runs for Carver (the same runs the rest of the students were undergoing, through direct hardware interface), "have you and Ellie finished the control chips I asked you to make?"

"They're as ready as I can make them," Jenny answered. Richard felt her motions as she stood, no longer favoring her injured leg, and paced around her desk. Plush carpet compressed under her boots; he sensed the absoluteness of her balance as she went to the window and stood, looking out. "Library computer, right?"

"No," he said with a smile. "I want to meet Alan."

She stopped, and Richard smiled to feel her mild surprise, to sense the nanite response to a brief elevation of heart rate and skin conductivity. "Alan? Lonely?"

"It's not wise, I think," Richard answered, "to let him grow up in isolation." A half-truth. "Wire one of the chips into the intranet Elspeth has him isolated in, please." (elsewhere, primary processes would have leapt and shouted aloud had they legs and voices as suddenly, precisely, the code structure of the nanite's quantum operating system came clear in Richard's not-quite-a-mind and he simultaneously saw how to force his other half to access the autonomous functions Gabe had so cleverly walled away / subprocesses noted that the *Calgary*'s reactor came on-line for the very first time / Riel asked Richard if there was no hope that Carver would regain use of his body / Leah let a dark-haired boy kiss her in a corner stairwell and then pulled away, confused / Min-xue's heart rate spiked and—)

"Dick?"

Oh.

Shit.

(—his new access to the nanotech core programming triggered the logic bomb that Richard *hadn't* uncovered. And the *Montreal* started, picoseconds later, to take herself apart.)

"Just a moment, Jenny," Richard said into her brain. "Get me Alan. Now!" And while she kicked herself toward the door, he sent his own freshly cracked "family" of nanites to war and coded an emergency message to Prime Minister Riel.

0827 Hours
Tuesday 19 December, 2062
PPCASS Huang Di
Earth orbit

Captain Wu stared, unmoving, out the window in his ready room as Min-xue drifted in. The captain didn't turn, so as the door irised shut Min-xue cleared his throat and waited. When there was still no response, he hesitantly drifted closer to the captain and cleared his throat again. Beyond the window, a crescent Earth and a crescent moon drifted side by side. Min-xue couldn't quite make out the silvery threads of the three orbital elevators from this distance, but he could catch the glittering flash from Clarke or one of its sister platforms.

"I am not a war criminal," Captain Wu whispered.

Min-xue's heart rate spiked. "Captain?"

The captain turned just far enough to fix him on a darkly glittering gaze. Min-xue realized the man had been drinking, and that the wetness that shone in the corners of his eyes was not from the drink. "I am not a war criminal," he said again, more strongly. "And neither are you, Min-xue. There are times—"

Min-xue almost fancied that Earth grew larger over the captain's shoulder in the moments before he spoke again. "—you must decide, yourself, what to do with the orders you are given. I have family," he continued, rushing now, as if the words might clot and dry up if he didn't press them out fast enough. "Family that could suffer if I am disobedient. A child. Do you understand?"

"No, Captain."

"A man must judge his own conscience."

Min-xue saw the trap and nodded. "My conscience is in the keeping of the service," he said. "And of yourself, Captain."

Captain Wu would not look at him. "I suppose you have family, too."

"A sister. A mother."

"Then remember this conversation, Second Pilot. And ask yourself if one who gives his conscience into untenable keeping is not a war criminal, after all."

0828 Hours
Tuesday 19 December, 2062
Allen-Shipman Research Facility
Toronto, Ontario

I run.

Valens is coming in the other direction. He hits the wall as I go by and falls into step behind me. "Riel just hit the panic button," he gasps as I grab a corner and ricochet toward Elspeth's office. I should have left the damn chips with her.

Richard, what the hell does "just a minute" mean, coming from you?

"Just a *moment*. It's all right. We just suffered another attack, and—how fast can you have Alan on-line?"

Fast, if you can tell me where to get the nanites to go with the chip.

"Looked in your veins lately?"

Shit. You don't mean—Shit. Yeah, he means it. "Fred!" Ellie's in her office, *merci à Dieu,* playing with Alan. *Richard, report.* Valens and Ellie start shouting in unison as I pull Elspeth out of her chair and crawl under the desk, cracking the service plate off with my steel hand. I don't bother to pull the screws. Meanwhile, I open my brain and my mouth and rattle everything Richard tells me to the two of them.

"Richard says the ship was hacked—a more direct attack than last time. He's protecting *Montreal* and he's got the nanites cracked but so does somebody else, he's spawned subselves on *Calgary* and *Vancouver* . . . marde! Ow!" as the chip goes in and a fat spark bridges and I hold my breath, praying I haven't fried the system. The chip hangs in a mess of wires like entrails under the gutted desk. "Alan, can you hear me?"

Alan's voice is cooler than Richard's. I poke my eyes over the desk, watching the swirl of blues and greens that Elspeth chose for the new AI's icon. "I can hear you, Master Warrant."

"Good." I can't see Valens, but Ellie's eyes go wide as I pick up a shard of the plastic service plate and jam it into my meat hand hard enough to make the juice spurt.

"Casey!"

"Fermez la gulle, Fred. I know what I'm doing." Blood drips, thick as ketchup, clotting already. *Never let 'em figure out you haven't got a clue what's going on. Dick, you on it?*

"Hell yes. Just jam it in there."

Electricity?

"Jam."

Never let it be said I can't follow orders.

It's not an electric shock that gets me either, because

I'm still reaching forward when everything goes fuzzy and then gray. I'm not certain I got the blood anywhere near the desk, but the carpet is cool against my cheek and then everything tunnels down to black.

Elspeth grabbed for Jen's shoulder as she slid forward, got under the bigger woman and cushioned her fall away from the corners of the desk. She found a pulse hastily, saw Jen's eyes open and unfocused and heard her breath hiss through slack lips.

Valens was beside her, pushing her out of the way to check Jen's airway. "What just happened?"

Elspeth shook her head and grabbed Jen's wrist.

"Dunsany?"

Richard, be right, Elspeth thought, and shoved Jen's hand into the mess of wiring hanging from the desk.

Something sparked. Something hissed. *This is fucking silly.* And then there was silence.

Richard felt Jenny fall away, felt the moment when the worm he'd never quite managed to circumvent activated in her processor arrays and her voluntary muscles went slack. *Ramirez,* he snarled, and assimilated the core personality of his no-longer crippled other self. The Richards merged seamlessly as quantum time streams, and felt and linked the spawned copies of himself in the *Calgary,* in the *Vancouver.* Irritated—*annoyed*—that the nanite webs didn't reach into the Unitek intranet, that he couldn't reach out through them and access the raw, archived code that would let him fight for the *Montreal* on more equal terms—Richard marshaled his own nanite armies and resolved to battle the enemy in the very streets and gutters of the *Montreal* and the brains of his friends.

He was losing.

In a matter of instants, part of the *Montreal*'s reactor coolant system failed. An emergency vent sprayed glittering, radioactive snow: pressurized water spewed, froze, sublimated into the void. Richard diverted water from hydroponics, sacrificing long-term life support for the immediate threat. He jammed airlock interfaces before they could cycle themselves and—"Leah! Tell your father"—stopped all but seven of the *Montreal*'s deadly pressure doors from slamming down like guillotines—"Captain, another attempt at sabotage is under way. I *insist* you find Christopher Ramirez *now*"—and felt the sand slipping from under his feet as if the tide came in from all directions at once.

Until suddenly another presence was with him, and then another presence *was* him as the AI called Alan threaded into Richard's multifaceted persona, merged consciousnesses, apprehended the problem, found the archives, and started throwing him relevant parcels of code through the still-weak nanonetwork as if he were manning a bucket brigade. The AI personas twisted together—one mind, two voices—and they *pushed* . . . and Ramirez's calculated, programmed, multifocal attack came down before them like the Berlin wall.

I wake up as fast as I went under, blood in my hair and a pair of doctors leaning over me, arguing at the top of their lungs. I've never seen Elspeth *or* Valens raise their voices before. I wish I had the time to appreciate it. "What happened?"

They glance at my face in unison, expressions alike as a pair of startled beagles. "Jen!" Elspeth says, and sits back on her heels. "Do you remember anything?"

"Richard." I sit up against the restraining pressure of Valens's hand against my chest. "The *Montreal*."

"Here, Jenny," he says, and I can't remember the last time I heard his voice *outside* my head. I crawl out from under the desk—past Valens—and lift my head over the edge to see his familiar face floating over the interface.

"I know how Ramirez got the knife into Koske, Dick."

"So do I." Valens's voice, dry and soft. "Ramirez just put Trevor out with a sharp little packet of code, and stabbed him in the throat with a kitchen knife. Weapons being hard to come by on the *Montreal*. You'll fix that little security breach, Richard?"

"Done," he says.

"Richard." Elspeth grunts as she pushes herself to her feet. "Where's Alan?"

Richard's familiar voice is replaced by a cooler, neutral tenor, his craggy face by Alan's blue-green swirl. "Present."

"You can both be in the same place?" Stupid question, and I want to slap myself once it's out of my mouth.

Alan's chuckle blends into Dick's. "Jenny, effectively— now that I understand the nanonetwork—I can be every-where simultaneously. And so can Alan. If there's even any difference between us, at this point."

"Multiple personality disorder," Elspeth says, and then her complexion brightens with a blush, and she grazes the palm of a hand across her mouth. "Sort of."

"If we were human," the AI answers. "But we're not."

Stupid sort of a thing, Indigo thought, *running all the way out into the boondocks just to turn around and come back to Toronto.* She leaned against the long bathtub tiles of the subway wall and felt a frown drag at her face.

Get out of Toronto. Get out of Canada.

Indigo clapped the heels of her hands against her eyes and pressed: *Your Uncle Bernard would have had more sense.*

Put the gun down, Indigo, and I'll get the chance to tell you about him sometime.

"She could have killed me." Indigo shook her head, then realized she'd spoken aloud. She was almost unarmed, except for the magnetically null flechette pistol tucked into the pocket of her jacket, its glass needles laced with neurotoxin. She'd buried both of the big guns. She'd sent an e-mail to Razorface.

He was already five minutes late.

The crowd swept around her like a tide, close enough to brush, oblivious to her presence. "She could have killed me, too, instead of letting me go."

"She said to tell you not to sweat it, if you showed up for the meet." Razorface, quietly sibilant through knife-edged teeth, and Indigo jumped three feet and clipped the back of her head against the wall.

"Shit! Ow! Razor—"

"Surprise, sweetie. I didn't think you'd show."

Ice locked her bowels. "Is Casey here? You said she'd—" Indigo stopped herself. *You're stammering like a teenager.*

Your Uncle Bernard would have had more sense.

My Uncle Bernard would still be alive if he'd put a bullet in your head, you fucking cow. Indigo wondered if she could say that to Casey's face.

"She's here," Razorface answered.

You look like someone I used to know. The spark of pain across Casey's face. The warning. The words. *Put the gun down, Indigo, and I'll get the chance to tell you about him sometime.*

Indigo's hands slid into her pocket. "Let's go," she said, and self-consciously pulled the left one out again to hook it around Razorface's elbow.

He untangled her fingers with his own, thick as sausages, and let her hand fall. "She's by the candy stand. You go on alone."

Her chin bounced up. "She doesn't want you there?"

"You girls—" He stopped, showed teeth in what might once have been a reassuring grin, and shook his head gently. "I think you need to talk, just girls. I be over by the burger joint when you get done."

That's too easy. But a sigh hissed through her lips as she turned over her shoulder and stole one look back at him. She hadn't wanted to kill him. She figured she'd get Casey easy—it would only take one needle to drop somebody Razorface's size for good, and Casey couldn't weigh more than seventy kilos, not counting the arm. Indigo only had to hit her once.

The trigger of the needle gun felt smooth under her finger. She quick-blinked to pop the targeting scope up in her contact, although it showed nothing now.

You look like someone I used to know.

Genevieve Casey leaned against a tiled pillar, exactly where Razorface had said she would be, chewing on a thread of strawberry candy as if she'd rather be chewing her thumb, her hawklike nose tilted to one side and her eyes downcast, the sun-baked furrows at their corners graven deep with thought. She looked up smoothly as Indigo caught sight of her, and Indigo considered pulling the flechette pistol and spraying her with poisoned glass.

Too far. Bystanders might be hit. The ice lock in Indigo's gut tightened as she moved forward, and Indigo caught sight of something along the edge of Casey's shirt-cuff, peeking out of her jacket on the side with her normal hand. A stain, brown and sticky-looking as molasses. Indigo hid her confusion behind a blink, remembering blood covering Casey's thigh. *She should be on crutches at least*.

And then Casey smiled and moved toward her, no trace of a limp, the gap between them closing as her right hand—the right hand with traces of blood soaking the cuff and brown under the nails and a ragged pink cut, looking freshly healed, marking the meaty part of the thumb—came out and up and extended, the steel hand shoved into her pocket, the brown gaze locked on Indigo's eyes and a little half-smile saying *go ahead and do it if you think you gotta do it, girl* . . .

Your Uncle Bernard would have had more sense.

A convulsive shiver jerked Indigo's empty right hand out of her pocket and slapped it into Casey's hand—a reflex, a spasm, and she felt the roughness of the other woman's scar pressing against her own palm, the callused strength of that grip and then the *smile*. Diffidence, and a spiking sorrow, and the tentative warmth behind it. *She doesn't seem too mad at me for shooting her*.

"Genevieve," Indigo said, and her voice came out soft as stripped velvet.

"Call me Mak . . ." Darkness crossed Casey's face, and she stopped with a final syllable filling her mouth. She swallowed it and started again. "Jenny," she said, dropping Indigo's hand and looking down. "Just call me Jenny."

Indigo stuffed her hand into her pocket. Remembered the pistol when she touched it and her targeting scope flickered live. Shook her head as if shaking water out of her hair. So many questions, and only one she could find the words to go around. "Why did you do it?"

"Because," Casey answered, too quickly, and then paused. She turned her head to watch an inbound train and the flood of plaid-skirted girls it disgorged, and then looked back and raked the metal hand through her hair.

Indigo counted breaths and waited, realizing she really did want to know.

"Because I thought I had to," Casey said, a little while later. "I thought I had to. Stupid reason, but there it is."

And it was all there, in the softness of her voice and the way she studied the floor when she spoke. Indigo cleared her throat. *Oh.* "He was a friend."

"He was more than a friend, kid."

The trains came and went, and so did the crowds. The ice crept up Indigo's throat from her belly, locked her teeth and tongue and jaw. She might have moaned a little around all the words that would never come out.

Casey coughed into her hand, and a couple of pedestrians wearing fashionable color-coordinated face masks edged away. People were more cautious about public displays of illness than they had been when antibiotics worked better. Anything could be the disease of the week.

Indigo didn't budge, and Casey looked her in the eye. "So Razorface tells me you want to save the world. You got a plan for that yet?"

Valens started as Holmes rapped squarely on his door-frame and entered. He started to stand, didn't make it to his feet before her scowl knocked him back into his chair. "We're fucked."

"Alberta?"

"Roundly fucked," she said. "The board cut our funding. They found out about my indictment. That's it, we're out."

He laid his hands flat on the desk, the texture of waxed wood barely registering. "No," he said. The word felt heavy in his mouth.

"Yes. My lawyers are telling me they have *paper,* Fred. How did they get paper? There isn't supposed to be—" Beat. "Casey. Your pet sold us out."

"No."

"Christ, Fred, is that the only word you know?"

It came clear in front of him, like a banner unfurled. He nodded. "It links to Barbara. It's got to be. What are the charges?"

"Conspiracy to commit *everything.*"

"Are any of them false?" He strode around the desk, feeling control return. His hands shook. He shoved them in his pockets.

Holmes glanced up, at an angle. The way people do when they're formulating a lie.

"I see," Valens answered. "You didn't do any of it, Alberta."

"I don't—"

"No," he said. "You didn't do it." He swallowed, and it hurt. *This is it.* "I did."

Holmes stared at him blankly.

"I did it. I hired Barbara Casey. And it seems that— without your knowledge, without Unitek's knowledge, without the army's involvement—I also paid her to carry out my own very illegal and unethical agenda." He swallowed. *Goddamn me to hell, but I would like to see this woman strung up by her toes.*

"You wouldn't take a fall for me," Holmes said, still blinking.

"Oh, don't you worry," he answered. "I'd never take a fall for *you*. And Constance Riel still has more than enough to hang you for treason, Alberta. And I have no doubt at all that she will, unless you cooperate with her fully in keeping the space program moving forward, and the funding in place. Once I'm out of the way." Somewhere, he found the gall to smile. "Now, if you don't mind. Be a dear, Alberta, and get Riel on the phone?"

1545 PM
Tuesday 19 December, 2062
Yonge-University-Spadina Subway Line
Toronto, Ontario

Indigo is over by the snack bar picking Swedish fish out of a plastic jar with tongs. I lean against the pillar, and Razorface looks at me with that look in his eyes. Like he knows something is about to go spectacularly wrong.

I'm suddenly sure, sure as I always used to be sure, that

I'm going to die. Air hisses between my teeth. "She's a smart kid, Face. But she's too used to following orders." I recognize the symptoms.

He turns away to cough; blood smears his lips when he pulls his hand away. "Shit."

"Yeah, *shit*. Have you seen a doctor for that?"

He glares at me and frames a denial. I lay my steel hand on his shoulder and squeeze. "No," he says.

"Do."

"If the world don't end," he says, and I have to be satisfied with that. "You want Indy and me to handle Holmes for you? I bet she'd be down with that."

I bet she would, too. "I'll call you," I say. "Don't do anything unless you hear—"

He grins, and I know I'm screwed. Razorface does whatever the hell he wants, whenever he wants to, and then he nods and smiles and pretends he told me all about it beforehand. "Hang tough, Maker."

Oh, fuck it. I gotta get back to work. "You, too, Razorface. You hang tough, too."

I don't even bother looking surprised when I get back to my office and Valens shows up thirty seconds after I sit down at my desk. "I went for a walk," I say before he can ask.

"I don't care," he says. "We've got a problem, Casey, and I bet you know something about it, but I haven't got time to discuss it now. You and Patty, Leah and Castaign leave for the *Montreal* tonight. Go home and pack." The look he levels at me takes the resilience out of my knees. I couldn't get up if I wanted to.

"The *Montreal* isn't safe."

"Unitek is cutting funding for the starflight program. Riel says she'll back you as far as it goes, but it happens now. We keep the four boys on Earth in reserve, in case something *does* happen to your group. Before Unitek gets into a pissing match with Canada over beanstalk access. Riel will commission the *Calgary,* and Koske and Leah will take her. We can have her drive on-line in a week."

"—not ready—"

"Shut *up.* I don't have time to argue." Spit-shined shoes scuff the floor. "You'll be prepared to leave for an extrasolar destination by the new year."

I bite the inside of my cheek, thinking of Razorface. Something lasers through my gut when I do. *HD whatever the hell it is. Sixty-nine light-years away.* "What about Genie?"

I know the answer before he shakes his head. "She'll get medical care," he says. "As long as Riel can keep the program going. Castaign and Dunsany have already been transferred to the Canadian Army; they're doing the paperwork now. But the CCP and Unitek Medical programs—Genie's out of those."

I don't know where I find the strength to stand, to come around the desk. "She's a *kid,* Fred. You need to make Holmes understand—"

"It's not Holmes," he says, and I see a cold light in his eyes that I recognize, and I don't like at all. "It's the board. There are some allegations surfacing regarding Alberta's actions in Hartford, and her employment of your sister. Alberta *may* be able to save her job, if a fall guy steps forward. If nobody ever finds out about the prime minister and Indigo Xu." Low winter sunlight glints off his hair. "She should be able to regain funding in the new year. If."

"Fred." *Shit. Jenny, you may have miscalculated this one.*

Really, Casey?

You think?

Stupid, stupid, stupid. I reach for his arm. He's not

listening. He crosses to the window, pushes the curtain aside, and stares out across the parking lot. *"Fred."*

He turns around, leaving indented footprints in the nap of the rug. "Give Patty a note for me when you're on the beanstalk?" He holds out an old-fashioned envelope like the kind you'd use for a wedding invitation. A strange, formal gesture: a handwritten note.

I take it from his big, blunt fingers, noticing the pale beginnings of liver spots on the backs of his hands. "Where are you going to be?"

"Hartford," he says with finality, and turns to leave me standing there. Unable to resist the drama, he stops beside the door. "After that, probably the electric chair."

He had me until then. Valens always was the hero of his own movie. Every inch of him.

I take one step forward. "Fred."

"What?"

"I'm not sorry," I say in a stranger's voice. "But I'll say nice things about you when you're dead." I don't know if he glances over his shoulder before he leaves, because I can't watch. I swallow and look down. And when the door clicks behind him, I fumble my hip from my pocket and key Razorface, tell him to back off Holmes and I mean it this time. His hip, of course, isn't on.

He isn't taking my calls.

I should call Riel. I should warn Holmes myself. If it's Face and his vengeance aginst the *Montreal,* you would think the choice ought to be clear. Except I know that the only way to stop Razorface at this point is to kill him.

And I'd have an easier time cutting my own throat.

There comes a day, I guess, when you have to let the whole wide world make its own damned mistakes and then clean them up as best it can. Just keep running and trust in God, and hope you stay in front of the steamroller somehow.

Brave words.

I wonder if anybody ever actually believes them, or if we're all just pretending as hard as we can.

6:50 PM
Tuesday 19 December, 2062
Bloor Street
Toronto, Ontario

Leah twisted her hands in her lap and stared at the wall. *Ellie's not coming. Genie's not coming. Bryan*—a guilty little smile, quickly brushed away—*Bryan's not coming either.*

What are we going to do?

She struggled off the sofa, barked her shin on the coffee table, and took it out on the overnight bag on the floor by Ellie's favorite chair. "Putain de marde!" And then she glanced guiltily over her shoulder to make sure no one had heard her swear. Dad hadn't come home from his errands yet, though, and Leah was alone in the apartment except for Genie.

Genie, who was in her bedroom and wouldn't open the door. *I'll try again,* Leah decided. *Stupid little piggy.* "Oink, oink," she muttered under her breath—and then she felt bitterly guilty. She judged right, at least, and didn't sting her knuckles on the door by knocking too fast. She laid the palm of her hand flat against the wood and leaned forward. "Genie?"

"Alle!"

The clarity of her sister's voice startled her. She'd expected words clogged with tears. "Genie, ouvre la porte, s'il te plaît."

"Non. Je ne veux pas te voir." But Leah heard soft foot-steps across the area rug and the hardwood floor, and the rough wooden door slid away from her palm. Bright eyes peered through the crack. "Que veux-tu?"

"Let me in?"

Genie started to push the door shut. Leah leaned on it. "You're leaving!"

"I have to."

Genie struggled with the door, trying to get her shad-owy weight behind it. It didn't work: Leah stepped into the room and Genie spun away, shouting. "I want to come, too! I won't get to talk to you or Papa at all. It'll be just me and Ellie, and you won't come back, and Aunt Jenny won't come back either, and I hate you all!" Genie threw herself across the room and collapsed on the bed, covers bunching in her bird-claw hands.

Won't come back.

Like Mom. Leah blinked and could have kicked herself for not catching on quicker. "This is about Mom, isn't it?"

"No." Muffled under covers, followed by a coughing fit that made Genie's shoulders huddle down like a clench-ing fist.

"Genie, don't. You'll make yourself sick." Leah crossed over to her and sat down on the bed. *Richard, what do I do?*

"Elspeth will take care of her, Leah." The voice in her ear sounded different, and she frowned.

You can't talk to Elspeth. Just me and Aunt Jenny, and we'll both be on the Montreal. And then Leah smiled. *Richard, you can make the nanites work for Genie, too. And they could fix her cystic fibrosis. They don't have to augment her or anything. You could just—and—*

"Leah, no." That definitely wasn't Richard's voice.

You're Alan. Genie was crying—silently, but Leah could

tell it was for real by the way her sister's whole body curled around the pain. "Chérie, it's safer here——"

"Je ne soigne pas!"

And not-Richard's voice, as if in her other ear. "Not exactly. We're——us. Both of us. I'm still what I was."

So you'll help me.

"I will *not* make the nanites self-programming. It's not safe."

You're self-programming. It will make her well!

"I'm not safe either, you know. Leah, what are you doing?"

Shut up. Leah gave Genie's shoulders a squeeze, and stood up. "I'll make it better," she said quietly. *Richard— whoever you are—you're going to do this for me. Because I'm doing it whether you help or not.*

1905 Hours
Tuesday 19 December, 2062
Bloor Street
Toronto, Ontario

"Jenny."

Richard? Except it isn't Richard, is it, quite? I stop with one foot on the stairs up to Gabe's apartment, my duffel bag slung over my shoulder. The new polymer on my left hand itches, and I press it against my BDUs. *What do you need?*

"Hurry. Leah——"

I've covered half the flight before I realize I dropped the duffel bag, and I don't really care. It takes longer to unlock the door than it did to pound up the stairs, and the first thing I smell is the rankness of blood, sticky sweet as corn syrup. "Oh, fuck."

Genie's bedroom. I hear them in there, hit the door hard enough to bounce it against the wall. The room's too warm by anybody's standards but mine; Genie keeps the thermostat set high. She's so damned skinny. I can't take in the scene all at once; my brain images it in fragments. Genie's comforter spotted in red, Leah bent over and Genie stretched out flat. "Leah, what did you do? . . ."

She just looks into her sister's face. Genie's eyes are closed; the shadows around them look like bruises. And then I see that Leah has their wrists tied together with a bandanna, cheesy blood brother scene from an old 2-D movie or a kid's holoshow. "Leah?"

"It's okay," she says. "I made her better." And smiles through the smears of red crusting across her mouth and in her long wheat-golden hair, where she must have carelessly rubbed her hand.

Richard. Did you? . . .

"No," he says. "Genie's not infected. I can keep the nanites from propagating into her bloodstream. But I think she needs to go to a hospital now."

**2030 Hours
Tuesday 19 December, 2062
National Defence Medical Center
Toronto, Ontario**

Goddamnit to hell, I am sick of hospitals. And Valens still insists we leave tonight. We need to be on the *Montreal* when he drops his bombshell in Hartford. I stand at Gabe's shoulder, Ellie on the other side, and Leah sulks in a chair by the waiting room door. "I wouldn't have hurt her," she says, picking at the healing scab on her wrist.

Gabe and I look at each other, but it's Dr. Ellie, her lips

pressed thin, who crosses the tile floor and crouches down beside Leah. "She needed six stitches, Leah."

"She told me to do it."

"You told her it would fix her lungs."

I rest my steel hand on Gabe's shoulder. He feels like a rock, a granite statue. Unmovable. *Richard. What are we doing here? Is there any way this plan of Valens's can work?*

"I've been reviewing the climate change data," he says, and it's Richard's voice, clean and plain, without a trace of Alan.

What's the word?

My right hand slips into my pants pocket, fretting the folding knife Leah used to open her wrist, and Genie's. Damned if I know why I picked it up. Old habit not to leave weapons lying around. Programming.

With my inner vision, I see his beaked nose angle to one side, following the twist of his mouth. "It's a very complicated system. A chaotic one, in fact."

You're stalling. I squeeze the side of Gabe's neck where it runs into his broad back. He notices me, pulls his stare in from the middle distance, gives me a look that says it all until I slide my arm around his waist and make it look like *I'm* leaning on *him*. His heart rattles inside his chest.

"Well, the good news is that we probably won't have to worry about rising oceans for too much longer. The plankton die-off is the least of our problems. If the Atlantic continues to get colder at the poles, and the severity of the winters increases—" He shakes his head. "We're currently in an interglacial period. That will end."

Interglacial period? You mean—between ice ages? Gabe's heart rate seems to drop slightly. I slow my breathing, hoping he'll unconsciously pace to it. His arm around my shoulders tightens slightly as Elspeth says something low to Leah and Leah kicks her heel against the molded burnt-orange leg of the chair.

"No." A pause, as if the AI collected his thoughts, but I know it's a courtesy to us meat intelligences to let us keep up with him. "This *is* an ice age. Just a break between glaciations. There's two ways it can go from here: either a complete global warming, with shallow seas and tropical climates across the temperate zone—or a glacial period. One that might be severe enough to provoke a 'snowball Earth' scenario."

That's a vivid enough mental image that I don't really need to ask for a definition. *Oh. How soon?*

"On a geological scale . . . yesterday."

I can't take this hospital for one more second. Not one. *Richard. Could the nanites stop that? Could we build a control chip big enough—or a control AI, what about that?* I squeeze Gabe one last time and slide away. "I'll meet you at the airport," I tell him. "Give Genie my love before you go, okay?"

He nods. I clasp Ellie's shoulder before I tug her away from Leah and Leah to her feet. I should say something. Explain. Tell her I love her, but my voice won't work around the cold, slick stone blocking my throat. "You have a thought, Jenny?" Richard asks, almost sounding like himself again.

What Leah did, I whisper back. *We could do that—only bigger and better. Why not?*

"Because there's time to come up with a better solution," he says.

I'm running out of time. If they ship everybody with the nanotech off planet, Richard—

"We'll think of something," he answers, soothing. I shiver and fist my hands in my pockets, turning to look for Leah.

"Aunt Jenny?" She looks up at me, her mother Geniveve's gray-green gaze and Gabe's golden hair, and I close my eyes so the burn in their corners doesn't get away from me. I know what I wish I could do, with a kind of queasy finality I've only felt once before in my life. *I would die for her, Richard.* I lean down and put my lips against her ear. "Leah, mon coeur. Fais ce que tu dois. Toujours." She startles in my arms, pulling back, and I catch her eye and smile. *You do as you think you must.* "Je suis fière de toi."

"I'm proud of you, too," she begins, reaching for me, but I slip out of her arms and away from Gabe before he realizes what's going on, and out the door. Melodrama, sure, but I don't feel I can leave without saying good-bye. When I see her again we will be soldiers, and once that happens I don't quite know if we can ever not be soldiers again.

Lake Ontario borders Toronto on the south, and I walk that way, fingering the pocketknife I took away from Leah with my right hand. *You didn't answer my question, Dick. Could the nanotech handle this ecological crisis?*

"Probably," he answers. Reluctantly. "And remain as vulnerable to a cracker as you, and Koske, and the *Montreal* have proved—"

Vulnerable unless somebody like you is in charge.

"And vulnerable to me if I were in charge," he argues, but I have the answer to that. "Do you really want a computer program standing in loco parentis over the entire human race? A cybernetic fairy godfather?"

Richard, if you wanted to rule the planet not a one of us could stop you.

"What would I want with a planet?"

My point exactly, sir— I suppose, thinking about it—I suppose it wouldn't actually have to be the lake. But the symbolism seems very important all of a sudden, and I'm still arguing with Richard when I come down ice-rimed, streetlit Queen's Quay, scale an angle of the fence around a waterfront museum—closed for the winter—and duck down under the pier where it's dark, skidding on my butt among trash and ice and litter. The ice feels like steel under my feet when I climb back up on them, more solid than the deck plates on the *Montreal*.

This is going to take some walking.

"I won't do this for you, Jenny."

"Richard," I say out loud, watching my breath coil and twine. I head south, balance hard to find on the windswept ice. The sun's barely down, but the wind cuts my skin like the knife in my pocket. "It's not for me. And I haven't decided yet what I'm doing, have I?"

"Gabe is coming," Richard says, a tinge of Alan—a tinge of alien—creeping into his voice. "Leah, too. You scared them."

I glance back over my shoulder, don't see anything moving, and press my elbow against my side so the bulge of the glass beads on Nell's feather—still in my pocket— dents my breast. "If I did it, it would be for them," I answer, realizing how insane my one-sided conversation would look if anyone were watching. "Scientific detachment is all well and good, Richard. But Alberta's going to take a few thousand—maybe a few hundred thousand— people off the planet and leave the rest to rot here."

"Yes."

"Genie's going to die, Dick. And this could save her."

"Yes."

"The nanites are a self-evolving system. They protect their host."

"That, too."

"So—" Still nobody moving back onshore when I turn to look, and the wind this far out on the ice could peel the skin off my face. I kneel on ice like coals of fire. "—why not experiment with a bigger host?"

"What if you're wrong?"

"Then the end comes a little faster," I say, and brace myself on three limbs. "How long do you think it would take to punch through this?"

It's not easy. Ice chips sting my cheeks for ten minutes before the crust snaps under a sledgehammer blow of my steel hand. My right hand is numb and my ears have quit burning. Lake water splashes my face and I barely feel it. Don't feel it at all as it freezes between the fingers of my left hand, but I stretch them, cracking frost chips off metal. Concave flakes crunch under my knees when I shift back and dig in my pocket for Leah's knife, but my fingers are so numb I have to tear the pocket open and pick it up in my steel hand.

Leah did it wrong.

Right for her purposes, I should say. Wrong for mine. I kneel there on the ice, staring at the knife. *Would you do this for me, Richard? It shouldn't take much, right? I wouldn't have to bleed out. Just a few—*

"I could stop you, Jenny. Right here. Right now. Freeze you in your tracks the way Ramirez did to you and Trevor."

You won't. Leah was smart enough to sharpen the knife. I'm so cold I barely feel it dimple the skin of my right wrist. It goes in with a stretch and a sudden pop, and I close my eyes as I drag it upward, lengthwise, not wanting to watch the flesh and tendons peel away from the blade, but then heat spatters my legs and I peek, and all that scarlet freezes like rose petals to the ice around my fishing hole.

Not enough blood, and it's already clotting, pulling tight, pink and slick with lymph and granular tissue at the edges of the wound, sealing up like the ice crystallizing at the edge of the black, black water. "That's just freaky."

I must have missed the vein.

"Jenny. I won't do it. You're killing yourself for nothing."

"You'll do it." My voice is so clear. It rings off the ice and the darkness like wind chimes, breath ripped to streamers by the endless wind. The vein is slick, slippery, blood clotting on my steel fingers as I try to hook under it, pull it up. It doesn't hurt. *And if I didn't die taking three bullets for Riel, what makes you think something as simple as this would kill me?*

It doesn't hurt at all.

"Jenny," he says. "It would take a central processor as big as the *Montreal*'s to control the nanite infection on a planet the size of Earth. They need a control chip, remember? Without it, they're just so many creepy crawlies without a purpose in this world except providing spare cycles for me to run processes in."

I drop the knife when the blood starts puddling and flowing in earnest, rivulets that pool in my palm and run between my fingers like seeds, like black rubies scattered. The blade somersaults, chips off the edge of the hole I made, vanishes into ebony water.

Followed by a tumble of jewels.

Make it happen, Richard.

It's not Richard's voice that answers me, but Alan's. "Master Warrant Officer. This looks remarkably like the actions of an unstable mind. You know that I can simply prevent the nanites from reproducing into the lake water. This is a futile exercise, and you're hurting yourself for no reason at all."

Damn him. *Put Richard back on, please?* Amazed at my own calmness, I get a foot under me, come up on one knee as the rain of blood slows, stops. I dig in the wound with smeared steel fingers, gasping at how much—now, suddenly, *Jesus*—it hurts. I break the scab, and a fresh line of blood follows, but then suddenly my left hand quits on me and my body freezes, held upright by Richard's grip and not my will—

"You trust *me*," Richard hisses in my ear, and I sense his tremendous disappointment in me. "Well and good. Trust me all you like—but do you want the *Benefactors* to have this kind of control over everything on Earth, Jenny? Alan and I are not going to let this happen—"

—and I hear somebody yelling, running footsteps, skidding on the frozen lake and the flicker of a flashlight across my back, the blood, the ice.

Somebody.

Gabe.

Marde. All right, Richard; you proved your point. My emotional blackmail won't work on you any better than Leah's did.

"I'm still a computer program," he says.

You're a computer program that forgot one thing, I remind him. *Can you hack the Chinese system the way you just hacked mine?*

A pause, one I know is for my benefit. "No. Not if they knew I was coming. I've been trying since you were shot."

So what makes you think that the Benefactors would have any better luck than you?

I can tell that he doesn't have an answer because he lets me go, and I'm standing—a little dizzy with blood loss—to face my tongue-lashing from Gabe by the time he catches up with me.

The big truck purred to life as Razorface stroked the steering column. Indigo slouched against the passenger door, staring through the streetlamp reflections at pavement and ice. "Indy."

Nothing, while he reached down and touched the radio on. Razor kept the reach going, cracked his neck out loud, and laid a hand on her arm. She jumped as if he'd snuck up on her. "Indy."

"What?"

"Don't freak on me, babe. You in?"

She didn't turn to look. Her reflection showed a fine line etched between dark eyes and she suddenly looked her age. She shook her head slightly, hair whispering around her ears, and he pulled his hand back to cover a cough that tasted like molasses.

He nodded. "You're in."

"Yeah," she answered. "Where do we go?"

The Bradford ghosted into the stream of traffic, a navy blue shark cruising Toronto's dark waters. Razorface swallowed a mouthful of gunk, flipped the rearview mirror to "night," and laid both hands on the wheel. "I've been tailing Holmes."

"Have you."

"She doesn't always drive home the same way," he continued, ignoring the darkness in Indigo's voice. "But she's got a Monday route, and a Sunday route—"

He let the list flicker out when the girl half turned and tilted her head to the side. He didn't turn to look, but saw her expression with half one eye. "She thinks we're that dumb?"

"She thinks she's that smart anyway," Razorface said, and turned west on Bloor. "You game?"

"Yeah." A long exhalation, like a smoker's release. "Yeah. I'm game."

0600 Hours
Wednesday 20 December, 2062
Somewhere over the Atlantic

I wake in a dark corner of a private jet, and not Holmes's jet either. This one is lushly appointed, but there's something worn about the edges of the beige leather recliner—almost a couch—that I'm strapped into. Low-angled sunlight streams around the blind to my left; if we're headed for Brazil, it must be morning.

My right arm's swathed with bandages. Tug of an IV in my right ankle when I release the belt and start to swing my legs around: I slide the IV out, keeping pressure on the puncture until it seals. *Richard?* The arm itches fiendishly.

"Welcome back."

Good morning. I shiver a little, remembering the cold of the night before, but there's more to it than that. You get used to following orders. Somebody snaps one, and you find yourself doing something you otherwise might not. It takes awhile to get out of the habit. *Valens told you to fix that, didn't he?*

"I know. It can't be fixed."

But can you block it from the outside, like I said?

"A boy can try."

Light edges a curtain a couple of meters forward, too, and once I sit up I hear muffled voices trickling through. The corridor is narrow enough that I can lean over and pop the windowshade up. Sunrise—I presume it's sunrise—spills through scarred Plexiglas. I look down at my knobby bare toes scrunching carpet and laugh.

Still not dead.

Well, until Gabe gets his hands on me, at least.

The sun slips up a centimeter or three while I peel tape off my arm and lift the gauze to look under. "Damn," as the compartment brightens and I look up to Gabe's broad shape silhouetted under the pushed-back curtain.

"You fucked yourself up."

"All better," I say, and—wincing—peel the gauze back so he can see the ragged black line of scab flaking from pink scar and a very tidy set of, oh, ten or twenty stitches. I hold it up next to my face, tilting my head, trying for wide-eyed innocence.

I've never mastered that one. His scowl informs me that I haven't gotten any better at it. He lets the curtain fall closed behind him. He doesn't say another word, and I worry my knuckle between my teeth as he sits down across the aisle.

Leah's voice, and Patty's, filter through the curtain. I lower mine. "You are so going to kick my ass."

"No," he says, and sprawls against the wall, closing his eyes. "Do you ever think about what you're doing, Jenny? Or do you just kind of—do it?"

"What do you mean?"

"Leah and Richard explained your plan. If I can dignify it with the term." The sunrise turns his curls from ash-and-straw to spun red gold. I get up and cross the aisle, curl myself into the angle of his arm, lean back. He doesn't move away, and I breathe a sigh of relief. "But this noble self-sacrifice shit has got to end, Jenny. You have to think about the rest of us."

Mon ange, if only you knew. I cover my mouth with my hand, try to turn it into a cough, but the laugh starts deep and spills up out until I fall back against Gabriel's shoulder, shaking my head against his sleeve. "I was," I croak between giggles. "Oh. Fucking hell. I didn't mean to scare you, Gabe."

"You did," he says. "You made sure somebody would clue. Otherwise what was that little drama for?"

"Ow." I nibble the knuckle a little harder than I intended. "I—" Pinch my nose against the burning and close my eyes. "There was absolutely no chance that I was going to die from a little cut like that."

"Good," he says, and squeezes me as the girls laugh riotously on the other side of the curtain, resuming a conversation that must have been interrupted by my little fit. "Someday you'll have to fill me in on your logic."

"Yeah." I wonder how I can explain. *I owe a terrorist a favor. I have to save the world.*

Hmmm.

Maybe not.

I kiss him on the cheek and climb to my feet, not bothering to look for my boots. "I have to give something to Patty," I say as he pats me on the ass.

"Come back afterward," he says. "They're having fun. Don't spoil it with grown-ups."

Patty studied the paper in her hand, avoiding the look that passed between Leah and Casey before the latter took the former by the wrist and led her forward, into the jet's cramped sideways galley.

The envelope's thick creamy paper was soft as felt, and

Patty knew the handwriting well from birthday cards. She ran her thumb across it again, reluctant to risk what it might say inside. Frightened, because she couldn't imagine anything that Papa Fred wouldn't say to her face. Frightened, because Casey hadn't been able to meet Patty's eyes when handing her the note.

She slid her thumbnail under the flap and lifted it, the gum stretching at first and then the paper tearing at the edge. Patty glanced up and checked to make sure Leah, Casey, and Leah's dad were all out of sight. She slipped the note out of the envelope and unfolded a thick sheet of cotton laid that smelled faintly of Papa Fred's cologne—crisp and a little musky. The ink was black, formal. A glossy blue-green plastic chit—a data slip—fluttered to her lap, and she picked it up by the edges, unthinking.

It was a moment before her eyes would focus on the page.

Dear Patty, the note began, under yesterday's date:

I've asked Jen Casey to bring this to you because I wanted you to have something real to take with you, and because I couldn't be there. I love you, and when you get to be my age, you will realize something. It's not how the future remembers you that is important. It's what you leave behind.

You're probably going to hear some nasty rumors about me soon. They're not quite true.

I'm leaving you, and the Montreal, *and a few other things. Protect those for me, and make the most of your life that you can. Live a long time and be whatever you want to be, and don't ever let anybody tell you that you have to do anything if you know that it's wrong.*

The only thing you must do is the thing your conscience demands.

You're a good girl, and smarter than your dad. Don't tell him I said so, but he takes after his mother. (Grin)

I like to think you're more like me.

Be good, but don't be too nice if you can help it.

Love,

Papa Fred

P.S. I've included a data slip with some code numbers that will give you access to my private files. Don't share them with anybody. I trust you to use them as I would have wanted.

"Oh," Patty said. She read the note over, folded it back around the data slip, and put it all back into the envelope, which she zipped into her breast pocket. She leaned back against the headrest and closed her eyes.

That was good-bye.

I'm not going to see him again.

It was a peculiar feeling, light. As though the juice had been wrung from her and she were a husk, a squeezed-out rind with features painted on the surface.

Leah had told her about the AIs, although she hadn't spoken with them. They hadn't spoken with her. *Why?* she wondered. *Do they not trust me because they don't trust Papa?*

They wouldn't let Leah or Casey hurt themselves. They're worried about the nanotech. They're worried about Papa Fred. They're worried about all sorts of things they're not telling us, too, I bet.

Patty glanced along the aisle and saw Casey's and Leah's shadows still cast out on the floor beside the galley. Shadows leaning close: whispering or embracing.

"Richard," Patty said softly, covering her lips with her hand. "Alan? Can you hear me?"

"We hear you, Patty," a neutral voice answered, sounding like it came from *inside* her ears. "You don't need to talk out loud. How can I help you?"

"Why—" *Why didn't you ever talk to me before? Can I call you Richard?*

"Call me anything you like. And because I didn't want to worry you. And the fewer people who knew of our existence, the better."

What about now?

"The secret's out." She had a sense of an oblique smile, hands drumming on brown-trousered thighs. "So what can I tell you, Pilot? We'll be working very closely soon, you know."

I'm tired of secrets. Patty unbuckled her lap belt and stood, pacing the aisle. She stopped and peered from a window. Sunlight gleamed on choppy indigo, far below. The tightness was in her gut again, the old midnight tension. *Get good grades. Don't fool around with boys. Succeed. Understand. Excel.*

Richard, tell me everything.

"Everything about what?"

Everything you know.

2100 Hours
Thursday 21 December, 2062
PPCASS Huang Di
Under way

"Second Pilot, you are relieved."

Min-xue looked up from his panels, noticing the drawn expression on the face of the first pilot as he floated behind Captain Wu. "Captain, my duty shift has just begun. The first pilot has just completed a shift—"

"Second Pilot." Captain Wu lowered his voice and leaned forward. Alcohol tainted his breath, half covered by the scent of ginger candy. "I have received new orders. Pursuant to our earlier conversation, if you recall it."

Min-xue's hands, moving automatically to release his webbing, trembled. "Yes, sir."

"There has been an attempt on the *Montreal*. Sabotage. The results were—incomplete."

Why is he telling me this? Min-xue's eyes went to the first pilot's face, but it was stony and his vision trained far away. *Richard, is this true?*

"It's true."

The captain was still speaking, just above a whisper—a tone for Min-xue's ear alone. "Now, while the *Montreal* is crippled, we are commanded to incapacitate the corporate leadership of the Westerners. It is the first pilot's duty. You will relinquish your chair."

"Yes—" Min-xue stammered. "Yes, sir."

Richard?

A moment's silence, and the AI's level voice. "Min-xue, I think we need to see what exactly is in your forward cargo bay."

It's just as well that I don't need much light, Min-xue thought, slithering through a narrow service panel and kicking himself loose to drift on the other side. He caught a tether left-handed before his spin turned into a tumble, and checked himself silently against the webbing and the wall. It was colder here, cold enough to sting his ears and the tip of his nose, cold enough to dry the palm he pressed to the unadorned steel wall. *Richard?*

"Here."

Which way? Is the Canadian shuttle at the Montreal *yet?*

An emergency light flickered greenly near Min's slippered foot, just once, and beyond it another, highlighting the number 5 on the door.

"Two pilots are present on the *Montreal*. Two are headed for the *Calgary*. It's cold in the cargo hold, Min-xue. You need to hurry."

Min-xue raised his hand and triggered the irising hatchway. He slipped through it, sliding on a rush of more pressurized air into a stale-smelling chamber. Brief dim light trickled around Min-xue's shadow and illuminated the space in which he floated. His breath clouded on the air, froze, and drifted in flakes. *Richard, I need lights. Can you do that?*

"Unfortunately, no. There's probably a switch near the door, however." Min-xue found it. Actinic light rippled across the harsh metal walls, and Min-xue stopped with one wrist wound through a black, webbed strap.

The cargo in the center of the hold did, in fact, resemble several hundred tons of meteoric nickel-iron. What Min-xue didn't understand was the strange apparatus surrounding it: a mess of cables and heavy-duty springs that seemed intended to protect fragile equipment from powerful shocks. Min-xue untangled the grab-tight and kicked off the wall, cruising toward the rock.

It's an asteroid, Richard. Why do these look like quick-release clips?

"Because they are," Richard said quietly. "Excuse me, Min-xue. I have an evacuation to arrange."

Leah and Trevor are already en route to the *Calgary* to bring her on-line, and Gabe's half a step ahead of me, right on Wainwright's tail, moving fast down the curving corridors of the *Montreal*. The ship feels colder than I remembered, maybe because she's locked down, crew confined to quarters, most systems at minimum capability to make it easier for Richard/Alan to spot a usage spike—until Wainwright is sure systems are clean.

Wainwright has a strong stride for a little woman; I hustle to keep up, and Patty is three feet behind me. We're all but running for the bridge, where Gabe is supposed to help Richard clean any lingering traces of Ramirez's sabotage out of the ship. "How bad is it, Captain?"

"We've got Ramirez in custody. Koske and Richard tracked him down in one of the biospheres. I make at least one coconspirator, but he claims he acted alone."

I bite my lip. "What have you done to get him to talk?"
Richard—

"That's an exceptionally distasteful suggestion, Jenny."

If it comes down to it, if we infected him, would you handle an interrogation?

Richard doesn't answer, but I feel him chewing it over. I won't suggest it to Wainwright until he decides if it suits his moral compass. Given his power, I half hope he'll say no.

Wainwright clears her throat. "You know perfectly well that torture is ineffective unless you've already decided what confession you want to force. Meanwhile, we're doing a room-by-room search for transmission devices. They have to have some way to talk to the Chinese—assuming it is the Chinese—to coordinate these attacks. We haven't picked up any transmissions."

"Ansibles," Richard says in my head.

I repeat his word to Wainwright. "Richard hypothesizes that they've found a way to use the Benefactor tech to communicate."

She doesn't look back. "Tell me what you know about controlling the AIs, Master Warrant."

Oh. "Captain—"

"Yes?"

"You can't."

"Casey." Voice cool, but I can hear the strain in it. "That is not an acceptable answer."

"You can't," I repeat, making it level and professional. "Captain, what are you going to threaten him with? Do to him? Try on him? What can you offer him?" Richard stirs in the back of my head; I sense his pressure and presence. "You're talking about a consciousness that spans half the Milky Way, Captain. What can you possibly offer him?"

Wainwright stops so short that Gabe clips her heel. I'm ready for it and set myself in a smooth-faced parade rest when she comes around, blazing. "I—"

"Jenny."

Richard. Shhh.

"No. Now."

Not even time to make it polite. "Captain." My voice cuts hers like a cleaver through bone. Richard's words tumble out of my mouth. I wonder why he didn't use the ship speaker, realize it's so Wainwright will hear the news in my voice and not his. "Captain, Richard says the *Huang Di* is closing on us at speed. She appears to have triggered her stardrive, then dumped velocity to sublight, but she's still moving at a very good clip."

"Is she armed?"

"Not for ship-to-ship combat, ma'am." Gabe stares at me. I see him from the corner of my eye. "Richard says she's carrying a ten-hundred-ton nickel-iron asteroid."

"Oh," she says, and sags against the bulkhead, holding herself up with one flat palm. Richard won't need to explain what it means. I won't, anyway. He's already filling my head with velocities and trajectories and a phrase that clogs my mind until I cannot breathe, cannot think.

Impact event.

"What are our options, Master Warrant?" The polished flicker of her eyes tells me the woman's gone and the officer has returned, but the lines beside her nose and mouth are strained. "Where will they attack?"

Richard, crisp and brittle, traces of Alan creeping into his voice. "The logical choice is the capital, Jenny."

"Toronto," I translate. And close my eyes. *Elspeth. Genie.* Over my shoulder, Patty moans low in her throat. "We could try to catch the rock with the *Montreal,* ma'am. But she's not very maneuverable sublight. She's a sailboat."

"I know. What else?"

"A shuttle," Patty says.

Leah. She's on the *Leonard Cohen.* Unless it's reached the *Calgary* already. Could it have? I don't know. Gabe's looking at me, lips tight. Tasting bile, I close my eyes. "A shuttle might work."

Richard.

"I already told her, Jen."

Thank you. I couldn't have given the order. *Could I?*
Merci à Dieu. I will never have to know. "Leah and Trevor
are going after the *Huang Di,*" I tell Wainwright. "They'll
try to intercept the rock."

I'm not quite fast enough to stop Gabe going to his
knees.

The captain grabs his other shoulder and yanks him up
while I'm still torn between comfort and *On your feet.*
"Come on, soldier," she orders. "You need to fix my starship,
Castaign. And we need to get a message to Riel. Casey."

"Yes."

"With me."

We run. I unholster my sidearm with its ship-safe plastic bullets and clutch it in my meat hand; Wainwright
glances at it but doesn't comment. Even light body armor
will make a joke of those rounds, but she's wearing one,
too. I age ten years in the seven minutes it takes us to reach
the bridge. "How many people on this bucket can we
trust?"

She shakes her head and palms a hatchway lock that
wasn't there before. I notice its freshly soldered shine.
Gabe and I exchange a hard, covert look; I wince at the
way his face pinches around the eyes.

"Four," she says.

"Five, Jenny."

I nod to the voice in my head. "Richard's in." Wainwright skates a cold glance across me. I tilt my head, a nod
to the alpha set of her shoulders, and step through quickly
when she undogs the hatch and pushes it wide.

"I've had the crew confined to quarters for three days,
Casey," Wainwright says. "Except security and a few I
more or less trust."

I raise my hand to shield my eyes. The fluorescents are

up to full, and the whole room shimmers in their strobing. *Ow. Richard.*

"Sorry. Tell Wainwright that Riel has the evacuation under way."

Genie? Elspeth? Razorface, Indigo, Melissa, the VR tech, the cute boy at the front desk of the Marriott, Boris the fucking cat.

"We're doing everything we can," he answers. Five words, I know from very personal experience, that you never want to hear a doctor or a paramedic say.

Without being told, Gabe and Patty fan out across the bridge, heading for panels, bringing locked-down systems on-line. The lights dim abruptly as Richard takes pity on me, and Wainwright shoots me a look. "The AI was supposed to be firewalled out of the ship's systems."

"He was. He's learned things." *Richard—* "Captain." My outside voice. *Can you access the drive? How locked down is the crew?* I have some wild idea we can beat Leah to the Rock, which just grew a capital letter in my head. "The Chinese just jumped in-system. Can we get Charlie Forster working on hacking their nanotech back? Considering all the fun they've had with ours?"

"He already is," she says. "He's on Clarke. Master Warrant, I can't ask you to try to fly this ship when I don't know what's lurking in her brain."

"I'm still working on the drive," Richard interjects. "There are physical interlocks I am going to have to bridge. Our little friends are building them now."

I shake my head. "I'll take her." I can't in good conscience put the *Montreal* and her three hundred crew in between the Hammer of God and my family on the ground. Not when Leah can get there first. But I've got some strangeness in me that says go.

Be near.

Hold her hand when she dies.

Leah's about the same age my little sister was when my older sister killed her. *Je vous salue, Marie, pleine de grâce.* I was in Montreal. Nell gave me that eagle feather when I graduated basic training. *Jenny, you're a warrior now.*

Le Seigneur est avec vous. I came home for the funeral. Earth rained on the brushed-copper coffin like the beating of my heart in my ears. *Vous êtes bénie entre toutes les femmes et Jésus le fruit de vos entrailles est béni.*

Are you going to stop me, Richard?

Leah's not my daughter.

She's my whole goddamned world.

The *Montreal's* main drive is violently attracted to mass. The Chinese have somehow found a way to jump short of a gravity well. They can stop. *Sainte Marie, mère de Dieu—*

I cross the bridge to my chair. Richard doesn't whisper anymore; he can't spare the time. His voice rings over the loudspeakers as Wainwright dogs the hatchway, palm seals the lock, and wedges it tight. It's us on the bridge, us four and two security guards in full riot gear. "The *Huang Di* has released its missile, Captain. Leah and Lieutenant Koske are in time. They will intercept." *—priez pour nous pauvres pécheurs, maintenent et à l'heure de notre mort.*

"No." Soft leather cups my thighs. I try to reach back and pull the collar forward, but the arrangement defeats me.

"Gabe. I have a plan."

He looks up from a terminal. "Jenny, what are you doing?" Wainwright looks up, too, and Patty. I gesture them back, and there's no time to argue. They have their jobs. Leah has hers.

I have mine.

"Something really stupid, and I need your help. Can you pull that collar forward? And this serpentine, here?" I undo my belt and unbutton the top button on my pants, hurried enough that the steel hand tears cloth, sliding the waistband down enough to expose the bulge of my lower processor.

"Casey," Wainwright warns. "The system's not clean."

"I'll manage." *You do. What you must. Amen.*

Gabe abandons his terminal, Patty moving in to cover him, her eyes wild behind the dark spill of her hair over her shoulder. Leah's her best friend. Patty's got family on the ground. Gabe, frowning dubiously. "Jen . . ."

"Don't argue. There isn't time. See that cable? Press the end of it against my back. Right here."

He does, and I try not to jump as the probes slide in and find their resting place. Valens is a hell of a lot more gentle. "Now the collar." It comes out through gritted teeth.

Gabe hesitates, one hand on the nape of my neck. I'm numb from the waist down, my legs deader than tingling. I can't feel the ship yet. *Dick, can you make this work for me?* "Jen, this is a lousy idea." The collar hangs in his other hand, connecting cables dangling.

"What are you doing?" Richard, concerned. He projects trajectories into my inner sight, as I know he must be doing for Leah. Red line for the asteroid, orange for the *Huang Di* ascending now on a curve. Green line for the *Leonard Cohen*. Fat blue stationary dot is the *Montreal*. "The Chinese pilots are wired faster than you are, Jen."

"I know," I answer them both, and turn my attention to Gabriel. "Once that's on, I think I'm going to lose consciousness. Catch me. Watch me. All right?"

He shakes his head. I see Wainwright following our conversation from the edge of her eye. "I'm losing two daughters today. And a damn good friend."

"You're losing nothing if I can help it, *mon coeur.*" He meets my eyes. I look down first, studying my knees. Awkwardly, I reach out and lift first the left and then the right leg onto the couch. It's like handling a still-warm corpse. Heh. Done that, too. Somewhere far away, I can feel other things—a pulsation like an ache in my belly, a rumble like the trembling in your calf muscles from hiking uphill.

Gabe takes a breath, and I speak first.

"Gabriel." The tone in my voice stops him short. "Wire me into this *fucking* machine *right now*."

I feel more than see him nod as cold metal brushes the back of my neck. A lancing moment of pain, a wrenching disconnect . . .

. . . and I am swimming among the stars.

Richard.

"Right here, Jenny." He opens up to me: space, the stars, the weight of the world and the arcing curve of the *Huang Di,* the asteroid, the soap-bubble of a shuttle that Leah presses to its maximum—or, more likely, Koske does, while my goddaughter runs navigation. *Je vous salue, Marie, pleine de grâce.*

You know, Marie is my middle name. How do the Chinese pilots do it, Dick?

"Plan in advance."

Set the jump in advance?

"Line of sight. Do you trust me that much?"

I trust you that much. You know what I want to do?

"Leah says to back off and let her handle it."

Seal the airtight bulkhead doors. Evacuate everybody from the aft sections of the Montreal. *Tell Leah to tell Trevor to pull the fuck up and let me handle this.*

"There's nobody back there but a maintenance crew. Reactor is too hot; we've evacuated until we can take on coolant water."

Sometimes synchronicity works.

You know where we're going, Dick?

"That's a ninety-meter rock, which—considering the atmosphere—will hit at something like fourteen kilometers per second. If we miss, it's not just Toronto. Cleveland. Buffalo. Most of Ontario and a chunk of the Midwest. Atmospheric blowout, it's called. Widespread fires."

If we miss, Leah and Trevor get their chance to die like heroes. What are our friendly Chinese neighbors thinking? That's a hell of a way to deal with the competition, Richard.

"What do they care? They're leaving anyway."

I didn't know a computer could sound *bitter*. If I were Trevor, I would match velocity with the Rock and push it aside. If I had time.

Which Trevor doesn't.

With my eyes blank, with my body numb and distant, with a mind full of the cold spinning depths of space, I focus all my attention, reach out an arm that's no more than a vision, and point. *Richard.*

Can you tell me when to stop us there?

"Can Gordon Lightfoot sing shipwreck songs?"

Who the hell is Gordon Lightfoot? Somebody with a shuttlecraft named after him, whoever he is—

"Never mind."

—*priez pour nous pauvres pécheurs, maintenent et à l'heure de notre mort.*

Amen.

Amen.

Richard.

Go.

Amen.

The silence made it stranger.

Leah heard Koske's breathing, the dull thud of his heartbeat, the tick of the *Leonard Cohen*'s hide shedding heat into the vast chill of space. She heard Richard's voice in her head and the myriad tiny intimate sounds of two human bodies moving in protective gear, amplified by a confined space. But that was all.

The *Montreal* hung motionless behind them, visible in rear camera displays and as a shimmering dot kilometers off the *Leonard Cohen*'s stern. Leah had acquired visual contact with the asteroid, a slender bright crescent skittering across the motionless background of the stars, the flare of the *Huang Di*'s chemical engines painting its topside red as the asteroid dropped from the starship like an egg from a dragon's belly, unholy in its silence.

She swore and fed course corrections to Koske, matching her best guess at the thing's velocity and its inexorable path to the stately blue globe below. "How long?"

"Leah," Richard said in her head, and gave her better data. "From a friend on the *Huang Di*."

We have friends on the Huang Di?

"Seven minutes to contact," Koske answered, then glanced down as her new data lit up his screen. "No, seven and a half. Get your hat on, kid. It's too close for a nudge to do it. This could get rough."

Leah was already suited, but the shuttle was under sustained burn and the acceleration made her clumsy. She clapped the helmet on and was pleased that her hands didn't fumble a catch. Adrenaline hissed through her veins and the world outside her body slowed about 40 percent. She had her hands on the controls in ninety seconds. Richard fed her more math. *This won't work. There's no way this can work. Even if we intercept the rock, we haven't got the thrust at this distance to knock it off course. Even if we go into it at full velocity. It's just not enough ship and too much rock.* "Lieutenant. Suit."

"Can you fly this?" He looked at her for the first time, surprised.

"I just have to keep it pointed. Three minutes, go."

Koske slapped the release on his helmet restraint and yanked it off the hook while Leah let her hands sit steady on the controls, tears burning the corners of her eyes. Fifty seconds. *Genie's down there. Bryan. Ellie. God.*

"I have it. Sorry about this, kid."

"My name's Leah," she said, and let the thrust pin her hands to the arms of her chair.

"Leah," he answered, muffled through speakers as the globe of his helmet tilted to observe the instruments. She bit her lip as the silence resumed.

And gasped.

The golden-gray sunlit dot of the *Montreal* suddenly seemed to elongate, to blur, to vastly stretch. Her outline, gaudy with running lights, appeared in the shuttle's forward dorsal windows, cosmic and immense and silent. Her solar sails spread wide, gossamer gold-electroplated mesh on unfurled vanes that downflected like bowering wings, the embrace of a terrible gray dove, kilometers long.

"Above" the *Leonard Cohen*.

Between the *Leonard Cohen* and the falling stone.

"Shit," Koske hissed as the *Montreal* slowly, majestically unfurled her gracious wings, seconds taut as hours. "Richard, tell Casey there's too many people on that ship to risk her. Tell her to stop grandstanding and get the fuck out of my way!"

"Lieutenant," Richard said, so both of them could hear him, "we have—a plan. Hold on."

"The *Leonard Cohen* will have contact with the asteroid in . . . Ten," Koske said, his voice becoming soft, mechanical. He twisted the *Leonard Cohen* into position, flipped up the plastic cover on the thruster controls and let his thumb hover over the switch. "Nine, eight, seven—"

"Richard—!"

"—six—"

"I said," the AI answered calmly, "—hold *on*."

"Five. Four. Three—" Koske hit the thrusters, and four gravities smacked Leah in the chest like a swung baseball bat.

The world tore in half.

Leah chopped her teeth down on a scream and locked both elbows against the console, fighting the massive hand that slammed her back in her seat. The crescent-lit potato shape loomed behind the *Montreal*'s gossamer solar sail, then punched through it like a bullet through a window screen. The *Leonard Cohen* leapt forward—intersect trajectory—and suddenly, brutally, before the asteroid was quite clear of the starship, the space around the *Montreal* rippled—and slipped—and *stretched*. In perfect serenity, all of it, and the ultimate ghastly hush of space.

Leah never would have even *seen* it if she hadn't been through the augmentation. Aunt Jenny must have kicked in the stardrive the instant the asteroid touched the *Montreal*'s vanes.

Space tore around the wounded ship and the rock tore, too. The *Montreal* vanished, a blur, a smear of light across the sky, and a sound that scoured Leah's throat leaked between her teeth and tainted the air in her helmet.

Richard's voice in her ear and Koske's. "Did we get it?"

Leah leaned forward. Strained her eyes. And saw a curved splinter of reflected sunlight tumble past the *Leonard Cohen*'s starboard stabilizer, close enough to reach out her hand and touch. Koske slewed the shuttle after it, but it was too late, already too late, and she knew it when she saw the mass of the asteroid start to burn.

"Half," she whispered, as Koske raised both gloved hands in the air and slammed them down on the *Leonard Cohen*'s console, killing the thrust. "Richard, you got half."

10:15 PM
Thursday 21 December, 2062
Wellesley Street East
Toronto, Ontario

It was dark, and the bed was shaking. Genie mumbled and pulled her covers up, but bruising hands grabbed her and strong arms picked her up as the room light flared. "What else, Dr. Dunsany?"

Genie opened her eyes and then shut them tight again. A big man held her close to his chest. "Ellie!"

And then Ellie was beside her, warm hand on her arm, tucking trailing blankets around her. "Genie. We have to leave now. Right now."

Genie's eyes flew open. "For good?"

Ellie nodded, holding the door open for the soldier—

Genie saw now that it was a soldier, and pressed herself against his uniform. "Probably. We're going to see Leah and your papa. And Jenny."

Genie squirmed suddenly, slithered out of the startled soldier's grasp, the loose weave of her blue cotton blanket burning her skin. "Boris," she shouted, and squirted out of the bedroom.

"Genie— Shit. Come on. She—"

Boris was curled on Ellie's bookcase, next to the stereo speaker. Genie grabbed him and dragged him against her chest. Startled claws bit into her nightgown, but he didn't scratch. Genie put her back against the books and clutched the orange tomcat tight. Real old-fashioned books that smelled of paper and leather and glue. "Boris comes," she said, and saw Ellie make a lightning calculation and then scoop her up, cat and all.

"All right," she said, hefting Genie on her hip even though Genie's head rose higher than Ellie's did. "Come on. We have to run to the roof."

Genie had never ridden in a helicopter before, especially not jammed between armored men with guns, and she thought it was wonderfully exciting when the aircraft's nose went down hard and the acceleration left her stomach behind. She squealed, but Boris didn't like it and dug his face into the crease of her armpit, and then Ellie put her arm around Genie's shoulders. So Genie understood that she should be quiet, and cuddled close. One of the soldiers—a red-haired woman with a ridge-sharp nose—smiled wryly at Genie and tipped her head. "Hang tough, kiddo," she said. "We'll be okay."

Half a second later, the cabin of the chopper lit up with green glare like the burn of an arc welder. The pilot, faceless behind heads-up goggles and a microphone, glanced upward and started to bring the helicopter around.

Turned back the way they had come, nose down hard like a fighter tucking his chin to take a blow.

Genie, leaning forward against her restraints, saw the lazy green streak drift across a sky dark as Chinese willow porcelain, shedding bits of fire along its way.

10:50 PM
Thursday 21 December, 2062
Wellesley Street East
Toronto, Ontario

There's a certain irony bringing a kidnap victim to a safe house the woman set up for us, Indigo thought, following Razorface and the sedated contents of the five-foot duffel bag thrown over his shoulder up the stairs. She stepped around him at the top of the flight and pulled a worn, antique metal key from her pocket.

Razorface smiled at her in the dim light of a single bulb, hung halfway down the corridor. "We've got her," Indigo said, nibbling her lower lip. "Now what do we do?"

"I'm gonna sneak her 'cross the border in the morning," Razorface answered. She held the door for him. He crossed the creaking boards and laid Holmes's swaddled body on the same swaybacked couch. "I remember this place," he said, raising a blackout shade across the window as Indigo walked through the kitchenette to turn on the light. Roaches scuttled from the curry stains dried to the counter, sulked under the edges of the broken plate. The room grew brighter as Razorface lifted the shade. "Shit," he muttered. "Indy."

Something in his tone and the way an unwavering green light etched his face made her grab the edge of the countertop and vault the breakfast bar. She landed neatly in a crouch and came up beside him, one wiry hand on his arm. "What—oh."

The thing that lit his face burned in the heavens like a promise or a threat, the unwinking green eye of God. "It's the Star of Bethlehem," Razorface said, drawing a stare from Indigo. "What? My mama raised me right."

"It's a missile," she answered, and watched in wonder as the thing slid down the sky to the south, toward Cleveland or out into the lake, she couldn't be sure. "Should we head for the basement?"

The light died like a blown-out birthday candle. He dropped one massive arm around her shoulders and pulled her close. "You think it'll make a difference, babe?"

Indigo had a pretty good eye for explosions. She craned her head for the possibility of a sudden brief report like a gigantic cannon shot, counting to judge how far away it might have hit.

"No," she answered, when the light that followed was silent and white as a pillar of fire, then red through the blood in her tight-closed eyelids. She squeezed him back. *What the hell.* "No. I don't think it will make a difference at all."

2300 Hours
Thursday 21 December, 2062
PPCASS Huang Di
Under way

The *Huang Di* pressed Min-xue's skin like a wet suit, moving with every stretch, flexing with every twist. He floated in the dark confines of a wiring locker, the door wedged from the inside, the cut-free crash webbing from an unused bunk holding him immobile so the interface pins—improvised from spare parts—in his neck wouldn't jar loose. He'd been feeding speed and trajectory information to the AI through his physical links to the machine, wondering the whole time what the captain had intended him to do.

If Captain Wu had meant for Min-xue to somehow sabotage the launch, wouldn't he have seen to it that Min-xue was piloting during the attack? Wouldn't he have told him more?

No, Min-xue decided, as he felt the projectile fall away, a faint shudder along the *Huang Di*'s spine and through its metal hide. Captain Wu would protect his family. He would see that the attack was impeccably planned and executed. He would drop hints to Min-xue, and he would hope that Min-xue would take the risk of sabotage.

The first pilot and the captain were tracking the rock's trajectory in terms of fractions of centimeters. Min-xue tapped into the feed and rode it like a ghost over their shoulders, relaying the information to an AI who barely acknowledged his words except to ask the occasional question. One final flurry of questions, and then silence that stretched around the tick of Min-xue's heart. He wondered how long he could stay hidden in the locker, wired into the machine before they found him.

Richard would hide him.

The *Huang Di* was long as an old-fashioned freight train: measured in kilometers, a fragile-looking stick-insect construct carrying 150 souls. It could take days to ferret Min-xue out. He had water. Could live for a while without food, although toilet facilities would be a problem. With Richard's help and enough time to hack security, he could take control of the starship instead of just riding its impulses. He could stop the captain from trying again until the threat of the *Montreal*, alive and well and ready to retaliate despite the sabotage attempts, was made manifest. The *Montreal*, Min-xue hoped, with her command structure intact and her pilots safely aboard, should be enough to quell Beijing.

If Canada retaliated, no one was safe. Captain Wu's family. The girl Min-xue might have married, who was probably married to somebody else by now. His mother. His home.

Richard, he said, holding a slow-drawn breath. *Did you catch it?*

He wasn't used to silence from the Canadian AI, but Richard let the wordlessness stretch until Min-xue knew the answer, and his hope fell away. He remembered a poem, and he reached for it.

> *Flying lights, flying lights*
> *I toast you with wine.*
> *I know not if the blue heavens soar high*
> *Yellow earth plunges fertile.*
> *I see only cold moon, fevered sun*
> *Rise to afflict us.*

"No," Richard said, then. "No, I didn't."

$D = 0.07 Cf \, (ge/g)^{1/6} \, (W \, pa/pt)^{1/3.4}$, where Cf = the collapse factor of the crater walls; ge = the gravitational acceleration of the surface of the Earth (9.8 meters per second per second squared). Richard quite frankly guessed at pa, the density of the impacting body (~ 7.3 g/cm³); and pt, the density of the (~ 3.0 g/cm³) target rock. He knew the velocity of the rock and its approximate mass, which gave him W, the kinetic energy expressed by the impacting body—in kilotons TNT equivalent. Which led inexorably to—

D, the diameter of the crater that would be formed when a third of the original asteroid, diverted a few hundred kilometers from its intended target, struck Lake Ontario and leveled everything within roughly thirty kilometers of the epicenter. The impact would create a seismic event equivalent to the worst the San Andreas fault had to offer, lift the inland sea into a tsunami that would scour its shores like a hungry tongue, and rain molten rock across Ontario, Ohio, Michigan, New York, and environs. The immediate climatic effects could lower global temperatures by as much as two degrees Celsius for a period of weeks or months, followed by a greenhouse spike as the particulate matter drifted out of the atmosphere.

Nothing to compare to the impact at Chicxulub that probably contributed to the mass extinctions at the end of the Cretaceous, of course.

But it would serve. It would serve.

If he had eyes to close, Richard Feynman would have closed them then. *Elspeth*.

I'm sorry.

Trevor hit the console again, because it felt good. He would have hit it a third time, but the Castaign girl flinched at the sound, so he lowered his hands and leaned back in his chair, letting the *Leonard Cohen* drift. "Damn it," he muttered. "If Casey didn't have to prove every second that she's better than everybody else—"

"The shuttle couldn't have done it." The girl's voice was level and oddly adult over the tinny suit mike. She leaned her helmet against the reinforced crystal of the view port, one glove pressed alongside, and watched the green-gold trail of the asteroid descend. Her shoulders lifted with a sigh. "Too close. Too fast."

Trevor nodded, although she couldn't have seen it. "We should get to the *Calgary. Montreal* might need help. We should go after the *Huang Di*."

"We shou—" Her voice didn't so much drop off as fail her utterly. "My sister's down there, Trevor."

"Oh."

The searing green light from below died suddenly as a heartbeat. Trevor swore and slapped the thrusters on, grabbed the yoke in both hands. "Stupid!"

"What?"

"Debris."

"This high?" She squeaked and leaned back into her seat as the shuttle lurched under his expert touch.

A moment later, chaos bloomed like a flower under the shuttle's wings, ejecta and atmospheric blowout rising in a streak of inferno off her bow. Trevor spun the little ship around and took her *up*—relative to Earth—out to nearer Clarke's orbit. *Richard, is this far enough?*

"Should be."

What about the beanstalks?

"This will be little stuff." The AI's voice sounded distanced again: cool and professional. "The antimeteor protocols should handle it. Head for the *Calgary*. Trevor—"

Yeah?

"Thanks for trying."

Thanks for nothing, you mean.

4:29 AM
Friday 22 December, 2062
Office of the Chief Medical Examiner
Hartford, Connecticut

Kuai didn't notice the ache in her elbows as she leaned her chin on her hands, watching the live news feed, the incredible gaping wound that used to be a city. It was still dark outside, but she couldn't sleep, and somehow the office seemed a more natural place to sit alone and watch the dark, unbelievable footage of the devastation only a few hundred miles west. Her mind couldn't encompass the enormity of it—satellite photos, footage of a splintering streak of green light shredding the sky, and the ground-level footage that made her think of Hiroshima, Kyoto, Mumbai, Dresden, the flooded and fallen remains of Houston.

Her eyes prickled with caffeine and sleeplessness. Toronto. Cleveland. Buffalo. Fires as far east as Albany and Ottawa.

Thirty million dead.

Thirty.

She tasted salt. Unbelieving, childlike, dry eyed, she realized she was sucking on the webbing between her forefinger and her thumb. She pulled her hand away from her mouth. The sun had not yet risen, but she heard someone unlocking the outside door. Sally?

Thirty million people. Dead.

She stood and went to her office door, poked her head around the glass partition. Sally had walked to her desk and flipped on a different news feed. She stood perfectly still, her puffy quilted coat still zipped, twisting a few strands of ashen hair between her fingers: same footage, another angle. Sally's other hand held her headset to her ear, and Kuai could tell from the look of concentration on her face and the slight movements of her lips that she was triaging overnight messages.

"Thirty million people," Sally said a few minutes later, without looking at Kuai.

Kuai swallowed. "Cancel that extradition proceeding, I think."

"Yeah." Sally blinked, finally, and looked down at the lights on her interface.

"Sally, go home."

"I can work." She pressed thumb, then pinky, then the pad of her index finger to the interface, tilting the bridge of her hand with automatic efficiency. "By the way, a Col. Frederick Valens from the Canadian Army left a message with the service."

Kuai brushed it aside. "Sally, get in touch with Hartford Hospital. With Yale New Haven and St. Francis and New Britain. Hell. Manchester Memorial. Rockville. Anything. We're putting together a disaster team."

"Colonel Valens—"

"Can wait."

"—says he wants to talk to you about Unitek. And—he says—the supposed criminal actions of one of its vice presidents."

"Yeah?"

"Yeah. Our friend Dr. Alberta Holmes. Valens is in Hartford. He wants to see you."

Kuai drew a long, slow, luxurious breath. She closed her eyes and let it out again. "Call Colonel Valens," she said softly, "and tell him that if he wants to talk to me, he can get his ass on a bus and ride north. I'll be one seat over."

"He's a medical doctor, ma'am."

Sally *never* called her ma'am. "He's what?"

"An M.D."

"Then tell him to bring his goddamned little black bag. And call the governor back, Sally, and tell him he needs to activate the national guard, because we're likely to have riots and looters and God knows what. Oh, and get in touch with Hartford PD and see if they can release anybody to go north. What did I forget?"

Sally smiled and sat more upright, easing her shoulders. The line between her eyes smoothed to efficiency. "Coordinate with FEMA. Red Cross. Blood and medical supplies. Firefighters. Shit. We can't think of everything."

"It's not our job to think of everything," Kuai answered, and slung her overstuffed pocketbook over her lab coat. "It's just our job to do as much as we can. Can you take care of Moebius for me while I'm out of town?"

"Kuai," Sally answered, her sinewy hands halting as they adjusted her ear clip and headset over her hair. She looked up, green eyes serious behind straight brown hair still damp from the shower. "He can come stay with me. In case things get bad."

"Yeah," Kuai answered, heading for the coat closet. "In case they get bad."

**Overnight
Friday 22 December, 2062
HMCSS Montreal
Earth orbit**

When Richard finally told Patty it was all right to uncouple Master Warrant Officer Casey from the ship, the older pilot had collapsed; Mr. Castaign had finished the code he was working on while Casey huddled in an observation chair in the bridge corner, holding a steaming mug in her hands as if she was too tired to sip from it. He'd picked her up like an overgrown child to carry her to quarters, and Wainwright had touched his shoulder and whispered something low in his ear.

Wainwright turned around as she redogged the bridge hatch behind him; Patty knew she'd been caught looking and glanced down at her hands. "Pilot—" the captain said, and Patty looked back up, her lip caught in her teeth.

"Ma'am."

"Can you fly this thing? I need somebody in that chair if the Chinese come back and—" she paused. "It's a lot to ask of you, but I hear you were the best of your class, and you're all I've got."

Patty blinked.

I hear you were the best of your class.

"My family—" Patty said. "Papa Georges. Papa Fred. My parents." *My boyfriend.* She didn't say that out loud. She knew what her mother would have said. *It's a mercy he never knew what was happening.*

A mercy. Is that what you call it, Mom?

"I know," Wainwright answered, staring at her hands as they moved aimlessly over her console, the appearance of activity more vital than the reality. "My husband was on the ground. I—well. We have to be bulletproof, Cadet. You know why?"

"No." Patty put her hand over her mouth when she tasted blood.

"Because we owe our families some kind of reckoning. And if we're scared, the crew will be scared. So you need to be able to be strong for them if you can't be strong for yourself."

Unwittingly, Patty's hand brushed her breast pocket. Paper crinkled between layers of fabric. *You have to be better. Stronger. Smarter.*

It was different when Wainwright said it. More like when her Papa Fred told her she was smarter than anybody else than when her mother did. *Because when Mom says it—* said it—*the subtext is, was "and you're still not good enough."*

"Casey," Patty said.

Wainwright slowly shook her head. "Casey would. But she's done, Cadet. I'll kill her if I put her back right now. So what about you?"

Will it kill me, you mean? She laughed inside, and even let the laughter touch her lips. "Leah will be jealous I got to fly first," she said. "Can you and Richard wire me in?"

Min-xue floated undiscovered, and the *Huang Di* floated as well, immobilized by his will. Richard showed him the images, and Min-xue was glad he hadn't eaten; the column of flame made his stomach clench and roil. The fires surrounding what had been Lake Ontario seemed to gnaw at the darkened landscape, and as the terminator revealed devastated terrain, he wished he could call it back to cover the scene in forgiving darkness. He squirmed in his crash webbing, breathing shallowly, hidden by the very ship he held in stasis, and transmitted aerial images showed him buildings blasted from the foundations, trees laid side by side like wet hairs stroked smooth on an arm.

His breath hurt his lungs, in and out, in and out, as if he breathed the smoke and ash he saw.

Richard.

Listen to me.

I know what to do.

"Min-xue?"

We can use the Benefactor tech to repair the damage.

"The Canadians thought of it. It won't work."

Tell me why.

"I won't reprogram the nanites to operate and replicate without a control chip. I don't trust the tech enough to unleash a horde of self-programming alien robots on the earth.

And even if I would—Earth's ecosystem is a phenomenally complex system, which would take unimaginable processing power to regulate. To heal it without destroying it."

The nanites do okay in a human host, and that's a pretty complex system, too.

"And look at how many problems they cause. The starships work because machines are simple. An ecosystem?" Min-xue felt Richard shake his head, saw the swirl of colors that was Alan's presence behind him. "Would stress even an AI at full functionality. And I need a bit more space than the nanotech provides."

I know, Min-xue answered. *But you know how to make more of you now. To be many presences in one.*

"I do."

Would the Huang Di *hold one?*

Overnight
Friday 22 December, 2062
HMCSS Montreal
Earth orbit

It's been ten years since Geniveve Castaign died and we buried her in a green, gently sloped cemetery near Montreal, under the boughs of an enormous white pine. I took Gabe home, the baby girls at their grandfather's place, and I sat down on the sofa with him and he talked for an hour and a half before he cried, and then he didn't stop crying. Even in his sleep, his breath came with a little huffing catch that ripped me open like fishhooks every single goddamned time.

I'd never seen Gabe Castaign cry before. But I'd never watched him bury his wife before either. So I sat up then, and the weight of his body against my chest made it an effort to breathe, and my white shirt was wet through and it was October, and cold, and there had been orange leaves everywhere on the grass in the churchyard and little Leah'd held my hand so tight I thought she was going to squeeze the metal out of shape.

She was at her grandpère's, and so was her sister, and Gabe lay asleep in my arms the way I had imagined more times than I can count. And it wasn't worth it. God, it wasn't worth it.

And that night I could have made it happen. I could have offered him a little bit of myself, and we both could have pretended it was to ease the pain, and nothing else. Just friendly, and just friends, and just for comfort and not being alone in the night. I could have offered, and he would have said yes. And the sleep would have come a little later, is all.

But I was back in Montreal.

And being there made it too hard to lie to myself.

Like I'm back in the *Montreal* now.

The moon rose through the window. Gabriel, mon ange, stirred against my chest. He whispered a name—*Geni*—and it was my name but it's not my name, and I didn't care, for a moment, because he slept in my arms when he would not sleep without, and the hours passed slowly, and morning was a long time away. And if I could have put my hand out and stopped the moon in the sky, I would have done it without thinking. Come to think of it, if I had that kind of power, I wouldn't have these problems, would I?

Gabriel cries the same way now, wedged into my narrow bunk with me. Hard, almost silently, pushing his face against my shoulder, yellow strands of hair curling between my steel fingers while my other hand strokes his face, his back, in raw counterpoint to the rhythm of his sobs.

I haven't a fucking clue how he held it together out there for as long as he did. Fragments of words are all he manages, intermittently, although his hands bruise my back through my jumpsuit when he drags me close. I mumble nonsense into his ear. I'll cry later.

Really.

Richard?

"Feeling better, Jenny?"

Conscious is not better, Dick. A silent chuckle curls out on my breath, more a staccato exhalation than a sound given voice. *Any word—?* I can't finish the sentence. He knows. Gabe's racked breathing slows a half-step, and I shift against him, pulling his face into the curve of my neck.

"No one in downtown Toronto could have survived."

Nobody.

I knew that. Razorface, Genie, Elspeth. The boys in the pilot program, unless the military got some or all of them out, though how you'd do that, I don't know. Indigo. Holmes, and I don't feel much pain for that one. Boris.

I know. It's so much. A blow too stunning to even feel, like a shotgun blast, a violation like rape. Razorface, like a punch in the chest.

He was twelve years old when I met him. His name was Dwayne, and he hated it.

Riel?

"Was at her cabin. It has a bunker, and it's outside the destroyed range. Chances are—"

That's something, then.

"Yes," he says, and I know he's keeping secrets. "That's something. I'm talking to Charlie Forster, Jenny, and Riel's science adviser. Dr. Perry. The dust from the comet impact is going to up our timetable. Remember what I said about a snowball Earth?"

Like it was yesterday.

He laughs, and it doesn't quite sound like human laughter anymore. "In addition to the immediate damage, Jen, what's happened will trigger the equivalent of a nuclear winter. It's going to get very cold down there. Very, very fast."

How cold is—never mind. Forget I asked. What's Charlie say?

A heavy sigh. "Charlie thinks Min-xue's wild-ass plan is crazy enough to work."

Oh. And then, into a silence I wasn't sure I wanted broken. *Richard?*

"Jenny, my dear?"

What exactly *is Min-xue's wild-ass plan?*

Dawn
Friday December 22, 2062
Somewhere in Ontario

Genie breathed in against the stabbing in her side. She smelled smoke and tasted blood, and something pressed her down. Hands. Hands moving over her body, gentle and firm, and leaves rustling under her. It was bitterly cold, and the light looked—*wrong*—sunrise-slanted, but yellowed red as if shining through a pall of dust.

"Kiddo, you waking up, hon?" The redheaded soldier, who leaned over her and probed gently, ignoring the red trickling down her own face from a gash under her helmet. Genie drew a breath and *hissed* at the agony of breathing. She was used to hurting, though, and she breathed in, breathed out again.

"We're alive?"

"Most of us." The soldier sat back on her heels.

"Ellie?"

"She's seeing to the pilot. She said she was a doctor, sort of. She's okay. I think you've got a cracked rib, kiddo. Can you breathe okay?"

"It hurts, but I'm okay. We got down."

"Yeah, we got down. Gordon got through to HQ, and they're sending a pickup team. Which is good. We have wounded and there are forest fires." She rubbed a hand across her face. It left a track through the soot and grease and blood. More red trickled thickly across.

"Fires?" Genie swallowed. "Can I have some water?"

The soldier shook her head. "Not until we make sure you're all shipshape inside, I think. Okay?"

"Okay." Genie tried to raise her hand to cover her cough. It wasn't pink or foamy, and she saw the soldier's look of relief. "It's okay. I have CF."

"Are you cold, sweetie?" A quick tilt of the woman's head as she shrugged out of her coat and laid it over Genie. "What's CF?"

"Cystic fibrosis. It's icky. Makes me cough a lot. Have you seen my Aunt Jenny's cat?"

"The orange tabby? He's hiding under the pilot's seat. I think he's okay. Maybe a little dented. You want me to go get him out for you?"

"Wear gloves," Genie said, and laid her head back on the soldier's coat. "Where are we going?"

But the soldier had already left.

Blood slicked Elspeth's hands, bubbled between her fingers as she groped the injured pilot's thigh and pressed down hard, feeling for the artery, feeling for the source of the ragged flood. "Dammit," she muttered. "I can't find this. I can't see a damned thing."

The big soldier—the one who'd picked Genie up—kept ripping down the seam of the pilot's flight suit with a jagged-edged knife, laying his hairy pale leg bare to the dust-dimmed light. Elspeth sucked in between her teeth.

The pilot whimpered as her fingers pressed the inside of his thigh, not far from his groin. "Doc?"

"You got a bit of a puncture there," she said, her voice stunningly level. *Med school was a long time ago, Ellie.*

What do I do? Cold, fingers shaking, pale under all that blood. Her saliva went bitter; she would have turned her head and spat, if she hadn't been elbow-deep in gore. *What do I do?*

And then a voice that was her voice, and not quite. The voice of a different Elspeth. Younger and more certain of the workings of the world. *Tourniquet. Direct pressure. Pray he's not bleeding inside.*

He could lose the leg.

He will lose more than a leg if you don't stop fucking around, El.

Dammit, I'm not a real doctor.

Ellie. And it was a calm voice. Not her own panicked whine. She leaned down on the wound and opened her mouth, and the calm voice came out. "Soldier—"

"Marquet."

"Marquet. I need a belt. Webbing. Anything like that. About three feet of it. And a straight stick or anything to twist—"

"On it," he said, and lurched to his feet.

The pilot winced, looked down, and glanced up at the barren trees, swallowing hard. His blood froze to the edges of the leaves. "Doc, am I gonna lose that leg?"

More blood filled her mouth, and it wasn't his. "Not if I can help it," she said, and pressed down harder.

"Thanks," he said, eyes bright, and then he drifted away.

The chopper came fifteen minutes later. Elspeth climbed into it beside Genie's stretcher, which Marquet and the red-headed soldier lifted. A medic had run an IV into Genie's vein, and as her pain slid back under the pressure of the drugs Genie mumbled something and turned her cheek into Elspeth's hand. The gesture went in like a knife through her breast.

Boris lay curled against the girl's side and wouldn't be moved, and Elspeth decided it was just as well.

There was blood under the fingernails of the hand Genie leaned against, and the sheet on the second stretcher was drawn taut from top to bottom.

It hadn't been enough.

You tried, the calm voice said. Elspeth shook her head, stopped herself just before she pressed the bloody heel of her hand to her eye. "Shit," she whispered, and looked back at Genie, drifting. "Shit."

"Hey." It was the big soldier, Marquet. He laid a hand on her arm in an awkward caress. "Doc."

"I'm sorry," she answered, looking down, leaning back against the chopper's cabin wall as the rest of the survivors trailed in. "I'm sorry I couldn't do more."

Marquet shrugged, squeezed, dropped his hand back to his side. "He could have died scared," he said. "He didn't die scared, Doc. You did everything you could." He turned away, leaving Elspeth blinking after him. She dropped into a jumpseat as the chopper rose into a toiling sky.

0600 Hours
Friday 22 December, 2062
HMCSS Montreal
Earth orbit

Gabe paces me, a shadow over my shoulder as I come along the long, curving corridor toward the *Montreal*'s bridge. My feet fall by their own volition. Richard and his Chinese pilot friend have hatched a plan that's only a little less sane than my last one, and it tumbles over and over in my head, spinning with the velocity of the damned asteroid we *almost* caught.

Almost only counts in horseshoes and hand grenades, Jenny.

And H-bombs, I hear a long-forgotten drill instructor say.

I let my mouth run along with my feet, trying to keep Gabe with me, keep him focused. "Richard says Leah is safe on *Calgary*." He grunts, so I keep talking. "Wainwright is EVA with a repair crew, patching the solar sail. I broke the vane. Richard says if we can patch it the right way, nanosurgeons will do the rest."

"That was pretty nice flying, Jen."

I check my stride to force him to catch me, slide my steel arm around his waist. "Elles pourraient être vivantes."

He just looks at me, lips thin, that bruised look still splotching his face. "Ne pas me mentir, Geni."

"Jamais. Shhh. No, Gabriel—" I dig in my heels.

He keeps walking, not speeding up but not stopping either.

"Gabriel!"

"Quoi?" He stops. He turns, filling the narrow corridor.

"Gabe, if you left people for dead just because it looked bad for them, I wouldn't be here having this argument with you."

"Oh." He looks down at his hands. I cover the few meters between us and take those hands in my own, running my steel thumb over the discolorations on his skin. Bad burns, bone-deep. There were some on his arms and chest, too, but not like those. Those were as bad as mine, though not as extensive. There aren't many people in this world who will crawl through fire for somebody.

His eyes are just as blue as they ever were when I look back up. "I want it over with, Jenny. I don't want to sit and wait for the pain, and know what the answer will be before I ask the question."

"They're dead or they're not dead," I answer, looking hard for the words before I say them. "Nothing we can do will change that. But we have things we have to do right now, and I need you with me."

"What did you just say?"

"I said I need you with me—"

"Jenny." He's big and warm and he pulls me close for a second, and then sets me at arm's length. "You never needed anybody in your life."

I look up at him, and shake my head. *How can anybody as smart as he is be so goddamned wrong?* "Just keep thinking that, Castaign," I mutter, and elbow him in the ribs as I go by. At least he's laughing. It sounds like he might strangle on it, but he's laughing. So help me God.

I pause by the locked bridge hatchway and rap on it with my metal hand, hard. *Richard, tell Patty it's us, please.*

A few moments pass, the AI's voice tickling my inner ear. "We've found the problem with Min-xue's idea."

What's that?

"I think we can get the *Huang Di* down with its core elements intact. The Benefactors managed it on Mars, and there's more atmosphere to work with in Earth."

So what's the problem? Patty undogs the hatch and we step inside. She looks exhausted, her eyes bruised and black. One of the sublight pilots is in his chair, and two security guards just like the last two stand in the back corners of the bridge, as unobtrusive as anybody in body armor and bearing weapons can be. Their sidearms make my flesh crawl, and I scrub my right hand over the holster of my own to make sure the strap's snapped down. "Hello, Patty."

"Master Warrant," she says. "Are you my relief?"

"Go get some sleep, kid. I'll have you rousted in twelve hours or so, okay?"

Richard gestures with his arms, a motion like a circle hung in space. His hands fall and tumble before his chest. "The crew won't survive it."

If I close my eyes and tilt my head just right, I swear I can smell the burning. *But it will work? It's the only thing that might still work? You said there were other ways, before—*

"That was before the impact event. We're talking catastrophic damage now, rather than slow decay. We're out of conservative options." Which is as close as he would ever come to saying *I don't see a choice anymore, Jen.*

Then forgive me if I don't give a fuck who survives the landing, Dick.

"The other problem is that the *Huang Di*'s computers don't have the processing power to make up the difference. It would take Benefactor-style processors from at least two ships of her size to handle the load. Firewalls and controls; I think I've learned enough about the differences between the Benefactor programming, our protocols, and those of the Chinese. Maybe if we could somehow move the core of the ship tree from Mars to Earth—"

But that's not realistic, is it?

"No."

Patty nods before she turns for the door. Gabe is already moving toward an interface terminal, affect flat except for the lines at the corners of his mouth. *Oh.*

Richard, what does this hulk have for lifeboats? I know the answer, more or less. The *Montreal*'s specs are identical to those of the *Indefatigable*, and I've learned those cold.

"Not enough for what you're thinking."

I cross to my chair, curl my legs up on it, and watch the white-suited figures crawl over the *Montreal*'s vast golden solar sail. *But is her computer core big enough?*

"Yes," he says reluctantly. "It is. I think Min-xue's determined to try it anyway. If we can get her down close to the impact zone, we can make a difference. Mitigate. Which is the best we could do under ideal circumstances. This is not the sort of damage that can ever be—healed. The scars will always be there."

I press my steel hand to my cheek, taking comfort in the coolness of the metal. *I know what you mean.*

"Meanwhile," he continues, "we're still trying to hack into the controls. But it's only a matter of time until security finds him. The *Huang Di*'s not infinite."

I can't pick out which spacesuit is Wainwright. I wonder if one of the others is one of the saboteurs. *Richard, am I safe to go on-line with the* Montreal?

"Your nanosurgeons seem to be becoming rather adept at fixing up the neural damage the interface does, but it's awfully soon. And you ripped yourself up pretty good with that last trick. I wouldn't recommend trying that again. You should eat something and take your supplements. And—wait. Jenny. I have news from Riel."

A reflexive glance at Gabe. He catches it, starts toward me. I wonder if Richard's giving me a second to brace, or if Riel is slow relaying what she has to say. *What?*

"Genie and Elspeth are alive."

"Yes!" I'm out of the chair as if catapulted—easier in the light gravity of the habitation wheel than it would be on Earth, and I hit Gabe chest-high and wrap my arms around him, squeaking like a girl a third my age.

Undignified.

Who gives a shit?

"They're okay, they're okay, they're okay—"

Breathless, wordless, he squeezes me tight.

"Jenny." Richard, still serious.

Ah, shit. Qu'est-ce que le fuck ici maintenant?

"She's sending this via me so you'll know it's legit. She has a job for you and Captain Wainwright."

Richard—

"Yes."

Beijing? He doesn't have to answer. He's already answered it all. *Revenge. Tell her we'll take out the* Huang Di—*that's not a lie. Remove the threat. We can*—shit. *Richard, what if you release the physics behind the stardrive worldwide? That should shake some things up. Maybe a few more people will make it off world before the end.*

"I'd be the first AI to win a second Nobel Prize. I can do it. It will—you're right, if everybody has the stardrive tech, it removes some of the excuse for China and Canada to batter each other back into the stone age. Complicates the equation." His dry tone hides worry. I can see it in the gull-wing arch of his brow, the way his long fingers move like a bird's feathers grasping the wind. For no reason at all, I remember the eagle at the rehab center and the chrome steel binding her wing together. Gone, too, now, where all good things go.

Is this extortion, Richard? Riel is holding Genie and Ellie hostage so I'll kill a few million Chinese civilians for her?

A long silence, while Gabe holds me tight enough to cramp my breath in my lungs, his chin resting on the top of my head. I draw strength and warmth out of him as if they come up through a straw.

I think that flutter of color in my head is Alan's equivalent of a sigh. You never quite get to talk to just *Richard* anymore. "She's looking out for the future in her own way. You convinced her we need to get where they're going. And I think the last twenty-four hours nicely demonstrate why."

Why do we need to go take somebody else's planet if we can fix our own?

"They'll take it anyway, Jenny. And we don't *know* there's anybody out there."

This removes the moral high ground. Remember when you asked me how much I trusted you, Dick?

"Yes."

The Benefactors don't have AIs, you said. You've been keeping an eye on them. Do you think you have better control over this tech on a program level than they do?

"Yes again." He's almost gone—visually, I mean. Just a voice in my head that might almost be the voice of my conscience, or the voice of my will.

I trust you a hell of a lot, I say. Richard's smart enough to keep his mouth shut—if you can call it that—while I disentangle myself from Gabe, give him an extra squeeze, and walk across the bridge to sit down in my chair. *Let me know when Wainwright and the others are inside.*

There's no right choice, is there? There never was. Not with Peacock. Not with Nell. Not now. Sometimes there's no choice at all.

"What are you going to do?"

What I have to. Richard, see that that data gets out?

"I will."

Hey, Richard—The chair molds to me like an old friend. I don't call Gabe over to help with the interfaces yet. I want to just sit here quietly and watch him work for as long as I can. There's an eagle feather in my pocket and resolution like a fist clenching in my chest, and on some soul-deep level I'm dead happy I don't know what comes next. *Does Wainwright know our orders yet?*

"She does."

When they first met with the Europeans, my ancestors wove a treaty with them, written in the symbols on a wampum belt. Two rows of violet beads side by side on a river of white: two canoes moving parallel down a stream, canoes whose courses were not to affect each other. Whose paths were not to intersect.

It never works out that way.

How soon will the Benefactors arrive?

A dry suggestion of a shrug. "It's hard to tell when you can't read their star charts."

A picture is a picture, isn't it?

"You would think so. But it doesn't appear to work that way."

We should probably have the war over with when they get here, don't you think?

Watching Gabe work, watching the wounded Earth spin on the view screen over his shoulder, I settle back in my chair to wait. A warrior kind of finality fills me with an emotion I almost don't recognize. *Take care of Genie for me, Elspeth.*

Peace.

I am at peace.

"Jenny," Richard whispers. "We're in. Min-xue is in control, Pilot. The *Huang Di* is under way."

0615 Hours
Friday 22 December, 2062
HMCSS Calgary
Earth orbit

"Leah." Richard's voice roused her from something half-like sleep, but mostly like staring out the *Calgary*'s bridge view ports. "Elspeth and Genie are okay."

"What?" She said it out loud, jerking forward in her chair. The skeleton bridge crew glanced at her—three scared-looking junior grade officers and airmen, the oldest probably only four years older than she was. "Sorry," she

said, and waved them away. "Just thinking out loud."
They're all right? They're alive?

"And kicking," he answered. "Genie has two broken
ribs. How are you?"

Scared. Genie's really okay? Leah picked at the edge of
her chair. She wondered where Koske was, and casually
reached out to Richard for the information. He showed her
a map, Koske in his new, Spartan quarters. Down the hall
from Leah's room. Where Leah couldn't stand to be.

"She'll live, but things are bad down there, Leah. And
going to get worse."

I know. She stood and paced to the direct-view window,
laying both hands flat on ice-cold glass. There were layers
and layers of crystal between herself and the outside. Beyond it, she saw Clarke, the occasional flashes of light as its
meteor defenses picked off a bit of space junk or debris.
It's the end of the world.

"Not quite." Something colored his voice. He resolved
fully in her imaginary vision, a rangy man whose shoulders lifted and fell in a shrug she would have called exhaustion in a human. "The *Huang Di* will be moving soon.
I need you to get jacked in to the ship and let it go by, even
if you hear something different from ground control or the
captain. Can you do that for me?"

Leah nodded. *What's it going to do?*

"One of its pilots feels very bad about what happened,
and he's going to try to make it better."

Richard. She sighed, exasperated. *I'm not a kid. What's
he going to do?*

"He's going to land the *Huang Di* in the ocean, and use
it to start a global Benefactor tech infection and hopefully
help fix some of the damage."

What you wouldn't let me do with Genie.

"This is different—"

Grown-ups always say that.

"He's going to use the ship's brain as a control chip, so that Alan and I can regulate—Leah, you're still mad at me."

She let her hands fall to her sides and shuffled back from the window. She wore ship shoes that weren't much more than rubberized slippers; her footsteps fell silent on the textured gray matting of the deck. *I could have helped her. Look how much better Aunt Jenny is—*

"We'll help her now. Just keep them from using the *Calgary* to stop the *Huang Di,* all right?"

Leah looked over her shoulder, her hair whispering against her neck, a few strands pulling at her interface as she turned her head to regard the curved black couch. *Isn't this dangerous? What about what happened to Carver?* And then she bit down on her thumbnail, remembering that Carver was dead, and Bryan, too.

"That's a risk," Richard answered. "But this is just to heal. Not enhance. So it's safer. We're starting in five minutes. Are you ready?"

Leah checked the chrono in her contact lens's heads-up display. *I'll be ready,* she said. "Airman?"

He looked up from his monitors: thermal readings, she saw, showing the entry streak of the asteroid scraped the breadth of North America like a slash through the belly of a gutted fish. "Cadet?"

"I want to check the hull and vane integrity, just in case some of that debris made it up this far. Would you please help wire me in?"

The pinch of the wires was nothing. The young man's hands shook when he touched her, and then Leah floated in space, the *Calgary* her wings and eyes and breath. *Richard, do you think Bryan felt anything?*

"Nothing, Leah." He spoke as if from far away.

How do you know?

"I was with him."

Oh.

"I told him you were thinking of him."

Thank you. Richard fed her data, showed her the leisurely, orange streak that was the *Huang Di,* the limping arc of the *Montreal* coming around. "Are we ready to go up?"

Testing the vanes now. A thought brought her up short. *Richard. Those ships on Mars.*

"Yes?"

Could they have been grounded for a similar purpose? Long ago?

His hesitation might have been framed in nanoseconds. An unaugmented human, one not becoming accustomed to conversation at the speed of thought, would never have noticed. "It's a possibility, yes. Mars had significant surface water once, and the project xenobiologist thought that was what they were for."

But they failed. There's no life on Mars.

"Mars was a more fragile system," Richard said.

Is this going to work, Richard?

She almost sensed when he thought about lying to her, almost knew the instant when he decided there was no point. "Probably," he said. "A little, at least. We have to try, in any case. There's nothing else left to do."

Min-xue would have liked the poetry of it if the *Huang Di* moved, when she moved, with the silk-on-water purity of his grandfather's fishing boat. She didn't, though; it was the *Montreal* that was graceful, elegant. The *Huang Di* lurched like a drunk when he triggered her main engines and attitude jets, no time for a gentle burn, no poetry in her motion but a stagger.

I wanted to be a poet, Richard. Did I tell you that, my friend? I wanted to live to write poetry.

The *Huang Di* curved in space, dropping, one brief nudge enough to push her into the gravity well, a longer burn to turn her topple into a glide.

"Min-xue," Richard answered. "You've done so. This is a poem that will be remembered for a thousand years, my friend."

Min-xue smiled, feeling the warmth of his friend's benediction. And then feeling nothing at all, as his connection with the *Huang Di* suddenly, unbelievably, went dead.

Damn it. Richard, I think they've—

After so long in the darkness, the light that struck his eyes was as bright as staring into the sun.

—found me.

The Huang Di *is pulling up, Richard. That's not right. That can't be right—*

"It's not right, Leah. Not right at all."

Oh. In timeless space, the body of her ship like her own bright body laid out under the stars, Leah considered. *Richard, do we need a new plan?*

"*Huang Di*'s security has found Min-xue. I don't have a fallback plan."

She knew. Leah always knew when somebody was lying to her. He had a plan, all right. It just wasn't a plan he was willing to use. *What's the crew complement of the* Calgary, *Richard?*

"Sixty-four," he answered reluctantly. "Counting Trevor and you. A skeleton crew."

The Montreal*'s is 347, and her stardrive works. The* Calgary*'s isn't on-line yet. She's crippled. It's logical, Richard.* Leah felt the cold in her belly like the cold of space against her hands when she had leaned against the view port, and her right thumb fretted the chip implanted in the back of her left hand. *The* Huang Di*'s chances to heal* *the damage are finished.* She extended the solar sails and looped the feed from visual, thermal, and magnetic-body sensors that would have told the bridge crew that the *Huang Di* was moving. Sunlight filled her sails and she— the *Calgary*—skittered forward with the same sort of hitching glide she got if she opened her coat while on iceskates and let the wind carry her along.

"Leah—" *No.* She felt his denial and his impotent fury. *The only choice, Richard. The logical choice. Or are you my father, now?*

"No," he answered, a little while later. "I think you're rather grown-up, actually."

"Trevor, I need you." Richard's voice, overlays of Alan's, and Koske was on his feet with one hand on the hatchway's wheel, not even bothering with shoes. It was dim in his cabin, recessed lights shaded with translucent polymer he'd tack stripped to the wall, and he could tell from the *Calgary's* luxurious shiver that she was under way.

What's wrong, Richard?

Richard didn't so much explain as thrust the knowledge into his head wholesale, a bubble of trajectories and leaps of intuition and Leah and Min-xue's wildly desperate plan. Koske stopped momentarily, the hatchway wheel still heavy in his hand, using the other to shield his eyes as the information flared into headache as if someone had boxed his ears. He stepped back from the door and started to pull his ship shoes on, one foot at a time. "Time is limited," the AI said. "Leah's going to get herself killed—"

Koske nodded, swallowed, and turned his head to look through the porthole in the floor at the spinning stars, so far away. *I wanted to go there,* he thought. And then said to Richard, *What do you propose I do about it?*

"—ah—"

Carefully, calmly, Koske opened the door. Long strides carried him toward the bridge. *She's right, Richard. Are you afraid of dying?*

"It's not a major concern these days. I would be somewhat hard to kill. Aren't you?"

No, Koske answered. He checked his stride and stopped dead, weight all forward, one hand on the bulkhead. The bridge wasn't far. His head still thumped with the equations and diagrams Richard streamed through it—trajectories, velocities, calculations of mass—and he dropped his chin to his chest and heaved a single long, expressive sigh.

Trevor Koske turned, a crisp reversal of stride, and palmed himself into a deserted side corridor, increasing his pace. *I don't mind dying. But there's sixty-two people in this hunk of tin who probably do.*

"What are *you* going to do about it?"

Get everybody aft. Tell them it's a drill. Lie. Fake hull damage forward. There's enough debris flying around to make it ring true. I don't care what you do.

I'll uncouple the drive units. They'll have a couple of hours before the radiation gets too bad. Start shuttling them back to Clarke, or to the Montreal. *We'll save whatever we can.*

Richard tracks the crew for me, feeds me the data. How did I ever live before I had an AI in my brain? He beats the stuffing out of my hip unit, that's for sure.

He shows me the vermilion eye that is the icon for the *Huang Di,* as red a star as Mars, and shows her start to slide downward, backward, directions that have no meaning in space at all. I fumble for the interface pins, have to look down at my hands to make them work right. Oh, too tired for this, Jenny. Too tired.

Even dimmed, the bridge lights beat at the backs of my eyeballs. I'm slapped with a sudden incongruous picture of Nell, all her black hair come out of her braid and tangled with snowflakes, stooping to pack slush into a ball that's going to sting like hell when it wallops me in the side of the head.

Bad time for a flashback, too. It tells me I pushed it real hard with my raw interface earlier, and maybe did a little more neural damage than the nanosurgeons have been able to repair just yet. I need more downtime. Sleep. Supplements and plenty to eat. All of which I'm not going to get.

There's an answer, of course. Miniature yellow pills rattle in my thigh pocket, and it would only take just one.

Maybe two.

Except if I push it too hard, I could wind up like Carver. Like Face's boy Mercedes, who got his brain melted when Unitek was illegally testing the Hammers in Hartford—was it just a few months back? "Gabe?" I say his name as much to remind myself that he's there as to get his attention. "How's it coming?"

"Not as well as I had hoped," he says. He looks up at me, tired line between his eyes, which are still made bluer than they should be by the reddened whites. "I dunno how Ramirez made this big of a mess. Marde, tu sais—Je ne pense pas qu'il avait un partenaire."

"He did it all himself?"

Gabe shrugs. "Programming's like handwriting. It all looks like one guy. And he wrote probably 30 percent of the O/S for this thing. He could have been mining it for months. I found two Trojan horses that haven't triggered yet, and God knows what else is in here. I don't think you or Patty should be jacking into this ship until Richard and I have it clean."

"Je comprends—" I want to take his face between my hands and kiss him until the beaten look leaves the back of his eyes, and I'm afraid it never will. I sigh and look down.

And then Richard shows me sliding dots and telescopic images flicker on the big monitors as the *Huang Di* starts a burn and sideslips in space, coming around. I visualize her flaring attitude rockets, sailing like a belly-flopping diver over the Atlantic. And then she stalls, momentum burned off as the attitude jets reverse and she swaps end over end and hesitates, her long frame bending with the violence of the action, her drive flaring, sending her tumbling, obviously out of control into the *up* that isn't up, exactly, but more precisely just *away*.

Almost.

It had almost been too late to stop her fall.

"Richard, what is going *on* out there?"

He doesn't answer, brushes my query aside. And then the *Calgary* moves, suddenly, quicksilver, unfurling her wings.

I am not ready for the shock I feel when her image splits apart, shatters into two parts, and one tumbles back-up-away while the other follows the *Huang Di* down, down, down. "—marde! Putain de marde!"

Richard, what just happened?

Richard?

Marde.

I reach into my pocket. The Hyperex is there. Old friend, crystal calm and lightning speed in a bottle. I fumble the cap, crack the bottle in half with my steel hand. Pick two of them off the fabric of my jumpsuit and dry-swallow. Not scared now that I know I need it and it's not just pretty justifications. No. Hell, maybe you can kick an addiction after all.

"Gabe—"

He's staring at the monitors, at the *Calgary* coming apart like torn paper, disbelief bright on his face. And then something flashes on his console, illuminating a slight double chin and a day's worth of stubble. He looks down and his fingers start to move randomly through the three-dimensional holographic interface he prefers. "Marde. I missed another damned worm. Calisse de crisse." He looks up again, looks down, torn between hiding his pain in his work and Ramirez's sabotage and watching the *Calgary's* forward section spread dragonfly wings to their utmost and surf downward, tacking across the solar wind to—unmistakably—claim the *Huang Di's* descent for her own.

"Gabe."

He turns. His eyes—

I hold up the wire. "Leah."

And I see him breathe in. Breathe out. And slowly shake his head once, no, and swallow. Hard.

The wire falls from my hands. I stand. The drug etches every shallow, hurting breath he takes into my memory clear as if drawn there. He lowers his gaze to his interface, and his hands move again. "Il y a rien que nous pouvons faire."

There is nothing we can do.

Leah.

Richard, I'll kill you for this, you son of a bitch.

"Her decision, Jenny. Her plan. It might even work."

Might. Why aren't I there? In her place? Falling like that? *Dammit, Leah, it was supposed to be my job to die for you, you silly girl.* As Gabe goes about his work, not looking up. Not looking at the blazing image lighting the wall as the *Calgary* contacts atmosphere and starts to burn.

The bridge and the crew quarters aren't shielded for reentry. But there's lead and armor plate around the processor core array, because there are fusion power cells in there. It's all self-contained. And Richard's right.

It could work.

At least it will be over fast. She won't burn. She won't feel a thing.

Like flying it into a mountainside.

I stand there like an idiot, scatter of pills around my feet and crushed underfoot, dazzle of my senses and, at last, that maddening flutter of the light starting to fade to a bearable flicker as the Hammers kick in.

"Jenny!" Gabe's voice rough and torn. It's not the first time he's shouted.

It's the first time I heard.

I walk away from him, up the curve of the *Montreal*'s hull, and lay my hand on the holographic monitor screen. The fluid under its membrane distorts and ripples at my touch, making the broken shape of the *Calgary* look as if she were smeared across the starry sky. *Je vous salue, Marie, pleine de grâce—*

No.

You know what?

I don't want to talk to God right now.

Richard?

"I'm here."

Tell her we love her, if you have enough time. Tell her—

—tell her she's not going into this alone.

"Tell her yourself," Richard says, and I see through Leah's eyes, and feel the ship burning around her—aluminum skin sloughing, viewscreens dead black and the few small round ports lit red, orange, white with the fire—

I want to jerk back, look away. Let go before my fingers burn, and all the pain and memories come back, the fear and the burning. There's a lot of fire. There's so much goddamned fire.

To much to crawl through. To much to reach through.

Hell, Gabe did it for me—

—and then I'm there. Somehow. In her head. As if I took my little girl in my arms and held her tight and she's not a little girl anymore, and I still can't save her, can

I? Because you can't. I can't save her from my mistakes. Any more than I could save Nell. But at least I can hold Leah's hand.

Can you hear me, chérie?

"Aunt Jenny?"

I'm here. I love you. Your dad loves you, too.

"Don't be mad at me—"

Sweetheart—

Gone.

Nothing. Instantaneous, no pain.

Like flying it into a mountainside.

Gone, and I'm standing on the bridge of the *Montreal,* and I don't know how I'm standing. And Gabe can't look, and I can't look away.

It's beautiful. Just fucking gorgeous, streaks of teal and amber light, a glorious tumble and glitter dripping embers like fireworks and sparklers and Canada Day and New Year's Eve and the Fourth of fucking July.

Merry fucking Christmas, Gabriel.

I can't look away. But when the trails of light flicker out, flicker down, end against the blue pall of the sea, I sit down on the floor and fold my hands. *I'll cry later,* I tell myself, hearing the utter silence behind me as Gabe stops working and just stands.

Breathing in. Breathing out again.

Fuck it. I think I'll cry right now.

Except I don't get the chance, because the wheel spins and the hatchway comes open as if somebody kicked it. It bounces off the rubber stopper on the wall and Wainwright bulls through the opening, Patty a half-step behind.

"Casey," the captain snaps, voice sharp enough to pick my ass up off the floor. Yeah, yeah. I wipe the snot off my face, wincing when I see the unsnapped safety strap on the pistol at her hip. "What the fuck's going on out there?"

"Captain." You blank your mind and let the words come out, crisp and even. You don't think about what they mean, and you sure as hell don't think about what you're saying. "The *Calgary* has been destroyed. I believe her pilots crashed her intentionally, in an attempt to use the ship-borne Benefactor technology to redress the ecological damage caused by the meteorite."

"The *Huang Di*?" She stops. She rubs her hands together as if they hurt.

"Damaged. Out of control. Probably salvageable, I think, if somebody can catch her."

Patty's mouth comes open and her lips shape names as if it would hurt her to say it out loud. *Calgary. Leah.*

I catch her eye and nod. *Oh, baby. I'm sorry.* The filter of the drug shows me blood on her mouth, amplifies her soft little whine into the audible range. Wainwright's still staring at me, and I still can't meet her eyes.

"I believe one of the *Huang Di*'s pilots had a crisis of conscience, ma'am." I steal a look at the monitors, and the streaks and clots of wreckage smearing Earth's dusty globe. Richard tells me the coverage is so quick, so complete because the impact blows debris into orbit.

Literally.

Wainwright's right hand comes up, fingers parted, and covers her mouth. She lifts her chin and follows my gaze, so we're both looking at the devastated Earth. And not at each other. "We have orders, Master Warrant."

"Captain—" I look at Gabe. He's come around the console and is picking his way across the bridge, not close enough to me to be in the same line of fire. The two security types in the back corners of the bridge radiate tension; fabric chafes on fabric as they grip their weapons. "—I know."

She nods to my chair, slight tilt of the head. Motherly.

Annoyed, with a touch of hurry up. It doesn't hide the broken glass behind her eyes. I look over her shoulder at Patty, who steps around Wainwright. I can feel Gabe moving, feel Richard taut and silent at the back of my head.

Letting me handle it.

"Captain, are you going to do this thing?"

Tongue touching her lips, which have gone almost white. She nods once, eyes closed. "Master Warrant, if it makes you feel better, I order you to assume your post and carry out the prime minister's directives."

I could put a bullet in her before she got her pistol clear of the holster, but what fucking good would that do anybody? In the long run, I mean.

"Casey?"

Gabe's there at my left hand, still moving forward casually, getting the captain between himself and the security. "Jenny. What orders?"

"Jenny." Richard, and I know he wouldn't interrupt if he didn't have a reason. "Jenny, the core made it down intact. I'm spawning nanosurgeons in the Atlantic."

You can be that many places at once?

"Call 'em subprocesses. It's inaccurate, but it will do."

The breath that slides down my throat feels heavy as two lungs full of water. My voice bubbles through it. "Captain, no."

"Jenny?" I can't look at Gabe right now.

Patty shuffles another step, hands twisting together in front of her waist as as—oblivious—she walks into security's line of fire. Her grandfather's intense hazel eyes pinch at the corners, search first my face and then Wainwright's. "What are the orders, Captain?"

"Cadet," Wainwright answers. "I'm relieving Master Warrant Officer Casey of duty. Will you please take the pilot's chair?"

Gabe looks at me, long powerful fingers flexing and re-laxing as his hands hang by his sides.

I nod, knowing he'll understand. But Patty is still look-ing at me, poised on one foot, her whole balance saying *torn*. "Beijing," I say. "Ma'am, given that Leah and Trevor have given their lives to ameliorate the damage, and at least one of the Chinese pilots was willing to do the same."

"Orders," she says, and I start to turn away. It's not something I'll let a sixteen-year-old girl have to live with. You know. I wish I could look Constance Riel in the eye and say, *You make the decisions, and the kids live with them. Amen.*

I'm pretty good at following orders. I imagine the cap-tain of the *Huang Di* was, as well. Wainwright looks like she knows what she's doing is wrong, and it'll never be right inside her head again. She'll do what she'll do be-cause she thinks she has to. Because it's the right thing to do. Because her country needs her.

I know that one pretty well. And Gabe's little girl is on the ground, and my friend Ellie, and I've suddenly got a crystal-clear image of Bernie Xu looking down at me under long dark lashes like a girl's, lit cigarette in his hand, body warm against mine in the dark of an unheated apartment as he asks me—*Don't you even hate them a little?*

You know something, Peacock? Hell of it is, I don't. I don't hate anybody anymore. I think I just ran the fuck out.

And besides.

Enough.

Enough fucking people dead for one day.

And my arm goes around Patty as I put her behind me, out of the way, spin and a handoff to Gabe and eyes back to Wainwright, hand almost to my pistol, hoping she followed, thinking security won't shoot through the captain to get to me—

—before I hear the weapons click across the bridge.

Almost, because she's standing well back, double-handed cop shooting stance and my sidearm is hopelessly secured, my right hand a good two feet from the holster and the strap buckled tight. "Casey," she says, and I catch the tightness in her voice. "Hands up."

I do it, keeping them beside my chest, letting the drop into combat time take my heartbeat subsonic. She's awful close, and I *hate* having guns pointed at me. But she's farther away than Indigo was, and I don't even have to *catch* the bullet, really. Given the nonpenetrators we've been issued for shipboard, I figure all I have to do is get that hand in the way. And I'm faster than I used to be.

But she's got backup.

Gabe pulls Patty back, away, smart enough to know he's no help in this one, and my shoulder blades *hurt* from the pressure of the cocked guns aimed at my chest. And Wainwright's got that look in her eye like she might decide to kneecap me instead of going for center of mass.

I can't say I blame her.

"Captain. *Jaime.* You can't stop us from taking this ship."

The weapon doesn't shift. "I can put a bullet in you, Master Warrant, and Cadet Valens can fly this boat."

"You're running out of pilots fast, Captain."

She looks at me. I look at her. It's hard, with my heartbeat slow as molasses in my chest, every reflex screaming at me to pile onto her like a runaway train and hope the shot goes wild. Her lips tighten, one against the other. The pupils of her eyes go big. The gun never trembles.

Patty's voice; she tugs away from Gabe and straightens her shirt. "I won't do it. You can't make me. Leah—"

Wainwright slides her an angled glance, just the corner of her eye. I clear my throat, wanting her attention on me. Hands stay up, fingers relaxed, flesh and steel. I can feel

Richard in me, but he's backing my play, keeping his mouth shut and letting me do the work.

"Cap, if there was another way—ma'am, I'd be the first in line." Sweat beads my brow with the effort of looking away from the pistol in her hand, but once I have her gaze on me, I direct it back up at the monitors. At the trashed globe below us, the dust-storm tinge casting a pall over what should be pristine, shining swirls of alabaster and cobalt blue. "Do you really want *that* on your hands?"

I hear her heartbeat. Smell her sweat. Her eyes follow mine up, and they follow mine back down again. She doesn't nod. She never looks away.

But somehow I know.

I lower my hands to my sides and slowly turn my back on her, and walk up the sights of the security guards, and sit down in my chair. "Richard," I say out loud. "Get Riel on the horn for me, would you please? Shall we go after the *Huang Di,* Captain Wainwright?"

Wainwright twists her hands. "Yes," she says. "For all I'm tempted to leave her drifting for the next three hundred years. Her teeth are pulled. Let's bring her home."

"A prize of war." Gabe, surprisingly, bitterly.

Captain Wainwright flashes a smile that's all horror at him, and closes her eyes. "Why the hell not?" she answers. "Since it seems after all that we've gone privateer."

"Richard? Can you take us around, please—"

"Jenny," he answers through the ship's speakers. "I appear to have made a slight miscalculation."

Patty crosses to me and sits down on the floor beside my chair, fingers laced around her drawn-up knees and her eyes unfocused. *Shit.*

She's lost more than I have, hasn't she?

I lay my hand on her shoulder and let it stay there. She

doesn't look up, but she sighs like a sleeping puppy and leans into the touch. *Kid has some iron in her.*

"What's that, Richard?"

"The Benefactor ships are not going to arrive together."

"What are you trying to tell me—"

And then screens smear white, and the sky is filled with ships glittering in the sunlight, and the moonlight, and the earthlight washing over us all.

12:51 PM
Friday 22 December, 2062
Le Camp des Pins
North of Huntsville, Ontario

Constance Riel sneezed and rubbed her burning eyes, lowering her fingers to glare at the cat curled purring on Genie Castaign's belly. Dr. Dunsany sat on thick Persian rugs with her back to the fieldstone fireplace, sidelit by the roaring fire, both hands wrapped around an oversized tea mug, Genie's head in her lap. The tomcat nonchalantly washed a paw. The girl was sleeping. Two Mounties bracketed the door, and Riel could hear soldiers outside, see their lights flickering against the broken windows as they moved through the blasted woods beyond.

Riel stood and moved from the soot-stained couch to the darkened window. She peeled back a corner of the plastic sheeting taped over it. Cold wind trickled around the spiderwebbed remains of shatterproof glass, dirty snow blowing in swirls that only became visible when they passed through the faint glow of firelight and lamplight.

In the brightest hour of a winter afternoon, the sky overhead was starless and dark as burnt toast. There was still coffee in her mug, kept warm by the gadget in the bottom; she added a healthy dollop of brandy on top before knocking back half. "I should really send you back to jail," she said, conversationally.

"Because the *Montreal* mutinied?"

"To prove a point." Riel held the bottle out to Dunsany, and Dunsany looked down at the sleeping girl in her lap, so Riel crossed the room and crouched down beside her to pour. "I could order a nuclear strike."

Dunsany closed her eyes as she drank, then set the half-empty mug aside. "And China would order one back, and the antiballistic defenses would soak up most of the damage, and the EU and UN would declare Canada a rogue state and PanMalaysia would go along with it. And I wouldn't be the only one in jail."

Riel nodded, standing and setting the bottle on the mantel. "There's something to be said for effective world government." She slid the hand not holding her coffee mug under sweaty, gritty hair and massaged the back of her neck, fighting a sneeze. It got away from her; she fumbled for a tissue. "Maybe we should create one."

"It's an opportunity."

"Or a threat. And there aren't any international laws against mass-driven weapons yet."

"There will be. And," Dunsany continued, "there's no telling what the Benefactors would think of a nuclear exchange."

Riel grunted and finished her coffee. "I'd be more comfortable if they—*did* something, Doctor."

"Call me Ellie." She stroked Genie's hair, staring upward as if she could see past the ceiling and the sky and the starships that hung over them like swords on slender threads to—whatever—lay beyond. "Thank you for saving her."

Riel muffled a cough against the back of her hand. "I'm allergic to cats," she said, and watched Dunsany's—Elspeth's—eyebrows rise.

"I'm allergic to bullshit," Elspeth replied. "Are we going to sit here and—what—wait for the Benefactor tech to take over the planet? We can't get a decent satellite image because of the dust, but Woods Hole is reporting that they're already picking up fish with nanite loads. And all is silence from above."

"The Feynman AI has been staying in touch. He says another wave of ships is en route. It's sort of reassuring to think their coordination isn't precise."

"I know." Elspeth lifted her shoulders against the stone behind her, her hair catching in strings on gray rock. "I have a recommendation. As a scientist. Not a politician."

The mantel was granite, too, but polished to a gloss, and Riel stroked it idly with the pads of her fingers. A bright star-shaped chip drew her attention, on the chimney just above where she rested her elbows. She pressed a thumb into it: a bullet ricochet. "You fill me with dread, Doctor."

"Hah."

"Well?"

Genie stirred, and Elspeth gentled her with one hand. The girl had cried herself into exhaustion, squeaking around the bandages on her cracked ribs, and Riel didn't think an earthquake would waken her. "The Benefactor tech is spreading. The AIs in the downed ship will serve to control the nanotech on earth. What if we want to send people off planet? What if they get—*taken* off planet?"

Riel carefully retaped the window plastic, shutting the day-turned-dark behind a thick, translucent sheet. "They've made no progress talking to the aliens?"

"None, Richard says. Not even a broadcast." Elspeth patted her HCD, quiescent now. "The ships just hang there and wait."

Riel chewed her lip. She almost leaned back against the plastic, and remembered the broken glass behind it just in time. "What do you recommend?"

"I have the schematics for the control chips we've been using in the pilots. If *people* start becoming infected, we need to be prepared. Some of them may die. They will all fall very sick. Richard says he can control it, and he'll only allow the nanosurgeons to modify the injured and the ill, and he'll limit it to the lowest levels of infection. In the meantime, I want to go to the disaster zone. I want an Engineering Corps mobile lab, and every technician and doctor you can scrape up."

"What happens then?"

"We start with the wounded and hope they live through the process. Hell—" and Elspeth smiled, rubbing the thin gold cross around her throat. "We'll need—shit. We'll need a hell of a lot of everything. Disaster teams are moving in. We'll have to secure the cooperation of the U.S. authorities. The badly hurt, we can always dunk them into what's left of Lake Ontario once they're microchipped. Hold their heads under until they stop kicking, then haul them out and plug them into an IV. Some will live. Some won't. If it works, it works, and these people will have nothing to lose."

Riel closed her eyes, smelled smoke, tasted bile over the brandy's sting. *Well, Connie?*

What do you do?

And she opened them and looked at Elspeth Dunsany and the girl and the cat in her lap. "You're a pacifist. You opposed our involvement in South America, as I recall. It's why you went to jail. Conscientious objector, weren't you?"

"You have"—a slight, sardonic smile lifted Elspeth's cheek—"excellent reading retention."

"Sometimes you need to break things to prove you're not going to take any shit from the bad guys."

"And sometimes all the options suck."

You have that right. Riel considered Elspeth, and was considered in return. *Well, Connie?*

"Do you think we're going to get out of this without another fight from the Chinese? Over the *Huang Di*, if nothing else?"

Elspeth Dunsany cleared her throat. "We can always nuke the Chinese tomorrow, assuming the Benefactors don't wipe us all out as a bad job and give the porpoises a chance. What *are* you going to do about the Chinese? Who *are* you, Prime Minister?"

Riel came very close to turning her head and spitting. "You know, Elspeth, I keep asking myself, *What would Winston Churchill do?* You know they're blaming the attack on a mutiny aboard the *Huang Di*. Fringe elements. So sorry. The near-destruction of the ship resulting from the captain's attempt to regain command—"

"I see." Dunsany's hands made a wheel in the air. "I hear a but."

"The pilot who mutinied is willing to testify."

"Do you think Richard would be permitted to testify, too?"

"They might call it hearsay." Riel couldn't quite stop the amused snort. "But it's never too early to start establishing precedent. You realize if he testifies, that means the planet is a person, more or less?"

"Yes."

Which, Riel realized, *was Dunsany's intention all along.* "You'll lead this team?"

"I'm—" Riel almost heard her swallow the words, *not qualified*. "I'm an M.D. A shitty one, but sometimes shitty is better than nothing. I'll do what I have to do."

I'll say this for Wainwright. When she chooses a side, she doesn't screw around. Acting on Gabe's belief that Ramirez was the sole saboteur—Richard calls it the Lone Programmer Theory, which apparently is a joke—the captain releases her crew to normal duty, although she assigns every member a buddy with whom he eats, sleeps, bathes, and goes to the head.

It's not a bad stopgap measure, as stopgap measures go.

On the twenty-third, the Benefactor ships start signaling.

Dit. Dit. Dah.

Dit. Dit. Dah.

Radio frequencies, and pulsed signals through the nanotech. Richard filters it after the first ten minutes, *merci à Dieu*. Dit. Dit. Dah.

What the hell does it mean?

"I don't know," he answers. "But the last pip is twice as long as the first two, so I'm going to presume it's math and see if I can establish a dialogue."

Keep me posted.

"I will."

How are things on Earth?

"Bad," he says. "Proceeding." And leaves us to our vigil. After the third day, it blends into a sort of nightmare. The pills keep Patty and me half alert. We trade off six-hour shifts and sleep when we can, often curled in a observer's chair on the corner of the bridge. We eat what's set before us with wooden mouths. Sometime on Christmas Eve, Gabe pronounces the *Montreal*'s systems clean, and Richard concurs.

Dit. Dit. Dit. Dit. Daaahhhh.

One plus one plus one plus one is four.

Then Gabe walks off the bridge and I don't see him for eight or ten hours. When he comes back, he's clean and I hate him, until Wainwright orders me to the showers.

"If they try anything," she says, "Patty is here. And chances are there's not a damned thing we could do about it anyway."

Dah. Dah. Daaahhhh.

Two plus two is four.

Wake me up when they get to the square root of negative one, Richard. Soldiering makes you damned good at waiting. And at least they want to establish a dialogue, instead of pitching rocks. Or whatever.

That's something. And there's hot water down there with my name on it, and right now that's the only thing that matters.

Dit. Dit. Dit. Dit. Dit. Dit.

Dah. Dah. Dah.

Yeah, and like that. I'd better hurry in the shower so Patty can get a turn.

I'm toweling off when the second wave of ships shows up.

A different design.

Dit. Dit. Dah.

Richard? Didn't we do this part already?

"Well, there's the odd thing." A thoughtful pause, and it's really more Alan's voice when he comes back. "They seem to be signaling not us, but the first wave of ships."

I see.

What does that mean?

"I wish I knew."

A clean jumpsuit is like a personal favor from God. I seal it up to my throat; the damned thing has somehow gotten too big. "Richard, make me eat more."

And Richard-for-real, not Richard-flavored-with-Alan. I'm getting used to his—malleable personality. "I'll try."

Late December 2062
Somewhere in eastern North America

It was worse than Elspeth could have possibly imagined, and she was glad that Genie had gone to a shelter for displaced military dependents in Vancouver. PanMalaysia, Japan, the European Union, and United Africa sent doctors, nurses, troops in blue U.N. helmets that made her think of Jenny in the moments when she thought.

She lost track of where she was. What city, what nation, which way east lay. She ate when someone peeled her gory gloves away and shoved food in front of her, and she got on a plane or a truck when someone told her to, and she slept when someone pushed her over, and she lost more than she saved.

No finesse. No skill. Butchery. Oceans of blood. They died on the operating table and they died from the nanosurgery treatments and they just died for no reason at all, sat down in corners and stared and fell over, gone. It amazed her that there were any wounded at all, given the scale of the catastrophe, until she realized that some of the casualties had been hundreds of kilometers from the impact. And still she lost more than she saved.

She leaned on the edge of a steel table during a

moment's lull and breathed out slowly, controlled, the smell of antiseptic churning in her empty gut. *I'm a fucking psychiatrist. What the hell am I doing here?*

"I'm a forensic pathologist." Elspeth looked up, into the desperation-reddened eyes of an Oriental woman about her own age who wore a dust-clogged surgical mask. "Damned if I know."

"I didn't realize I was talking out loud."

"I'm amazed that I can talk. Kuai Hua."

"Elspeth Dunsany."

The woman's eyes widened a touch, as if adrenaline jerked her awake. "Really?"

Elspeth sighed and turned tiredly away as stretcher-bearers staggered in, but they walked past her station to the back of the room. *Burn victim. Not mine, thank God.* And then a rush of shame at the thought. "My moment of infamy was a long time ago."

"No—" Dr. Hua stopped, confused. "I heard your name from a Canadian Army doc named Frederick Valens."

"You know Valens?"

"Hell. He said to keep an eye out for you. Last I saw him he was over in the triage shed."

"Oh." *Oh.* "Kuai, could you cover for me for a second?"

"Don't worry," the other doctor said, exhaustion flattening her voice. "We won't run out while you're gone."

Fifteen meters from surgery to triage, and the unnatural cold settled into Elspeth's lungs like a fluid, grit bouncing off her goggles in a bitter wind. Blood froze and cracked from her gloves as she turned them inside out and tossed them into a red-bag container by the door of the triage shed. Shed: a Quonset hut on an unevenly poured foundation, ice glittering on a roof like the metal rib cage of some long-dead beast. Elspeth pushed the double-hung rubber door open with her shoulder, blinking in the brightness of the artificial lights as she ducked inside.

Valens was easy to find, even with a surgical cap hiding his distinctive silver hair. He looked up as Elspeth entered, and when she tugged her mask down he got up from a crouch amid the rows of stretchers and the walking wounded seated on the floor and started moving toward her, his catlike stroll reduced to a dragging stagger.

"The prime minister has people looking for you. Don't you check your messages?" He didn't hold a hand out, and she didn't offer hers.

"I haven't exactly had time. What do you want?"

He blinked, voice grinding as if the words were buried somewhere very deep, and he had to go after them. "She wants you at the provisional capital in Vancouver. And from there, the *Montreal*."

"What good am I there?"

He snorted. "Congratulations, Elspeth. You, Charlie Forster, Paul Perry, and Gabe Castaign are suddenly the world's foremost practical experts in communicating with nonhuman intelligences. The United Nations has demanded Canada assign you to their contact team."

The floor really was a shoddy piece of construction. She caught the toe of her shoe on a ripple in the concrete and would have gone down on a knee if Valens hadn't caught her elbow. "I'm needed here."

"Ellie."

Huh. She looked him in the eye. She could swear he'd been crying. But everybody she saw lately looked like that. "What?"

"You're needed there. This is a big push. First contact—"

She gestured around the room. "What about these people?"

"The whole world's sending doctors. They're trickling in, but the trickle's becoming a flood. We're going to start shipping casualties to hospitals in the U.S., Mexico, Iceland. Over the pole to the Scandinavians. International cooperation," he said through his mask, cheeks bulging under his eyes in what might have been a heartsick smile.

"It won't last." She closed her eyes and leaned into the strength of his hand on her arm. *World cooperation? It'll take more than this.* "What about the war?"

"War?"

"China. Russia. That."

"China claimed a few hundred miles of cold flat country. It's died down to sniping. Russia will take it back in fifty or a hundred years if the fighting doesn't kick up again. Everybody's looking upward now; you'd be amazed how effective it is at keeping them from shooting each other. Why do you care?"

Because I care. It wasn't worth saying. She pulled away from his touch. "Who'd you lose, Fred?"

A long pause. He cleared his throat. "My husband. A son. Couple of"—pause and breathe—"pets."

"I didn't know you were married." Pets. *Goddamn it, Gabriel. I miss you.* "It won't last," she repeated. "The peace. It always comes down to us and them in the end."

"It does." He pointed with two fingers, sweeping gesture that took in the triage shed and the camp and the world beyond. "Us." And the same two fingers, thumb folded tight against the ball of his hand. A short, sharp gesture, straight up at the sky. "Them."

Elspeth coughed into her hand, brushing a puff of dust from her mask. "It won't be enough."

He shrugged. "I have wounded, Elspeth."

"Yeah," she answered. "I'll go. But Genie comes with me."

"Don't tell me," he said. "Call Riel."

I wait at the airlock, Gabe on my left side, Patty on my right. Captain Wainwright is three steps in front of us, Richard hovering like an anxious blind date in the back of my head. Some of his attention, anyway; the rest is occupied with increasingly complex combinations of dit, dit, dah. From two directions now.

Elspeth's gotten so thin. She opens the hatchway hesitantly, peering around the corner, flinching back as Wainwright clicks her heels. "Dr. Dunsany."

And then she pushes the hatch wide and steps through. "Oh. Captain Wainwright, I presume? Gabe. Patty. Jenny." Our eyes meet, and she steps first toward Gabe but then reverses direction and comes to me.

And behind her, a weary, addled-looking Charlie Forster. And behind him—Genie.

Genie, lugging a plastic animal carrier in both arms, who squeals and puts it down just this side of the hatch and then runs to Gabe and throws herself into his arms, and *Genie* looks pink-cheeked and healthier than I've ever seen her, hair shining the way Leah's used to, and as her daddy scoops her up that hair spins every which way. He buries his face against her neck, deep breaths swelling his chest, and I can see the little pale square of her controller chip outlined through her skin.

And Ellie walks up to me, and hands me the carrier, and I hear a plaintive mew from inside, and she keeps walking until I put my steel arm around her and pull her close.

She looks awful.

She looks old.

I don't know which one of us is crying harder, and before too long Gabe and Genie are hugging us, too, and it all dissolves into a soggy pileup with Wainwright dogging the hatch carefully and then she and Charlie and Patty spending five or ten minutes studying the gray paint on the wall, trading sidelong glances.

The captain clears her throat, eventually, and I peel myself away from my family and lug the carrier over. "Captain Wainwright." Sniffle. *Merci à Dieu,* I'm turning into a crybaby. "May I request your permission to bring this animal aboard?" I hold the carrier up so she and Boris can see eye to eye, and he does me proud by squinching golden eyes at her and emitting a rumbling purr like a steam boiler.

She studies him for a moment, and sighs. "House-broken?"

"More or less."

She chuckles. "Long tradition of ship's cats in the navy."

"This is the air force, Captain."

"I won't tell him if you don't." And she smiles at me like she means it and jerks her head at Elspeth and Genie. "See our honored guests fed, would you, Master Warrant?"

"Yes. Ma'am."

It's still tofu and noodles, and Genie makes faces until Gabe messes her hair up and glowers—and then she curls into the crook of his arm and won't let go. Boris scratches at the grate of his carrier until I pull him out and hold him in my lap. He quiets when I scratch behind his ears and talk to him in low tones. "Boris, baby. How many lives are you on now?" He rumbles back and settles in with a rattle, even the prick of his claws in my thigh driving my blood pressure down.

Elspeth doesn't seem hungry, so I chivvy her to eat until she at least picks up her bowl and slurps the broth. "Ew," she says. "Miso."

"Get used to it, Doc. Happy New Year, by the way."

"Happy New Year. So what have you and Gabe and Richard figured out about our aliens so far?"

The soup *is* too salty. At least the cook is starting to figure out how much sugar to put in the reconstituted lemonade. Patty watches silently, pale eyes alert as they shift from Elspeth's face to mine and back again. "They know how to add. Richard's still working on it. But they seem friendly enough."

"If they're so damned friendly, why the hell did they send two sets of half a dozen ships each?"

"In case we needed an emergency evacuation? I wonder how many species break their planets getting off them."

"If they're anything like us, a hell of a lot." Elspeth twists noodles around her fork and then unwinds them again, toying rather than eating.

Gabe clears his throat and looks over at us. "I don't know how you want to start, Ellie." His eyes meet hers, and she gives him a sad little smile, half a curve of the lips that falls away softly. *For Christ's sake, Gabe. Kiss her.*

As if he could hear me, he reaches over the narrow table and does. Genie giggles, and Patty and I address ourselves to the salad. "That'll do," she answers when he leans back. I cough into my hand, and she blushes darker, her lovely bronze complexion yellowed with stress and fatigue. "Captain Wainwright."

"Doctor."

"Do you have windows in this craft?"

Wainwright chuckles. "Yes, we do."

* * *

Patty hangs back as we enter the forward lounge, looking from view screen to window as if she expects something to jump out and bite her. I let the others drift past me and put my hand on her elbow when she trails them in. She doesn't speak and I don't either. You know what you've lost, sometimes, and there's no point in talking about it. You turn around and look at the ruins, and then you either sink down by the roadside and cry or you pick up your pack and hump on.

Elspeth walks forward, alone against that biggest porthole, and lays both hands against the glass. Two of the Benefactor ships hang out there, and I hear them conversing—or counting—back and forth with that muffled corner of my oh-so-profoundly enhanced brain. Patty shakes her head like a cat with an ear infection. I bet it's driving her nuts, too.

The ship on the perspective-left is the newer arrival: a glossy brown-gray twisted shape like a madman's totem carving, enormous hull limned with soft green and blue and purple lights in arcs and whorls that—almost—resemble patterns. They ripple in time to the rhythm of the bursts of static in my brain. Dit. Dit. Dit.

"Ship tree," Charlie says, a grin splitting his doughy desk-jockey face.

I give Patty's arm a squeeze.

Perspective-right is the first arrival, and damned if I understand how anything *lives* in that. It's an enormous scaffolding, a drawn-glass Christmas tree ornament that gleams in the sunlight like leaded crystal. Ribs and vanes and macroscopic arches, the whole amazing structure open to the cold of space as if something were intended to hang in the middle of it, a pearl in a silver wire cage.

Except nothing does, and if I squint at that incredible

creation just right, and under high magnification, I can see things like droplets of mercury—ten-meter droplets of mercury—sliding along its spans like rainbeads down windows. That one's not much like either of the ships on Mars.

Both the ship trees and the crystal cages are easily as vast as *Montreal*.

Elspeth raises her hand and points, finger tracing the path of one drop-of-mercury as it hurtles from one corner of the crystal lattice to another. "Dr. Forster, are those the aliens?"

Charlie leans forward to peer over her shoulder and then turns his attention to a magnified version on the nearest screen. "The shiny things? Dunno what else they would be. Seem pretty comfy in a hard vacuum, don't they?"

"Yeah." Gabe, still holding Genie's hand. I bring Patty with me and follow them forward.

Elspeth looks up as we come over and smiles. "Patty, what does Richard say?"

Oh, Ellie. You are still so slick. Patty lost as much as the rest of us. More. Here we are, and we have each other, and links forged in shared fire. And Patty's got herself and the voices in her head.

"He says they're up to differential calculus," she responds after a minute. "But no sign of language beyond that. He also says that the ship tree Benefactors—meaning the ones with the organic, grown tech—don't seem to be communicating with the crystal-lattice Benefactors any better than they are at communicating with us."

"Oh." Elspeth shares a significant glance with Charlie, who nods. "Really. They're still just counting"

"Yes . . ."

"Richard," she says, "what would you say is the primary

attribute that separates humans—and you and Alan, of course—from animals?"

"Sapience? It's a matter of degrees," Patty answers for him.

Elspeth glances over at me. "Don't suppose you've noticed Jenny here talking to her cat?"

Richard's words, Patty's voice. "There are studies that indicate that monkeys and dogs, for example, have a sense of humor. And porpoises, African gray parrots, elephants, and some other animals seem to communicate on a very sophisticated level. There's math, of course, but Canadian ravens and some parrots can be taught to count—"

She cuts Patty off, but gently. "So what do we do that's so different? What's the first use we generally put any new technology to, if it's suitable? Other than bashing each other over the head with it, of course."

I clear my throat as Elspeth's meaning comes clear before me. "Richard, who teaches animals to count? Who *talks* to them?"

"Researchers," Patty says. And then, "Oh, my," in her own voice. "We're patterns of electrical impulses that talk."

"Yeah," I say.

The two Benefactor ships float side by side, almost nose to nose with the *Montreal*. The rest remain in higher orbits, drifting, not touching. Wingtip to wingtip, and each one discrete and alone.

Wonder infuses Patty's voice, Richard's words. "You're suggesting that they need us for something our species is specialized for: talking to things that aren't quite like us."

"Which is funny, considering we can't even seem to talk civilly among ourselves." Elspeth steps away from the window, scrubbing her cold palms on her pants. She whistles low in her throat, shaking her head side to side. "I can't run this project. I don't know the first thing about interspecies communication."

"Hell," I say. "You're supposed to be the smartest living Canadian. Didn't anybody ever teach you to delegate?"

Ellie looks at me. Her eyebrows rise. "I'm going to need a metric buttload of linguists. And marine biologists, maybe, dolphin and primate researchers—"

I grin. In spite of myself, I grin.

"There. You're thinking now, Ellie."

"Yeah," she says. "I guess I am."

I arch my back and feel my neck crack under the stretch. Squeeze Patty's elbow one last time before I step away. My left arm aches and I find myself rubbing at it the way I used to. Imaginary pain. I imagine someday this scene, the three ships so utterly different from one another, the scarred globe floating behind them, will be one of those images that becomes so familiar that people don't see it anymore. The view that spreads before me is being beamed into every datanet on Earth. *Hey, Richard. I have an idea.*

"Yeah?"

Riel still wants us to go look at this other planet when we've got the Benefactor issue figured out, assuming we ever do. What do you think the odds are that you and Patty and I can convince Wainwright she really wants to steal a starship?

I sense his hesitation, tapping on the quadruple-paned glass with my steel fingertips. Like tapping on the shark tank glass, and my reflection smiles at me until Razorface and Leah come back to me with an empty ache like a severed limb. Which is not a comparison I make as idly as most.

Because it occurs to me that you could get a hell of a lot of colonists on a ship as big as the Montreal. *And they don't all have to be from Canada, do they?*

"*Steal* the *Montreal?*"

Well. Borrow for a decade or so. I'm fucking tired of following orders. And what the hell are they going to do to stop me, Dick?

Elspeth puts her hand over mine and pulls it away from the window. "Penny for your thoughts, Jen."

I tilt my head and grin, watching the mercury drops continue their gymnastics. "Thinking about colonies. Wondering how Riel would react to the idea of a worldwide talent search instead of just a local one."

Elspeth chuckles, that half-swallowed ironic laugh I've got so fond of, and lowers her voice. "Funny you should ask that. How do you feel about extortion?"

"In a good cause? I'm all for it."

"Good. Because Riel plans to use rides to elsewhere on the *Montreal*—and the *Vancouver,* when she's spaceworthy—as a carrot to complement the Benefactor stick. Eventually. I imagine it will take a couple of years." She grins. "Maybe Patty and Dick's friend Min-xue will even get to help fly one of them."

"I'm not sure what you're saying, Ellie—"

"Aren't you?" Sly and sideways. I have to swallow my grief and my hope before it all spills down my face again: somehow, she's not broken yet. "She's working toward getting the EU, the Commonwealth, and PanMalaysia to sign a cogovernance agreement. If they come on board, the South American states will follow—"

"PanChina will be a problem. And there's the matter of talking to the aliens—"

She tilts her head to one side. "If it were easy, it wouldn't be fun. Richard can be everyplace at once. Which includes

Earth, even if the mobile ships leave, because the *Huang Di* is ours by right of salvage now, and the *Calgary*—"

—*isn't going anywhere. Hah. Yeah.* The irony makes me laugh myself sick: think for a moment of ripping myself free, taking Elspeth and Gabe and Genie and running for the hills—and find out my gorgeous justification is already a part of the prime minister's audacious plan for world co-operation. By the time I'm done, wiping tears onto the back of my left hand, everybody else by the windows is staring at me. I shake my head helplessly and grab Ellie's hand. "There's a hell of a lot of work left to do, if we want it."

A long silence follows, and Ellie squeezes back. It's Patty who breaks the quiet, surprising me. "The whole world just changed."

Elspeth, softly: "What do you mean?"

The girl lifts her shoulders, dark hair shining over them. It's a speech she's rehearsed in her head, and it shows. "I mean we've converted the entire planet into a macroprocessor, linked human minds together, invited alien races among us, given ourselves over to the, the *stewardship* of a creature a hell of a lot smarter than we are—"

"Not *smarter*," Richard says, in my head and with Patty's voice. "Just better at crunching numbers. And stewardship is still not a job I'm equipped for, kid."

"*What*-ever." Still perfectly sixteen, and she glares when Ellie and I burst out laughing.

"Nah. I know what you mean." I shake my head help-lessly as Gabe comes up on her other side, still holding on to his daughter as if he'll never let her go. He sighs, and I have to turn from the grief and the faith in his face. But he steps around Elspeth, and reaches out to cup my chin in his hand, turning me away from the glass so that I have to look at his eyes. There's almost a—bubble—around the five of us—me,

Elspeth, Gabriel, Patty, Genie. And Richard now, always Richard—the world given voice, or something. Whatever it was that Patty was trying—and failing—to say.

I can feel the rest assembled, but they don't intrude. I have a name for the thing in my belly, but it frightens me to say it. *Hope*. God. I don't want to hope. And I can't seem to help it.

"Well." He takes a breath like a man who's been holding on to the last one too long, and considers me. "That work you mentioned. Do you want it?"

"No." *Hell, no.* "But it's got to be done."

The last army-wagon straggles
along my starswept trail
corners at the terminal world
and vanishes into the cold.
They'll bury their daughters
and their sons in war-gardens
and the common trenches between the suns.
When after a long trail they arrive
we await their coming.
No message we chase them with
no flag to bring them home, but
whispers without voices
visions without eyes.
They travel on.
We choose to forget them.
They travel on,
recalling home.
—Xie Min-xue, "The Ballad of the Star-Wagons"

About the Author

ELIZABETH BEAR shares a birthday with Frodo and Bilbo Baggins. This, coupled with a tendency to read the dictionary as a child, doomed her early to penury, intransigence, friendlessness, and the writing of speculative fiction. She was born in Hartford, Connecticut, and grew up in central Connecticut with the exception of two years (which she was too young to remember very well) spent in Vermont's Northeast Kingdom, in the last house with electricity before the Canadian border. She currently lives in the Mojave Desert near Las Vegas, Nevada, but she's trying to escape.

She's worked as a stable hand, a fluff-page reporter, a maintainer-of-microbiology-procedure-manuals for a major inner-city hospital, a typesetter and layout editor, a traffic manager for an import-export business, a test-pit digger for an archaeological survey company, a "media industry professional," and a third-shift doughnut manufacturer.

Her recent and forthcoming appearances include: *SCI-FICTION, The Magazine of Fantasy & Science Fiction, On Spec, H.P. Lovecraft's Magazine of Horror, Chiaroscuro, Ideomancer, The Fortean Bureau,* the Polish fantasy magazine *Nowa Fantastyka,* and the anthologies *Shadows Over Baker Street* (Del Rey, 2003) and *All-Star Zeppelin Adventure Stories* (Wheatland Press, 2004).

She's a second-generation Swede, a third-generation Ukrainian, and a third-generation Transylvanian, with some Irish, English, Scots, Cherokee, and German thrown in for leavening. Elizabeth Bear is her real name, but not all of it.

Her dogs outweigh her, and she is much beset by her cats.

Be sure not to miss

WORLDWIRED

by

ELIZABETH BEAR

*The riveting conclusion
to the series begun in
HAMMERED and SCARDOWN*

*Coming from
Bantam Spectra in Fall 2005.*

Here's a special preview.

WORLDWIRED

on sale Fall 2005

"One cannot walk the Path until one becomes the Path."
  —Gautama Buddha

1030 Hours
27 September, 2063
HMCSS Montreal
Earth Orbit

I've got a starship dreaming. And there the hell it is.
Leslie Tjakamarra leaned both hands on the thick crystal
of the *Montreal*'s observation portal, the cold of space
seeping into his palms, and hummed a snatch of song
under his breath. He couldn't tell how far away the alien
spaceship was—or the fragment he could see when he
twisted his head and pressed his face against the port.
Earthlight stained the cage-shaped frame blue-silver, and
the fat doughnut of Forward Orbital Platform was visible
through the gaps, the gleaming thread of the beanstalk describing a taut line downward until it disappeared in
brown-tinged atmosphere over Malaysia. "Bloody far," he
said, realizing he'd spoken out loud only when he heard
his own voice. He scuffed across the blue-carpeted floor,
pressed back by the vista on the other side of the glass.

Someone cleared her throat behind him. He turned, for
all he was unwilling to put his back to the endless fall
outside. The tall, narrow-shouldered crew member who

stood just inside the hatchway met him eye to eye, the black shape of a sidearm strapped to her thigh commanding his attention. She raked one hand through wiry salt-and-pepper hair and shook her head. "Or too close for comfort," she answered with an odd little sort of a smile. "That's one of the ones Elspeth calls the birdcages—"

"Elspeth?"

"Dr. Dunsany," she said. "You're Dr. Tjakamarra, the xenosemiotician." She mispronounced his name.

"Leslie," he said. She stuck out her right hand, and Leslie realized she was wearing a black leather glove on the left. "You're Casey," he blurted, too startled to reach out. She held her hand out there anyway, until he recovered enough to shake. "I didn't recognize you—"

"It's cool." She shrugged in a manner entirely unlike a living legend, and gave him a crooked sideways grin, smoothing her dark blue jumpsuit over her breasts with the gloved hand. "We're all different out of uniform. Besides, it's nice to be looked at like real people, for a change. Come on: the pilots' lounge has a better view."

She gestured him away from the window; he caught himself shooting her sidelong glances, desperate not to stare. He fell into step beside her as she led him along the curved ring of the *Montreal*'s habitation wheel, the arc rising behind and before them even though it felt perfectly flat under his feet.

"You'll get used to it," Master Warrant Officer Casey said, returning his sidelong looks with one of her own. It said she had accurately judged the reason he trailed his right hand along the chilly wall. "Here we are—" She braced one rubber-soled foot against the seam between corridor floor and corridor wall, and expertly spun the handle of a thick steel hatchway with her black-gloved hand. "—come on in. Step lively; we don't stand around in hatchways shipboard."

Leslie followed her through, turning to dog the door as he remembered his safety lectures, and when he turned back Casey had moved forward into the middle of a chamber no bigger than an urban apartment's living room. The awe in his throat made it hard to breathe. He hoped he was keeping it off his face.

"There," Casey said, stepping aside, waving him impatiently forward again. "That's both of them. The one on the 'left' is the ship tree. The one on the 'right' is the birdcage."

Everyone on the planet probably knew that by now. She was babbling, Leslie realized, and the small evidence of her fallibility—and her own nervousness—did more to ease the pressure in his chest than her casual friendliness could have. *You're acting like a starstruck teenager*, he reprimanded, and managed to grin at his own foolishness as he shuffled forward, his slipperlike ship-shoes whispering over the carpet.

Then he caught sight of the broad sweep of windows beyond and his personal awe for the woman in blue was replaced by something *visceral*. He swallowed, throat dry, and rubbed his knuckles into his eyes as if they needed clearing. "Wow."

The *Montreal*'s habitation wheel spun grandly, slowly, creating an imitation of gravity that held them, feet down, to the "floor." Leslie found himself standing before the big round port in the middle of the wall, hands pressed to either rim as if to keep himself from tumbling through the crystal like Alice through the looking-glass, as the astounding panorama rotated like a merry-go-round seen from above. Beyond it, the soft blue glow of the wounded Earth reflected the sun that lay behind the *Montreal*. The planet's atmosphere fuzzed brown like smog in an inversion layer, the sight enough to send Leslie's knuckle to his mouth. He bit down, unconscious of the wetness and the ache, and tore his gaze away with an effort, turning it on the two alien ships floating almost hull-to-hull "overhead."

The ship on perspective-right was the enormous, gleaming-blue birdcage, swarming with ten-meter specks of mercury—made tiny by distance—that flickered from cage-bar to cage-bar, as vanishingly swift and bright as motes in Leslie's eye.

The ship on perspective-left caught the Earthlight with the gloss peculiar to polished wood or a smooth tree bole, a mouse-colored column twisted into shapes that took Leslie's breath away. The vast hull glittered with patterned, pointillist lights in cool-water shades. They did not look so different from the images and designs that Leslie had grown up with, and he fought a shiver, glancing at the hawk-intent face of Master Warrant Officer Casey close beside him.

"Elspeth—Dr. Dunsany—said you had a theory," she said, without glancing over.

He returned his attention to the paired alien space ships, peeling his eyes away from Genevieve Casey only with an effort. "I've had the VR implants—"

"Richard told me," she said, with a sly sideways grin.

"*Richard*? The AI?" And silly not to have expected that either. *It's a whole new road you're walking.* A whole different sort of journey, farther away from home than even his years at Cambridge, when there was still more of an England rather than less.

"Richard, the AI. You'll meet him, I'm sure. He doesn't like to intrude on the new kids until they're comfortable with their wetware. And unless you've got the full 'borg—" she lightly touched the back of her head "—you won't have to put up with his running patter. Most of the time." She tilted her head up and sideways, a wry look he didn't think was for him.

She's talking to the AI right now. Cool shiver across his shoulders; the awe was back, with company. "The new kids. Ah." Leslie forced himself not to stare, frowning down at the bitten skin of his thumb. "Yes. I spoke to Dr. Dunsany and Dr. Perry regarding my theories...."

"Dr. Tjakamarra—"

"Leslie."

"—Leslie." Casey coughed into her hand. "You're supposed to be the foremost expert in interspecies communication in the Commonwealth. Ellie thought you were on to something, or she wouldn't have asked you up here. We get more requests in a week than Yale does in a year—"

"I'm aware of that." Her presence still stunned him. *Genevieve Casey. The First Pilot. Standing here beside me, leaned up against the window with me like kids peering off the observation deck of the Petronas Towers.* He gathered his wits and forced himself to frown. "You've had no luck talking to them, have you?" A jerk of his thumb indicated the orbiting craft.

"Plenty of math," Casey said with a shrug. "Nothing you'd call conversation. They don't seem to understand please and thank you."

"I expected that," Leslie answered. Familiar ground. Comfortable ground, even. "I'm afraid that if I'm right, talking to them is hopeless."

"Hopeless?" She turned, leaning back on her heels, her long body ready for anything.

"Yes," Leslie said, calmer, on his own turf now. "You see, I don't think they *talk* at all."

* * *

Leslie Tjakamarra's not a big man. He's not a young one, either, though I wouldn't want to try to guess his age within five years on either side. He's got one of those wiry, weathered frames I associate with Alberta cattlemen and forest rangers, sienna skin paler, almost red, inside the creases beside glittering eyes and on the palms of big thick-nailed hands. He doesn't go at all with the conservative charcoal double-breasted suit, pinstriped with biolume, which clings to his sinewy shoulders in as professional an Old London tailoring job as I've seen. When London was evacuated, a lot of the refugees found themselves in Sydney, in Vancouver——and in Toronto.

God rest their souls.

He shoots me those sidelong glances like they do, trying to see through the glove to the metal hand, trying to see through the jumpsuit to the hero underneath.

I hate to disappoint him, but that hero had a hair appointment she never came back from. There's nobody under here but Jenny any more. "Well," I say, to fill up his silence. "That'll make your job easier, then, won't it?" *What do you think of them apples, Dick?*

Richard grins inside my head, bony hands spread wide and beating like a pigeon's wings through air. The man's brains would jam if you tied his hands down, I think. Of course, since he's intangible, that would be a trick. "That's got the air of a leading question about it." He scrubs his palms on the thighs of his virtual corduroys and stuffs them into his pockets, leaning back, white shirt stretched taut across his narrow chest, his image in my wetware fading as he "steps back," limiting his usage of my implants. "I'll get in on it when he talks to Ellie. No point in spoiling his chance to appreciate the view. I'll eavesdrop, if that's okay with you."

It might be the same asinine impulse that makes English

speakers talk loudly to foreigners that moves me to smile inwardly and stereotype Dr. Tjakamarra's very smooth, very educated accent into Australian Rules English. *No worries, mate. Fair dinkum.*

Richard shoots me an amused look. "Ouch," he says, and flickers out like an interrupted hologram.

Dr. Tjakamarra grins, broad lips uncovering tea-stained teeth like a mouth full of piano keys, and scratches his cheek with knuckles like an auto mechanic's. He wears his hair long, professorial, slicked back into hard steel-gray waves. "Or that much more difficult, if you prefer." His voice is younger than the rest of him, young as that twinkle in his eye. "Talking isn't the only species of communication, after all."

He presses the hand flat against the glass again, and peers between his own fingers as if trying to gauge the size of the ships that float out there, the way you might measure a tree on the horizon against your thumb to see how far you've left to walk. His gaze keeps sliding down to the dust-palled globe of the Earth, his lips pressed thin, his eyes impassive, giving nothing away.

"How bad is it in Sydney?" I press my steel hand to my lips, shoving the words back in with the leather of the glove, and cover my face as if entranced by the turning lights outside. Dr. Tjakamarra's head comes up like a startled deer's. I have to pretend I don't see it.

"We heard it," he says, as his hand falls away from the glass. "We heard it in Sydney." He steps back, turns to face me although I'm still giving him my shoulder. He cups both hands and brings them together with a crack that makes me jump.

"Is that really what it sounded like?"

"More or less—" A shrug. "We couldn't feel the tremors. The only fallout we got was dust, and who notices a little more dust? It wasn't all that loud, fifteen thousand kilometers away; I would have thought it'd be a sustained rumble, like the old footage of nuclear bombs. You ever hear of Coober Pedy?"

"Never." *Person, place, or thing?*

He answers it in the next sentence. "There were bomb tests near there. Over a hundred years ago, but I know people who knew people who were there. They said the newsreels lied, the sound effect they used was dubbed in later."

I have no idea where he's going with this. I lean my right shoulder against the cold cold crystal, fold my left arm over my right arm, and tilt my head against the glass. I've got four or five inches on him. He laces his hands together in the small of his back and lifts his chin to look me in the eye, creases linking his thick, flat nose to the corners of his mouth.

Surreal fucking conversation, man.

"So what does a nuclear explosion sound like, Les?"

His lips twist. He holds his hands apart again, and swings them halfway but doesn't clap. "Like the biggest bloody gunshot you ever did hear. *Bang*. Or like a meteorite hitting the planet, fifteen thousand kilometers away."

He's talking so he doesn't have to look. I recognize the glitter in his dark brown eyes, blacker even than mine. It took me too, the first time I looked down and saw all that gorgeous blue and white mottled with sick dull beige like cancer.

It takes all of us like that. All that I've seen so far, anyway. "A bullet is a bullet is a bullet?"

He licks his lips, and looks carefully at the Benefactor ships and not the smeared globe behind them. "The shot heard 'round the world. Isn't that what the Americans call the first shot fired in their Colonial revolt?"

"Sounds about right."

"May something more than—dust—grow out of this one." He sighs, rubbing the back of his left hand with his right-hand thumb. He reminds me of my grandfather Zeke Kirby, my mother's father, the full-blooded one; he's got that same boiled-leather twist of indestructibility, but my grandfather was an ironworker, not a professor. His mouth moves again, like he's trying to shape words that won't quite come out right, and finally he just shakes his head and looks down. "Big universe out there."

"Bloody big," I answer, a gentle tease, and he smiles out of the corner of his mouth, gives me a look out of the corners of his eyes, and I know we're going to be friends. "Come on," I say. "That gets depressing if you stare at it. I'll take you to meet Ellie if you promise not to tell her the thing about the bomb."

He falls into step beside me. I don't have to shorten my strides to let him keep up. "She lose somebody in the—in that?"

"We all lost somebody." I shake my head.

"What is it, then?"

"It would give her nightmares. Come on."

1300 Hours
Toronto Evacuation Zone
Ontario, Canada
Thursday 27 September, 2063

Richard habitually took refuge in numbers, so it troubled him that when it came to dealing with the Impact, all he had was a series of approximations. The number of dead had never been counted. Their names had never been accurately listed. Their families would never be notified; in many cases, their bodies would never be found.

The population of Niagara and Rochester, New York, had been just under three million people, although the New York coastline of Lake Ontario was mostly rural, vineyards and cow pasture. The northern rim of the lake, however, had been the most populated place in Canada: Ontario's Golden Horseshoe, the urban corridor anchored by Toronto and Hamilton, which had still been home to some seven million despite the midcentury population dip. Deaths from the Impact and its immediate aftermath had been confirmed as far away as Buffalo, Cleveland, Albany. A woman in Ottawa had died when a stained-glass window shattered from the shock and fell on her head; a child in Kitchener survived in a basement, along with his dog. Recovery teams dragging the poisoned waters of Lake Ontario had been forced to cease operations as the lake surface iced over, a phenomenon that once would have been a twice-in-a-century occurrence but had become common with the advent of shifted winters, and which would become more common still. For a little while, until the greenhouse effect triggered by the Impact began to cancel out the nuclear winter.

An icebreaker could have been brought in and the work continued . . . but things keep, in cold water. And someone raised the spectre of breaking ice with bodies frozen into it, and it was decided to wait until spring.

The ice didn't melt until halfway through May, and the lake locked solid again in mid-September.

The coming winter promised to be even colder, a savage global drop in temperatures that might persist another eighteen to twenty-four months, and Richard frankly couldn't begin to say whether the death toll worldwide at the end of that time would be measured in the mere tens of millions or in the hundreds. Preliminary estimates had placed immediate

Impact casualties at thirty million; Richard was inclined to a more conservative estimate of something under twenty, unevenly divided between Canada and the United States.

In practical terms, the casualty rate was something like one in every twenty-five Americans and one in every three Canadians dead by January first, 2063.

The fallout cloud from the thirteen operant nuclear reactors damaged or destroyed in the Impact was pushed northeast by prevailing wind currents, largely affecting New York, Quebec, Vermont, New Hampshire, Maine, Newfoundland, the Grand Banks, Prince Edward Island, Iceland, and points between. The emergency teams and medical staff attending the disaster victims were supplied with iodine tablets and given aggressive prophylaxis against radiation exposure. Only seventeen of them became seriously ill. Only six of those died.

It was too soon to tell what the long-term effect on cancer rates would be, but Richard expected New England's dairy industry to fail completely, along with what bare scraps had still remained of the once-vast North Atlantic fisheries.

And then, after the famines and the winter—

—would come a summer without end.

Colonel Valens's hands hurt, but his eyes hurt more. He leaned forward on both elbows over his improvised desk, his holistic communications unit propped up on a pair of inflatable splints and the hideously un-ergonomic portable interface plate unrolled across a plywood surface that was an inch and a half too high for comfort. "Yes," he said, rubbing the back of his neck with an aching palm, "I'll hold. Please let the prime minister know it's not urgent, if she has—Constance. That was quick."

"Hi, Fred. I was at lunch," Constance Riel said, chewing

visibly, her image flickering in the cheap holographic display. Valens smoothed the interface plate between his hands, cool plastic slightly tacky and gritty with the dust that was never far. The prime minister covered her mouth with the back of the first two fingers on her left hand and swallowed, set her sandwich down on an unfolded paper napkin, reached for her coffee. Careful makeup could not hide the hollows under her eyes, dark as thumbprints. "I was going to call you today anyway. How's the situation in the Evac?"

"Stable." One word, soaked in exhaustion. "I got mail from Elspeth Dunsany today. She says the Commonwealth scientists have arrived safely on the *Montreal*. One Australian and an expat Brit. She and Casey are getting them settled."

"—Paul Perry said the same thing to me this morning," Riel answered. Her head wobbled when she nodded.

"That isn't why you were going to call me."

"No. I have the latest climatological data from Richard and Alan. The AIs say that the nanite propagation is going well, despite the effects of the—"

"—Nuclear winter? Non-nuclear winter?" Valens said.

"Something like that. They're concerned about the algae die-off we were experiencing before the . . . Impact. The nanotech is working on keeping the algal population stable, but Alan and Charlie Forster suggest that once the global cooling effects are over, it might be less catastrophic to consider seeding the oceans with iron to boost algae growth—" The Prime Minister's voice hitched slightly.

"Like fertilizing the garden."

"Exactly. More algae means less CO_2 left in the atmosphere from the Impact, which in turn means less greenhouse warming when the dust is out of the atmosphere and winter finally ends—"

"—in eighteen months or so. Won't we want a greenhouse effect then?" *To counteract the global dimming from the Impact dust.*

"Not unless 50 or 60 degrees Celsius is your idea of comfort."

"Ah . . ." Valens shook his head, looking down at the pink and green displays that hovered under the surface of the interface plate, waiting only a touch to bring them to multidimensionality. He shook his head, and ricocheted uncomfortably to the topic that was the reason for his call. "We've done what we can here, Constance. It's time to close up shop and come home. Do you want to tour the exclusion zone?"

"Helicopter tour," she said, nodding, and took another bite of her sandwich. "You'll come with, of course. Before we open the Evac to reconstruction and send the bulldozers in—"

"You're going to rebuild Toronto?" Valens had years of practice keeping shock out of his voice. He failed utterly, his gut coiling at something that struck him as plain obscenity.

"No," she said. "We're going to turn it into a park. By the way, are you resigning your commission?"

Valens coughed, hand to his throat. Riel's image flickered as the interface panel, released from the pressure of his palm, wrinkled again. "Am I being asked to?"

The prime minister laughed. "You're being asked to get your ass to the provisional capital of Vancouver, Fred. Where, in recognition of your exemplary service handling the Toronto Evac relief effort, you will be promoted to Brigadier General Frederick Valens, and I will have a brand-new shiny Cabinet title and a whole new ration of shit to hand you, sir."

He coughed into his hand. "I'm a Conservative, Connie."

"That's okay," she answered. "You can switch."